D0507094

Full Figured 3:

Carl Weber Presents

Full Figured 3:

Carl Weber Presents

Brenda Hampton and Nikki-Michelle

www.urbanbooks.net

Urban Books, LLC
78 East Industry Court
Deer Park, NY 11729

ISBN 13: 978-1-60162-315-7
ISBN 10: 1-60162-315-1

First Trade Paperback Printing September 2011
Printed in the United States of America

10 9 8 7 6 5 4 3 2 1

Distributed by Kensington Publishing Corp.
Submit Wholesale Orders to:
Kensington Publishing Corp.
C/O Penguin Group (USA) Inc.
Attention: Order Processing
405 Murray Hill Parkway
East Rutherford, NJ 07073-2316
Phone: 1-800-526-0275
Fax: 1-800-227-9604

Who Ya Wit 2

By

Brenda Hampton

Chapter 1

The verdict wasn't in yet about Roc being the man I needed him to be. At the age of forty-two I had allowed very little room for error in my relationships, and the drama Roc had previously brought my way, he could do no more. Somehow or someway he managed to get out of the ten-year bid he was sentenced to at Bonne Terre Correctional Facility, only completing a year and a half. He mentioned that his lawyer had gotten the sentence reduced, but there had to be more to it. Either way, I was very glad about that, and the thought of him being able to be a father to our daughter, Chassidy, truly pleased my heart.

It was only two days ago that Roc stepped into my kitchen, claiming to be a free man and asking if I was still down with him. I really didn't know what to say, but I remember my mouth hanging wide open.

"I'm not sure who I'm down with right now, Roc. There is a lot at stake and I just don't know if I can trust you again. I know that your son's mother, Vanessa, is still in the picture, and what about your conniving uncle, Ronnie? I don't know if I can deal with some of the mess I put up with before, and I'm sure you understand my concerns."

"I do, but let's face it . . . you've never trusted me. Vanessa won't be no problem for us and neither will Ronnie."

I could have laughed at his response, only because he knew that was a lie. "It would be so wrong of me to go there with you, so I won't. Just . . . just give me a hug, and the only thing I will say right now is that it's good seeing you."

"Same here, especially since you only came to visit me once. You were wrong for that, as well as for not bringing my daughter, either. But you're right . . . our issues need to be put off for another day and time. I'm here, so come give me the hug I've been waitin' for."

I moved closer to Roc, and as soon as his arms eased around my waist, the feelings for him that I was unable to release came back to life. I wasn't sure if this connection I had with him would be everlasting, or if it was just me wanting to make this thing work because of our child. That answer would come soon, but there was no doubt whatsoever that I was happy to see him.

It was scorching hot outside that day, but Roc spent much of his time trying to get to know Chassidy. He played with her in her swimming pool, chased her around the spacious backyard, watched TV with her in her *The Princess and the Frog*—decorated bedroom, and even cut the grass for me. It was good seeing the two of them together, and for her first time seeing him, she took to him very well. Later that day, we left my home in St. Louis, and followed my son, Latrel, back to college at Mizzou. After staying with him for a couple of hours, Roc, Chassidy, and I returned home. Chassidy was exhausted, so I laid her down for a nap, and then went into the kitchen where Roc was sitting shirtless at the glass-topped kitchen table, sipping from a Coke can and eating some barbecue-flavored potato chips. The calories would do him no harm, and the muscular frame that he had before did not compare to the one he now had. His biceps looked bigger, his chest was carved to perfection, more tattoos covered his arms, and the daily iron pumping had definitely paid off. He was dark as midnight, still very sexy, and clean-cut as ever! I couldn't ignore the fact that seeing him always made my panties moist and my palms sweat. Aside from the way he made my insides tingle, there was so much that I needed to say. I didn't quite know how to say it, but it was now or never.

With Roc being in prison, certain things came to my mind about what kind of person he now was. Was he still the young man who lived in the fast lane, selling drugs and having sex with many different women? Was he still willing to do whatever his Uncle Ronnie wanted him to do, and was Roc willing to do jail time for Ronnie again? Was movin' and shakin' still his occupation, and what could he offer me? Basically, had he matured at all, and, at twenty-seven years old, did being in prison redeem him? I sat across the table from him, eager to continue our conversation from earlier.

"So, in other words, you're telling me that you're a changed man. I don't have to worry about Vanessa ringing my phone or confronting me, as she did before. I don't have to concern myself with Ronnie calling me out of my name or putting a gun up to my head, right? And what about you? Can you promise me that you are done with shaking and moving? If not, Roc, I want no part of this."

Roc squinted, staring deeply into my eyes. "You don't have to worry about nothin'. All of that shit is in the past, ma. I'm done with all of that mess, jus' . . . just give me a chance to show you what's up. I promise you won't regret it. I've had time to reflect on some things, and my goal is to live a better life. I tried my way before, so let's roll with your way."

I wasn't sure if Roc could handle doing things my way. My way consisted of him getting a job, helping me take care of our daughter, leaving the drug game behind him, making sure there was no drama from his son's mother, and distancing himself from the people around him who helped bring him down, particularly Ronnie: the uncle who Roc had looked up to as a father figure. The one who supposedly made a way for Roc and had gotten him in to the drug game. He was the one who Roc had taken the fall for and wound up going to prison for. I hated Ronnie with a passion, and I could never see him being an inspiration to Roc, or Roc distancing himself from an uncle he loved more than life itself.

That night, all I allowed Roc to do was hold me in his arms, while questioning his early release and his future plans. He insisted that with lots of money and a damn good lawyer, anything was possible. As for his future, he wasn't sure. Lord knows I wanted to have sex with him, but I wasn't sure about us yet. My life had changed in so many different ways since he'd been gone, and honestly, I hadn't forgiven him yet for choosing to take the fall for Ronnie, instead of being there for his child. I was in a different place in my life and I couldn't afford any setbacks.

My career with the STL Community College was going strong, I had pulled myself out of debt, and my children were happy. Latrel was now a junior and I was as proud of him as any mother could be. He drove home almost every other weekend just to be with me and spend time with his sister. He also spent some days with my ex-husband, Reggie, who had divorced me because he'd fallen out of love. That's what he'd said years ago, but he was now regretting his decision. We rarely spoke to each other these days because he remained upset with me about Chassidy. In no way did I care about how he felt about me, and his only worries should have applied to his messed-up life.

According to Latrel, Reggie was in the midst of tying up his second divorce, which was more costly than the one he had with me. I only asked for what was due to me, but his new wife, she wanted it all! The house, cars, part ownership of his real estate business, and $10,000 a month in spousal support. I couldn't believe all that she was asking for, and, to my recollection, Reggie didn't have that much money to dish out. I truly wished him the best with his situation, but that's what he got for marrying a woman he had only known for one year.

That situation, in itself, made me wise up even more. I didn't want anyone to take what little I had, and I wasn't trying to share much, either. My house was for me and my children. My car was for me only to drive. I was perfectly fine with the way things were going, but I couldn't help but sit at my desk at work, thinking about how Roc would impact my life going forward. I had briefly spoken to him yesterday, but he seemed busy, trying to move his things from the penthouse he once had to a condo he was now living in on the south side of St. Louis.

I wiggled my fingers on the side of my face, eyeballing the phone on my desk and contemplating calling him. Why? Because he said he was busy, and since he hadn't called me back, maybe that meant he was *still* busy. I wanted to allow him all the time he needed to get settled, so I quickly dropped my thoughts about calling him and got back to work.

Working for the vice president of Student Activities was challenging. My boss, Mr. Anderson, was a serious black man who kept me on my feet. He was in his mid-fifties, and had a wife and three kids, but made little time for them. Normally, he worked six days a week, hoping that I would do the same. From the beginning, I made it clear that I could only work Monday through Friday, never on the weekends. My family was too important to me and they definitely came first. Mr. Anderson understood that, and that encouraged me to give him my all. We got along very well and it turned out that losing my previous job was the best thing that had ever happened to me. My salary increased by $15,000, it helped with my bills, and I was in no way upset about that.

As my mind was consumed with calling Roc, the ringing phone interrupted my thoughts.

"Mr. Anderson's office. How may I help you?"

"Desa Rae, this is Sherri. Is my dad around?"

Mr. Anderson would never tell his kids when he was going out of town. And it wasn't my place to tell them, either. "No, he isn't, Sherri. He's out of the office today, but you may want to try his cell phone."

"Okay, thanks. I'll do that, but, in the meantime, how's Latrel doing?"

"He's fine. I had hoped the two of you would go out on another date, but he told me how busy the both of you are."

"Unfortunately, but I had every intention of calling him soon. You know I'm in med school and I never have time to do much of anything."

"Oh, I understand, sweetie, and you definitely don't have to explain anything to me. I'm sure Latrel understands too. Call him when you can. He did mention you the other day and I'm sure he would be happy to hear from you."

"I sure will. Let me call my dad now, and be sure to tell Latrel I'll call him soon."

I told Sherri that I would, but shame on me for lying. Latrel hadn't mentioned her at all, and he actually told me that the two of them didn't click. Personally, I thought Sherri was perfect for Latrel. She was smart, funny, cute, and had goals that made her family proud. The fact that she was a virgin made me appreciate her more, and she reminded me a lot of myself. I made a mental note to call Latrel to see if he would be willing to take her out again. I knew it was none of my business, but I would forever and always be looking out for who or what was in my son's best interest.

Mr. Anderson was out for the entire week. I was pretty much caught up on all of my work, but just to keep busy, I started merging a letter that wasn't supposed to go out to the students until next week. Next to me was a pretty red basket, filled with chocolate chip cookies. I had already eaten three of them, and I couldn't believe how much my appetite had increased since Roc had been home. I'd probably picked up five pounds in two days, and couldn't stop snacking. It was probably my nerves, and even though I hated to go there, I wondered if he was still okay with the *weight* thing. He did compliment me on how beautiful I was, but it was hard to hide the ten pounds I had packed on over the last few months. Since Latrel had been coming home a lot, I was cooking and eating more. Chassidy loved pizza, and it had become one of my favorites, too. Surely, it was hard to get those pounds off, and the once/twice-a-week workout that I was doing appeared to be a waste of time. My hips were more curvaceous and my thighs had gotten thicker. I guess the weight was going to the right places, and, for that, I really couldn't complain.

Double checking, I pulled a compact mirror from my purse, gazing at my reflection. Yeah, I still had it going on, and even the chocolate on my teeth from those cookies wasn't enough to make me think otherwise. I licked the chocolate, then pressed my lips together to spread my gloss that was barely there. I teased my feathery, long hair and batted my lashes at the prettiest woman I knew—me. I smiled and placed the compact back into my purse. Ready to finish up my letters, I scooted the black leather chair up to my cherry oak square desk that was neat and spacious. I barely had to leave my desk for anything, as the four-in-one HP printer, fax, copier, and scanner was right beside me. Stack trays for my letters were to my right, and pictures of my children were to my left. My drawers included everything that an administrative assistant would need to do her job, including the chocolate Hershey Kisses that I had stashed away for my cravings. I shook my head, knowing that I needed to stop.

Instead of resuming with my chocolates and the letter, I reached for the phone to call Roc. *What the hell?* I thought. If he was too busy to talk, then he would say so. The phone rang twice before he answered.

"Say, baby," he immediately said. "I'ma hit you up in about ten minutes. I'm in the middle of doin' somethin'."

Well, crack my face, why don't you? "Uh, okay. I'm at work, so call me here."

"Will do."

He hung up, leaving me to wonder what was up. Seemed like that spark he once had for me wasn't there anymore. I knew that the time we spent away from each other would make us feel differently, but was he still excited about me? I hoped that my small transformation from a size fourteen/sixteen to sixteen-plus wasn't a factor, but with men you just never know. Just in case, I grabbed my basket of cookies, aiming it toward the trashcan to throw the cookies away. When the aroma of sweet and thick chocolate chunks hit me, I quickly changed my mind, putting the basket back on my desk. I put one of the cookies in my mouth, closed my eyes, and let it melt. No need letting the cookies my best friend, Monica, had made go to waste that.

"Mmmmm," I said, indulging myself. "If you don't like it, Mr. Roc, too darn bad."

Less than five minutes later, the phone rang again. By looking at the caller ID, I knew it was Roc.

"Desa Rae Jenkins," I said, wiping my mouth with a napkin.

"Dez, it's Roc. I was just callin' you back. What's up?"

"I didn't want anything. Just checking to see if you got settled into your new place. Did you?"

"Just about. I still have a few things to do, but for the most part I'd better get used to makin' my condo feel like home. It's a li'l cramped for my taste, but a nigga gotta do what he must do to stay out of jail."

"I'd say so, and changing course, as well as leaving the drug game behind, will be very beneficial. You think?"

Roc was silent and all I heard was a deep sigh on the other end.

"Roc, are you there?"

"Yeah, I'm here. But, before we get off on the wrong foot, let me say somethin' to you, all right? I know I've made some mistakes, but there are no guarantees that more mistakes won't happen. All you need to know is that I'm goin' to do my best to stay on the right track, but even my best may not be good enough for you. If we hook up again, and I truly hope we do, please don't nag me about my decisions in life. They are mine to make and mine only. If you can't handle that, then don't waste your time."

Oh, no, he didn't just try to tell me off, did he? I knew he was busy trying to get everything in order, and I figured his situation could have been frustrating. In knowing so, I remained calm. "I just want the best for you, that's all. If my comment offended you, I apologize."

"Yes, some of your comments, with an s, offend me. Especially when I wanted to taste your pussy the other night, and all you wanted to do was tell me what you expected me to do. That shit is a turnoff, ma, and I'm not down with nobody tryin' to give me orders. I've been takin' orders for the last year and a half. Had enough of that shit and it's timeout."

Okay, I messed up so I had to lighten the situation. "Forgive me, as it's the motherly thing in me that always kicks in. So . . . does this mean I'm in trouble? I hope so."

Roc laughed out loud, and it put a smile on my face as I visualized his deep dimples and Lance Gross attributes.

"Big, eleven and a half . . . maybe twelve inches of trouble."

"Wow, I'm impressed. Didn't know a penis could grow that fast, but I'm willing to take whatever you got. When can I get it is the question?"

"It's all yours and all you have to do is say the word. My place or yours? Today or tomorrow? Morning or night? A bed, table, shower, or the floor?"

"I'll let you decide. Just let me know, so I can make some arrangements with our beautiful daughter."

"Yeah, you may have to do that because I don't want her around to witness all the hollerin' and screamin' I may cause you. Come to my place tonight and I will make sure all of the floors are clean."

"Can't wait," I said with excitement, picking up a pen. "Address, please."

Roc gave me his address and directions to his place near Tower Grove Park. Afterward, I called Monica to see if she would watch Chassidy for me and she told me to bring her over for the weekend. I thanked her and told her I would drop off Chassidy around 6:00 P.M. I couldn't wait to see Roc, and, unfortunately for me, yes, I was in trouble. The only person I'd had sex with was a man from work I'd met named Greg. We went out a few times, but I wasn't feeling him at all. He was boring to be with and I had to pretend as if I were enjoying our dates. I thought that having sex with him would help to break the ice, but that did nothing but turn me off more. He was the same age as me, very nice, but not for me. He continued to pursue me for a while, and just recently backed off. Thank God. I guess Roc had spoiled me. I knew it would be difficult to find a man who was capable of making my body do what he did, and, for the record, it was time for me to have some fun that seemed long overdue.

A few hours later, I was at home standing in front of my bed and observing the three outfits I had laid out. One was a red stretch dress with a V-dip in the front. It came with a black belt that tightened around the waist, and I had the perfect black heels to match. The other outfits were a one-piece, strapless white jumper, and jeans with a burnt orange button-down shirt from Ashley Stewart. I must have stared at the outfits for an hour, debating which one would fit me best. While in thought, I snapped my fingers and hurried into my walk-in closet. I scanned my clothes, then came across the flowered sundress I wore the first time Roc and I had sex. He loved my dress, so he said, but more than anything he appreciated the easy access. I slid the dress over my body and stepped into my yellow flip-flops that matched. *Now, why didn't I think of this before?*

I thought, and hurried to grab my purse and keys so I could go.

On the drive to Roc's place, I couldn't stop thinking about what the night had in store for us. I hoped like hell that I was still capable of pleasing him. I mean, with Greg, my sexual performance was just okay. In no way did being with him encourage me to give it my all. Roc always got the best sex out of me, and right about now, I needed something good in return. I couldn't wait to see him, so I put my foot on the accelerator and sped up.

By the time I reached Roc's place, it was 8:15 P.M. I told him I'd be there around eight, but the battle with my clothes delayed me. I wanted to check on Chassidy again, so I dialed out on my cell phone to call Monica.

"She's perfectly fine," Monica said. "And if all you're going to do is call here the entire weekend to check on her, then I'm going to stop answering my phone."

I smiled, as my best friend knew how protective I was of my children. "What is she doing? Did I forget to put her *Princess and the Frog* pillow in her bag?"

"No. She's cuddled up next to me, resting peacefully with her pillow beside her. We were watching *Up* and those beautiful little eyes were fading by the minute. Tomorrow we're going to go check on my parents and I'm taking her to Incredible Pizza with my two nieces. They're spending the night, too, and the girls will have lots of fun. Trust me."

"I do trust you and you already know that. You know how I am about my babies."

"Yes, I do, and I'm the same way. Have fun with Roc this weekend, and don't worry about Chassidy. I hope everything goes well, even though I'm not sure yet about his return."

"I'm not sure, either, but I'm here. And the way my hormones are raging, there will be no turning back."

We laughed and Monica knew exactly where I was coming from. "What did you wind up putting on?" she asked.

I looked down at my sundress with blooming flowers, fearing to tell her. "A simple sundress."

"A sundress? Which one?"

"The yellow one with the white flowers and thin straps."

"Ugh, the one that looks like a balloon? You couldn't find anything else to put on? Girl, that dress is for cleaning up around the house. I can't believe that was the only—"

"Good-bye, Monica. I'll call to check on you and Chassidy tomorrow."

Monica was still talking and laughing about my dress. I hung up on her, but I was sure she would understand. Feeling a bit nervous, I looked at the address I wrote on the paper, comparing it to what looked to be a newly built two-family flat: one upstairs, the other down. The landscaping was beautiful and the huge picture windows on the front gave the property a luxurious look. I slowly walked to the door, already biting my nails. I couldn't understand why I was so uncomfortable with this, especially since I had gotten to know Roc so well. I took several deep breaths before ringing the doorbell. Almost immediately, I could hear Roc's hard footsteps coming down the stairs.

"Who out there ringin' my bell?" he playfully asked.

"Desa Rae."

"Who?"

"You heard me, Roc. Stop playing."

"You're late."

"And?"

"And if it were me, you would be all in my shit. So I'm gettin' in yours."

"Well, that's why I'm here. I was hoping that you would get into . . . well, something."

He opened the door with a heart-melting grin on his face. He wore a pair of dark denim jeans that hung very low, showing his light blue boxers and rock-hard abs. His eyes scanned my dress and his grin got even wider. So did the door. "Damn, baby, you . . . you out here lookin' like a dyme piece. Please come in."

I stepped inside, blushing. "I thought you would like my dress, and I have no complaints either."

Roc shut the door, and then turned to face me. His eyes dropped to my lips, and even though we had kissed the other day, this time was starting to feel different. I was feeling a bit more at ease, and when his hands went underneath my dress to touch my bare ass, I felt relieved. He backed away from our intense kiss.

"Did I tell you how much I love this dress? Seein' you in it always makes my dick ready to aim and shoot."

I rested my arms on his shoulders, already feeling his hardness. "I think you appreciate what's underneath my dress more, but that's just my opinion, of course."

He winked and continued to feel my ass. "Both. And to be honest, I appreciate all of it. Every single inch of it."

I could in no way argue with that, and his tongue went in for the kill again. My hands roamed his rock-hard body and I could feel my temperature rising. As we were both indulging ourselves, Roc eased back on the steps, pulling me on top as he leaned back. I could feel cool air on my butt, as every bit of it was now exposed.

I paused from the intense kiss, looking eye to eye with Roc. "Aren't you going to show me around first?

We could talk about how your day went or how mine went before we start screwing each other's brains out, right?"

"As hard as my dick is right now, we gon' have to save the chit-chat for later. And trust me when I say you will get the tour you've been waitin' for in just a few minutes."

Roc attempted to raise my dress over my head, but I backed up. I stood, looking at him leaned back on the stairs, resting on his elbows.

"Can we at least get up the stairs? I need way more room than this and it's not like I weigh a buck-zero-five."

"You were the one who always told me to be creative, and work with what space I have. You do remember tellin' me that, don't you?"

I couldn't deny my own words, but the stairs were not my cup of tea. I started up the stairs, ignoring Roc as I passed by him. When I reached the top, he stood closely behind me. I could see into the small living room that was to my right, and the bedroom that was down the hallway to my left. Roc wasted no time removing his jeans and tossing them down the stairs. He pulled the top of my sundress apart, ripping it straight down the middle. Wondering if I cared? Hell no, I didn't. My thick breasts were now exposed and so was my shaved pussy. Roc peeled the sundress away from my body, tossing it down the stairs as well. In no way could I make it to the living room or his bedroom, so I lay back on what I assumed to be a very clean, carpeted floor. Within seconds, Roc rested his body between my trembling legs, allowing me to feel a big piece of hard meat that I couldn't wait to enter me. He started in on my wobbly breasts, squeezing them in his hands and sucking them at the same time. I was on fire, and all I could do was rub my hands all over his sexy dark body that had me hooked! I could already feel my juices boiling over, and when Roc slipped his finger inside of me, I gasped out loud. He made many rotations, causing my groans to increase. I couldn't take the foreplay much longer and was in a rush to receive the satisfaction I had waited on for almost two years. I reached down, touching his monstrous dick that made my mouth water.

"Baby, pleeease put on your condom. Hurry, okay?" I begged.

Roc removed his fingers from inside of me, bringing along a small flood of my juices. He sucked his wet fingers and kneeled between my legs. Putting me into position, he placed my legs around his back. He lightly rubbed his hardness against my slit, causing my eyelids to flutter. As he toyed with my insides and circled his head around my clit, I felt so weak for him.

"Do I have to use a condom?" he asked. "I really don't want to and I'm dyin' to feel the real deal."

The foreplay he delivered was feeling so good to me, and stopping the action would have been a crime. I guess I was about to commit one, because there was no way in hell he was entering me again without a condom. Him being incarcerated put a bit of fear in me and having sex with numerous women in the past concerned me too. I reached down, moving his hardness away from me.

"Please. Let's do this the right way. I know you understand my concerns."

He shrugged. "I don't, but when we're finished, I'm sure you'll tell me."

I kept quiet, as I in no way wanted to ruin the moment. Roc stood up, making his way down the long hallway and into his bedroom. I sat up on my elbows, observing him open his drawer and break open a condom package. I was in awe looking at his side profile, and the sight of his bulging muscles made me hungry. I got off the floor and made my way to his bedroom. He had barely put the condom on before I moved him back to the bed and kneeled on the floor in front of him. I held his hardness in my hands, preparing myself to please him in every way possible.

"Nice room," I said, not paying much attention to the room, but more so to my grip on his stick.

"I knew you would like it," he replied, looking at his goods with a wicked grin.

I covered his package with my mouth, making sure it hit the back of my deep throat. Due to his size, that wasn't an easy task. Roc dropped back on the bed, allowing me to have my way with him. Almost immediately, I brought him to an eruption.

"Dezzzz," he whined. "Daaaaamn, baby, you're guuuud at that shit."

I gave him minimal time to regroup, expecting him to return the favor. I eased my way onto the bed, straddling my thighs across his face. My pussy lowered to his thick lips and he already knew what to do with it. As his tongue dipped into my overly heated tunnel, all I could shout was, "Welcome home, baby, I'm so glad you're home!"

Thing was, would I feel the same way tomorrow?

Chapter 2

I slowly opened my eyes, slightly remembering parts of a dream I'd had about my mother. All I remembered was her sitting at a table, telling me to be very careful about my choices. She was holding Chassidy in her arms, and, for some reason, Reggie was standing beside her, laughing. It was a very weird dream and I was so glad to come out of it. I yawned and sat up to observe my surroundings. I was still at Roc's place, but he was nowhere in sight. His room was lit up by a picture window that had no curtains at all, letting the bright rays from the sun come in. In front of me was a flat-screen television, sitting on an entertainment center. A microfiber wavy black chaise was next to the queen-sized bed I was in, and a dresser with a mirror was to the left of the bed. A ceiling fan in the shape of a palm tree hung from above, and the beige-colored walls looked freshly painted. The whole room was quite simple, and, to be honest, it was nothing like his penthouse.

Feeling a bit woozy, I pulled the soft blue sheets away from my body and sat up on the edge of the bed. Yes, Roc had sexed me all night and my coochie was real tender. More than anything, I needed a shower. I also needed to find something to put on, since my pretty flowered dress was now history. There were two doors in Roc's bedroom, also the exit door. I didn't know what was behind the other two doors, but when I opened one, I saw a very long closet lined with clothes.

Shoes, mainly tennis shoes, were everywhere and so were plenty of boxes. I could tell Roc still had some unpacking to do. I reached for the first thing I saw, and that was a long purple and yellow Lakers T-shirt. After I put it on, I opened the other door. That one led to a bathroom. Inside was a stand-up shower, double sinks, and a toilet. Toothpaste, cologne, and soap were on the sink, and I only saw two towels. I looked at myself in the long mirror, teasing my wild hair. I didn't have a brush to straighten it, but my fingers were doing the job. Once my hair was in place, I splashed cold water on my face, patting it dry with my hands. I wanted to brush my teeth, but my toothbrush was in my purse. I couldn't remember where I had left that, and I assumed it was somewhere near the stairs.

I left the bathroom and started down the hallway to find Roc. Almost immediately, I could hear voices. The floor squeaked a little, but I halted my steps just to listen in on the conversation.

"I'm tellin' you, them fools had me fucked up," Roc said. "I was one nigga they didn't want to pull them gates open for, and I wanted to spit on that white son of a bitch who opened it. But all I did was smile at his ass and salute! Adios, muthafucka, I'm out!"

I heard hand slapping, then another voice chimed in. "That's how you gotta do 'em. And the fact that you never showed fear, nor did yo' ass get in any trouble, it fucked them up. I told you Watts was gon' make a way out of no way, but I had to pay that fat sucker a bundle of dough. It was worth it though, baby boy, and you know I will always have yo' back."

Hand slapping sounded off again, and, unfortunately for me, I knew that voice all too well. It was Ronnie. Why Roc would want us underneath the same roof, I don't know, but I continued to listen, hearing another voice.

"I do think it's a good idea for you to lay low for a while. Ronnie, me, and BJ got this and you know we gon' hold it down for you."

"Just like you held down Vanessa while I was away, right? Sippi, you know I'm still bitter about that shit, but it takes a ho to show her true colors when a nigga locked up."

"I hit that bitch twice and if you got a beef about it, take it up with her. She the one who came at me. I'm not gon' turn down no available pussy. Besides, you told me she was just your baby's mama, nothin' more, nothin' less. Correct?"

I inched forward, waiting to hear Roc's response.

"She ain't shit to me no more, but a long time ago I would have given her ass the shirt off my back. She couldn't get a damn gummy bear from me now."

I heard laughter and that's when I decided to make my presence known before I got busted for creeping. I also wanted to make Ronnie aware that I feared him in no way, and since Roc had no intention of keeping him away from me, why not show my face? I took a deep breath, but just as I made my way to the living room, the floor loudly squeaked. Everyone turned, looking in my direction. Seeing Ronnie made my flesh crawl, and the other young man who Roc referred to as Sippi, oh my God! I wanted to run! If Vanessa had slept with him, she was out of her mind! He was tall, muscular, and had long dreads and a rugged goatee. His hazel eyes were frightening and damn near matched his gold grille. I didn't mean to stare, but I sure wouldn't want to see him in a dark alley.

Roc stood up, tugging at his cargo shorts to pull them up. "Say, baby," he said, sucking on a toothpick. "You already know Ronnie, but this is my boy, Mississippi. Sippi, this is Dez. Chassidy's mama."

Normally, I would have extended my hand, but . . . okay, what the hell? I reached out my hand and Sippi barely touched it. He threw his head back. "Sup. Glad to meet you."

Ronnie hadn't said a word and I ignored him, turning my attention to Roc.

"Honey, I was looking for some towels so I could take a shower."

"Damn, ma, you wasn't gon' wait for me?"

"No. Besides, you're busy."

Ronnie stood up, face twisted and cutting his eyes. He reached in his pocket, pulling out a wad of money that was too thick for his ashy hands to hold. Diamond rings were on each finger and a platinum and gold watch glistened on his wrist. He cut the wad in half, dropping money on the table. "My move," he said, looking at Roc. "You already know what I told you and I won't say it again. The next move is yours."

Dressed in an all-linen, cream-colored suit and diamonds in both ears, Ronnie proceeded toward me. He put his hands back into his pockets, jiggling his keys.

"Desa Rae, risk-takin' Jenkins. I see you back in business, but I wonder for how long. This time, I suggest that you don't overstay your welcome." He winked, looking very identical to Roc. "As that would please me more than you know."

Ronnie going to hell would have pleased me, and it was obvious that he still had a beef with me for taking up too much of Roc's time. Particularly keeping him away from the drug game. Before I could say anything, Roc intervened. I was sure he remembered what happened the last time the three of us were together, and I knew he was in no mood to see another gun upside my head. Trying not to go there again, I kept quiet, giving Roc an opportunity to address his out-of-control uncle.

"Man, lighten up and chill," Roc said, moving next to Ronnie. He kept staring at me, and I stared back. Roc swayed his hand in front of Ronnie's eyes, and he smacked Roc's hand. "Don't put your gotdamn hands near my face, nigga! I don't give a fuck who you are. You out of line." I was surprised, as Roc in no way backed down. Now his face was twisted up and his forehead showed thick wrinkles. "Muthafucka, yo' ass the one out of line. If I didn't touch you, nigga, don't touch me. Show a man some respect in front of his woman and don't be treatin' me like no punk."

Sippi got between Roc and Ronnie, but from the way he was gazing at Roc, I could tell he had Ronnie's back. Lord knows I didn't want to get into the middle of this, but I had to put forth some effort to calm the situation.

"Look, Ronnie, I apologize if my presence makes you uneasy. I will do my best to stay out of your way and I don't want you and Roc arguing—"

"Shut the fuck up talkin' to me, bitch," he spat, keeping his eyes on Roc. "I see you done got some extra balls in prison, but you'd betta cut them suckers off and get back to just havin' two. Watch yo' tone with me, youngblood, and the next time you slip up at the mouth, I will bust you in it."

Roc tapped his lip with his finger. "Are you threatenin' me? Right here, old school, go ahead and put it right there."

I witnessed the mean mug on Ronnie's face and saw his fist tighten. My stomach dropped when he slammed his fist into Roc's mouth, staggering him backward. In no way did he fall, but as he quickly charged forward, Mississippi stopped Roc dead in his tracks. He placed his gun on Roc's heaving chest.

"Don't touch him, Roc!" Sippi yelled. "Back the fuck up!"

There was no way for me to just stand there, and when my eyes shifted over to the phone, Sippi turned the gun toward me. All I could think was, *Not again.*

"If you move, you die."

"Y'all muthafuckas trippin'," Roc said, wiping a dab of blood on his lip with his hand. He seemed calm as ever, but I wasn't. My stomach was rumbling and my hands had a slight tremble. All kinds of things were roaming in my head and all I could think of was my dream. Why did I continue to inject myself into this mess? I didn't know.

"Put that shit down," Ronnie said, giving Sippi an order. "You need not act unless I ask you to. As long as that fool got my blood running through his veins, don't you ever pull a gun on him! You got that shit?"

Sippi nodded and had already lowered his gun. Ronnie turned to Roc again, poking at his chest. "You and me gon' holla later. We don't do this, Roc, 'cause you ain't bigger than me yet. A wise man can go a long way in this world, and he also knows to never put pussy before partna. I hope you understand what I'm sayin', and don't you ever bite the hand that feeds you and feeds you well."

Roc cocked his neck from side to side, saying not a word. Ronnie and his goon headed down the stairs and I was relieved when I heard the door shut. Roc stormed by me, making his way down the hallway and into his bedroom. When I got to his room, he was laid back on the bed, looking up at the ceiling with his arm across his forehead. I figured it was time for me to go.

"I'll be out of your way in a minute. I had a nice time last night, but I'm discouraged by what just happened. You know how much Ronnie despises me, so why didn't you just wake me up and ask me to leave?"

"Good-bye, Dez. I'm not up for a bunch of your irritatin'-ass questions."

Roc was as stubborn as stubborn could get, but so was I. I was also a person who had to have answers when I wanted them. I walked over to the bed and lay sideways next to him. To put him at ease, I dabbed the blood on his lips with a Kleenex, then pecked his lips and put his arms around my neck.

"Listen, can we please not get off on the wrong foot? You just made that suggestion yesterday and I don't want my feelings for Ronnie to get in the way of what I feel for you. I hope you don't either, and for the sake of our child, let's do our best to get along. It would really mean a lot to me, Roc, and I promise that I will not pressure you about our relationship, or about what you decide to do with your life. I just want to be happy and have fun. I can't think of a better person I would enjoy myself with more than you."

Roc turned his head, then used his finger to touch the side of my face. "You're right. I'm sorry that happened in front of you, but shit like that happens all the time. We'll be drinkin', smoking herbs, and laughin' about that shit tomorrow, so no big deal. I apologize for how Ronnie is, and I really need to make sure the two of y'all keep your distance."

"Please," I laughed. "And how can you laugh, drink, and smoke blunts with someone who treats—"

Roc placed his finger on my lips. "Let it go, Dez. Puttin' my hands on Ronnie would be like fightin' with my own father. He's dead and you know Ronnie's been like a replacement. So sometimes I gotta chalk that shit up and take it. You would never understand and I'm not goin' to waste my time explainin' it to you. Now, if you're leavin', good-bye. If you prefer to stay, I have some other suggestions."

I smiled, wondering what his *other* suggestions were.
"You're right. I don't understand, but tell me about your
other suggestions. I have some idea, but I just want to
be sure."

Roc rolled on top of me, playfully kissing down my
neck. "I have to straighten out my closets, get my kitchen
in order, bring my dinin' room table up from the basement, and unload a few more boxes. Will you help me?"

"Hmmm, don't know yet. I thought you may have
something in this for me."

Roc stopped kissing my neck and pecked my cheek.
"I always got somethin' for you. Once we get finished
with the house chores, I intend to tackle some of your
sweet pussy all night long and into the next morning."

"Wow. Are you sure about that? If my memory serves
me correctly, you were the one who threw in the towel
last night because you were tired."

"No, I wasn't tired. I was just givin' you a break. You
were startin' to lose your voice, and I assumed you got
tired of screamin' my name."

"That's because your dick is sooo good and I love
hearing myself say your name."

Roc blushed. "I like hearin' you say it too. Hearin'
you say 'Ohhh, Roc, baby' is like music to my ears. Let's
go ahead and handle our business with the unpackin'
first, then I'll let you turn on your music. I'll turn on
mine too, and the way your snatch talks to me, my music may get a bit louder than yours."

"Tuh, it always does. You just don't know how loud
'Daaaamn, Dez, baby, keep fuckin' me like this' is. Your
words are way louder than I could ever get."

Roc chuckled. "I don't be sayin' no dumb shit like
that. And if I do, that's because I be under the influence."

"Under the influence of what?"

"A sexy-ass, lovin' woman who I couldn't stop thinkin' about while I was in prison. We gon' do this shit, ma, and before all is said and done, I'm goin' to make you my wifey. For better or worse, no doubt."

"And I'm going to enjoy watching you try."

We kissed, and before I made another move, I got up to take a shower. Roc left me at peace and I stood in the shower thinking just how much of myself I was willing to give. In no way did I know, or even want to predict my future with Roc, but being with him again felt special—with the exception of my setback with Ronnie.

For the next several hours, I helped Roc get his place in order. Like I'd said before, it in no way compared to his penthouse, but his new place was nice. It was shaped like an L, with the living room, dining room, and kitchen being on one side, and his bedroom on the other. He had two bathrooms and a basement that had to be shared with the other tenant. Not much furniture adorned the space, and Roc said that was because he wanted to keep it simple. He wasn't sure how long he was going to live there, but it was imperative that he removed himself from his previous location.

Around 4:00 P.M., I took a break to eat some barbecue from Red's that Roc had gone to get us on West Florissant Avenue, and to call Monica. She didn't answer, so I left a message on voice mail, telling her to call me soon. I wasn't sure if she was trying to avoid me, but I was a little worried since I hadn't heard from her all day. Roc was still going from room to room, making sure everything was to his liking. He had no organization skills at all, and since he kept stopping to answer his phone calls by hitting the Bluetooth on his ear, I gave up. The loud hip hop music was working me, too, and I could feel a headache coming on. I plopped down on his bed, and turned on the TV to watch the news. I could hear Roc talking to someone on the phone, cursing and laughing some more. I closed my eyes, trying to soothe my headache, but that's when he came into the room.

"Uh, what are you doin'? I thought you were supposed to be helpin' me."

I yawned. "I was, but I got a headache, plus I'm tired. You've been slacking anyway, and you have talked on that phone more than you've done anything else around here."

"Nigga, let me get at you later," he said, then hit the button on his Bluetooth. "I ain't talked to some of my boys in a while, so they were just callin' to see what was up. Sippi out runnin' his mouth about me and Ronnie, too, so everybody just wanted to make sure everything straight."

"Is it?"

"Yeah, I already talked to that fool. We good."

I had no comment, but I did ask Roc to turn down the music. He did as I asked, then sat on the bed next to me.

"Say. If you don't mind, I want to take Chassidy and Li'l Roc to a picnic with me. They need to get to know each other and I hope you don't have a problem with that."

The thought of Chassidy being anywhere near Roc's crew in no way sat right with me. I didn't know how to say it without offending him, but Chassidy wasn't going anywhere with him, without me. "I don't mind Chassidy getting to know her brother or relatives, but where is this picnic supposed to be? Am I invited?"

"It's next weekend at Fairground Park. He havin' a barbecue bash and I want to bring my kids to show them off. I don't care if you come or not, but you don't really click with my peeps. You know how we get down, and I don't need you there watchin' my back and rollin' those pretty eyes."

"Yes, I witnessed today how you get down, and unfortunately, Roc, I don't want Chassidy exposed to that kind of foolishness. Have all the fun you want, please, but I'm not comfortable with her being surrounded by a bunch of people getting high, drinking, pulling guns on each other . . . You know what I mean. I would love for us to have a picnic, and the kids can join us. How about that?"

Roc got off the bed, seeming a bit irritated. "Chassidy is my daughter too, Dez, and whether you like it or not, she will get to know her peeps. All of them ain't ghettofied Negros and plenty of them are down-to-earth, normal people. I have a serious problem with people who look down on others, so correct yourself on that, all right? I'ma do this picnic thing with you, but there will come a time when you gon' have to ease up on our daughter."

I was already getting to a point when I knew it made sense for me not to comment. This was one of them, but Roc was so wrong about me easing up on Chassidy. No way, no how would I subject her to anything like what happened today. Roc would have to come to grips with it, and this was the one thing I wasn't willing to budge on.

After I took two aspirin, I lay back on the plush pillow to take a nap. Roc let me get some rest and I was glad about that. I was still puzzled why Monica hadn't called me back, but when I checked my phone, she had. She said that they were having a good time, and she'd see me tomorrow. The only reason she'd missed my call was because she couldn't hear her phone ringing, due to the loud arcade games at Incredible Pizza. I smiled, thinking of my daughter having fun, and fell asleep.

What seemed like hours later, I was awakened by a loud boom. I jumped from my sleep, noticing that Roc was lying next to me, asleep as well. His arm was around my waist and the room was partially dark. I looked at the alarm clock on the dresser, and it showed 9:45 P.M. Since Roc was still sleeping, I figured I was just hearing things. My eyes searched the room for a while, then I lay back to watch the TV. A few seconds later, the booming sound happened again. This time it was constant and sounded like someone banging hard on the door. I shook Roc's shoulder to wake him.

"Roc, wake up. I . . . I think someone is knocking at your door."

He was groggy as ever and all he moaned was, "Huh?"

"Someone is at your door. Don't you hear that?"

Roc forced his tired eyes open, listening for a knock. He heard several, and that's when he threw the covers aside.

"Wait right here," he said, slowly getting out of bed. He turned on the lights, causing me to squint. Wearing nothing at all, he grabbed his housecoat, and then opened up a drawer. I noticed him put his gun in his pocket and then he made his way down the hallway.

"Who is it?" he yelled. "And why in the fuck you bangin' on my damn door like the police?"

I had already started to bite my nails, and being with Roc at his place was starting to become a problem. I had never spent the night with him in his territory. In the past, we always stayed at my house. There was a possibility that I would resort to staying at my house only. I was trying to give him the benefit of the doubt, but this was getting ridiculous.

As I was in thought, I could hear a female's voice yelling and screaming. Yes, Roc told me to stay where I was, but I was never one to listen to his orders. I got out of bed, wearing his white long T-shirt I'd changed into before taking my nap. His white socks were on my feet and I teased my hair to straighten it. I made my way to the top of the stairs, looking down to see what was up. The door was wide open. Roc stood on one side, and his son's mother, Vanessa, was on the porch. She looked up at me, causing Roc to turn his head in my direction as well.

"Good-bye, Vanessa. If you don't stop all of this clownin' and shit, you gon' regret it."

She tried to come inside, but Roc held up his arm to block her from entering. "Nigga, move your damn arm! Let me in! I see why yo' ass ain't been answerin' your stupid-ass phone."

Roc slightly shoved her back, but she kept charging forward to get inside. "I haven't answered my phone because I told you I don't fuck with you no more. What's so hard for you to understand about that?"

Vanessa ignored Roc, and when she ducked underneath his arm, she made progress to the second step. Roc grabbed her waist and tossed her back out the door like a paper doll. I felt bad for her, and in no way was I going to stand by and let him go overboard with her.

"Roc," I said. He turned his head toward me. "Just come inside and close the door."

As his attention was on me, Vanessa lifted her foot like a punter in the NFL, kicking him right between his legs. When he doubled over and grabbed himself, she slapped the shit out of him. He was caught off guard and she ran inside again. This time, she almost made it up the stairs. She lunged out at me, but immediately went tumbling back down the steps. Roc grabbed her ankles, and she hit the steps so hard, I knew she had to have broken something. Roc reached for her hair, squeezing it tight and jerking her head.

"Bitch, didn't I tell you to exit? I can't be nice to yo' ass for nothin'! You just ain't satisfied unless I got my foot up yo' ass, are you?"

"Let me go, muthafucka! I hate yo' ass, Roc! I hate your fuckin' guts!"

Roc slammed her face into the wall, and I swear that every breath in my body left me. I could in no way watch things go down like this, so I hurried down the steps to pull him away from her.

"Is this what you want?" he said, turning her around and holding her in a headlock. She couldn't say a word, as his grip was too tight. "What's that?" he said, seething with anger. "I can't hear you. You was just talkin' all that shit, but yo' ass ain't sayin' nothin' now."

Tears were pouring down Vanessa's face and she couldn't open her mouth if she tried. I reached out, trying to remove Roc's arm from her neck.

"Don't touch me, Dez! Go back upstairs and stay the fuck out of this!"

I ignored Roc, still trying to loosen his grip. Finally he let Vanessa go, and her body was so weak that she dropped to the floor. I was so angry that I turned around and headed upstairs to go. With my back turned, Vanessa rushed up and grabbed the back of my hair, pulling me backward. Thank God for the banister, as she moved so quickly that I would have been on my butt. Roc grabbed her again, this time twisting her arm hard behind her back.

"I will break this muthafucka off! Let her fuckin' hair go."

The pain must have been too much for Vanessa to bear, because she let go of my hair in an instant.

I pointed my finger in her face, fuming. "Touch me again, and Roc won't be the only problem that you have. And trust me, he's not nothing compared to me," I spat. I kept it moving up the stairs and didn't even turn around to see what would happen next. If Vanessa thought that I was her problem, she was sadly mistaken. Her problem was with Roc; then again, so was mine. I went into the bedroom, closing the door behind me so I wouldn't have to listen to what was happening. I wondered why Vanessa wouldn't just leave, and if a man said that he didn't want to be bothered, then why force the situation? My mind went right to Latrel, and I wondered if he had ever been in a situation where a woman had hit on him like Vanessa had done to Roc. Would Latrel do what Roc did? I seriously doubted it, but his father and I had taught him to always defend himself. No matter what, I didn't like what was going down with Roc and Vanessa, and as soon as they settled their differences, I intended to leave.

About ten minutes later, the bedroom door flew open and Roc came inside. I was sitting against the headboard with my knees pressed close to my chest. Roc looked at me, and then went over to the dresser to put the gun back inside.

"Before your mouth starts goin', Dez, I don't want to hear it. You know nothin' about my situation with her, so keep your comments to yourself."

I got off the bed, and reached for my keys and purse on the nightstand. My flip-flops were already next to me, so I slid into them. I made my way toward the door, but stopped before exiting.

"Enjoy your evening, Roc. No, I don't know much detail about your relationship with Vanessa, but I do know this, a man should never hit a woman, but I guess you felt as if you had to do what was necessary. That's your decision to make, but through my eyes it makes you look really bad. I can't help the way I feel, even though she works the hell out of me."

His mouth dropped open. "You saw for yourself what she was doin' and you're damn right I'm goin' to always defend myself. That bitch has tried to shoot and stab me before. She gangsta like that and some women you have to handle in a different way. She'll be all right, and when you keep gettin' your head bumped enough, you'll eventually learn somethin'."

I couldn't help but to shake my head. "If you've continued in a relationship with a woman who has tried to shoot or stab you, then you're getting what you deserve. The wake-up call obviously came awhile back, but too bad you missed it. Trying to cut her off now may not work in your favor, and head bumping will get you nowhere but back in jail. I hope you know that."

Roc didn't respond, so I walked out the door. He shouted my name as I made my way down the hallway.

I turned with an attitude. "Yes."

"Being with me will not be easy," he said, now standing in the doorway to his bedroom. "What you see is what you get. I'm not goin' to sugarcoat nothin' and you need to decide if you're wit' me or not. I can't have no woman who thinks she can walk in and out of my life when she gets ready. I need one who knows my situation and accepts it. As you can see, much of this shit is beyond my control. I'm tryin' to get rid of the bad seeds, but they won't disappear as quickly as you want them to. Think about what I'm sayin' and get at me when you've come to grips with the way I do things."

"Do your bad seeds include Vanessa and being in the drug game? I just want to be sure that's what you're referring to."

"Exactly. Just don't expect everything to change overnight. In due time, they will. For now, all you need to know is I'm not sexually involved with Vanessa and I've had no part in sellin' drugs. I hope you're at least happy about that."

I shrugged, somewhat knowing that Roc was just saying what he did to please me. If anything, I had hoped being in prison had taught him a lesson. The verdict was still out, so, "Possibly happy," was all I could say. In no way did I want to leave Roc under these conditions, but what had happened today left a sour taste in my mouth. I closed the door behind me, and as I made my way to my car, I noticed my passenger's side window was cracked. "B.I.T." was spray-painted on my door. I let out a deep sigh, as the truth was now staring me in the face. Roc was home, and I had a feeling that it wasn't such a good thing after all.

Chapter 3

I talked to Roc every day for almost two weeks straight, but had not been back to his place. He hadn't come to mine either, but since we had planned to have a picnic, he was on his way over with his son. He was upset about what had happened to my car, but not as much as I was. He promised to give me the money to pay for the damages, but I knew where his money was coming from. According to Roc, he was no longer "hands on," but his condo and any money that he had was given to him by Ronnie. This concerned me, and I had plans to see what I could do to help him earn his own money. I had already contacted my insurance company to have my car taken care of. The window was fixed right away, but I had to wait another week for the paint job to get done. Until then, I drove around in a rental, and kept my car in the garage. What a stupid thing for a woman to do, and, at this point, I had very little sympathy for Vanessa. A fool she was, and along with her pulling my hair, I considered this strike number two for her. There was only so much one could tolerate, and my patience with her was wearing thin.

It was a Saturday afternoon, and I had put together some ham and cheese sandwiches, chips, fruit cups, and cupcakes for us to eat on our picnic at Forest Park. I made Chassidy and Li'l Roc some frozen Mickey Mouse Popsicles and hoped they wouldn't melt too quickly. For entertainment, I dusted off two fishing rods in my garage that Latrel and Reggie used to go fishing. I bought Chassidy a smaller one and picked up some bait while I was at the store. I figured we could do a little fishing, just to have some extra fun. It was about eighty-five degrees outside, so I dressed Chassidy in a pair of jean shorts and a pink T-shirt. Pink and white Nike tennis shoes covered her feet, and her hair was sleeked back into a neat ponytail, tied with a pink ribbon. I guess I was being biased, but she was quite adorable. I wore my blue jean stretch capris, a plum-colored T-shirt, and tennis shoes. My hair was also in a ponytail, because I wanted to be comfortable.

I stood in the kitchen, making sure I had everything packed and ready to go. All I was missing was the insect repellant, so I hurried to the closet to get it. Chassidy followed me, trying to keep up. She was such a happy child, and giggled as she chased me.

"Girl, you can't keep up with me," I teased. When the doorbell rang, I couldn't keep up with her. She rushed to the door, but I was right behind her. Roc had a new steel gray Lincoln Navigator, and I could see it parked in the driveway. I opened the door, inviting him and his son to come inside. The first thing he did was ease his arm around my waist and peck my lips.

"What's up, sexy? You know anytime a woman can dress down and still look good, she one bad mamma jamma."

His compliments always made me blush, and seeing him period genuinely excited me. He reached for Chassidy, picking her up and kissing her cheeks.

"Muah," he said. "Hey, beautiful. Girl, you know you lookin' more and more like yo' daddy every day."

I cut my eyes, as sometimes the truth was hard to admit. Li'l Roc was still standing by the door, so I reached out my hand to his.

"Hi," I politely said. He wouldn't smile at all, but did reach out to shake my hand. "You are so adorable. How old are you?"

"Five," he responded, but pouted right after.

"Are you okay?" I asked.

"Leave his knucklehead ass alone," Roc said. "I had to get in his shit in the car and now he got an attitude."

I closed the door. "Well, come on inside and let's go in the kitchen. I'm just about finished getting everything together and we can leave in about ten minutes."

Roc carried Chassidy in his arms, tickling her and making her laugh. Li'l Roc followed us, and when we got to the kitchen, I offered him a Popsicle. He declined, moving his head from side to side, still pouting.

Roc commented again. "When somebody offer you somethin', what are you supposed to say?"

"No, thank you," Li'l Roc replied, then slightly rolled his eyes. Roc put Chassidy down, then stepped up to Li'l Roc, poking at his chest. I definitely knew where that came from.

"You need to get yo' shit together. Do you remember what I told you in the car?"

Li'l Roc nodded and listened. "I meant what I said and I will not repeat myself again. Get it together, all right?"

Li'l Roc nodded again, this time without pouting. Roc pointed to Chassidy. "You know who that is right there?" Li'l Roc shrugged his shoulders. "That's your li'l sister, Chassidy. She got it goin' on like you and me, don't she?" He nodded again. "Always have her back, 'cause that's blood right there. The same blood runnin' through your veins runnin' through hers." Roc crossed his fingers. "Tight like this, okay?"

Li'l Roc crossed his fingers and repeated what Roc said. "Tight like this."

Roc rubbed the top of his son's head. "Now, that's what's up."

It appeared that everyone was back on the same page, so I gave Roc the picnic basket, blankets, and pillows to put in his truck. As we stood outside loading up, he looked at me like I was crazy with the fishing poles in my hands.

"Where in the hell are you goin' with those?"

"We're going fishing. Have you never been fishing before?"

"If I have, I can't remember. But I thought we were supposed to be havin' a picnic."

"We're doing that too, but we can also catch fish as well."

"Are you cookin' the fish later on tonight?"

"Nope."

"Then what's the purpose?"

"The purpose is to have fun with the kids and with you."

Roc cut his eyes at me, and after the kids were strapped into their safety seats, we left. Roc had no concern for our ears and he blasted the music as high as it could go. I looked back, seeing Li'l Roc bobbing his head and Chassidy, with a frown, covering her ears. Definitely, like mother, like daughter; like father, like son.

"Now, you already know what I'm going to say. I think you raise the volume on that thing just to irritate me."

Roc smiled and bobbed his head, ignoring my hint. A few minutes later, he turned down the volume.

"Before I forget, look in the glove compartment and get that envelope," he said.

I reached for the envelope in the glove compartment, noticing several hundred dollar bills inside.

"That's for your car. Sorry about that, but payback gon' be a muthafucka."

I put the envelope back into the glove compartment and closed it. "My car is already taken care of. Thanks, though, and I appreciate your kindness. I'm almost afraid to ask, but have you talked to her since then?"

"We don't talk anymore. All we do is cuss each other out. Yes, I've had the pleasure of cursin' her ass out because she came over again, tryin' to bring mo' noise. This time, I didn't open my door, so she had to handle her business on the other side."

"Well, that was a smart move. Just be careful and I know I don't have to tell you to watch your back. She has some serious issues, and if you've been dealing with that mess for . . . how many years?"

"Seven. And, yes, we have always had a rocky relationship, but don't ask me why. All love one minute, hate the next."

"I guess it be like that sometimes."

As much as I wanted to know about Roc's relationship with Vanessa, I really didn't care about it. I already knew what it consisted of, and the answer was a whole lot of disrespect. Shame on both of them for being in a battle for love for that damn long.

When we arrived at Forest Park, I could see a cozy spot from a distance. It was underneath a shaded tree on a slight hill. A few feet away was a pond where several people were already fishing. The kids had plenty of room to run around and play. I predicted we would have a decent time.

Roc carried most of our things to the designated spot and I held the kids' hands. He laid the blankets on the green grass and dropped the pillows on top. I blew up two huge balls for the kids, using an air pump. They couldn't wait to play with them, and when I suggested eating first, they refused. I sat on the blanket next to Roc, who was already laid back on one of the pillows. A cool breeze was coming in, making it so relaxing.

"Aren't you going to eat something?" I asked Roc. I pulled out the ham and cheese sandwiches, showing them to him.

"What is that? Ham and cheese? No, thank you. Had enough of that shit in jail. What else you got in there?"

I pulled out the chips, fruit cups, and cupcakes. "Okay, which one?"

Roc turned to his side, resting on his elbow. He reached for the fruit cups and a small bag of Doritos.

"Thanks," he said with a smile. He looked so sexy in a dark blue wife beater, cargo shorts, and Jordans on his feet. I wasn't the only one who could dress so simply, yet look spectacular. All day I had wanted to kiss him, just to let him know that I wasn't bitter about what had happened at his place. I took the opportunity, and leaned in to give him a lengthy, juicy kiss. He reached up to the back of my head, holding it steady and softly rubbing my hair. My eyes closed, as kissing him always seemed so perfect. Chassidy interrupted our kiss when she came over and reached for a cupcake. I opened the package for her, and gave Li'l Roc a bag of chips he was reaching for. When I asked if either of them wanted a Popsicle, both of them said no.

"Why doesn't anyone want a Popsicle? It's hot and I thought they would help to cool us down."

"Shit, then give me one," Roc said, looking down at his goods. "I definitely need somethin' to calm me down right about now."

He wasn't the only one, so I gave him one of the Popsicles and kept one for myself. The kids ran off to play again while Roc and I slurped on each other's Popsicles. "Remind me to thank you later," he said. "This pic-nookie was an excellent idea, and who would have thought I'd be havin' this much fun?"

The Popsicle juices were dripping from his lips, and you better believe I was there to suck them. He was working my lips and Popsicle too, and we couldn't help but laugh.

"You know if the kids weren't with us, I would lay you back on this blanket and fuck somethin' up. Feel how hard my dick is right now."

"I don't have to feel it. I can already see it through your shorts. Calm down, baby, and you know I'm going to take care of that real soon."

"Soon? Shit I was hopin' you'd take care of it for me now. Let me play with those titties, touch your pussy or somethin'. That will calm me down real quick."

I watched Chassidy and Li'l Roc continuing to play with their balls and chasing each other. They seemed to be having a good time, so I responded to Roc's suggestion. "Not out here, okay? There will be so much time left for that later."

Roc moved over, straddling his legs behind me as we both sat up. He wrapped his arms around my waist and nibbled on my ear.

"Be creative, Roc," he said, repeating those words I'd said before. "Work with what space—"

I turned my head to the side. "You are not going to let me forget what I said to you about being creative, are you?"

"Nope. And I'm goin' to live by those words, especially when we're together."

His hands eased up my shirt, touching my lace bra. My nipples had already become erect, and when he softly shaved his hands across them, I could feel my breasts tighten.

"See," Roc whispered in my ear. "This looks totally innocent, but brings great pleasure. Keep smilin' and lookin' at the kids playin' and they will pay us no mind."

I couldn't believe I was letting Roc massage my breasts and get me so aroused in public. There weren't too many people around, but it did feel pretty awkward. His touch felt good, too, so I couldn't complain about that.

Roc placed his lips on my earlobe and whispered in my ear, "Damn, these titties soft as hell. I wanna suck them, though. Can I?"

My body was tingling all over, but sucking my breasts would be going too far. "No, Roc. This is as far as we go and this is quite enough."

"Aww, you ain't no fun. All you gotta do is throw these covers over your head for a minute or two. We can pretend that we're wrestlin' or playin' around."

My eyes were still focused on the kids, but my mind was elsewhere. "No," I laughed. "Absolutely not. And is this your idea of a pic-nookie?"

Roc lowered his hands from my breasts, causing the tingling to go away. "Exactly. Now answer this question for me. Are you wet yet?"

I turned my head to the side as he rested his chin on my shoulder. "What? What's it to you?"

"I know you are, just by how hard those nipples were. Keep on grinnin' and watchin' the kids. Sit Indian style, and I'm gon' bend my knees. Pull up the blanket, and lay it across your lap."

"You got this all figured out, don't you?"

Roc didn't answer, just bent his knees and remained straddled behind me. I reached for the blanket, covering myself from the waist down. Roc touched my hips, and then eased his hands underneath the blanket. He popped the buttons on my capris and his fingers dipped into my wetness. His touch always made me gasp, so I did.

"I knew you would like it," he whispered in my ear. "Chill and . . . And how in the hell did you get this wet so fast? Damn, baby, this shit feels too good."

My eyes fluttered and all I could do was suck in my bottom lip. "Please don't talk anymore. You will make me jump on top of you soooo quick and fuck your brains out."

"That's what I want you to do."

"But I can't," I whined.

"Then chill and just let me finish."

I took a few deep breaths, as Roc's fingers were turning circles inside of me. I mean, he was working it like a professional, flicking his fingers fast and causing my insides to feel as if they were being tickled. We could both hear what his actions were doing to my insides and my juices were causing a stir.

"I love the sound of that," Roc whispered again. "Don't you hear it?"

I nodded, squeezing my stomach tightly and tightening my legs. I looked at the kids coming our way and dropped my head. "Hurry, baby, they're coming."

"So are you," Roc said, but my come didn't get there fast enough. With the kids only a few feet away, Roc pulled out, leaving me high and dry . . . well, actually, wet as ever.

Chassidy jumped into my lap and Roc stood up. "I'ma go over here to this bathroom," he said, smiling. "I'll be right back." He looked at Li'l Roc. "Man, do you need to go to the bathroom?"

Li'l Roc said no and stayed with me and Chassidy. They reached for the cupcakes, allowing me time to get up and button my capris. I felt very sticky between my legs, and when I got Roc home, I intended to make him pay for what he'd done.

Roc was in the bathroom for several minutes, and when he came back I didn't even have to ask what took him so long. "That was a good one," he whispered to me as I was trying to untangle the string on the fishing rod. "I let go of some mad-ass sperm and you should have seen it."

"Uh, thanks for sharing with your nasty self. You are so nasty and I can't believe I let you do that to me."

"That's 'cause you nasty too. Now, what's up with these fishin' rods?"

"I'm just trying to untangle this one. If you would get me some of that bait over there, I would appreciate it."

As Roc got the bait, I kept my eyes on Chassidy and Li'l Roc. He threw his ball hard at her face, causing her to fall on the ground. She hit the ground pretty hard, and that's what made her cry. I dropped my rod and went to go pick her up. Roc had seen what had happened as well, and he tore into Li'l Roc.

"Nigga, what's wrong with you?" Roc said, punching his chest. "Why you do yo' sister like that?"

I couldn't believe Roc's punch didn't cause Li'l Roc to shed one tear. It sounded off pretty loud to me, and calling him a nigga just . . . It just bothered the hell out of me.

"Speak when I'm talkin' to you, fool!" Roc demanded of his son.

Li'l Roc didn't say a word, just mean mugged his father as if he could tear him apart. That made Roc even madder and he grabbed him by his shirt.

I quickly put Chassidy down and touched Roc's shoulder. "Look. I know this is your child, but he didn't mean no harm. Kids have accidents all the time and it's no big deal. Please don't talk to your son like that. There is a better way to handle children when they get out of line. Chastising him by punching him is not the way."

"Fuck that. He needs to man up and take responsibility for his actions. I'm not raisin' no punk, Dez, so you can get that shit out of your head."

"There will come a time when he needs to man up, but you need to let a five-year-old be a five-year-old. Now, please let go of his shirt. You can do whatever it is that you want to do with your son, but not in my presence."

Roc let go of Li'l Roc's shirt. "You lucky today, but get your butt over there to your sister and apologize. And if you ever treat her like that again, I'ma put—"

I covered Roc's mouth, but he moved my hand away. "Put my foot up your ass!"

Li'l Roc apologized to Chassidy, but she couldn't care less. Yet again, I was pretty darn upset with Roc about his actions, but, for now, I left the situation alone. I told Li'l Roc and Chassidy to follow me down by the water, and showed them how to toss their rods into the water. At first, Roc was too mad to say anything, but after he realized that nobody was tripping but him, he finally got his act together. He helped Li'l Roc toss his rod, and the farther it went into the water, they gave each other high-fives. Chassidy could barely throw her rod, and after a while, all she did was chase the ducks that had come over to us. She was trying to pet them, and so was Li'l Roc. A few minutes later, Roc had a tug on his rod, and the two of them reeled in a fish. It was a mid-sized pan fish and was wobbling all over. Roc pulled it out of the water, watching it flop around in the grass. He and Li'l Roc both looked kind of scared of it.

"Now what?" Roc said, looking down at it.

"Touch it," I said. "Pick it up and touch it, before we throw it back in the water."

Roc frowned, but reached down to pick it up. The fish slipped out of his hand, causing me and Li'l Roc to laugh. I hurried to pick up the fish, inviting the kids to touch it. Li'l Roc hesitantly touched it, but said that it felt slimy.

"Yes, it does," I said, pointing out different parts of the fish. "These are his fins, his tail is right here, and these are scales. He's called a pan fish because he's just big enough for you to fry him in a pan. Can you see his eyes? What color are they?"

Li'l Roc moved closer, observing the fish and touching him again. "They look blue. Are we going to take him home to cook him?"

"No, I think we'd better put him back into the water. He really likes it there, but maybe we can try to catch another one that looks different. Great job on catching this one and thumbs up!"

I gave Li'l Roc a high-five and he was all smiles. I let him throw the fish back into the water and he did. He was anxious to catch another one, but, unfortunately for us, we stood in the hot sun for at least another hour and didn't catch a thing. Afterward, we played ball with the kids and lay out on the blanket, laughing and talking as if our lives had not missed one beat. Chassidy was getting antsy, so I suggested packing up and leaving.

The drive home was noisy as ever. The kids were talking and so were Roc and I. I really enjoyed my day with him, and looked forward to many more days like this to come. When we got back to my house, I cooked dinner, we watched a movie, the kids took showers, and then we called it a night. Chassidy had fallen asleep on Roc's lap, and wherever her *The Princess and the Frog* pillow lay, so did she. He carried her to her room, and I got the guestroom prepared for Li'l Roc. Latrel had so many action figures, video games, puzzles, etc. in his room in the basement, so I took Li'l Roc downstairs so he could gather some things to take to the upstairs guestroom with him. He picked up Latrel's Xbox and also got some games. He liked the big puzzle pieces of *Iron Man,* so I picked those up too. All kinds of books lined Latrel's bookshelves, so I picked up two books I figured Li'l Roc would like.

"Do you like to read?" I asked.

"No, I hate books."

"Why?"

"Because my teacher makes me read them at school."

"Then you must have a very, very smart teacher. She just wants you to be smart too, and I do as well. Reading books is so good for you and it's an excellent way to feed your brain. Your brain has to eat, you know. And when you feed it, wowww, so many wonderful things can happen to you. Remember that, okay?"

Li'l Roc nodded and we carried the items up to the guestroom. I could hear Roc talking to someone on his phone, so I let him handle his business with whomever and got Li'l Roc situated for bed.

"Now, you can watch the television and play with the puzzle tonight. Your dad can hook up the game for you tomorrow, but I want you to get some sleep. I hope you're comfortable. Do you like lights on or lights off?"

"Lights off!" he yelled, pulling the covers over his head.

"Well, okay." I smiled, turning the lights off on my way out.

"Miss Dez," he said.

"Yes."

"Thanks for being nice. My mama said you were a mean B."

I was stunned, but then again, no, I wasn't. "You're welcome. And I'm glad that you got a chance to see that I'm not mean."

He smiled and I walked down the hallway, shaking my head. How dare Vanessa say something like that to her son, with her dysfunctional self? What a poor excuse for a mother.

When I got to my room, Roc was sitting in my chair, laughing at what someone was saying on the other end of the phone. I went into my closet, stripped naked, and gathered my things for a shower. I tossed my nightgown over my shoulder and slipped into my house shoes. Leaving the closet, I eyeballed Roc and his eyes got wider. He licked his lips and tried to cut his conversation short.

"Uh, say, man . . . hold that thought." The person on the other end kept talking, and I watched Roc nod his head. I made my way to the bathroom and turned on the water in the shower. Wasting no more time, I got inside and started to lather myself. A few minutes later, Roc joined me. I had the pleasure of lathering his body, and the look of the white, sudsy soap against his black sexy body was priceless. I dropped the soap, pressing my body as close to his as I could. My arms rested on his shoulders, and before I said anything, I delivered a passionate kiss that locked our lips for minutes.

"Mmmm," Roc said, backing away from me. "Let's hurry this shit up so we can get to the bed."

"I say be creative and work with whatever space you have."

He smiled and rubbed his hands up and down on my backside. "Then I say bend that ass over and let's get this shit started."

After Roc strapped up with a condom, his wish was my command. We tore it up in the bathroom, but being in the shower didn't allow us the space we needed. The bedroom definitely did, and as Roc fucked me doggie style on the bed, I couldn't get enough. I threw myself back at him, as he tightly squeezed my hips. I massaged my own breasts and was on cloud nine feeling his hard, long meat slide in and out of me. His rhythm was perfect and the way he eased in from different angles was impressive. I felt defeated, and pulled on my hair.

"You . . . you got me, Roc. I am hooked on the way you do this pussy. You treat it so well and I loooove it!"

"I'm hooked like a muthafucka too. I crave for this shit, baby, every gotdamn day of my life! Nobody makes me feel like this. Nobody!"

I could feel Roc's dick thumping inside of me and I knew what was coming next. "Daaammmn, Dez, baby, why you fuckin' me like this."

"Ohhh, Roc, I'm there. Just . . . just keep at it, baby, and I will give you something special to remember."

I cut loose on Roc, coating his shaft and leaving his balls dripping wet. He held on tightly to my hips, and we both fell forward, completely out of breath. Slowly, he rolled over next to me, trying to gather himself.

I rested my head in my hand, looking over at him. "Do you think the kids heard us? We were pretty loud, you know. Maybe you should go check on Li'l Roc. I'm surprised you didn't go tuck him in."

"With your door closed, I doubt that they heard us. As for tuckin' him in, please. He don't need to be treated like no baby and those days are long gone. And if they did hear us, Li'l Roc knows what's up."

"What does that mean?"

"It means he knows what it sounds like when a woman and man are havin' sex. It also means stay put 'cause it ain't yo' business."

I reached over, rubbing his chest. "You know, I often wonder how the two of us are going to make this work. It's like we've come from two different worlds, trying to pull it together to create one that will make sense.

Do you think it's possible for us to do it? I mean, the way you want to live your life is so different from the way I want to live mine. I'm forty-two years old, Roc, and even though I sometimes think this is just about us having fun, there's so much more to it than that. I have very strong feelings for you and there are times that I feel as if I'm in love. Then I ask myself if I could be serious, because this thing between us is complicated in many ways. Am I analyzing things too much? Do you ever think or feel how I do?"

"All the time, ma, but I'm hopin' that these feelings that we have for each other keep us together, no matter what. We gon' have to learn to compromise on some things, especially you. I'm usually down for whatever, but you the one who set in your ways. Never will I make you feel hoodwinked, bamboozled, or led astray. My shit is out there for you to see, and you have to decide what's up."

"Let's be real, Roc. You haven't been that open and honest with me about everything. I'm left to assume a lot, and not once have you said where you would like for our relationship to stand. I mean, what are we? Friends, companions, lovers . . . What? I need to know, only because I want to know what I can and cannot expect from you. Does that make sense?"

"We can be whatever you want us to be."

"No, that's bullshit and you know it. I already told you that I would never pursue a relationship with a man who wasn't ready, but are you ready to give me all that I may require?"

Roc was silent for a while, and I already knew this was a conversation he didn't want to have. "I would love to give you everything you require, but I got some loose ends to tie up. I planned on doin' so, and I can assure you that it will be taken care of soon."

"Loose ends meaning women? Just how many women are you seeing?"

"I'm not sexing nobody but you, but I still got some close friends here and there. It ain't nothin' serious about the shit and most of them fell off when I went to prison."

I sat up in bed, pulling the covers up over me. Roc followed suit and both of us sat against the headboard. "So, let me get this straight. For the record, you are only having sex with me?"

Roc turned to me with a very serious look on his face. "No one but you."

"Are you sure?"

"Positive."

"Why only me?"

"Why not you? I'm one hundred percent satisfied with how you put it on me, and I seek no one else to give me what only you can."

I shook my head, not even telling Roc that in no way did I believe him. If he was telling the truth, he was going to have to forgive me for giving him no credit. There was just something about him that made me not want to trust a word that he'd said. Then again, he was so into this thing with us that maybe I was wrong for feeling as I did. At this point, I wanted to pull my hair out for not being able to put my finger on the doubtful feeling I had inside. I don't know why I had such a skeptical feeling, but I knew my gut didn't lie.

Chapter 4

For the last month and a half, things had been pro-
gressing very well. Roc and I were spending an enormous amount of time together, especially with the kids.
Latrel had been home twice, and he and Roc got along
well. We went everywhere together and it was such a
joy to see all of us on the same page. I had not been
back to Roc's place to visit, but he had spent plenty
of nights at my house. Maybe even more than he had
been spending at his, and he often brought Li'l Roc
with him. Latrel was overly thrilled about me and Roc
getting back together. So thrilled that when I asked if
he'd call Sherri to take her out again, he promised me
that he would.

Another good thing that happened was that I'd
gotten Roc a job in the mailroom where I worked. I
wasn't worried about Greg working there because our
so-called relationship was over. Roc didn't deliver the
mail on my floor, and that was a good thing. In no
way did I think it was a good idea to have him around
twenty-four-seven, because he seemed like the kind
of person who sometimes needed space. I did too, so
whenever he didn't call for a couple of days, I was okay
with it. As long as we didn't go weeks without speaking
to each other, that was fine by me.

Mr. Anderson had been back from his business trip,
and as usual, he had me running around the office like
a chicken with its head cut off. I was standing in an-

other VP's office, waiting on him to sign some papers that Mr. Anderson needed right away. Dressed in my silk purple ruffled blouse and hip-hugging gray skirt, I waited for Mr. Blevins to end a call. He held up one finger, nodding his head and whispering that he'd be with me in a minute. Just to give him privacy, I exited his office, taking a seat in a chair that was right outside of his door. I crossed my legs, looking at my bare legs and high-heeled black shoes. As soon as I looked up, I saw Greg coming my way. I did my best to avoid him by turning my head in the other direction as if I didn't see him. That, of course, didn't work.

"Hello there, Miss Thickety Thick," he said, checking me out. I hated to be called that, and it bothered me that he always referred to me as being thick. True to the fact or not, he didn't have to always say it. I stood, just to address him appropriately.

"Hi, Greg. How are you?"

"Sexy lady, I would be so much better if you would agree to go out on another date with me. I hope that's not asking too much."

I didn't want to hurt Greg's feelings, but he really wasn't my type. He wasn't a bad-looking man, but he was a bit too thin for my taste. He was kind of nerdy, too, and he was very much the opposite of Roc. "Let me think about it, Greg. I am seeing someone else right now, but it's nothing serious."

He swiped his forehead and smiled. "Whew, I'm glad to hear that. I hope you call soon and you know I'll be waiting."

I heard Mr. Blevins call for me, so I told Greg I would talk to him later. When I walked back into Mr. Blevins's office, he had the papers signed, ready to give back to me.

"Sorry for your wait," he said. "Tell John I'll see him around seven and do not be late."

"Will do." I smiled.

I returned to Mr. Anderson's office, and he had his back turned while on the phone. He didn't hear me come in, but I could hear him whispering something over the phone. Now, as his administrative assistant, I knew what his phone calls were all about. I knew what his so-called extended business trips were about too, but it wasn't my place to say one word. As he laughed at the caller, I cleared my throat. He quickly swung his chair around, abruptly ending his call. I handed the papers from Mr. Blevins to him.

"Mr. Blevins said he'd see you around seven and don't be late."

Mr. Anderson slapped his forehead. "Oops, I almost forgot about that. Thanks for reminding me." He looked at his watch. "Have you had lunch yet, or would you like to run across the street with me to get a bite to eat?"

"I'll pass. I'm trying to watch my weight a little, so I'm going to just grab something quick from the cafeteria. Thanks, though, and if you don't mind, I'm leaving in about five minutes. Is there anything else you would like for me to do before I go?"

"Nope. Just close my door on your way out. If I'm not back when you get here, I will see you tomorrow."

"Okay. Thanks again."

I left Mr. Anderson's office, closing the door behind me. He was really too nice to me, but at times could be a flirt. When I first started working for him, all he did was compliment me on how I looked and his stares made me uncomfortable. I didn't mind the compliments, but it was the way he said them that made the difference. One day, I pulled him aside, telling him how

I felt and assuring him that I was in no way interested in married men. I didn't care much for dating much older men, either, so we got that conversation out of the way real quick. Since then, he chilled and we continued to get along just fine. He didn't say much about his daughter, Sherri, going on a date with Latrel, and I said nothing about it either.

I removed ten dollars from my purse and headed to the cafeteria to get something to eat. A couple of times I had been to the gym with Roc. Since I had been cutting back on eating so much, I felt myself losing a little weight. It wasn't much to brag about, and it wasn't like I had really been trying.

The cafeteria was crowded with some of my coworkers, as well as students. Normally, I sat with three other ladies from another department, Val, Bethany, and Emma. They were much older ladies, and I think Val was the only one who was in her forties like me. Emma waved so I could see them, and after I paid for my chicken salad and fruit, I went over to the table to take a seat. They all spoke and I spoke back.

"What's cooking with you, girlee?" Bethany asked. She was an older white woman who was nosey as hell. Val and Emma were black, but they were just as nosey.

"Nothing much. Mr. Anderson got me running all over the place today, and my feet are killing me," I joked.

"You know us admins can relate, but it's so much better working for a man than it is a woman. Jackie is a pain in the ass!" Val said.

We all laughed, only because her boss, Jackie, had a reputation for being a force to be reckoned with. Still, I disagreed that it was much easier working for a man, and we spent thirty minutes debating the issue.

Only a few times while I was in the cafeteria did I see Roc, and today I hadn't planned on it. Emma, however, nudged me and the other ladies to get our attention.

"Have you ladies seen or heard of the Mailroom Mandingo?" Bethany said.

I kind of, sort of, knew where this conversation was going, but I played clueless. "No, wha . . . who are you talking about?"

"The new chocolate hunk in the mailroom. Oh my God, Desa Rae, you have got to turn your head to see him. He is freaking gorgeous and hot as ever." Bethany fanned herself.

I was surprised by her actions, but Val and Emma agreed with her. "I can't believe you haven't seen him, Desa Rae, and where in the heck have you been hiding?" Val asked.

I slowly turned around, just to look in the direction of the ladies' eyes. Yes, I did see Roc standing by a soda machine, debating what kind he wanted. How in the hell he made a simple mailroom uniform look so enticing, I didn't know. Pants were fitting his thighs in all the right places and the short-sleeved shirt clung to his muscular frame. The young woman behind him who was waiting to get her soda, her eyes were glued to his butt.

"Are you all talking about the young man at the soda machine?" I asked.

"Yes," Emma said. "What a piece of artistic work."

We all laughed and I couldn't help what I was about to do. I turned to the ladies. "He is fine, and see, I'm the kind of woman who when I see a man I want, I will go after him." I looked at Val. "Give me a pen and piece of paper."

Her mouth hung wide open. "Noooo," she whispered. "Are you going to confront him?"

"Yes, and I'm going to give him my number. Hopefully, he'll call me and we can indulge in some sweaty sex or something. Hurry, before he walks away."

The ladies sat almost speechless. "Wha . . . Well, he's already moved to another vending machine," Bethany said. "If you want to catch him, you'd better hurry."

Val hurried to give me a piece of paper and a pen from her purse. "I can't believe you're doing this. That's being a bit aggressive, don't you think? A woman should never approach a man, and I don't care how gorgeous he is."

"I beg to differ. My mother always told me to go after whatever it is in life that I wanted and never let a good opportunity pass you by."

The ladies sat in disbelief as I got up from the table, making my way over to the vending machines. By now, the other chick had kicked up a conversation with Roc, and she seemed to have his attention. Not for long. I crept up from behind, lightly tapping his shoulder. He turned, smiling to play it off.

"What's up?" he asked.

I held up the piece of paper and pen. "Nothing. I just wondered if I could get your sevens or possibly get you to come to my house and lay me tonight?"

The young woman he was speaking to, her eyes bugged and she pursed her lips. When Roc replied, "You can have anything you want," she walked away. He eased his arm around my waist, and when I looked over at the table where the ladies were sitting, their eyes were popping out of their heads and mouths were covered with their hands. I shrugged as if I were shocked by Roc's actions too.

"Why you playin'?" Roc asked. He pecked my lips and all I could do was laugh. I took his hand, asking him to follow me.

I didn't even notice Greg sitting close by until he spoke out. "It looks pretty serious to me."

I ignored Greg, but Roc stopped. "What you say?"

Greg repeated himself. "I said the relationship looks pretty serious to me. Only a few hours ago, Desa Rae said she wasn't in a serious relationship. Obviously, that wasn't true."

Roc looked puzzled, and I couldn't believe Greg was trying to put me on blast. "Greg, please. It is what it is, okay?"

He shrugged. "Whatever. Hey, your loss, not mine."

I moved forward, but Roc stopped me again. Luckily his voice wasn't that loud. "What in the hell was that all about? You fuckin' that nigga or what?"

"No. I'll tell you about it later. Right now, I want you to meet some of my coworkers." I stepped up to the table and couldn't decide who looked the most shocked.

"Girlee, wow, do you move fast?" Bethany said. "If I would have known it was that easy, I would have taken the initiative."

I decided to let the women off the hook. They'd heard me speak of Roc before, but no one knew he had been in prison. "Ladies, this is Chassidy's father, Roc. I know you all remember me mentioning him, right?"

The ladies' tongues were tied until Roc reached out, shaking their hands one by one.

"Oh, Desa Rae, you made us all look like fools," Val said. "But nice to meet you, Roc, and you are really a handsome young man."

"Appreciate the compliment," Roc said, blushing. "I do have to get back to the mailroom, but you ladies enjoy your lunch."

Everyone said good-bye to Roc, and I was surprised that, before he walked away, he gave me another peck on my lips. "See you later, baby," he said.

"No doubt," I said, watching him walk away.

"Desa Rae Jenkins," Emma said. "How . . . what . . . why . . . and where did you meet him? He is rather young, isn't he?"

I sat back at the table. "He's twenty-seven, but don't let his age fool you."

"I can sit here all day long and listen to you tell me how great the sex is, but I have a feeling that you will not spill the beans," Bethany said.

"Unfortunately not, but I will say this, age is just a number and a number don't mean jack."

The ladies laughed and we quickly changed the subject from bosses to men. Of course I was a little late getting back from lunch, and thank God Mr. Anderson had already checked out for the day.

Normally, Roc got off at 3:30 P.M., and I didn't get off until five. He went home and so did I. Sometimes, we'd meet up to get a bite to eat, and other times he'd meet me at my house. As I was driving home, my cell phone rang and it was him.

"What's the play for today?" he asked.

"Not sure. I'm not really hungry, but after I pick up Chassidy, I'm stopping at Monica's house to see her. I won't be long, but I should be home by eight. Are you coming over?"

"Nah, not tonight. I think I'm gon' just chill."

"Did you cash your check yet?"

"I dropped it in the bank. Never thought I'd see the day that I, Rocky Dawson, would be gettin' a paycheck, but anything for my Dez."

"I hope you're not working because of me. I hope you're working for yourself. You have to admit that it feels pretty good to make money the legit way, doesn't it?"

"Listen, I'm grateful, but I didn't mean it the way I said it. And if you think I'm supposed to be over here jumpin' up and down over a $960 check that I make every two weeks, I'm not that moved. Grateful, but not moved."

I had to slam on my brakes, almost hitting the car in front of me. I had jumped through hoops to get Roc that job in the mailroom, and with a police record like his, it damn sure wasn't easy. He was being ungrateful, and twelve dollars an hour was not bad at all. With the economy as bad as it was, millions of people would kick butt to hold his position. I couldn't even respond, so I didn't. I hung up on his butt, and when he called back, I didn't answer. No doubt, I'd pay for my actions later.

I picked up Chassidy from daycare and was on my way to Monica's house in Maryland Heights. When I got there, I was shocked to see Reggie's car in her driveway. I wondered what the hell was going on, and I couldn't wait to get out of my car to see what was up. I rang the doorbell, with Chassidy on my hip. Monica opened the door, whispering that Reggie had just come over and needed someone to talk to.

I went inside, whispering back at her, "What in the hell does he want?"

She shrugged. "He called out of the blue, looking for you. I told him you were on your way over here, and the next thing I knew, he just showed up."

I swallowed the lump in my throat, unprepared to see Reggie again. The last time we spoke, he chewed me out about Chassidy and ridiculed me for moving on with my life. I guessed since his second marriage had failed, maybe he was ready to talk like he had some sense. Monica's house wasn't the place to have this conversation, and how dare he just show up out of nowhere? I made my way to the kitchen, with Chassidy still on my hip. Reggie had his back turned, but his good-smelling cologne lit up the entire place. He was dressed in a brown suit with a peach shirt underneath. His wavy hair was perfectly lined and I could see his clean-cut beard from the side. He heard Chassidy's voice and quickly turned all the way around. Seeing me too, he stood up and grinned.

"Hello, Dee," he said, reaching out to hug me. I gave him a half hug and patted his back. Monica entered the kitchen, offering to take Chassidy into another room so we could talk.

"She may be a little hungry, Monica, so grab her veggie dips from my bag."

Monica got the veggie dips from my bag and left the room with Chassidy.

I sat across the table from Reggie, seriously wondering what the hell was up. He clinched his hands together, pausing before he finally said anything.

"You look really nice. Not that you ever didn't, but I guess I was a fool for not realizing a good thing when I had it," he said.

Reggie waited for me to respond, but I didn't. I folded my arms, and continued to listen.

"I . . . I just had this dying urge to see you. I stopped by the house a few times, but I could tell you had company. That's why I reached out to Monica. When she said you were coming over, I couldn't resist."

"Okay, so now that you've seen me, now what? I'm confused, Reggie, and what is this all about?"

"I want my life back. The life that I once shared with you and Latrel, I want it back. We were so happy together, and even though I didn't understand what it was that I was going through at the time, I now know that leaving you was one of the biggest mistakes of my life. I'm not asking you to drop everything right now for me, but I want you to think about it. Have you been on stable ground since we've been divorced? Can you honestly say that you have been happy with the person you're with? Roc is not the one, baby, and you know that he's not. All I'm asking for is another chance, and I have spent the last several months trying to figure out the best way to come to you about this. My life has been in shambles and I need a woman like you to help me piece it back together. You're the only woman capable of doing it and the only woman I have truly ever loved."

Reggie said a mouthful and I didn't even know where to start. Years ago, he left me high and dry with very little reasoning other than he'd fallen out of love. I went through hell without him, and he ripped our marriage apart, all for another piece of ass. There was a time that I would have given the world to hear him say what he'd just said to me, and even though Roc may not be the one for me, neither was Reggie. I was absolutely sure about that, and I did my best to spare his feelings, especially since my heart went out to him.

"I have very few words for you right now, Reggie. Obviously, you are going through something because of your failed marriage. I definitely know how that is, but traveling backward is not the solution to your problem. Besides, I'm not in love with you anymore. I care deeply for you and I wish that we could have a better relationship because of our son. You didn't seem to want that and all I can say is . . . is, honey, I have moved on. I may not be all complete yet, but one day I will be. I don't see you in my future in the way that you want us to be and I'm sorry to have to say that to you."

Reggie lowered his head, and rubbed his forehead. "I knew you were going to possibly say that, but just think about it before you—"

"There's nothing to think about. I'm sorry."

He sighed and rubbed his beard. "What's the story with you and Chassidy's so-called father? Are you in love with him? The two of you are like night and day, and I can't believe you're still dealing with him. Please don't continue in that relationship, for the sake of your daughter. In the end it will not be worth it."

"I haven't predicted our ending yet, and the verdict is still out on whether I'm in love with him. But whatever happens with us, I have very few regrets. He has given me a precious child, and, like you, there will always be a place in my heart for him. Now, I don't know what else to say to make you feel better, but you may want to try counseling like I did. It helped and I'm sure it can help you too."

Reggie sat silent for a while, and moments later he backed up from the table. He tossed his suit jacket over his shoulder and looked at me while shaking his head. "If you change your mind, you have my number to call me."

I said not one word and watched as Reggie made his way through the living room and left. Shortly after, Monica came in with her lips pursed.

"Now, he has some nerves," she said, taking her seat at the table. Chassidy was on her lap.

"How do you think I feel? I wanted to say something awful to him, but I felt bad for him. Reggie is only reaping what he sowed. Monica, you know I gave that man my all, and why in the hell would I even think about going back to him?"

"No, why would he think you would? I tell you, men are something else, and at forty-three years old, I am still trying to figure them out."

I threw my hand back. "Don't even waste your time trying. The things they do we will never understand."

"I agree. Meanwhile, what is up with you and the Rocster? I know things have been going well, but I'm concerned about you, Dee. I still haven't been able to swallow what happened at his place that day and I don't want you putting yourself in any more dangerous situations like that."

"I haven't been back over there since. Roc doesn't mention Vanessa or Ronnie around me, and I really couldn't tell you what's up with either of them. As long as they don't come to my house, we cool."

Monica got up from the table and asked if I wanted something to drink. I told her Pepsi would be fine and she got me one from the fridge. She also gave me a couple of my favorite Hershey's chocolates with almonds.

"Right on time," I said, opening one up. "Thank you."

Monica sat back down in the chair. "How's the job thing coming along? Does Roc like it?"

"I'm not sure yet. Today he said something over the phone that kind of pissed me off. I mentioned the job and he said, 'anything for you.' Then he said that $960 every two weeks wasn't much to rave about. I thought he was being very unappreciative and I hung up on him."

"That wasn't the appropriate thing to say, but he has probably made that kind of money in an hour on the streets. Give him time, and as long as he's trying, why are you upset with him?"

"Because I wish he would do this for him, not for me. I wish he would get that, but I don't think he does. I'm not mad at him. I was just taken aback by his comment. In an effort not to start an argument, I hung up."

Monica cut her eyes and pulled a twenty dollar bill from her purse. She laid it on the table. "I bet you twenty dollars the argument that you didn't want to have will find its way to you tonight. You can't treat him like that, and you already know that Roc ain't the kind of man who will sweep that under the rug."

I told Monica to keep her money. I knew more than anyone that she was right.

As soon as I pulled in the driveway, Roc was already at my house waiting for me. I had stayed at Monica's house until 9:00 P.M. and was pretty tired. When I got out of my car, he stepped up to me.

"Yo' battery on your phone went dead, right? Or, did you hang up on me, which one?"

Ironically, just as I was getting Chassidy out of her car seat, my cell phone rang. I was sure it was Monica, checking to make sure we safely made it home. I ignored Roc and the phone, making my way to the door with Chassidy asleep on my shoulder.

"Well, we damn sure know it wasn't the battery," he said.

I sighed, really not in the mood for an argument. "Would you mind unlocking the door for me, please? Chassidy is heavy and so is my purse."

Roc unlocked the door, then tried to take Chassidy from my arms.

"I got her. I'm going to go lay her down, and then you can yell at me all you want to, okay?"

"Hurry up then."

I carried Chassidy to her bedroom and Roc headed to mine. I tucked her in bed, kissed her cheek, and turned on her nightlight. When I got to my room, Roc was sitting in his favorite chair with his hands behind his head.

"First things first," he said. "Who the fuck is Greg?"

I blew Roc off, throwing my hand back at him. "Greg is a nobody. That's exactly who he is."

"Really? A nobody who came out and said what he did today. Did you tell him you weren't in a serious relationship?"

I was stunned that Roc was even going there, and could tell he was in the mood to argue. I stood, folding my arms, and defended my one-month relationship with Greg. "I dated him while you were in prison. We went on three dates, I wasn't feeling him at all, and I stop returning his phone calls. Anything else?"

Before he could respond, his cell phone rang. He looked to see who it was, then answered. "What, muth-afucka? I'm in the middle of somethin', nigga, and I told you I would call you back." He paused, smiled, and then laughed. "Quit lyin', fool. She did what?" He paused again, listening and shaking his head. "All . . . all right. Let me hit you back in a bit. Before I go, did you take care of that for me?" He paused. "Cool. No doubt. In a minute, all right?"

Roc hung up and walked over to the closet as I was gathering my things to change clothes and shower. "Okay, so you dated him a few times. Did you up the pussy?"

If I spoke the truth, I suspected it would cause a lot of problems tonight. It really wasn't his business anyway, so I said what I felt like saying. "No, I did not up the goods because, like I said before, Greg is not my cup of tea. I was bored, and being with him gave me a chance to get out of the house, hopefully to have some fun. Unfortunately, that didn't happen. Now what?"

"Why did you hang up on me?"

"Because you were sounding ungrateful and I didn't like it."

"So when you don't like what I have to say, you hang up the fuckin' phone? Since when?"

I shrugged, making my way out of the closet. Roc moved aside to let me pass by him.

"So we goin' out like that?" he said, reaching for his keys in his pocket. "That's cool and I'ma holla at you real soon, okay?"

Roc left the room, and moments later I heard the front door close. I was going to apologize for hanging up on him, but since he had left, I picked up the phone to call him. He answered right away.

"What?" he snapped.

"I'm sorry for hanging up on you, and maybe I should—"

He hung up on me, and when I called back, he had turned off his phone. I was too tired to deal with any drama, so I called it a night, hoping and praying that my little white lie wouldn't catch up with me. Not only that, I hoped I wouldn't regret getting Roc a job, especially working with someone I was involved with. While I made no promises to Roc about ever being there for him when he was in prison, something told me all of this would come back to haunt me.

Chapter 5

Roc was really trying to play me shady, and for the next week and a half, he did not pick up the phone to call me. I called him, though, only for him to either cut me short or tell me he was busy. While at work, he avoided me altogether. I tried to catch up with him a couple of times in the mailroom, and when I did, he pretended to be so busy. I couldn't believe all of this was going down over a stupid phone call and there had to be more to it. What? I didn't know, but I was sure time would tell.

On Thursday, we had just come out of a meeting and I was on my way to the bathroom. I had to go real bad, but was approached by Roc before I went inside.

"We need to talk," he said with a disturbing look on his face.

"I've been trying to for a week and a half now, but you've been avoiding me."

"Handle your business and meet me across the hall in the stairwell."

"Give me a minute," I said, going inside of the bathroom. I quickly used it, and as I washed my hands, I wondered what Roc wanted to talk about. Maybe it was something with his job, and I guessed it was no secret that he didn't like it that much. After drying my hands with a paper towel, I dropped it in the trash. I headed across the hallway and into the stairwell where

Roc asked me to meet him. He was sitting back on the stairs, looking at me with a hard stare.

"What's going on?" I asked.

"You're a gotdamn liar, that's what's up."

His tone caught me off guard and my brows scrunched inward. "What are you talking about?"

"You know damn well what I'm talkin' about. You fucked that nigga, and you still been fuckin' his ass. He told me what was up, Dez, and why did you lie about the shit?"

I swallowed, wondering exactly what Greg had told Roc, if anything. "He told you what? And you believed him?"

Roc stood up, moving very close to me. "Are you callin' him a liar? I will go get that muthafucka right now, Dez, and have him repeat what he told me. Ain't no way in hell he knows what your bedroom looks like if he ain't been in it. Ain't no fuckin' way he knows how your pussy feels if he ain't had it! Ain't no cock-suckin' way he knows that you have a mole on your right thigh if he ain't hiked up your damn dress and seen it for himself. So tell me, baby. Who's the liar? You or him?"

I looked into Roc's fiery eyes, regretting what I had said the other day. I looked so guilty, and I really wasn't guilty of anything but a lie. There was no telling what Greg told Roc, and in no way was I in a position to defend myself. "Twice," I said, already knowing that he'd feel betrayed. Still, I didn't want to lie again. "I had sex with him two times, only when you were in prison. If he told you we have recently been intimate, that was a lie."

"Yeah, kind of like the one you told me." Roc sucked his teeth and put his hands into his pockets. "You know what? I thought you was about somethin'. You ain't shit, ma, and you just like these other fake-ass bitches out here. Then you always tryin' to judge me like yo' ass all that. You played me shady, baby, and you best believe there are consequences for that."

Deep down, yes, I was hurt because I felt as if this was on me. "I apologize for not telling you the truth, but please don't talk to me like that, or refer to me as one of your fake bitches. You're way out of line. The only reason I wasn't truthful with you about me and Greg is because I didn't want to argue with you that night. We had been getting along so well and I didn't want to go there with you."

Roc looked me over and threw his hand back at me. "To hell with you, ma. You ain't even worth my time. I don't believe shit you say, and whatever the hell was up with you and that nigga, you should have said that shit the other night. Regardless."

I defensively crossed my arms in front of me. "And you have always been so on the up and up with me, right? Please don't stand there and pretend that you have been honest with me about every single thing, knowing you haven't."

Roc snickered and let go of the doorknob he had touched. "That's right. Play the blame game and throw that shit back at me. Blame me for your fuckups, baby, but that's the oldest damn trick in the book. Find a new plan and another play toy, too. To hell with this job, and do me a favor, ditch my number, and if you need anything for Chassidy, have Latrel call me."

Roc opened the door, but I couldn't allow us to go our separate ways over something so ridiculous. I reached for his arm, but he snatched away.

"Not now, not never. Touch my arm like that again and you will really see a side of me that you won't like."

I could see the anger in his eyes, so I let it be. Roc walked out the door, and even though I wanted to go after him, I didn't. I also wanted to go and confront

Greg, but I didn't do that either. I headed back to my
desk and tried my best to get some work done.

When Friday rolled around, I went to the mailroom
to see if Roc had come into work. His boss said that Roc
had called in sick. I figured that was good news since he
at least called in, and hadn't told his boss that he quit.
In no way did I want this to be permanent, so around
noon, I asked Mr. Anderson if I could leave early. I told
him I had many errands to run, but I was actually on
my way to Roc's place so we could quickly resolve this
matter.

I arrived at his place around 1:00 P.M., and when I
rang the doorbell it took him awhile to answer. Finally,
I could hear him coming down the stairs. He opened
the door with no shirt on and his gray jockey shorts.

"I'm busy," he said.

"Do you have company? If you do, I'll leave."

He stared at me, then turned to make his way up the
steps. I entered, locking the door behind me. I went
up the steps and saw him lying back on the couch with
his feet propped up on the armrest. He focused on the
television, as if he were all into it. The room had a very
smoky smell, and I couldn't tell if it was marijuana or
smoke from the Black & Mild cigar that was lying in an
ashtray. I sat on the loveseat that was across from him
and placed my purse on the table.

"Can I please talk to you without you getting upset
with me over something so ridiculous?"

Roc continued to look at the TV, pretending to ignore me. He had a toothpick in his mouth, dangling it
around.

"I said I was sorry, and how dare you not forgive me
after all of the things you've done to me in the past? I'm

not here to play the blame game, but I did forgive you in the past for some of the things you've done. If my lie was so bad and you refuse to forgive me, fine. I made the mistake and I'll have to deal with it. But please don't quit your job and do not give up on your daughter. I'm not going to involve Latrel in our mess and you should always be there for her, no matter what."

Roc removed the toothpick, then looked over at me. "Are you finished? Let me know when you're done, so I can walk you out."

His eyes shifted back to the TV and the toothpick went back into his mouth. This was becoming so irritating for me, and I took a deep breath. I combed my feathery hair back with my fingers and gripped it in the back. "I'm not going to kiss your ass, Roc. If that's what you want me to do, I'm not. You can pretend that you have been so on the up and up with me all you want, but I know better. I know you've been over here tying up your so-called loose ends, and what about Vanessa? After all of those years together, now all of a sudden it's over? Please. Who do you think I am? I wasn't just born yesterday."

This time, Roc didn't even look at me when he spoke. "You finished yet?" He picked up his watch on the table, looking at it. "You don't have much time, so hurry up and say what else you gotta say."

Okay, if drama was what he wanted, then drama was what he was going to get. I stood up and snatched my purse up from the table. "Yes, I'm finished. And to hell with you, too, Roc. Don't call me, either, and as a matter of fact, I'm going to get my darn number changed."

"Sounds good to me," he said, sucking on the toothpick.

He sure as hell knew how to get underneath my skin, and his nonchalant attitude was doing more than that.

I picked up a pillow from his loveseat and threw it at him. It bounced off his chest, and knocked his ashtray and watch on the floor. That surely got his attention and he jumped up from the couch. He held out his hands and stepped up to me.

"What you want, Dez? You want me to kick yo' ass, is that it?"

"No," I said, blinking away water that rushed to the brims of my eyes. "I want you to listen to me and understand that I have no desires for any man but you. We will always have some disagreements, but don't treat me like I mean nothing to you. I need for you to man up and stop acting so darn childish."

Roc sucked in his bottom lip, and when his phone rang, he ignored it. "Good-bye, Dez. What you need is a grown man, and obviously you've found one in old boy at your job."

"Fine, forget it. You're not listening to me and I'm wasting my time." I moved away from Roc, slightly pushing him back so I could make room. He reached for my wrist, squeezing it tightly.

"Watch where you're steppin', and if you think a li'l crocodile tears are enough to move me, then you got me all fucked up. I don't care nothin' about no tears, or those fake cracks in your voice."

"Then what do you want from me, Roc? Do you want me to get on my knees and beg for your forgiveness? What? I'm confused." I stepped forward, this time stepping on his feet. He pushed me back on the loveseat, and, yes, I lost my balance.

"You may not know what I want," he said, removing his boxers. "But I damn sure know what you want."

Roc used his foot to kick open a compartment on his coffee table. He reached for a condom package and put the condom on. He then pointed to his dick, which was hard as ever.

"This it, ain't it? Just like the others, this all you want from Roc, don't you? When he ain't around to give it to you, you take your ass elsewhere, right?"

I knew Roc was trying to compare me to Vanessa, but that was in no way the case. He was so wrong about me, but I let him get whatever it was off his chest. I sat up, but he lay over me so I couldn't move. All I could think about was the last time he forced himself on me, and I regretted that he was about to go there again.

"Please don't do this, Roc. Sex is not all I want from you and you know it."

"Then what do you want? You still haven't told me, and fuck all that talkin' and listenin' shit. What's really up?"

"I want whatever it is that you want. Now get off me. You're hurting me."

"So damn what? And since you won't keep it real with me, I'll tell you what I want. I want to know why you ain't told me that you love me. I've been home for four months, and you ain't said shit. I'm spendin' all my time with you, tryin' to do right by you, and all you've done is lie to me and complain. What's holdin' you back this time? Tell me so I can understand what the fuck is up. Is it Greg, Reggie, some other mutha-fucka, or what?"

I closed my eyes, taking a moment to think about Reggie. No, he wasn't holding me back; it was all about Roc. "None of the above. I'm just afraid, Roc, that's all."

"Afraid of what?" he said through gritted teeth.

"Afraid of being hurt again. I'm so afraid that you're going to hurt me and leave me and Chassidy without you. I can't let my guard down, only because I know how easy it is for you to choose Ronnie over us. Vanes-sa doesn't even concern me as much, but your dedica-tion to Ronnie scares me. I had fallen in love with you and you just . . . just said to hell with me and your child, and took the fall for him, choosing to go to prison. I was angry and it's so hard for me to believe that you will never play us like that again. I don't trust you, and it's difficult for me to tell you that I love you, even when deep in my heart I know I do."

There, I said it, and now he knew it. I tried to fool myself into believing that this was just fun, but I knew it was more than that. Roc had ownership of my heart and all I could do was hope like hell that he wouldn't break it. He lifted himself off me, allowing me to sit up. He sat on the table in front of me, rubbing his hands up and down my thighs.

"Listen, I'm not goin' back to jail, so that decision will never have to be made again. You and Ronnie on different levels, and in no way can I compare the love for him to the love I have for you. I do love you too, Dez, but holdin' back on me like you've been doin' makes me uneasy. In a relationship, I need a woman who is willin' to give her all. She needs to accept me for who I am and not try to change some of the things about me that will never change. I told you I'd meet you halfway, but I feel like I gotta go all the way with you. Then lyin' to me about some dumb shit ain't even cool. If it had been me, you'd be all over me, talkin' shit. I'm not thrilled about you havin' sex with that fool while I was in prison, but you made no promises to me whatsoever. As far as I knew, you'd moved on with your life, but I damn sure wish you would have been there for me."

I bit my nail, already admitting that he was right. "So, I guess this means I'm in trouble, huh?"

Roc cut his eyes, slightly grinning. "Hell, yeah, you in trouble. Big trouble, and I'm not gon' give you no dick, either. I told you that's what you wanted and you tryin' to play it down like that ain't it."

I pouted. "At the moment, I told you I didn't want the 'd' and I meant it. I do, however, need for you to hold me, touch me, make love to me, and give me a big ol' piece of the man I've fallen in love with. I want this to work so badly, but we've got to be open and honest with each other. I can do it, but do you think you can handle that for me too?"

"Yes," he quickly said. His cell phone rang, and he picked it up from the table, seeing who the caller was. "Hold that thought," he said to me, then answered his phone. "BJ, make it quick. What's the address?" Roc wrote down an address on a piece of paper. "'Preciate it. Now, don't call me back for the next hour." He looked at my thighs. "Maybe two. Two or three hours, and tell Ronnie I'm busy."

Roc ended his call, and for the next several hours, we kept ourselves pretty busy. Being with him felt so right, but there was still a big part of me that was so afraid to give him my all. I had to work hard at doing so, and maybe now that everything was out in the open about our feelings for each other, it would be easier for me. The only other concern I had was the constant phone calls. Knowing that Ronnie was involved, it always put up a red flag.

Chapter 6

Latrel was home for the weekend, and I was excited because he and Sherri had already been on one date and were due to go on another. I had invited her over for Saturday morning breakfast and she was on her way.

As for Roc, we were getting along so well that it was almost kind of scary. It had been a month since our unfortunate disagreement. He was back to work and I was very happy about that. He did, however, bring up the idea of Ronnie and me calling a truce, just to put him at ease. He told me that he expressed to Ronnie how important I was to him, and there was no way for him to keep the two most important people in his life away from one another. That conversation led to him asking me to go to the wedding and reception of his cousin, Andre. Ronnie would be in attendance, and even though I really didn't want to go, I agreed to do it for Roc. Loving him meant that I had to accept his family too, but it didn't mean that I had to put up with any nonsense. Hopefully, Ronnie wouldn't get out of line, and as long as he didn't say anything to me, I suspected it would be all good.

On Saturday morning, I had a packed house. Latrel was in the basement still asleep, Roc was in my bedroom, Chassidy was in her room, and Li'l Roc was in the guestroom. Monica had come over at 5:00 A.M. to help me with breakfast and Sherri was expected to show up at 8:00. I enjoyed having company and the house felt so lively. The smell of maple syrup was in the air, and I was standing in front of the stove, flipping buttermilk pancakes. Monica was setting the table, and we both had on white aprons as if we were working in a restaurant.

"I really do love the new dye that you put in your hair, Monica. The auburn looks pretty, and how did you get your hair to have so much body? Let me guess, Pantene shampoo and conditioner?"

Monica came up to me, moving her head from side to side so her hair could swing. "Uh, no, ma'am. Pantene is not for me. I'm a Dark & Lovely kind of gal. You should try it, but since your hair is always bouncing and behaving, I doubt that you will."

Monica swiped the back of my hair, trying to mess it up. I held up my spatula in defense. "Girl, you'd better back up before I cut you. You know I will hurt you for putting your hands on me."

Monica picked up a Jimmy Dean sausage and put it into her mouth. "You've been around Roc for too long. Put that darn spatula down and get back to flipping those pancakes before they burn."

"Don't blame that shit on me," Roc said, coming into the kitchen with white silk pajama pants on. They hung low on his waist and he was without a shirt. Yes, Monica was drooling, but she quickly closed her mouth and pretended to be occupied with setting the table.

Roc came up to me, kissed my cheek, and grabbed a sausage as well. "As I was saying . . . Dez was gangsta before I met her, so don't go blamin' me for bein' a bad influence."

"You got that right," Monica said. "I was just trying to make an excuse for her."

I threw my hand back at Monica and hoped she wouldn't get started on stories about our younger days. "Baby, why are you up so early? We won't be finished for at least another forty-five minutes."

Roc folded his arms while leaning against the counter next to me. "All I could smell was IHOP and I knew somethin' good was cookin'. Besides, I didn't feel that warm body next to mine and I couldn't get comfortable."

"I know how that is," I said, giving him a kiss.

"I'm gon' take a shower and put on some clothes. Hopefully breakfast will be ready when I get back. If not," he said, picking up another sausage, "you in trouble."

"I'll be sure to take my time. But if you and Monica keep eating up all of the sausage, I'm going to be standing here until noon, cooking."

Roc swayed his hand across my ass and squeezed it. "Umph, umph, umph," he said. "If only you knew what you do to me, especially in the mornin'."

He left the kitchen, shaking his head. Monica couldn't wait to add her two cents. "If you would like for me to finish up while you go get you a shot or two, I will be more than happy to take over."

I laughed at Monica trying to take the spatula from my hand. I bumped her with my hips, telling her to move aside. "Would you move, please? I've already had enough *shots* and don't need another one right now."

Monica leaned her backside against the counter, biting her nail and looking in the direction of my bedroom. "I don't see how you do it, Dee. I would be in that room, right now, wearing him out! Girl, Roc is so handsome, and he really missed his calling as a model. That Polo guy better watch out! He'd better hope Mr. Roc never comes for his job."

We laughed and I couldn't agree more. "I told him the same thing, but he let a good opportunity pass him by."

"How are things going with Chassidy? Has she gotten any more bites from any modeling agencies?"

"Not in a while. I haven't had any recent pictures of her taken, but I'm going to soon, especially since the holidays are coming up. I'm going to make sure I take plenty of pictures."

"Good idea."

Monica helped me with breakfast and we were all done by 7:35 A.M. I woke up Chassidy and Li'l Roc, getting them both ready for breakfast. Roc had showered, but had lain across the bed and gone back to sleep. I figured he needed all of the rest he could get, especially since we had plans to go to his cousin's wedding at three. Latrel was going to watch Chassidy, and Roc was taking Li'l Roc to his grandmother's house. We had arranged to stay at a hotel for the night, only because the reception was there as well.

The doorbell rang and Latrel had gone to get it. Everyone was all seated at the table, with the exception of Roc. Sherri came in, looking very classy in her nicely fitted stretch jeans, stilettos, and silk shirt. Her hair was cut short and her makeup was on like a work of art. Latrel still didn't seem excited about her, as I had hoped, and in no way did I understand why. She was so polite, and had come in with a yellow flower and card in her hand.

"Good morning, Ms. Jenkins," she said, giving me a hug. "Thank you so much for inviting me over, and these are for you."

"Aww, that was so sweet of you," I said, hugging her back. She spoke to everyone around the table and I got up to get a vase for my flower. Latrel helped Sherri with her chair, and everyone was waiting on me to bless the food.

"Would you hurry it up?" Monica said. "These pancakes are stacked so high and they're about to fall over. Me and Li'l Roc hungry, shoot!"

Monica was sitting next to Li'l Roc and he laughed at her while kicking his feet underneath the table. Monica picked up her fork and started hitting it on the table, chanting, "Hurry." He did the same thing and so did Chassidy. Everyone laughed, and as soon as I put my flower into a vase, I blessed the food and we started to eat.

The kitchen was rather noisy, as everyone was talking and the television was on in the background. Li'l Roc and Chassidy liked to watch the cartoons, so they were tuned in. Monica was asking Sherri all kinds of questions, but she was sharp with her answers and truly impressed the heck out of me. I wasn't trying to jump the gun or anything, but I could really see someone like her as my daughter-in-law. Up until now I wasn't so sure, but her presence truly lit up the room. I noticed Latrel's demeanor too, and I could tell he was starting to let his guard down as well. He had mentioned another girl at school who he was dating, but hopefully he'd begin to see the light.

"So, Sherri," Monica said, cutting into her pancakes. "What do you think of our president? Obama is wonderful, isn't he?"

Sherri shrugged. "He's okay. He's kind of growing the deficit too fast for me and I hope he will manage to get all of this spending under control. Besides, I didn't vote for him. I voted for John McCain."

Monica damn near choked on her food and she kicked me underneath the table. "John McCain? You're a Republican?"

All of us had stopped eating, waiting for Sherri to answer. Now, I had nothing against Republicans, but *we* were all very progressive Democrats. "Yes, I'm a Republican, but if we don't come up with a decent candidate in 2012 to defeat Obama, I'm not sure if I'll be voting at all."

I was trying hard to hold my peace, but *some* political talk was hard to ignore. This time I kicked Monica underneath the table and I could see steam coming from her ears. Latrel spoke up before either of us did.

"Time to change the subject," he suggested. "Everyone is entitled to their opinion, but no one can ignore or deny Obama's efforts to get this country back on track. We didn't get to this point overnight and he can't fix all of our problems overnight. Anyone expecting him to can, frankly, and no offense to Republicans, Sherri, but they can go to hell."

Monica smiled, but I held mine in. Latrel said exactly what I would have said, but I didn't want Sherri to feel uncomfortable because she had different views. I did change the subject, and when we started talking about reality TV shows, that had all of us cracking up. Even Latrel.

"I don't see how y'all watch that stuff," he said. "Most of it is fake and it is all for the ratings. The more outrageous those people are, the more people watch."

"That's the purpose," Monica said. "But them Kardashian sisters be working me. I be like . . . go somewhere and sit down, even though I can't get enough of them!"

We laughed, all agreeing again.

Breakfast lasted for about two hours, and Monica stayed in the kitchen with me to clean up. Everyone else was downstairs in the basement and the loud music was causing the floor to vibrate. I had gone in the bedroom to check on Roc, but he was still asleep. We'd had a long night, so I closed the door so he could get some rest.

"Latrel needs to turn that music down," I griped, making my way back into the kitchen. Monica was putting the dishes in the dishwasher and had already made progress on the messy kitchen.

"It is rather loud, and Miss Republican probably down there shielding her ears from the lyrics."

I hit Monica with a towel. "Be nice. Republican or not, she's still a nice young lady. She has a good family background, and the young lady is going to school to be a doctor. Thus far, she's the best thing Latrel has brought into this house, and I'm not going to complain."

"Well, I wonder if she's using any of that money Obama made available for college students, or if she's using those healthcare benefits that were extended to kids still in college under their parents' insurance plans."

"You got a point, okay? But let it go, Monica." I laughed. "Girl, let it go! I feel you, and I know none of it makes sense."

Unfortunately, Monica kept it going, this time putting her hand on her hip. "And then . . . she had the nerve to come in here with that flower, sucking up to you with a cheesy card. I wanted to throw up, and she blew it with me right then and there."

I covered my mouth and couldn't believe how upset Monica was about Sherri. When Roc came into the kitchen, she finally changed the subject.

"Did you get enough rest?" Monica asked. "I hope so, and I got you a full plate of pancakes, maple sausage, grits, cheese eggs, and biscuits right there on the table."

"Thanks," Roc said, smiling and taking a seat at the table. He now had on a pair of shorts and a white wife beater so Monica was able to contain herself a little better. She and I kept cleaning the kitchen, talking here and there as Roc ate his food. I didn't hear his cell phone ring, but his Bluetooth lit up, meaning that he had a call. I continued to talk to Monica while listening to him raise his voice at someone who was asking for money.

"It's the day of the gotdamn weddin' and those fools still beggin'? As much money as I've given up, this should have been my weddin'. You tell his ass I ain't got it. Fuck that. Niggas need to get they shit together." Roc paused, trying to eat his food and talk at the same time. All of the cursing was working me, but I had gotten used to it. "Look, I'm just a groomsman. Holla at the best man, or call Ronnie and ask him for it. I will predict that you'll be wastin' your time and he gon' say the same damn thing. A weddin' can go on without flowers."

Roc ended the call and Monica and I left the kitchen, leaving him at peace. We sat in the hearth room that was attached to the kitchen.

I wiped across my forehead, sitting on the sofa. "I am soooo tired. I don't know how I'm going to make it through this day. I at least need to get in one or two hours of sleep before the wedding."

Monica looked at her watch. "It's almost noon, and you don't have much time. I'm glad you found something nice to wear and I love the dress you picked out."

"I like it too, and I was a little bit worried because these hips of mine always get me in trouble. I've lost a few pounds, but if I start moving in the other direction, I'm going to have to have my clothes special made. With my waistline being smaller, it's hard to find clothes that fit me the right way."

"Yeah, that's a shame, too, because you do have a very nice shape. I know you may disagree, but you're blessed that everything is proportioned in the right places."

I'd heard that many, many times before; that's why I rarely complained about my weight. Roc seemed happy with it and that was a good thing. I watched as he put his plate in the sink, stretching his arms. Right after, Latrel, Sherri, and the kids came upstairs, and when Latrel put Chassidy down, she and Li'l Roc came over to me. I hugged them both, but couldn't help noticing Sherri staring at Roc and him staring at her. Latrel introduced the two of them and they both gave fake smiles. Li'l Roc got Roc's attention when he went over to him and tapped his leg.

"Daddy, what time am I going over to my granny's house?" he asked.

"In a li'l bit." Roc reached in his pocket and gave Li'l Roc his phone. "Call her to make sure she'll be at home."

Li'l Roc took the phone and went into another room to call her. Latrel and Roc kicked up a conversation, but Sherri couldn't keep her eyes off Roc. I couldn't keep my eyes off them, and Monica's eyes were on me.

"Yeah, like Prudential, she wants a piece of the Roc," Monica whispered. "She's got the hots for him, and how disrespectful for her to stand there looking at him like that."

"So I guess she's not allowed to look at a nice-looking man when she sees one, huh? Please give that young lady a break."

Monica sat back with her lips pursed and legs crossed. Sherri headed our way, informing me that she was about to leave.

"Thank you so much for inviting me over, Ms. Jenkins," she said, hugging me again. I stood up and thanked her for coming.

"You are welcome to come back anytime. Usually, Latrel comes home every other weekend, and I hope the two of you keep in touch."

She had her fingers crossed. "He did ask me to go on another date with him next week, so we'll see." She giggled, and after she told Monica and Roc good-bye, Latrel walked her to the door.

Time was moving fast, so Monica was on her way out and Latrel had offered to take Li'l Roc to his grandmother's house. He and Chassidy were going to see Reggie, and then he had plans to take her to the movies. I gave away plenty of kisses and hugs before sending everyone out of the door with a good-bye. I went into my bedroom, falling back on my comfortable bed and wanting to stay there. Roc climbed on top of me, pecking my neck.

"Mmmm," he mumbled. "I am so glad that everybody is gone. We still got a li'l time to shake somethin' up in here before we go, don't we?"

"Unfortunately not. As tired as I am, I would just lie here like a dead duck and let you do all of the work."

"That sounds like a plan to me, and just bein' inside of your pussy excites the hell out of me."

I slightly pushed Roc's chest back so I could look into his eyes. "Tonight, okay? You have all night to do whatever you wish, but please let me get at least an hour of sleep in before we go."

"That hour is going to make you more tired, but go for it. I'll let you get some rest and wake you up around one-thirty so you can get ready."

"Thanks, snookums."

Roc eased his way off of me and stood up. "Don't start that shit. You haven't called me that in a long time. That only means you want somethin' from me."

I laughed, as he was so right. I turned sideways, holding my head up with my hand. "I didn't want anything, but I did want to ask you something."

"What's up?" he asked, folding his arms in front of him.

"Did you know Sherri? I mean, there was just something about the way you looked at her and she looked at you."

Roc hesitated, then bent over on the bed to come face to face with me. "Remember that lie you told me about Greg? I'm not gon' do you like you did me, but, yes, I do know Sherri."

My stomach tightened, and I was almost afraid to ask how, but what the hell? "Do you mind telling me how you know her?"

Roc tapped the side of his temple with his finger. "Well, let's see. A few years back, I met her at a party and we got to know each other."

"As in sexually? She told Latrel she was a virgin, but I guess that was a lie."

"Ay, that's how women do it. Big lie. I owned and boned it several times, and she wasn't no virgin when I hit it, either."

Yes, I was starting to frown, even though this was before my time. "Why did the two of you stop seeing each other?"

"It was just a fuck thing and fuck things don't last for long. She wanted more, but I wasn't givin' more. She stopped callin' me and the rest is history."

"Truthfully, was it before or after you met me?"

"I don't always remember timelines, baby, but it was at least a year, maybe two before then. What difference does it make? Ain't nothin' poppin' with me and that chick."

I reached over to my phone on the nightstand, dialing Latrel's cell phone number. He answered right away.

"When is your next date with Sherri?"

"I told her next week, Mama, but I don't know—"

"Cancel it."

"What?" he laughed. "What did she do now? I guess Monica got through to you, huh?"

"No, she didn't. I jus' . . . I just don't think she would be good for you, that's all."

"Mama, now you know I don't like you getting in my business like this. And just because she's a Republican, it doesn't mean she's a bad person. Don't be like that, and you have always taught me not to judge people, even though you tend to do it a lot."

"I know, but forgive me. It's not because she's a Republican, it's because she was intimate with Roc before. Didn't she tell you she was a virgin? I don't want you to involve yourself with a woman who lies to you."

Roc was standing in front of me, shaking his head. "Ain't that about nothin'," he said. "You know you be killin' me."

I smiled at him and put my finger over my lip, asking him to be quiet.

"I can see why that would concern you," Latrel said. "But it doesn't concern me, especially if it happened a long time ago. Either way, the only reason I took Sherri out on those dates was because of you. She was decent, but in no way is she my type. I will soon show you my type, and I have been dating her for the past eight months. The only reason that I didn't tell you was because I didn't want to hear your comments about who I should or shouldn't be dating. Good-bye, Mama, and have a good time at the wedding."

I quickly sat up on the bed. "Eight months? Why didn't you say anything? Is she black, white . . . what? I hope she's . . . Well, you already know what I'm going to say, and make sure she is not a Republican. Please."

"I'm hanging up, Mama. I don't like to talk while I'm driving and if you want to put your precious cargo at risk of having an accident—"

"Bye, Latrel. I love you."

"Me too."

Latrel hung up, and as expected, Roc was still staring at me. "He's my son, Roc, and I couldn't let him make a big mistake like that one."

"Right, you're so right. I feel sorry for that man, and he will never find the woman of his dreams, waitin' on you to come around."

I pulled my shirt over my head, tossing it on the floor. "I guess he won't," I said. "And I guess that will only lead to me being in trouble again."

Roc winked at me, then jumped on the bed. "I knew you'd find a little time to fit me into your schedule. Lie back, baby, and swoop those pretty legs into position."

I did as I was told, and rubbed my hands on Roc's carved chest. "Do . . . Don't you think we fuck too much?" I said bluntly. "Every time I look up, there you are, looking down at me, smiling and stroking away."

"Then maybe you should turn around more often and let me get at your pussy from the back. Besides, I know you ain't complainin'."

I turned on my stomach, resting my head comfortably on a pillow. Roc straddled my legs, bending one of them so he could have easier access.

"Hike that ass up a bit so I can get at it like I want to."

I hiked up my ass, and he pulled my cheeks apart. When he entered me, I squeezed my eyes, and let out a deep sigh of relief. I thought about how good he made my insides feel, and confirmed that I wanted to feel him inside of me forever.

"Nooo complaints," I assured him. "And you could fuck me like this forever."

"That's what I thought and it's somethin' that I definitely know."

Cocky or confident, it didn't really matter. Roc was giving me what I wanted and that was summed up as sexual satisfaction.

The sex session delayed us. By the time we got ready and arrived at Roc's cousin's church on Grand Boulevard, it was 3:45 P.M. The wedding hadn't even started yet, and since Roc was one of the groomsmen, that was a good thing. He drove like a bat out of hell getting there, only to be told that the minister hadn't shown up yet. I sat by myself in the crowded church that was filled with who I assumed to be many of Roc's relatives and friends. The church was beautifully decorated with turquoise, black, and white. I could tell someone had put a lot of money into the wedding, and I guessed the money for the flowers had come through. Beautiful lilies were everywhere, and each pew had a bundle of carnations with pearls. A big picture of the bride and groom was propped up on the stage on an easel, and the dim lighting made the sanctuary look even more elegant. The pianist started doing his thing, but for at least ten minutes, he seemed to be tuning the piano. I crossed my legs, looking down at my black silk and leather heels with pleats near my opened toes. The half-shoulder mustard-colored silk dress I wore tightened at my waist and hugged my curvaceous hips. It was knee-length level, but inched up a bit when I took my seat. My hair was pinned up, giving me a very classy look that kept others staring. Whenever someone smiled at me, I smiled back. One older lady in particular, she came over and stood next to me with her cane.

"Oooo, young lady, you're so very pretty," she said. "What gentleman in here do you belong to?"

I could only thank her and laugh. "Thank you for the compliment, and you are beautiful too. I'm here with Rocky Dawson. He's one of the groomsmen."

"You mean Roc?" The lady smiled. "Nobody calls him Rocky anymore, and he hates that name. I'm a longtime friend of the family, and we all go way, way back."

The lady stood next to me, going on and on about the Dawson family. I asked if she wanted to take a seat next to me, but she insisted that she was sitting elsewhere. Almost fifteen minutes later the pianist asked everyone to take their seats, and that's when the elderly woman walked away. By now, there was no place next to me to sit, and more people had crammed into the church.

The wedding got started, and instead of the groomsmen coming down the aisle, they all walked in at once and stood in front of the church. There were eight men total, all very handsome men, with the exception of Ronnie. Well, he was nice-looking too, but I couldn't stand him. To me, of course, Roc looked the best. The black tuxedo fit his body perfectly, and along with his fresh haircut and trimmed hair on his chin, my eyes stayed glued to him. I couldn't help that I was sitting in a church, thinking about what had transpired only a few hours ago. My mind was definitely in the gutter, and God would have to forgive me.

My attention turned to the bridesmaids coming in, and then to the flower girl and ring bearer. The bride was also pretty, but I wasn't going to say anything about her having on too much caked-on makeup. Whoever did her makeup needed to rethink his/her career. Other than that, she was perfect.

As the ceremony was in progress, I occasionally looked at Roc and he looked at me. We smiled at each other, but I also noticed his attention focused elsewhere. I followed the direction of his eyes, only to see Vanessa sitting in one of the pews with another man next to her. I thought I'd seen the man before, then I quickly realized it was that goon Mississippi who was at Roc's place that day. His dreads had been cut off, and even though he looked a little better, he still wasn't all that great looking to me. I wondered if Vanessa was now seeing him, and I guessed as close as they were sitting, it was obvious. I didn't know how well that had gone over with Roc, but I really wanted to know how he felt about it. I suspected the day would get interesting.

The "I do's" were exchanged, so were the rings, and the broom had been jumped over. The wedding party was asked to stay to take photos, and instead of waiting around, I left to go use the bathroom, plus call to check on Latrel and Chassidy. The hallways were so crowded that you could barely move, and when I got to the bathroom, a line was outside of the door. I dug in my purse to get my phone, and I would be lying if I said I didn't hear the word "bitch" from behind. I turned, seeing Vanessa standing only a few feet away with three other women. To be honest, she looked really nice in her lavender sheer-like strapless dress with a small slit on the thigh. Her long hair was pulled away from her face, bumped up a bit, and clipped in the back. All I did was cut my eyes at her, and started to move in another direction. I was glad to see Roc exiting the sanctuary. He saw me and motioned for me to come his way.

"I want you to meet some people," he said. I made my way up to him and he eased his arm around my waist. He introduced me to several of his cousins, aunts, uncles, and some friends. He was all smiles, and seemed really proud to have me with him. I was kind of shocked by his reaction. More so by his arm that he never removed from my waist. People were taking many photos and I couldn't tell you how many times we had to stop and pose for the cameras. I had even posed in two pictures with Ronnie, and you best believe that he was on one end and I was on the other.

Everyone was starting to leave the church to make their way to the reception. I still needed to use the bathroom, so I interrupted Roc, talking to a couple of his friends.

"Say, honey," I said. "I'll be back, okay? I need to go to the restroom."

Roc held my hand, asking me to hold up a second. He exchanged a few more words with his friends, then they walked away. He then turned to face me, while wiggling his bowtie away from his neck.

"It's hotter than a mug in here," he said. "So, what did you think?"

"Think about what? The wedding?"

"Yes, the weddin' and my peeps. They ain't as bad as you thought they would be, are they?"

I smiled, thinking how surprised I was that he had some very nice and down-to-earth people in his family. I then reached out to help him remove the bowtie he seemed to have trouble with. It came loose and Roc placed it in his pocket. He wrapped his arms around me and I wrapped mine around him. "I think the wedding was beautiful, you looked so very, very handsome, and your family is everything I imagined them to be. Wonderful people."

Roc laughed. I swear his bright white teeth against his dark skin was a combination that set me on fire. "Quit lyin'. You are such a good liar, but you good."

He pecked my lips, only encouraging me to go for more. As we kissed, an older man interrupted us and held up his camera. He flashed it, making us laugh.

"Boy, you got yourself somethin' right there," he said, squeezing Roc's shoulder. "Good God Almighty, and if you can't handle all of that goodness, be sho' to let me know!"

"Will do, Cousin Freddy, but I'm positive I can handle it."

Freddy walked away, sucking in his lips and eyeballing me. I couldn't help but blush from his compliment.

"I really need to get to the bathroom," I said. Roc let go of my hand, and thank God the bathroom wasn't that crowded. After using it, I washed my hands while checking myself in the mirror. My lip gloss had gotten light, so I removed my tiny purse clutched underneath my arm to find my gloss. I must have forgotten it at home, so I snapped my purse back together and left the bathroom. No sooner had I walked out than I could see Vanessa, who had already made her way up to Roc. She was close to his face, pointing her finger and gritting her teeth. Several other people were standing around, and didn't she know how much she was embarrassing herself? Roc slapped her finger away from his face and that's when he saw me coming. He looked over Vanessa's shoulder at me.

"Are you ready to jet so we can go to the reception?" he said, trying to ignore her.

She quickly turned around with a mean mug on her face. I stepped around her, and stood next to Roc. She couldn't help herself from reaching up to hit him. This time, however, I grabbed her wrist, catching it in midair. Her eyes widened, as she couldn't believe I was protecting Roc.

"That will land you on this floor, and I don't think you want to catch a beat-down in no church. Take it up with Roc later, and if you don't, you will regret it."

She snatched her wrist away from me, and before any words could come out of her mouth, the man standing next to Roc pushed her backward. She almost fell, but charged forward again. This time, he squeezed her arm, ordering her to leave.

"Move out of my way, Steve! That bitch don't put her hands on me. She don't know me and I will kick her ass! I'm just tryin' to talk to Roc!"

"Wrong place," Roc said with a smirk. "Wrong time." He looked at Steve, who seemed to have control over her. So many people there were shaking their heads, and the whole scene was quite embarrassing. "Please do somethin' with her," Roc said to Steve. "Throw her ass in the river for all I care, but get her the fuck out of my face."

Vanessa called Roc all kinds of son of bitches, you muthafucka this and that. She was being pushed in one direction while we walked in another one. As soon as we walked out of the church doors, Mississippi was standing outside, talking to a gathering of other young men and several ladies. Roc was holding my hand, but I guess he couldn't help himself from saying something.

"Sippi, you need to go inside and calm your bitch down. She clownin', and if you care about her like yo' hatin' ass say you do, then go handle that."

Sippi pointed to his chest. "Nigga, you talkin' to me? I know you ain't talkin' to me."

Roc tried to let go of my hand, but I squeezed it. He snatched away, making his way up to Mississippi. I knew this day was too good to be true, and didn't somebody recognize that we were in a church? I called out Roc's name, but he ignored me. A few people had already started to move out. Many stayed to watch as Roc stood face to face with Mississippi with tightened fists.

"You damn right I'm talkin' to you, you fake-ass muthafucka. Now what, nigga? Yo' move."

Mississippi didn't have a move, especially since Ronnie and three of his henchmen walked up from behind him. He gripped Roc's shoulder, massaging it.

"Calm down, baby boy. There won't be no bloodshed today. G'on and take yo' pretty young thang to the reception and enjoy yourself. Sippi ain't mean no harm, did you?"

Roc hadn't moved, and he waited for Mississippi to respond. "Roc know he my boy, but he don't need to be comin' at me about some dumb shit over no trick."

"One who ain't even worth it, so we gon' leave this shit right here at the front door of the church," Ronnie said. "Squash this and let's move out. We got a party to go to."

Mississippi held up his fist for Roc to pound and squash it, but Roc cut his eyes and walked away. He took my hand, and, at a speedy pace, walked with me to his truck. Honestly, I didn't feel like going to the reception, and this ongoing drama with Roc was working my nerves. And then for Ronnie to suggest that they leave the drama at the church door—please. God was probably shaking His head at all of us. There was no denying that every time I attempted to be a part of Roc's circle, something tragic almost happened. I prayed for him and definitely for my safety.

Roc sped off the parking lot, only to be stopped by Ronnie, who stood in front of the truck, holding up his hand. He strutted around to the driver's side, and Roc lowered his window.

"You good?" he asked Roc.

"I'm fine. That fool was the one trippin', not me."

"I don't give a shit about him. All I care about is you. I don't want no shake, rattlin', and rollin' goin' on, so calm down and sleep on it."

Roc nodded, and before he rose his window, Ronnie looked over at me.

"Sup, Desa Rae? You lookin' lovely as ever. Glad you decided to come. When you and my Roc gon' tie the knot?"

Roc smiled and put his hand on the switch to raise the window. "Man, stop talkin' shit. You high, drunk, on crack, or what?"

I leaned forward to address Ronnie. "You look awesome too, Ronnie, and as for me and Roc tying the knot, not a chance in hell. I only use him for sex."

Ronnie laughed and backed away from the car. Roc looked disturbed by what I said, and I was bothered by what he'd said as well. That's why I responded the way I did. We couldn't get off the parking lot before he tried to tear into me.

"Not a chance in hell, huh? And all I'm good for is sex? You shot me down like I wasn't shit."

"I knew you were going to say that, but it was no worse than you saying Ronnie was high, drunk, on crack, or whatever if he thought we'd ever get married."

"I was just playin', and I told you that's how we talk."

"Well, I guess I'm learning from you, and, at the time, I couldn't think of a better response either."

I playfully shoved Roc's shoulder, and, just to irritate me, he blasted his music. I turned it down, feeling a need to ask him a few questions.

"Snookums, I don't really want to bring this up right now, but please tell me what is up with Vanessa. Why does she always carry on like that? Has she always been that way?"

"She's a crazy and deranged woman. She actin' like that cause I don't fuck with her no more. She didn't always act like that, but she definitely ain't got it all upstairs."

"Well, it's been awhile since you've been out of jail. Almost six months to be exact, and I don't understand why she doesn't accept the fact that you've moved on."

Roc stopped at the red light on Lindell Boulevard and looked over at me. "I don't know either. But since you showed her how gangsta you can be, next time you see her, why don't you ask her? I can't answer why she's a nutcase. Some people are just that way when they don't get what they want."

"Gangsta, no. I just don't have time for games, that's all." I touched the side of Roc's face. "Besides, I didn't want her messing up that handsome face. Not today anyway."

"No worries here. But I don't believe for one minute that you ain't got a li'l hood in you. It's there, and ain't no way you'd be messin' with me if it wasn't."

I threw my hand back at Roc, but he was on to something, because I did graduate from the one and only Charles Sumner High School. I did have my suspicions about why I thought Vanessa reacted the way she did. I couldn't believe any woman would constantly be carrying on the way she had been if she wasn't still someway or somehow involved with Roc. Maybe it was just me, but the next time I saw her, yes, I very well would ask.

The wedding reception was just as nice as the wedding was. It was in a ballroom at the Renaissance Hotel where we were staying the night. It was even more packed than the wedding was, and you would have sworn that Roc's cousin and his new wife were celebrities. I was having myself a good time. The people who sat at the table with me were funny, as well as entertaining. There was something about the way an older man cracked jokes, and the one next to me was on a roll. He was talking about everybody and their mama, including Roc and his bright white teeth. I even danced with the old man a few times, but when Roc cut in, the dance floor belonged to us. I still hadn't learned how to dance, but as long as Roc kept me close to him, I was perfectly fine.

"You feel it, don't you?" he said, pressing his hardness close to me.

"As a matter of fact, I do. In front of all of your relatives and friends, I feel how hard you are. I may have to bend over to give them something to watch."

He blushed. "Ooooo, you so nasty. But you know I love it, don't you?"

"I hope so. Now, how much longer are we going to be? My feet are killing me and I'm getting very tired."

"I'm gon' be awhile, but if you want to go upstairs to our room to get some rest, go right ahead. I'll be up later. Not too late, though."

That didn't sound like a bad idea, so I got the keycard from Roc and gave my good-byes to his family. I made my way to the elevator, on my way up. The door was about to close, but someone put his hand between the doors to make them open wide. It was Ronnie. He stepped onto the elevator with me.

"Going up?" he asked.

I nodded, feeling very uncomfortable being alone with him. We pushed the sixth floor button at the same time.

"I had a damn good time today," he said, sucking his teeth. "How 'bout you?"

"Great time," was all I said.

The elevator opened and he extended his hand, inviting me to exit first.

I walked down the hallway and Ronnie followed me. The keycard had door number 612 written on it, so I followed the arrows and made my way to it. When I found it, I stopped and Ronnie stopped behind me. I quickly turned.

"Is there something I can help you with, Ronnie?"

"Jus' . . . just open the door. I need to go inside and holla at you about a few thangs."

I folded my arms, and in no way was going inside of the room with him. "Whatever you have to say, you can say it out here."

"It's private, Desa Rae, and I'm not gon' hurt you. I just want to get at you about some things with Roc, particularly about him gettin' out of the game. I'm concerned about some things he's been bringin' on himself, as a permanent move like that can do more harm than good. I'm sure you understand."

I really didn't want to let Ronnie inside of the room with me, but I also didn't want to stand in the hallway discussing Roc. I told myself that if Ronnie tried anything stupid to kick him hard in his nuts and run!

I opened the door with the card and went inside. The suite was very nice, but I didn't have time to check it out like I wanted to because of Ronnie. He removed his suit jacket, then took a seat in one of the chairs by a window. I stood close by the bed with my arms folded.

He cleared his throat and rubbed his hands together. "Let's not pretend, Desa Rae. You don't like me and I damn sure ain't got no love for you. You've managed to get at my li'l nigga's heart and I'm not quite on board with that shit. I've thought about several schemes to get rid of you, and when anybody starts messin' around with my money, I gotta do what I gotta do. You know what I'm sayin'?"

"No, Ronnie, I don't know what you're saying. I don't understand how I'm messing with your money, and quite frankly, I haven't spent one dime of what belongs to you. As for your schemes to get rid of me, please let me know if that was a threat so I can get a restraining order against you and make the cops aware of this situation."

Ronnie chuckled and swiped his hand on top of his head. "Roc slippin', Desa Rae, and when you slip, eventually you fall. When you fall, you fall six feet under. He slippin' 'cause he ain't focused on what needs to be done. I've lost a lot of money in the last several months, and while you got him out here at a two-bit-ass job, makin' twelve or thirteen lousy dollars an hour, I'm losin' mo' money. While he busy over there playin' house with you and yo' gotdamn family, my family ain't gettin' takin' care of. Now, I'm bein' as nice as I can possibly be about this, but you and that baby girl need to quickly make way out of St. Louis. Tell that nigga somethin' came up, and you gotta go. If you don't, well, see, I would hate for somethin' tragic to happen." Ronnie shrugged. "Can't say who it will happen to, 'cause I don't know yet. But if you fall back, everything will be peaches and cream."

I stared at Ronnie and couldn't even respond. All kind of hate for him was running through me, and I had never felt like this for anyone in my life. I didn't even know fools like him existed, but sadly enough, they did. I went to the door and opened it.

"Please get out," I said. "You will have to do what you wish because I will never take orders from you."

Ronnie slowly stood up and stretched. With venom in his eyes, he walked to the door, looking me over. He reached his hand up, touching the side of my face. Before he could say anything, I smacked it away. He chuckled out loud and left. I slammed the door behind him, not sure if I would tell Roc about this incident.

Chapter 7

For whatever reason, I kept what Ronnie had said to me a secret. I hadn't said one word to Roc about the letters I'd been getting in the mail, threatening my life. All they said was:

You die, bitch! Your days are numbered!

The letters started after my confrontation with Ronnie. Someone was constantly calling my house and hanging up, and when a man ran into the back of my car the other day, I was quite shaken up. It seemed as if he just wasn't looking where he was going, and after the police came on the scene, everything checked out. Still, I was paranoid. I wanted to go to the police about this, but without any evidence against Ronnie, what could they really do? I intended to watch my back, and I did tell Roc to be very careful about his surroundings too. He assured me that he would. I did my best to make sure he spent plenty of days and nights with me, away from the drama that seemed to happen when he was on his turf. Roc seemed as if he had a new attitude about life, and he had not missed any more days at work. I was happy for him, and definitely happy about the way things were going between us.

Christmas was just around the corner, and for Thanksgiving I had dinner at my house. Everyone from the breakfast crew was there, with the exception of Sherri. Latrel had finally brought his girlfriend home to meet me, and I held off on making any comments. All I could say was I liked her, she seemed nice, and she was African American. At this point, I realized that it didn't even matter. As long as he was happy, I was. Until he intended to marry someone, I told Latrel he would never hear my mouth again.

Things were going so well that I had even started talking sensibly to Reggie again. He was in counseling and told me how much it was helping him. We hadn't laughed together in quite some time, and when he came over one day, apologizing again for what he'd done, I was okay. I was pleased that he'd realized his mistakes, but made it clear that we could never turn back the hands of time. He understood.

On Christmas morning, I got a call from Roc, telling me that he wasn't feeling well so he was staying at home. I was looking forward to our time together, and so was Chassidy. She wanted to give Li'l Roc his gift and I wanted to give him the ones I had bought him too.

"I hope you feel better," I said over the phone to Roc. "And if you come over, I promise to take care of you."

He let out a hacking cough, and asked me to hold while he spat. "I'm feelin' so miserable I can't even move. I'll get at you on the weekend, promise. Now let me talk to Chassidy so I can wish her a Merry Christmas."

I gave the phone to Chassidy, very disappointed that Roc wasn't coming over. While she talked to him, I turned to Latrel, who was coming up from the basement on his way over to Reggie's house.

"Where's Roc at?" Latrel asked.

"He's not feeling well today. Said he wasn't coming over until the weekend."

"I've been feeling a little under the weather too, but I took some Tylenol Cold & Flu last night. I feel much better."

I touched Latrel's forehead, just to see if he was running a fever. He wasn't. "Well, go ahead over to your father's house. Tell him I said hello and don't forget to get his presents underneath the tree."

"I won't. But since Roc isn't coming over, why don't you and Chassidy go over to Dad's house with me? It's not like you doing anything else."

"No, I don't think that's a good idea. Have fun and I'll see you later."

Chassidy gave the phone to me, and Roc had already hung up.

"Can Chassidy go with me then? I mean, it's Christmas, Mama, and she don't want to be cooped up in the house."

"We weren't going to be cooped up. I had planned on baking some Christmas cookies and chocolate cupcake bears."

"I don't want to leave you by yourself, but if you don't want to go with me, at least let her go."

Chassidy always loved going with Latrel, so I put on her clothes and told the two of them to have fun. It wasn't the first time I was alone on Christmas, and I suspected it wouldn't be the last. Besides, my house had gotten kind of messy, so I decided to spend my day cleaning.

Around noon, I was taking a break from vacuuming the floors and sat breathlessly at the kitchen table. I had a tall glass of ice-cold water in my hand, guzzling it down pretty quickly. The news had just come on, and at the top of the hour there was breaking news. Apparently, there was a murder in St. Louis and a police officer had been shot at as well. The person identified was a twenty-nine-year-old black man by the name of Craig M. Jackson. I somewhat ignored the story, because it disturbed me that so many black men were getting killed. It always made me think of Roc, and as the reporter wrapped up her story, she repeated the name. This time, she said that Mr. Jackson also went by the name of Mississippi, and if anyone had any information they were asked to call the number on the screen.

Almost immediately, my heart dropped to my stomach. I couldn't believe Mississippi was dead, and less than a month and a half ago, he and Roc stood outside of the church, arguing. I wondered if there was any connection and my gut was sending off signals that there was. I rushed to my bedroom to put on some clothes, and, yes, I wanted some answers. I didn't think Roc was capable of murder, but he damn sure knew something about this.

When I got to Roc's place, I started to use the key he had given me awhile back, but instead I knocked. I got no answer, so I knocked again. Finally, after knocking for at least five minutes, he opened the door. I immediately noticed a small bruise underneath his left eye and a scratch on his neck. No, he didn't look happy to see me and the cold stare in his eyes said so.

"Can I come in?" I asked.

He covered his face with his hand, wiping down it. "Dez, I'm tired. I was upstairs sleepin', tryin' to work off this cold."

"I won't be long."

Roc turned and headed up the stairs. He went back into his bedroom and got underneath the covers. The room was partially lit by the sun's rays coming through the window, but I turned on the light.

"What happened to your eye?" I asked.

"I ran into somethin'."

"And the scratch on your neck?"

"Somethin' bit me and I kept scratchin' it."

"Roc, stop lying. I thought we didn't go there with each other like that anymore."

He sat up in bed and put his hands behind his head. "Are you over here because I didn't come to your house for Christmas? I told you I wasn't feelin' well and nothin' else needs to be said."

"What happened to Mississippi?"

He cocked his head back. "Who?"

"Sippi. The one you got into it with at the wedding. The news reported that he was murdered. I thought you may know something about it."

Roc shrugged. "That's what that nigga get. No love lost here, and if I did know somethin' about it, so what? What you gon' do, call the police on me or somethin'? You runnin' up in here like you tryin' to get info for a reward."

"I don't know what I would do with the truth, but I want to know if you had anything to do with it."

Roc didn't answer. He reached for a Black & Mild cigar next to him and lit it. "So you don't know what you would do, huh? I feel you, ma, but just so you can sleep at night, no, you don't have a murderer lyin' in bed next to you and runnin' up in that pussy. I don't get down like that. Sippi had a whole lot of haters, as well as enemies. Ain't no tellin' who put two in his head, but it damn sure wasn't me." Roc defensively held out his hands. "Could have been anybody. Now, please, please can I get some rest? If it makes you feel better, I will stop by tomorrow. Promise."

Roc took a few more puffs from the Black & Mild, then put it out in the ashtray. I watched as he threw the covers back over his head, trying his best to ignore me. I really wasn't in the mood for this on Christmas Day, so I turned to leave. As I walked down the hallway, I stopped dead in my tracks. The news hadn't mentioned anything about Mississippi being shot twice in the head, and how would Roc know that? I turned, making my way back to his room, clearing my throat.

He snatched the covers off his head and sighed.

"I'm going to get out of your hair soon, but I wanted you to know that your cough is already sounding better. Let me know what kind of medicine you used, as it seems to work magic. Pertaining to Mississippi, I don't really care what happened to him, as I firmly believe you reap what you sow. But the news didn't mention that he was shot twice in the head. The only person who would know that is the killer, or *the one* who made the order to have it done. That's just something for you to think about while you're resting."

Roc held out his hands again, staring at me with a cold expression. "I said it wasn't me."

I left the room with nothing else to say. I knew Roc had something to do with it, but he would never tell. This secretive life he lived was killing me and there was so much about it that I didn't want to know, then again I did. I figured the truth behind all of it would hurt me, as well as, someday, Chassidy. I never wanted to sit her down and tell her what kind of man I suspected her father to be. A killer? I wasn't sure yet, but I prayed on my way out that it simply wasn't true.

I had gotten about two miles away from Roc's place when I saw a familiar face driving in the opposite direction on Grand Boulevard. It was Vanessa. I didn't think she'd seen me. When I got to the light, I quickly made a U-turn just to see where she was going. She drove a white convertible BMW and I wasn't about to let it get out of sight. That thought was short-lived, as the light turned yellow and she rushed through it. I had to stop at the light and it seemed to take forever. I tapped my fingers on the steering wheel, already feeling the knot in my stomach tighten. I tried to loosen the knot by taking deep breaths, but the deeper my breaths got, the knot seemed to tighten more. The light changed, and Vanessa's BMW was out of my sight. That in no way mattered, and when I got to Roc's place, her car was already parked out front. She must have been inside, so I waited to see how long she'd stay. I couldn't believe that I was spying on Roc, but there were some things that I needed to know because he wasn't telling. *Do I stay out here?* I kept asking myself. *Or do I go to the door?* I sat in the car, debating with myself, and had also thought about just going home. That's what I should have done, but it didn't seem like much of an option. Before I knew it, I had been sitting in the car for about forty-five minutes. I had hoped that Vanessa would've come out by now, but she hadn't. I was so hurt inside, but my hurt wouldn't allow me to shed one tear, even though my throat felt as if it were burning, and my hands were starting to tremble. I took another deep breath, eventually saying, "Fuck it."

I got out of my car, making my way to the door. I fumbled around with my keys in search of the one Roc had given to me. I knew he had plenty of guns inside, and there was a possibility that I could get hurt. I figured Vanessa was the kind of woman who would protect her man at any cost, but I didn't care. I was numb and wasn't thinking clearly right now. I turned the lock, slowly pushing the door open. Immediately, I heard loud rap music playing, and it wasn't until I got midway up the stairs that I heard Vanessa moaning as if she were in tremendous pain. My entire body felt weak, and my legs felt as if I had been running a marathon. At that point, I knew I had all of the answers I needed. I wanted to turn around to leave, but this was an out-of-body experience that I had never felt before. I kept on moving up the stairs, and when I almost reached the top, I turned to my right. That's where all of the action was taking place. Roc was sitting up on the couch with no clothes on, leaning back and looking helpless. Vanessa's near-perfect naked body was straddled on top of him. Her back was facing him and she was giving him one hell of a ride. His head was dropped back and eyes were squeezed tight. So were hers. Seeing his dick plunge into her insides made me ill. His hands roamed her ass and he had the nerve to smack it. Then he eased his hand around to her clitoris, teasing hers like he often teased mine. She was near tears. All she could do was tell him how much she loved him. I'll be damned if he didn't respond, "Daammn, baby, I love how you do this shit! Keep on fuckin' me like this, and *nobody* makes me feel like you do!"

I'd heard it all before and could have fallen down the stairs as I quickly made my way out. As weak as my legs were, I almost did fall. I didn't care that I probably had their attention, and by the time I reached the porch, it was obvious that I did. Roc called after me, but I kept it moving. I hurried to my car, and he chased after me with a towel wrapped around his waist. Dick was still probably dripping wet from the festivities. As he crossed the street, a car almost hit him but swerved out of the way. The driver blew his horn, yelling profanities out of his window.

"Fuck you too," Roc said, running up to my car. He banged on the window, telling me to lower it. I looked in my side mirror making sure it was clear to pull off. It was, so I did.

I was a nervous wreck driving home. I kept smacking away my falling tears, fighting my pain. I don't know what it was about me that always tried to play the tough role, but this time, Roc had broken me down. I don't even think my divorce from Reggie had hurt this bad, only because at the age of forty-two, going on forty-three, I found myself in a very similar situation. The choices I had made had cost me dearly, but anyone could say what they wanted; I in no way deserved this. Bullshit came at any age, and some men would never stop bringing it. It was up to me to do better and I knew it. Sadly, I took a risk and in no way did it pay off.

As soon as I got home, I rushed inside and hurried to take off my clothes. I turned on my shower and got inside to let the warm water pour down on me. I had a sponge in my hand, scrubbing my skin hard, attempting to wash away the touch of Roc's hands. I knew the scrubbing was doing me no good, but I felt like the water was cleansing my mind, body, and soul. I closed my eyes, thinking of every single time he'd touched me, and couldn't get the thoughts of what I had just witnessed at his place out of my mind. Finally, the tears streamed down my face and I cried harder than I had ever cried before. I asked myself over and over again, *Where did I go wrong?* At the end of the day, I knew I had no one else to blame for this but myself. I'd let my guard down, and how in the hell did I allow myself to trust a man like him? That was one big mistake, and I should have seen this coming. He toyed with my feelings before he'd gone to prison, and this time was no different. He couldn't give up Vanessa if his life depended on it, and there was no telling who else was in the picture. Like in the past, I bet he'd been running from one woman to the next, pretending as if I was the one who had changed his life around. I hadn't changed nothing, and today proved to me that Roc was the same man that he'd been before. Damn! Why me?

I stayed in the shower until the water had turned cold. By now, my body was quivering and I was a complete mess. I was sitting on the seat in my shower with my head hung low and my hair dripping wet. My hands covered my face and I felt like I couldn't even move.

"You . . . you left the door open," Roc said. I heard the shower door slide open, but I didn't say a word. Right now I could have killed him. I often wondered what made Vanessa as angry as she was, and now a part of me understood her actions. Being screwed over and lied to by a man definitely wasn't any fun.

"Dez," Roc said, touching my hand and trying to move it away from my face. "I'm sorry. But can I tell you why I did what I did?"

I really didn't care, only because there was nothing he could say that would ever repair this kind of damage. I removed my hands from my face, trying to wipe my face clean. Roc squatted down beside the shower, trying to explain his actions.

"Maybe I should have told you this, but I've been upset with you for a while. Only because you didn't tell me that Ronnie approached you at the hotel, basically threatenin' my life and yours. I couldn't understand why you didn't say nothin' to me, but it bothered me that you didn't. As a woman who is supposed to love me, you need to have my back. When somebody—anybody—get at you with some shit like that, it is imperative for you to say somethin'. You made me feel as if I couldn't trust you, so I was like fuck it. I felt as if you wasn't givin' me your all, so I decided not to give you my all."

I still had nothing to say. Roc could sit next to me and explain his mess until he was blue in the face, and it wouldn't even matter. He knew damn well that he had never stopped seeing Vanessa. Whether I had told him about Ronnie or not, what happened today would have happened anyway. Roc reached for the faucet to turn off the water. He squatted next to me again.

"The truth about Vanessa, here it is. Yes, I was dippin' and dabbin' in that every blue moon. Nowhere near as much as you think, only because I wanted to do right by you. When I found out that you neglected to tell me about your conversation with Ronnie, I went back to the woman I felt safe with. Vanessa would lay her life on the line for me, Dez, and anytime Ronnie has said some shit that affected me, she's told me. Even so, I didn't want to be with her. I wanted to be with the woman who was helpin' me grow into a better man and encouragin' me to live a better life. The one who captured my muthafuckin' heart like no one had ever done before. I'm so sorry for what your eyes witnessed today, but I did it because I was hurtin' inside too."

Roc waited for a response, but I still didn't have one. Obviously, he was with the right woman if she was willing to lay her life on the line for him, because I wasn't willing to do so. I closed my eyes again, rubbing my forehead and hoping that he would leave.

He stood up, placing his hands into his pockets. "Lastly, I wasn't the one who killed Mississippi, but, yes, I do know who it was. He owed someone close to me a lot of money, and shit happens when you don't pay up. The bruise underneath my eye and the scratch on my neck was from Vanessa. She was upset because I told her I was spendin' Christmas with you and Chassidy. I didn't want to come over because I knew you'd question me about my marks. When Vanessa came to my place, I was upset with you, again, about not knowin' what you would do with information about

Mississippi. It's shit like that, Dez, where you leave me with too many unanswered questions about you. If this is a wrap, so be it."

Roc left the bathroom, and I wasn't sure if he had left. When I heard the front door shut, I figured he had.

Chapter 8

I stood in the foyer, reading another letter that had been mailed to me. The words were a little different this time.

Yous a dead Bitch

it said with a smiley face sticker. I tore up the letter and threw it in the trash. A part of me felt as if the letters were coming from Ronnie, but could a man as old as he was act so darn childish? I wasn't sure, and the thought of the letters coming from Vanessa had crossed my mind as well.

While in the kitchen, I gazed out at the backyard, watching Latrel and Chassidy make a snowman. Seeing them together always pleased my heart and I had to do whatever was necessary to protect them. In this case, calling the police to report the letters wasn't an option, and I didn't want to involve them because I'd have to mention Roc. I'd never had a gun in the house, but a few weeks ago I'd gone to get one. If I had to use it, I would do it in a heartbeat. Ronnie didn't seem like the kind of man that I could take lightly, and I was starting to worry more about his threats. Maybe it was a good thing that Roc and I weren't seeing each other anymore, but the letter that came today proved that someone wasn't backing down. No doubt, Ronnie hated me with a passion, and to be honest, the feeling was very mutual.

As soon as I took a sip from my coffee, the phone rang. I picked up, but no one answered.

"Hello," I said again. No reply. "You know, I could get my number changed, but I won't. Whoever this is, you don't scare me. Show your damn face, you coward. And when you do, you'd better believe I'll have something waiting for your ass."

I slammed down the phone. Even though I was afraid, I would never show it. I just took a deep breath, hoping that this matter would quickly resolve itself.

Like in the past, Roc called to say he would give me time to get my thoughts together and not pressure me about what I ultimately decided to do. Time was in no way what I needed, because I already knew that our relationship was a done deal. It was hard for me to swallow, and I knew that I still had to deal with Roc because of Chassidy. I also had to see him from time to time at work, and, by now, I had expected him to give up on his job. In no way did he need to be working, and it was obvious that there was still some moving and shaking going on behind the scenes. With him keeping his job, I figured he was just trying to prove something to me.

The new year had swooped in so fast, and, if you blinked, you missed the month of January. My birthday was in March, and I couldn't believe that I would be turning forty-three. I didn't quite feel it yet, and didn't look it, either. That was a good thing.

In August of this year, Latrel would finally be a senior. He wouldn't graduate until the following year, but time had definitely gotten away from me. He was still playing basketball, but he seemed to focus more on his engineering degree. His visits home had slacked up a bit, simply because he was starting to spend more time with his girlfriend. I was a little upset about that, but Latrel had a life to live and I had to accept that. Reggie had been griping about how much time Latrel had been spending with his girlfriend too. When he told me Latrel had mentioned getting married, I was stunned.

"Married?" I said over the phone, talking to Reggie. "Are you serious?"

"Very. I'm just warning you. I have a feeling about this one. There is something in our son's eyes that I'm seeing and I know what that means. He's in love with Angelique, and I would put some money on it."

"I think he's in love too, but I don't know about this marriage thing. It's too soon. He hasn't even known her for a year yet, has he?"

"He's known her for a while, but they started dating a while ago. I didn't call to get you uptight, and like I said, I just wanted to warn you."

I thanked Reggie for the heads-up, and eyeballed the phone after I ended our call. I picked it up to call Latrel, then decided to put it back down. *What's gon' be is gon' be,* I kept telling myself. I didn't know why I seemed so frustrated about this, but I guessed I just didn't want Latrel to make the many mistakes that his father and I had made.

It was back to work for me on Monday. When I got to my desk, there was a note on my computer. The note was from Roc, asking me if he could stop by after work to see Chassidy. It had been a little over three weeks since I'd had a conversation with him about her. Even though I debated in my mind what to do, I didn't want to keep them apart. I immediately called Roc's cell phone and he answered.

"Yes," I said. "That will be fine."

"I can come over?"

"Roc, you are welcome to come and see your daughter anytime you wish. She misses you too, and I would never prevent you from being a part of her life."

"'Preciate it. I'm leavin' work early today because I gotta go handle some business. I'll see y'all around six, no later than seven."

"Sure."

I kept myself busy at work just so I wouldn't think about my situation with Roc and Chassidy. I had a feeling that he was going to use her to get to me, and I had to make sure he could never slip through the cracks. A part of me still felt a little vulnerable, but that didn't stop me from cutting off my connections with Roc. Regardless, we had to make peace with this situation and realize that it wasn't about us anymore, it was about our daughter.

Around 6:30 P.M., the doorbell rang and I made my way to the door. Chassidy and I had been in the kitchen finishing dinner, where I had some fried pork chops, string beans, and mashed potatoes. I opened the door and Roc came inside with a teddy bear and card in his hand.

"Before you chew me out, the teddy bear ain't for you. It's for Chassidy, all right?"

I smiled, inviting Roc inside. He went into the kitchen, giving Chassidy her teddy bear and opening her card so he could read it to her. I started to clean up the kitchen, and before I had finished, Roc had taken Chassidy to her room so they could have some alone time. This situation felt so awkward. In the past we could always sit around each other, laughing, joking, and having fun. I certainly didn't want to give Roc the wrong idea about us, and, for now, things had to be left as they were.

Roc played with Chassidy for a while. They watched TV in the den together; he helped her put together a puzzle, and chased her around the house with a hand puppet. I was lying across my bed, reading a book, when she came running in the room screaming because Roc was trying to scare her with Oscar the Grouch.

"Roc, don't scare her with that thing," I said.

"She's not scared. We just playin'." Roc stood at the end of the bed and Chassidy jumped into his arms. It was getting late, so he carried her to her room, telling me that he was going to tuck her in.

Fifteen minutes later, he came back into my room and stood in the doorway. "I just wanted to let you know that I'm leavin'. Thanks for lettin' me stop by, and I figure maybe I can make arrangements with you to drop by on Tuesdays and Thursdays, if that's okay with you. I know how you feel about her comin' to my place, and since things ain't always smooth on my home front, I'd rather come over here to spend time with her."

"You know I'm not going to argue about that, and Tuesdays and Thursdays sound fine."

Roc hesitated, then walked farther into the room with his hands in his pockets. "Are you ready to talk to me yet about what happened and about what you've decided to do? I'm real interested in what you got to say."

I lowered my book and took off my reading glasses. "There's no need for us to talk about what happened. It's over and done with. You already know what I've decided. I'm not going to continue to play this back and forth game with you. It gets tiresome, and, for an old lady like me, it's played out."

Roc snickered and moved closer. "What you got planned for your birthday, *old lady?* Can I take you out to dinner or somethin'?"

"No, but thank you. I'll be right here on my birthday, and if it falls on a Tuesday or Thursday, maybe I'll see you then."

"It's on a Tuesday. Enjoy your book and I'll see you tomorrow at work. Remember tomorrow is Tuesday, so I'm comin' back this way again."

Every single Tuesday and Thursday, Roc showed up to spend time with Chassidy. Sometimes, I would leave and go to Schlafly Library or the Galleria, just to give them some time alone together. No doubt, he'd kept his word about spending time with her and about keeping his job. Sometimes, he brought Li'l Roc with him to visit, and the farthest they would go was to some of the playgrounds in my neighborhood or to the grocery store to buy junk. I had become more relaxed with the situation and was glad that Roc hadn't suggested doing more than what he was already doing.

The day of my birthday, Mr. Anderson had ordered me a cake and many of my coworkers had come to my desk to get a piece. Monica had sent me some flowers, and so had Latrel and also Reggie. Needless to say, my desk was full of love and I felt pretty darn special. I packed up everything around 3:00 P.M., leaving for the day. I picked up Chassidy early from daycare and headed home to cook dinner. Since it was Tuesday, I knew Roc was coming over and I suspected that he would bring Li'l Roc with him. We had spoken earlier and I mentioned that I had plenty of cake left. Arriving at his normal time, Roc got there around 6:30. Li'l Roc was with him and he couldn't wait to tear into the cake I had placed on the table. I told him and Chassidy to have at it, and what did I say that for? Cake was everywhere, leaving me with one big mess to clean up. As I walked over to the sink to get a rag, Roc asked me to follow him into the den. I was still able to keep my eyes on the kids, so I went to the den to see what he wanted. He gave me two boxes and a card.

"Here," he said. "This is what Li'l Roc picked out for you. He would have given it to you, but, as you can see, he's too busy with that cake."

I opened the card first, reading what Li'l Roc had written in his own handwriting:

Happy Birthday Miss Dez. I love you very much and thank you for being like a 2nd mama to me. Sometimes I wish you were my 1st mama but I know you can't be. Thanks for my little sister 2 and you are a wonderful family.

I closed the card where he had written the names of me and Chassidy on the images of the woman and little girl on the card. My eyes watered, but I held back my tears. I swallowed the lump in my throat and opened the box, which contained a cross with diamonds. I was so touched, and stood up to go give Li'l Roc a hug and kiss.

"Wait a sec," Roc said. "Can you open my gift before you go back into the kitchen?"

"I told you not to do anything for me, Roc. And I don't want you spending your money on me, either."

"I didn't spend that much money on you, so just chill, all right?"

At his request, I opened the other box, and couldn't help but smile when I saw my favorite sundress inside. I knew he had to go to hell and back to find one exactly like the one he'd torn, and his efforts impressed me.

"Thank you," I said, looking up at him.

"Are you goin' to wear it for me tonight? I hope so."

I had no response and ignored his question while I opened the envelope inside of the box. There was a beautiful card, along with a cashier's check for $12,000. I held it in my hand, wondering what it was for.

"I've been saving my checks for Chassidy's education. That's my hard-earned money, so I don't want you trippin' with me about it. Every dime that I make will be for her, all right?"

I was speechless, and this was a very tough situation. I loved and appreciated so much about him, but then there was a side of him that I could in no way cope with. Roc stepped up closer to me and reached into his pocket. My heart dropped, as I thought he was going to pull out a ring. Instead, he pulled out a piece of folded paper. He unfolded it, then let out a deep sigh.

"You'd better not laugh at me. And if you do, I'm never doin' this shit again."

I didn't know what the note said, but in no way would I laugh at something he'd written. "Go ahead," I said, watching him look over the paper. "Read it."

He cleared his throat. "What is Black love and what does it really mean to me? For years, I thought that Black love represented drama and disrespect. In order to get somewhere as a black couple, there had to be pain or no gain. My partner didn't have to show love, 'cause she didn't know love. And if we ever had to go to blows with each other, then that just meant we were angry because we couldn't bear to be without each other. Yeah, that's what I thought, but for all of these years, I have been wrong about Black love. Dead wrong. Now, I know better, 'cause true Black love is alive in me. I feel love like I have never felt it before, and it's so energetic that it takes over my mind, body, and soul. It makes me laugh when I want to cry, it makes me strive harder when I want to give up, it causes me to be real with myself, as that is sometimes so difficult for me to do. Even in my darkest hours when I feel hopeless, or if I don't want to go on, the feeling of Black love picks me up and lets me know that I must move forward. Yeah, I finally get it, but I hope Black love don't give up on me, because I will never give up on it."

Roc folded the paper and seemed embarrassed to look at me. "That was nice," I said with tears in my eyes. "I have to ask, but did you write that? I mean, you just don't seem like the type of person who—"

"Yes, I wrote it. I know it was corny and everythang, but I just wanted to share with you my thoughts that I often write on paper. I did a lot of writin' when I was locked up, too, and these are my real thoughts, ma. I wanted to take this opportunity on your B-day to share that with you, even though we got some serious problems in this relationship."

"Thanks for sharing, your words were beautiful. I really don't know what else to say, but I will never give up on Black love either."

I stood up, giving Roc a hug. He squeezed me tight and kissed my cheek. "You've had your back turned, but when you turn around, please do not be mad at me."

I quickly turned my head and more cake was everywhere. Li'l Roc and Chassidy's mouths were full and their hands had cake squeezed all in between them.

"Why didn't you say anything?" I said, rushing into the kitchen to clean up the mess.

"I was lookin' down at my paper. I just looked up and saw them." Roc followed me into the kitchen. "Man, you know better," he said to Li'l Roc. "Get down from that chair and go wash your hands."

"Don't blame them," I said to Roc. "You're the one who should have been watching them."

I squeezed the cake with my hand, smashing it into Roc's face. He tried to move back, but I caught him off guard. It was smeared all on his cheek and Li'l Roc and Chassidy were laughing. I was too.

"Oh, so you think that shit is funny, huh, birthday girl? I got somethin' for that ass."

Roc picked up the entire cake and started following me around the kitchen. "I'm sorry," I laughed. "Please, put that cake down. If you throw that at me, Roc, that mess will be everywhere. You'll have to clean it up and . . ."

I tried to run out of the kitchen, but I wasn't fast enough. Roc pushed the cake forward, but when I held up my arm, it flipped backward and most of it got on him. The sheet that the cake was on hit the floor and we had one gigantic mess. Roc was still trying to get after me, and as I circled the kitchen island, I laughed when he slipped and fell hard. Before he could say anything, the light on his Bluetooth flashed and he hit the button. He then swiped his cake-filled hands together, rubbing them on his jeans.

"Speak," he said with a smile on his face. Seconds later, his smile vanished quickly. "What?" he yelled. "Nigga, I can't understand a word you're sayin'." Roc paused to listen, then hurried off the floor. "All right," he snapped. "Calm the fuck down! I'm on my way."

He looked at me. "I gotta go. I'll be back to get Li'l Roc later, and I promise I'll be back."

Roc rushed to the door and I rushed after him. "Wha . . . what happened?" I asked.

He yanked open the front door, staring at me for a few seconds with a confused look on his face. "Somebody shot Ronnie."

Roc rushed out, and it wasn't long before I saw his truck speeding down the street.

I slowly closed the door, feeling bad for Roc but unsure about my feelings for Ronnie. Yes, I hated him with a passion, but did I really want the man to die? There were times that I wanted to kill him myself, but those were just thoughts of the anger I felt inside. Hopefully, he was in the hospital and the situation wasn't that serious. I said a quick prayer by the door, and went into the kitchen to clean up the mess.

It was getting late, and after I cleaned the kitchen, I tucked the kids in bed, spending a little more time in the guestroom to thank Li'l Roc for my birthday present. I also read him a story. He had fallen asleep on me and when I looked at the clock it showed 1:00 A.M. I yawned, leaving the guestroom and making my way into my bedroom. Worried, I called Roc's cell phone, but got no answer. I left a message for him to call me back.

I hadn't found anything to wear for work tomorrow, so I went through my closet and picked out a skirt and blouse. I laid them across my chair, dropping the shoes that I wanted to wear on the floor. For whatever reason, I couldn't get Ronnie off my mind. Was it a possibility that my enemy was killed on my birthday? Well, you know that old saying: be careful what you wish for, right? I surely wanted to take back my wishes, only because I knew the loss of Ronnie would be devastating for Roc. I looked up, praying and reneging on what I had said about the man, now wishing him well. I had no idea what losing Ronnie could do to Roc, and the thought of it made me nervous. I cleared my head, quickly changing my clothes so I could get some sleep.

At 3:45 A.M., I heard the doorbell ring. I had just gone to sleep, so I pulled the covers back and rushed out of bed. I could see Roc's truck in the driveway, so I immediately opened the door. He came in so fast that it scared me to death. So much blood was on his shirt, and he staggered inside, appearing to be in much pain. I touched his chest, fearing that he'd been shot, and trying to help him keep his balance.

"Have . . . have you been shot?" I yelled in a panic, still touching all over his bloodstained shirt. "Oh my God, Roc, what happened?"

He staggered into the living room, falling back on the couch. His arm dropped on his forehead and he squeezed his eyes tightly together. His entire face was wet from tears and his breathing was very fast. "He died, Dez. Ronnie died on meee!"

I had never, ever seen Roc like this, nor had I ever witnessed any man crying so hard. My hands trembled as I reached out to touch his body that wouldn't stop shaking.

"It'll be okay, honey. I'm so sorry. Really I am."

Roc wailed out loud, tightening his fist and slamming it into the couch. I really did not know what to say or do to help him. Putting my arms around him only caused him to push me away.

"Just leave me the fuck alone," he cried. "Back up and give me some gotdamn breathin' room!"

I backed away from Roc, giving him the space he requested. Seconds later, Li'l Roc came into the living room after hearing Roc's loud voice.

"Why you crying, Daddy?" he asked tearfully.

Roc didn't respond. He just kept on sobbing and pounding his fist while screaming, "Damn."

I took Li'l Roc's hand and he looked up at me. "What's wrong with my Daddy, Miss Dez?"

"He lost someone very special to him," I said. I continued to hold Li'l Roc's hand, walking him back to the guestroom so he could get back in bed. "Give your dad time to cool off and he'll tell you about what happened soon."

Li'l Roc looked up at me again. "Did Ronnie get killed? Was it Uncle Ronnie?"

In no way did I want to answer Li'l Roc's question. I wasn't sure about his relationship with Ronnie, and the last thing I wanted was to bring a child to more tears. "I'm not sure. But get some sleep for me, okay?"

I noticed Li'l Roc wipe a tear, as he must have shed a few for his father. I had done so as well, and after I tucked Li'l Roc back in, I stood outside of the door to gather myself. I took several deep breaths, then made my way back into the living room where Roc was. He was sitting on the floor with his knees bent, shielding his face with one hand. With his back resting against the couch, I got on the floor and sat next to him. I put my arms around him and laid my head on his shoulder.

"Don't worry. You'll get through this and I will do whatever it takes to make sure you do. If you need me for anything, I'm here."

Roc leaned forward, removing my arms from around him and making sure my head left his shoulder. He squeezed his stomach and continued to break down on me.

"This shit hurts, ma. Losing that muthafucka hurts. He's all I had, Dez. Now what the fuck I'm gon' do?"

Roc rocked back and forth while I rubbed his back. He had me to depend on, but with us limitations had been put in place. I knew that the love he had for Ronnie in no way compared to what he felt for me. All I could say to him was, "You still have to live for you and you have so much to live for. Your children need you, just like you needed Ronnie. Don't give up, and I love you so much."

Roc stayed in the living room and I tried to find out who killed Ronnie and why, but got no answer. I didn't press the issue and didn't leave his side until morning. I was too tired to go to work, so I called in sick. I also called Roc's boss, telling him that Roc had a loss and wouldn't be in for a few days.

Ronnie's funeral was scheduled for Saturday, and I had barely talked to Roc since he left on Wednesday afternoon. When I asked if he knew who had killed Ronnie, he said no and refused to talk about it. Our phone calls were short and he seemed to be so out of it. He invited me to attend the funeral with him, but, to be honest, a big part of me didn't want to be there. I knew how much Ronnie disliked me, and I felt as if going to his funeral would be very disrespectful on my behalf. In no way was I happy about what had happened to him, and I truly wished that this whole situation had turned out differently. But I just couldn't relay those words to Roc. He needed me, and if the shoe were on the other foot, I know he would have been there for me.

I told Roc that I would meet him at the funeral, and, ironically, it was at the same church as the wedding. When I pulled into the parking lot, as expected, the funeral was packed. I was very nervous, and had anticipated sitting in the far back, out of the way. With all of the people standing around, I wasn't sure if I'd see Roc. I just hoped he knew I was there to support him. I walked into the church, dressed in my black linen short-sleeved dress that had a waist-length jacket to go with it. Pearls were around my neck and adorned my wrist as well. My hair was pinned up again and I wore very little makeup. My black heels made me tall, but even so, I hiked myself up on the tips of my toes, looking over the many people in front of me to see if I could find Roc. I didn't see him so I made my way into the sanctuary, taking a seat in the far back. Ronnie's shiny black and chrome casket was already up front and on both sides of the church were pictures of him. I swallowed again, feeling so uncomfortable. I couldn't understand why I continued to put myself in these kinds of situations, but a lot of it was because of Roc.

My eyes wandered around, looking at the hundreds of people piled into the church. The middle section was for the family, so the ushers started to bring in chairs. Moments later, I looked to my right and saw Roc standing next to me.

"Why you didn't let me know you were here?" he said with a very saddened look on his face. His eyes were red, and puffy underneath.

"I figured you would know I was here."

He reached out for my hand. "Come out here with me. The family ain't comin' in until last."

I wasn't family, but instead of saying it, I took Roc's hand. We made our way through the crowd, where people were rubbing his shoulder, telling him everything would be all right, and giving lots of hugs. That made Roc very emotional, and every time we stopped to talk to someone, he squeezed my hand. I figured he thought I was going to let go, but I didn't.

The funeral was under way, and the long line of family members proceeded to go into the church. Roc and I were seated in the very first pew. I kept praying for God to give me strength so I could pass it on to Roc. His legs were trembling and his eyes were glued to Ronnie's casket. Every few seconds, he'd let out a deep breath and sit back. Then he'd let out another and lean forward. He was very fidgety and I reached for his hand to calm him. I held on tight, occasionally rubbing his back and patting his leg.

Midway through the funeral, it was pure, deep torture. The cries in the church were getting louder, the singing choked me up, and one person after another stood up to tell how Ronnie had caused such an impact on their lives.

"Y'all just don't know," a young man stood in front of the church saying. He was crying his heart out. He pointed to Ronnie's casket. "That man right there, he took care of everybody. You could ask him for anything, and he would do it, no questions asked. We lost a hero, but I'm gon' be thankful that I got a chance to know who the real man was."

So many people in the church vouched and hollered, "Amen."

Roc tightened his fist and whispered, "Say that shit, man, say that shit again." He rolled up Ronnie's obituary, tapping it against his hand. At one point, he seemed to calm down, and reached his arm back to rest it on top of the pew. I looked up at him, but it was almost as if I were looking through him. This was a different Roc sitting next to me. A much colder one.

According to the obituary, it was now time to view the body. This was the part that I hated so much. With us being rather close, there was no way for me to avoid it. I prayed, yet again, for strength. The funeral directors opened the casket, and all I could picture in my mind was Roc lying there. From a short distance, I could see Ronnie laid out in his black pinstriped suit and burgundy accessories. Roc was staring at him again, and it wasn't long before the people in the church erupted with more hollering and screaming.

"Jesus Christ," one lady shouted, covering her mouth and damn near fainting. I had never seen so many men cry in my life, and another man dropped to his knees in front of the casket.

"Why you leave us like this, man? Why?" he screamed. "You was supposed to be a soldier!" The ushers had to carry the man out, and, one by one, some of the visitors kissed Ronnie, placed items in his casket, or fell all over it in tears. Shouts of pain rang out, and when Roc dropped down to one knee, I stood up behind him. Several men came to his aid, trying to hold him up. Eventually, they had to carry him out of the church as well. I followed, wiping my tears and hoping that this torture would all be over with soon.

Nearly two hours later, it was. We were now at the gravesite at St. Peter's Cemetery on Lucas and Hunt, where Ronnie was soon to be put into the ground. I stood, holding Roc's hand, looking at all of the people there to pay their last respects. Yes, Ronnie may have been hated by some, but he was still loved by many. The proof was in the pudding, and now he was in the hands of a man who he would have to answer to for the good, bad, or maybe ugly. I said one last prayer for him and made my way with Roc back to his truck. He plopped down in the driver's seat, looking dazed. Another man was riding in the passenger's side, and he got into Roc's truck.

"Are you coming over?" I asked, standing beside Roc's truck. "I'll cook you some dinner."

"Nah, I'm goin' home."

I touched the side of his handsome face, rubbing it. "Okay. If you need anything, call me. Take care, baby."

Roc shut the door and I made my way to my car. I could see Vanessa staring at me from afar, and at a time like this, she had the nerve to confront me.

"I see you're not ready to give up on Roc just yet, huh?" she said.

I sighed and quickly turned to face her. "Vanessa, please stop with the childish games. If Roc is your man, so be it. Why are you constantly approaching me with your nonsense? I know why. Because you know, like I do, that all we are to Roc is some pussy. He doesn't know how to love you, nor does he love me. The only person he has ever loved is now gone, so stop wasting your time with this. Because no matter what you do, Roc is going to be the man you've known him to be for all of these years. Too bad you haven't figured out what kind of man you have on your hands. I have, and that's what you're so afraid of. So stop fighting with him, and instead figure him out. Then you can decide how you wish to proceed in your relationship with him, and in no way will what you decide affect me. That's just a little something I think you should know."

She pursed her lips and put her hands on her hips. "Roc does love me and he can get pussy anywhere. No matter what, he always comes back to me, and that's just something I think *you* should know."

I reached for the door handle on my car, as this chick just wasn't getting it. "Don't chalk it up as love, Vanessa, as it can always be mistaken for convenience. His security blanket you may be, but after a while a blanket gets worn and tired and gets thrown away. I regret to inform you that, personally, I think your days are numbered. Simply because a woman doesn't have to keep fighting for what's hers, she only fights for what's not. Obviously, Roc is not yours."

I got in my car, because this wasn't the time or place for the kind of action I knew she wanted. I couldn't help but to wonder where things would go from here now that Ronnie was gone. Would Roc now become the Head Negro In Charge, or was this the right time for him to move away from the bullshit and be done with it? Just from observing and noticing all of the people coming up to him, along with Vanessa and her continuous mess, I wasn't so sure.

Chapter 9

I guess it didn't take long for my question to be answered, and, just for the record, Roc had been fired from his job. His boss had come to me this morning, telling me that Roc had taken too many days off and failed to call in to say why. I knew he hadn't been coming to work, and every time I spoke to him, he said that he needed more time to get himself together. Basically, he didn't feel like working, so he wasn't coming in. His Tuesday and Thursday visits had come to a halt, and the last time I'd seen him was at the cemetery that day. In no way did I want to pressure him, and when he asked for space, I gave it to him.

Besides, on my end, I had an even bigger fish to fry. My weight had been fluctuating and the stress I had been under was causing me to eat more. Since I hadn't been working out with Roc, I had packed on seven pounds and wasn't too happy about it. My self-esteem had plummeted, and I just couldn't get out of this funk I was in. In addition to that, Latrel had finally broken the news to me, telling me that he wanted to get married. I was livid, because he hadn't even finished college yet. He still had one year to go, but he refused to wait.

"What is the rush?" I asked, talking to him over the phone while I was on the treadmill at Gold's Gym. This weight was coming off of me, and the last thing I needed was to feel uncomfortable about how I looked.

"There is no rush. I've known her for a while and I'm in love. We feel now is the right time to do it, and before we go back to school in August, we will be married. Either you're on board or not, Mama. It's going to happen and I'm not going to argue with you about this. Just be happy for me, all right?"

"I'm trying to be, Latrel, but I don't understand why you can't just finish school first. That would make so much more sense. Give this relationship *thingy* a little more time."

"I'm not on your time, I'm on my time. Angelique agreed to marry me and I'm not going to wait to do it."

"She's pregnant, isn't she? Why don't you just come out and say it, Latrel?"

"I would tell you if she was, but she's not. Look, I'm not getting anywhere with this conversation. I'll be home next weekend and we can talk more about it. I have to get to class, so bye, Mama."

He hung up, leaving me fuming inside. In no way was I against him getting married, but Latrel needed to wait. He was moving way too fast, and just two years ago he was claiming to be in love with someone else. It reminded me so much of the situation Reggie had put himself in. I was concerned about Latrel following that path. I called Reggie at work, ready to chew him out for . . . nothing.

"Would you please talk to your son?"

"I have, Dee, but it's his life and we have got to let go. I know how hard this is for you, but, baby, it is his choice. We got married right after college, and if he wants to do it a year sooner, so be it. Why are you stressing yourself over this?"

I started to walk faster on the treadmill. "I don't know. I guess . . . I guess I'm just afraid of losing him."

"You will not be losing him. As I see it, you're gaining a lot. You'll finally have a daughter-in-law to go shopping with and to chat with over the phone. She'll—"

"Ughhh. I don't need anyone to go shopping with and chat with over the phone. I have Monica for that and no one will take her place."

Reggie laughed, trying to convince me that this was the right move for Latrel. I wasn't buying it, and when I called Monica to vent, she told me the same thing. I guess it was time for me to get on board, but then again, maybe not.

The weeks had flown by, and I was so sure that Roc would have made some time for Chassidy, but he hadn't. Basically, he had cut her off and I didn't like it one bit. I was very upset with him, and even though I figured he was probably still going through a hard time, his approach was wrong. She had been asking about him and I really didn't have a legitimate answer as to why he had stopped calling and coming over.

Friday after work, I decided to go get my answer. I remembered the turmoil that going to his place brought me the last time I paid him an unexpected visit, but I was prepared to deal with whatever. He wasn't my man and this was all about how he intended to move forward with his daughter. I wanted what was in her best interest, and if Roc had decided not to be a part of her life anymore, I needed to know that.

When I arrived at his place, I knocked, getting no answer. I rang the doorbell; no one came. I waited, and, yes, I contemplated using my key. That would be such a bold move, and if the shoe were on the other foot, I would have a fit. Still, that didn't stop me from putting my key in the door and going inside. Just like the last time, the music was up very loud. This time, however, I called Roc's name to let him know that I was inside.

"Roc, are you in here? It's me, Dez."

I got no answer as I made my way up the steps, fearing to look into the living room and witness what I'd seen before. This time, the living room was empty, but it was a mess. Clothes were everywhere. Smoked blunts were in an ashtray, and empty beer cans, as well as liquor bottles, were all over. It looked like somebody had been partying and partying hard. I checked the dining room and the kitchen, but they both were empty. Two of the kitchen chairs were tilted back on the floor, and empty bags from London & Sons Wing House were on the table. I picked up the chairs, placing them back underneath the table. Afterward, I turned, making my way down the hallway to his bedroom. I felt very uneasy. As I slowly walked, the floor squeaked loudly. Seconds later, I heard Roc's voice coming from his bedroom.

"If you make another move, I swear I'll kill you."

I stopped in my tracks with an increased heart rate. "Roc, it's me. Dez."

I got no response, but as I inched my way to the door, I peeked into his bedroom. He was sitting up in bed. His gun was aimed in my direction, and when he saw me, he dropped it into his lap. The room was partially dark, because he had put up some curtains to cover the window. I turned on the light, and just like the rest of his place, everything was a mess.

"What's going on, Roc?" I asked, walking farther into the room. The smell of marijuana nearly burned my nose and it was very strong. Roc's eyes were bloodshot, and I had never seen the hair on his head, as well as his facial hair, look so scruffy.

He scratched his head and I could hear how dry his hair was. "Ain't nothin' goin' on. Just chillin', that's all."

I sat on the bed in front of him, looking around at his messy room. "It looks like something has been going on. Did you have a party?"

"Nope. And if I had, I would have invited you."

"Don't do me any favors." I chuckled. He didn't laugh, and all he did was clear his throat.

"I . . . I'm not going to stay long, but I stopped by because you haven't called or come by to see Chassidy. She misses you, Roc, and I do too. Have you given up on your daughter? I know things haven't been going well with us, but I at least thought you'd still see about your daughter."

Roc sat back on the bed, resting against the head-board. "Yep. I've given up on everything. Ain't no place in this world for a man like me, so I'm here in my own space, doin' my own thing."

"So, in other words, you're hiding out? From what? Me? Chassidy? Who?"

"I'm not hidin' out. I just don't want to be out there right now. I like right where I am and this shit is peaceful, ma."

"Well, I definitely don't want to interrupt your peace. I know how it is when you feel the need to be alone. I was the same way when I lost my mother, so I can understand how you feel." I touched the side of his face and rubbed it. "Just know that I'm here for you, and don't give up on life, okay? Chassidy and I really miss you and I want you to be well."

He said not a word, just glared at me in a trance. I stood up, willing to leave Roc at peace. When it came to healing, people were on their own time and they dealt with the loss of a loved one how they wanted to. I figured Roc would come around, so I wasn't too worried. I gave him a hug and he barely hugged me back. Needing no answer as to why, I made my way to the door. I reached for the light, turning it back off.

"Dez," Roc said, halting my steps.

"Yes." I turned to see what he wanted.

"I . . . I did it all for you. For you and Chassidy. I just wanted to let you know that."

My brows scrunched inward. "Did what for us? What did you do for us?"

I saw a tear roll down his face and he swiped it away. I moved closer, asking the same question. Roc looked into my eyes, sucking his teeth.

"He was gon' kill you, baby." He spoke tearfully. "You and my daughter, and I . . . I couldn't let him do it. I couldn't, Dez, and I had to make a decision. He was days away from doin' it, and when I found out about the letters and phone calls from my boy Ned, I . . . I had to take action."

It felt as if cement had been poured over me. I couldn't move. I opened my mouth, but no words came out. Roc lowered his head and squeezed his forehead.

"Please forgive me, but I can't be around you and Chassidy anymore. It hurts too bad and it reminds me of what I had done to him."

I looked at the gun in Roc's lap, realizing that he must have been over here contemplating suicide. What a messed up situation to be in, and there was no doubt in my mind that Ronnie was coming for me. This was so very tragic and I never thought or believed that it would have resulted in this. I slowly sat down on the bed, moving the gun away from Roc's lap. He began to tell me how he had Ronnie set up, and the paranoia he'd felt from doing so. He even let me listen to a tape that was given to him by Ned, where Ronnie clearly had planned to do away with me and Chassidy the day after my birthday. I was to be blown away at the front door, and directions were given to do away with anyone else in the house and make sure the little girl, Chassidy, didn't live. I was stunned that any man could be so cruel, but then again, I wasn't. This was one time that I had passed the correct judgment on a person, and it pleased my heart, more than anything, knowing that Ronnie was now in hell.

I could see the pain Roc was in for making such a difficult decision. I put my arms around him, thanking him repeatedly for basically choosing our lives over Ronnie. "Please don't be so hard on yourself," I said tearfully. "I am so grateful to you for what you did, and one day you will realize that you did the right thing. Thank you, baby, thank you. I love you so much, and you don't know how much Chassidy and I need you."

I had a tight hold on Roc, but his hold on me wasn't so tight. He begged me not to tell anyone the truth and did his best to convince me that him not being in Chassidy's life was a good thing. According to him, there was no way for him to be the father he needed to be to her, and if anyone ever found out the truth about what had happened to Ronnie, we could all lose our lives. In no way did he want that to happen, so he asked me to please understand why it had to be this way. Of course, I disagreed.

"I will give you all the space and time you need, but you're not going to do this to us again, Roc. You promised me that you wouldn't give up on us and I'm going to hold you to that promise. I will never repeat a word of this to anyone, and at the end of the day, you made a choice that saved the lives of two people who didn't deserve to die. I know it hurts, but it was a brave thing to do."

"Maybe so, but I'm not feelin' it right now. I . . . I really don't want to talk about this anymore. All we're goin' to do is disagree about Chassidy and I have to do what I feel in my heart is best. Chassidy will one day get it. She's so young right now, and by the time she turns ten, she won't even remember who I am."

The thought of what he said choked me up even more. How could he continue to easily walk in and out of our lives like this? My mouth hung open and my throat ached from the thought. "How can you say that? Every child needs their parents, and if anybody knows that it should be you. How dare you sit there and give up on her like that? I guess this is so easy for you, as it wouldn't be the first time you've done it. Chassidy loves you and she has gotten to know—"

"What about you?" Roc asked. "Do you *really* still love me too, Dez? Ain't this got somethin' to do with you? This not all about Chassidy, so let's be real. What about us getting back together? You ended this shit with me over some pussy. Pussy that don't mean shit to me no more."

I looked down, fumbling with my nails. "I . . . I love you, but I can't be with a man I don't trust. You make this so hard for me and I don't want to keep being with a man who hurts me all the time. I appreciate all that you've done, but it's not enough."

He quickly fired back. "Not enough! I had Ronnie killed." He paused, unable to say it again.

"I know," I said, standing up and squeezing my forehead. I was so confused and debated with myself about what to do, as well as say. "I just don't know about us being together, Roc, and that's a separate issue. Give me time, and I'll deal with it as it comes. Meanwhile, I hope you think about what you're saying about your child. Focus on being there for her, and I can't tell you how much she needs you. She will always need you and that's never going to change."

"I have thought long and hard about Chassidy. This is best for everyone, and even though you may not see it now, you will soon. Now, please. I got a headache right now and I need my peace. Lock the door on your way out."

I couldn't believe what Roc was saying and I threw up my hands in defeat. "Fine," I said, picking up my keys so I could go. I wasn't going to sit there and beg Roc to be a father to his child. Like so many other mothers, I could easily do this by myself. I should have known that it would come to this. Stupid me, and there I was again having hope and faith about this situation turning out differently. I abruptly walked down the hallway, hoping that Roc would call my name to stop me. He didn't. Then, something else hit me. My thoughts were sometimes late, but accurate. I went back into his bedroom.

"You're telling me all of this because you're leaving St. Louis, aren't you?" I asked.

He didn't hesitate one bit. "Yes."

"When?"

"Soon."

"How soon? Days, weeks, months. . . ."

"Days."

I stood, shaking my head, feeling the huge lump in my throat that wouldn't go away even when I swallowed. "And you weren't even going to tell me, were you?"

"No, because I knew you wouldn't understand."

I was stunned, angry, disgusted . . . all at the same time. This in no way made sense to me, but it clearly confirmed that Roc had love for no one. I reached into my purse, pulling out something that I knew would come in handy. I read Roc's own words back to him, hoping that he would reconsider. "What is Black love and what does it really mean to me? For years, I thought that Black love represented drama and disrespect. In order to get somewhere as a black couple, there had to be pain or no gain. My partner didn't have to show love, 'cause she didn't know love. And if we ever had to go to blows with each other, then that just meant we were angry because we couldn't bear to be without each other. Yeah, that's what I thought, but for all of these years, I have been wrong about Black love. Dead wrong." I looked up at him, just to make sure he was paying attention to me. He was. "Now, I know better, 'cause true Black love is alive in me. I feel love like I have never felt it before, and it's so energetic that it takes over my mind, body, and soul. It makes me laugh when I want to cry, it makes me strive harder when I want to give up, it causes me to be real with myself, as that is sometimes so difficult for me to do. Even in my darkest hours when I feel hopeless, or if I don't want to go on, the feeling of Black love picks me up and lets me know that I must move forward. Yeah, I finally get it, but I hope Black love don't give up on me, because I will *never give up on it*."

I tore the paper in shreds, watching each piece slowly drop to the floor. "Like everything else, I guess that was a bunch of bullshit too. Good-bye, Roc. Have a nice life."

Chapter 10

For the next several months, my life remained Roc free. He stuck to his guns, and it was confirmed by a very credible source that Roc had moved out of his condo and had left St. Louis. I felt dissed all over again, but I kept it moving. Like the last time, I threw myself into work, focused on my children, lost weight again, and put the past behind me. There was nothing that I could do to change the past. I had regretted that I hadn't made better choices, for me, and for my daughter as well. Because of me, she would not know the man she often called her father. She would be left with a very vague memory of him. I was so sure she would one day wonder what she, herself, had done wrong to cause him to abandon her. In no way was this her fault, and I would someday tell her that all of this was on me. No matter how I looked at it, or tried to spin it, it was on me for making bad choices.

Latrel's wedding was the following day, and, by now, he had my full support. I had completely changed my attitude. If I couldn't get this thing called Black love right, I was counting on him. He truly loved Angelique and I was looking forward to her becoming a part of our family. I liked her mother and father a lot, and even though they were divorced like me and Reggie, they still got along well.

***

The day of the wedding, Monica picked me up early so we could go to Forest Park, where the wedding was taking place. I wanted to be sure everything was in order. Angelique wanted an outdoor wedding, but, unfortunately for all of us, light rain was in the forecast. The sun was shining bright for now, but I wasn't sure how long it would last. I prayed for God to hold off the rain for as long as He could, or just long enough for Latrel and Angelique to say, "I do."

When we got to Forest Park, everything seemed to be in place. The chairs had already been set up. The gazebo sat up front, decorated with many beautiful red and white flowers. Angelique had wanted a horse and carriage to bring her in, and I checked with the wedding planner just to make sure it was a go. She said it was. After tying a few big ribbons and bows around several of the trees that would show in the pictures, Monica and I left to go get ready. We both got ready at my house and Latrel and Reggie got ready at his place.

"I can't believe you are finally letting your son go," Monica said, pulling Chassidy's dress over her head. "And I just knew you'd request to be his best man, instead of Austin."

I threw my hand back at her, continuing to look in the mirror while glossing my lips. "I haven't let him go and I will never let him go. I may play second fiddle for a while, but Angelique knows who the real boss lady is."

We laughed.

"I'm sure she does, and I must say that I'm glad she's a Democrat," Monica gloated.

"Uh, sorry to bust your bubble, but she's not."

Monica cocked her head back. "Then what is she? Latrel needs to call this mess off right now, 'cause he don't need to be marrying no woman who belong to a Tea Party."

I reached over, patting Monica on her back and whispering. "She's registered as an Independent, so calm down, okay? And as far as I know, she doesn't belong to no Tea Party."

She playfully rolled her neck in circles. "And just how do you know all of this?"

I put my hand on my hip, twitching my finger from side to side. "Because I already did my homework. Spent hours on the Internet, Googling her name and finding out everything that I could possibly find out about her. She did have a racy picture posted on her Facebook page, but everything else checked out."

"Ooooo," Monica laughed. "You are so, so bad. I saw that picture too. Did you see that she had a judgment filed against her for not paying her credit card bill?"

My eyes widened. "Don't you tell me that, girl. Did you check her out too?"

"I sure did," Monica confirmed with a serious look on her face. "As soon as you told me Latrel was getting married to her, I got busy. She's pretty clean, but not paying your bills may not be a good sign."

"Are you sure it was her?"

"Let's go check and make sure."

We laughed, running over to my computer and checking the information Monica had found. "See, right there," Monica said, pointing to the information given for a person name Angelique S. Branson who owed $7,385 in credit card debt.

"Umph," I said with my hands on my hip. "Scroll down." Monica scrolled down, but I immediately realized that Angelique's middle name was Lashay.

"Monica, that's the wrong person. Her middle name is Lashay."

"Is it?"

"Yes," I said, walking away from the computer, playfully swiping my forehead. "I'm glad about that, and I damn sure didn't want my son paying for no big bill that she'd made way before his time."

"I know what you mean, but shame on us." Monica laughed. "Both of our asses were in big debt when we got out of college. If I recall, Reggie did have to pay for those Visa credit cards you racked up on, didn't he?"

"If you won't tell, I won't tell." I snickered. "Now get your shoes on so we can get the heck out of here. You're going to have me late for my own son's wedding. You know I wouldn't miss this for the world!"

The wedding was in progress and Angelique's father had just given her away. She stepped up to Latrel, who looked handsome as ever, tightening her arm with his. Monica sat next to me and Reggie sat behind us. He had brought another woman with him, and all I did was say hello. Monica saw me already getting emotional, so she slipped me some of the Kleenex she'd already had in her hand. I dabbed my watery eyes, pleased by how happy Latrel looked, and smiling at Chassidy, who was the flower girl and just couldn't keep still. She was swaying from side to side, and every chance she got, she waved at me. I waved back and several people laughed. Then, all of a sudden, the lady who was sitting to my right moved and I looked up, only to see Roc take her seat. He was razor sharp. Dressed in a black single-breasted tailored suit that traced his sexy frame. Two diamond-studded earrings were in his ears and his hair was trimmed to perfection. Minimal hair suited his chin, and I would have loved to see him on the cover of *GQ* magazine. I swear he could give Lance Gross a run for his money, and Roc would come through slightly on top.

"Glad I didn't miss too much," he said, sitting next to me. I watched him wave at Chassidy, and she smiled, waving back. She was about to run over to us, but I whispered for her to stay where she was. Roc smiled. "Latrel would have killed me if I didn't make it." He looked over at Monica. "Hey, Monica. What's up?"

No doubt, we were both shocked to see Roc, and Monica could barely get the word "hello" out of her mouth.

Roc cleared his throat, crossing one leg over the other. I looked at the sparkling diamond watch on his wrist and two diamond rings on his finger, wondering what he'd been up to. My mind quickly got back to the wedding and it remained my focus for quite some time.

As the wedding vows were being exchanged, everyone was taking peeks up at the cloudy sky. The dark clouds were slowly moving in, so the minister decided to hurry it up. Angelique and Latrel exchanged wedding rings, and after it was all said and done, they laid a big kiss on each other. The rain held off for as long as it could, and it had started to drizzle. I was glad, only because it helped to cover up the few tears that had fallen down my face.

"That was so beautiful," Monica whispered. "Shame on us for underestimating Angelique."

"No. Shame on you."

The minister shouted, "I give to you Mr. and Mrs. Latrel R. Jenkins."

Everyone stood and applauded as they ran down the middle aisle, shielding themselves from the rain that was picking up. Latrel paused for a moment, mouthing that he loved me and nodding his head at Roc. I blew a kiss to him, sealed with approval.

Giving the wedding party time to leave, I held my tiny purse over my head, trying not to let the rain damage my hair too bad. The carriage and horse had brought Angelique to the wedding, but she and Latrel, along with the wedding party, were leaving in limousines. They rushed to the limousines, getting ready to take the short drive over to the reception that was at a nearby indoor banquet room. After everyone got into the limousines, the guests started to leave. By now, the rain was coming down pretty hard so everyone was rushing.

"I'll see you in the car," Monica said, squinting from the rain. She looked at Roc. "Are you coming too?"

"It depends. But I need to talk to Dez for a minute."

"Okay, but don't be long." Monica gave me a quick hug, then ran off to the car.

I continued to hold my purse over my head, but it did me no good. My hair was getting flat and I could feel my heels sinking in the ground. As for Roc, he was completely drenched. He reached out his hand to move my hair away from my face, gazing at me with his lowered, hooded eyes.

"You look so sexy," he said, blinking his wet eyelids. "Damn, you're gorgeous."

"Too bad being beautiful has never stopped me from getting hurt. What's going on, Roc?"

"I'ma make this quick, but, uh, I just wanted to tell you that I moved, but not too far. I live in Kansas City, Missouri now, and I wondered if you and Chassidy would consider movin' there with me? I'm ready, baby. I am so ready to do this shit with you. I got my shit together, got a job, and lookin' forward to startin' a new life with you. I want you as my wife, and the sooner, the better. Tell me what you're thinkin'. Can we do this shit or what?"

I lowered my head, knowing deep inside that I still loved him so much. I had been miserable without him, but had done my best to ignore the void in my heart. I felt like we had been to hell and back, but the time had come for us to stand still. I slowly moved my head from side to side. "I'm sorry, baby, but your timing couldn't be more off. I believe that people come into your life for a reason, season, or a lifetime, and your season is over. Obviously, you were never meant to be my lifetime, and the way you continue to walk in and out of my life shows it. If I allow you to, you will continue to come and go as you please, but not anymore, Roc. You hurt me too bad this time, and I can't let you do it again. The one thing I regret is letting you back in. I could have prevented all of this from happening to me twice. I soooo wish things could have turned out differently between us, but the ball was always in your court, never mine. I truly wish you well, and take care of yourself."

I reached out, just to give Roc a hug. He didn't hug me back, but that was perfectly okay with me. I ran off, shielding myself from the rain with my hand, and intending not to look back.

"Black love," Roc shouted. "No matter what, you can't fight it! It's there, Dez, and it's always gon' be between you and me."

I turned, just to get one last glimpse at his handsome self standing in the rain. I had to respond. "You're so right about Black love, Roc," I shouted back. "It's out there and I'm not giving up because one . . . two men didn't get it right. Keep the faith, and I hope you don't give up on true Black love either!"

I hurried to open the door to Monica's car, and hopped in on the passenger's side. My eyes connected with Roc's as he continued to stand motionless in the rain. While it may not have worked out between us, I was so serious about not giving up on love. No matter what age a man was, or I was for that matter, Black love was still out there and I was determined to find it.

Monica pulled away from the curb and I let out a deep sigh. I was pained that my season with Roc was over, but eager to see what my lifetime had in store for me. After this much experience with relationships, I felt ready to meet my soul mate. It wasn't Reggie, and unfortunately, it wasn't Roc either.

TELL ME ABOUT IT!

By
Nikki-Michelle

(for Sam and Michelle)

Chaper 1

My life has always been mundane and for the most part, I have been okay with that. Mundane has kept me free from most of the dramas of life, women, and men. I have no man and no desire to have one. I have been that way for the last four years. The last man I dated was so busy lying that even he didn't know when he was telling the truth. It wasn't like he did a lot of lying about cheating, not to say that he wasn't, but it was other simple things that irked my nerves. Like, why lie about your grades in school or why lie about why you haven't taken your car to the shop to get it fixed yet? Simple stuff like that irked me.

I liked to stay to myself mostly because that meant no worries of trust and people issues, but it seemed as of late the drama followed me to work. *Come on five o'clock.* I kept chanting that inside of my head all day! I was tired, sleepy, and cranky as hell. I had to do way more work than I was being paid to do and the slackers that worked with me annoyed me too. I had been in the same cubicle for four years at this simple entry level position at Atlanta's top marketing and advertising firm. B&G Marketing and Advertising had almost been run into the ground by the former executives and CEO. With all of the sex scandals and sexual harassment lawsuits being thrown at the company left and right, it's a wonder we are still standing.

"You okay over there Chyanne?" Justin asked when I answered my earpiece.

We were working on some research and analytics for this contract that the company had just acquired. We had landed a major deal with a big production company in Atlanta to do all of their marketing and advertising so it was imperative that we get this done on time. There were seven floors in this building, not including the basement. And the whole sixth and seventh floors had been fired. All the old executives were out. They didn't leave one.

I nodded. "Yeah I'm good."

"You sure, girl? Because you are as quiet as a damn mouse."

He laughed and swung his invisible hair. Justin was as gay as gay would ever get. Let him tell it, he was more woman than me and that was no easy feat since I was what America considered full figured. A big girl some called it. My thirty-six double-D's made me curse them at times and my thighs touched when I walked, but they were not overlapping each other. I was a size sixteen and could squeeze my big ass, and I mean that literally, into a fourteen. Hell just last month I had lost myself and was pushing a size eighteen. I quickly threw away juice and everything that wasn't chicken or fish. I mean don't get me wrong, I had no problem with being super thick, but I didn't want the diabetes and high blood pressure that ran in my family either. I was deathly afraid of being taken out of here like that. So no, I didn't have washboard abs, but damn it, I made my clothes look good!

"Yeah. Just trying to get this report done," I answered.

"You know why everyone is walking on eggshells around here today, right?"

Justin was also a gossip queen.

"No."

"Bitch, I swear! You are so clueless sometimes," he fussed. "We could have a hurricane in this bitch and your ass wouldn't notice."

I giggled a bit. "Shut up and tell me!"

"Well, today is the day that the new CEO makes his debut on the first floor."

I turned to look at Justin and he made a dramatic effect, nodding his head and turning his lips down. His cubicle was right across from mine. The new CEO had been here for weeks cleaning house.

"Oh really?"

"Yes Ma'am. That's why that sour pussy bitch Lola has been prancing around here all morning. How much do you want to bet she has already sucked his dick?"

"Are they firing people down here too?"

"Seems like it girl! You know that girl Andrea right?"

"Yeah."

"Well she just filed another sexual harassment claim against the company and John's old white ass."

"Damn! His old cripple dick was getting with and at everybody huh?"

"Yes Ma'am! But bitch let me tell you, that new CEO is sexy as fuck. You hear me?"

I kept typing and laughing, while Justin kept talking. "Girl that thang came down here early this morning before you got in and I almost dropped down and sucked his dick for fun."

"Ewww Justin! Really? Save me the graphics will you?"

He laughed a little. "Girl that fucker is fine! You hear me and he's a brother."

"If he's a brother and he's that fine then he's probably down low gay. You know how they do."

I expected Justin to agree but I heard his line click. When I went to glance over at him, my eyes stopped at the waist and blue suit pants of someone standing directly in front of my cubicle. I got annoyed and looked up into hazel brown eyes. He had a bald head with a smooth baby face. Dimples were easy to see, evenly placed on each side of his cheeks. He had thick eyebrows with long curly lashes that gave his eyes an exotic appeal. He stood in a wide legged stance with his arms folded across his chest. His expression showed something that I couldn't read. I removed my earpiece and looked back up at him.

"Chyanne, is it?" He asked. I could tell he was from New York. His accent was thick.

I nodded. "Yes, it is."

"Is there anything you want to ask me about my personal life?"

Everything and person in the place was quiet. Even the clocks seemed to have stopped ticking.

"No sir, there isn't."

I assumed this was the CEO.

"You sure? Because you could have fooled me."

"I said I didn't," I snapped.

The way his eyebrows lifted told me I had touched a nerve with my tone of voice.

Before walking off he said to me, "Before you leave today, I need to see you in my office."

His whole demeanor, attitude, and accent grated my nerves. Even the way he strutted over to the elevator worked me. He must have come in from the stairs because he sure didn't come off the elevators or I would have seen him. Justin cut his eyes over at me and mouthed the words 'I'm sorry'. I shrugged and went back to my report. I was a little antsy for the rest of the day. It was well known around here that I didn't take any mess or hold my tongue, but the proof was in the pudding. Out of the five degrees I have, a Master's in business and a BA in marketing is what got me this job, and yet here I was in an entry level position. I finished all of my reports at around 4:00 p.m. and since I was set to leave at five, I packed up my belongings and headed to the elevator. Hell if he was going to fire me, it was going to be on their time. I could see a few people eyeballing me, wondering if they could have my hours once I was gone. I stepped onto the elevator and rode it up to the seventh floor. I caught my reflection and saw my fro was all over the place. I had one of those wild manes that would make Angela Davis's fro look like a baby fro. I ran my hand threw it to try and give it a better look. That didn't help. Oh well.

I gave myself the once over. I had on all black everything; black cropped dress shirt, black wide legged dress pants, and black six inch caged Chanel booties. I could feel my phone vibrating in my purse. It was probably April. She was my best friend. Had been for the last five years. I'd call her back later. After I find out if I still had a job or not. The elevator stopped with a ding and I stepped off onto the seventh floor. I made no qualms in speaking to anyone. Even when the guard asked me who I was there to see, I kept walking right past him.

I rounded the corner and walked down the long corridor. I could see Lola in his office. Mr. McHale's office was big enough to house a small family. The only thing that wasn't made of glass was his big cherry oak wood door. He had the blinds pulled up. Smart move. Guess he didn't want any trouble. Judging by the way Lola was acting, she had probably already sucked his dick like Justin said. Lola annoyed me too. She was light, bright, and darn near white. She had a honey blonde weave with a Kelly Rowland body and a Kim Kardashian outlook on life. By the time I made it to his office, she was coming out and heading back to her desk. The rude trick didn't even speak. She cut her fake honey golden eyes at me and shook her head with a smirk that said she knew something I didn't know. I ignored her and without knocking walked right into the CEO's office. He stopped what he was doing, quirked an eyebrow, and tilted his head. I could tell he was either surprised that I had come early or surprised that I had walked right in.

"Have a seat Chyanne," he said to me.

Like hell I was. If he was going to fire me, I was not going to sit down for it. I watched as he turned and put some papers away in a file cabinet behind him. When he turned back around to see me still standing by the door, he stopped mid stride and looked at me. I watched as he calmly pulled his big black desk chair back and sat down.

"Will you please have a seat? This shouldn't take long," he said to me.

"If it won't take long there is no need for me to sit."

He frowned a bit and this time the expression on his face showed annoyance. I could care less. He inhaled and exhaled before brushing his fingers across his lips. He had full lips. Thick lips. My eyes were drawn to his lips.

"Look, I understand what you all had to deal with before I got here, but that's not the case with me. So if you would, please, have a seat."

I switched my purse from one hand to the other and made my way over to the black cushioned wing back chair in front of his desk.

"Good! Now first things first. You're fired."

I closed my eyes and sucked in my bottom lip to keep from snapping.

He kept going. "Now tell me why a woman with three degrees, a Master's in Marketing, a BA in business, and Associates in accounting, is still in entry level after four years?"

I looked at Lola as she pranced through the doors with bright red pants that looked like they were painted on. They were so tight I could see all that she had been blessed with. She handed him a file and switched back out. He told her thank you and turned his attention back to me right after moving his eyes from her assets. That woman had a gap so big in between her legs that I could fly a 747 through it.

"Care to answer my question," he asked me as he put the file on the desk and clasped his hands together. He licked his lips and stared at me.

"I don't know. Maybe it's because I don't lay on my back for positions," I shrugged for dramatic effect. "You know how it is."

He smiled and leaned back in his seat. "Well I was firing you from one position to offer you another but since you don't fuck your way up the corporate ladder I guess I can keep my offer."

I looked at this man to see if he was serious. The fact that I couldn't read his face pissed me off. For some reason the way he looked at me unsettled me. I felt my blood pressure spike. This was the point where I should have turned back around or quit or resigned or something, but I stayed there after he smirked and told me he was joking. I took the position he was offering and prepared myself for a new break in my career.

Chapter 2

"I am beginning to hate dating in Atlanta!"

That was April. We were sitting at the bar in Club Miami and once again the boyfriend she had been seeing for about two years turned out to be a lying, cheating, blah blah blah. This was beginning to be the norm for her and I always asked her why did she just have to have a man? Because as soon as one threw her away like a used tampon she was out looking for another. April was thirty-five with three teenage boys. One was a senior in high school and the two twins were freshmen. So when she called me once again I became the dutiful friend. I pulled on some high waist wide legged black slacks with a black ruffled blouse that tapered to my waist and pushed my breasts up a little more. Slid my feet in my black and gray platform six inch heels and pulled my fro back into a puff ponytail. We both hopped in my car and here we were.

I sipped from my Ciroc and lime. "Girl please. You'll be right back at it tomorrow."

"Not this time. Do you know he had the nerve to tell me phone sex is not cheating?"

I laughed. "Well, technically it isn't."

April looked at me. She was a light skinned thick chick from Louisiana, with about five feet six a short spiked platinum blonde pixie hair cut. Her chocolate brown eyes gave me a look that said she wasn't in a playing mood and I don't care what she said. The fact that we were in a bar only a few hours after her break up meant she was on the prowl again. The short denim skirt with the five inch heels and half shirt said the same thing.

"Well that may be the case, but the fact that the bitch could tell me about my brand new Egyptian cotton sheets closed the deal," she said, sipping from her drink and looking around the club.

The music was too loud. Some fool was screaming through the speakers talking about "Oh let's do it"! This was one of the reasons I didn't like coming out. The only time I hit any club was when April was going through one of her moments. Other than that she and whoever she was dating were inseparable. I was an afterthought.

"Damn! He had the girl in your house?"

"Yeah, some young ass bitch. She's about your age. Young and fucking dumb," she spat.

I was about to ask her was that a shot at me. She always had some something snide to say at or about me. But it seemed like the only one dumb here was the thirty-five year old woman sitting across from me who couldn't keep a man. But I would shut up for now. We sat quiet for a while and I zoned out. My mind had drifted off to work. For three weeks now I had been in a new position at work. Aric, that's what he insisted on being called, had promoted me to his executive assistant. This pissed a lot of people off including Lola who had been demoted to my old job.

We had been working all kinds of late hours trying to get the company back on track. I would like to think that we were doing a pretty bang up job. We had contracts coming back in left and right. Aric had other executives following his lead and I guess more assistants were following mine. For a while it was just me and Aric on the seventh floor after five. I had become so accustomed to staying late that I had started to bring a change of clothes after the work day to be more relaxed in. Last night was the night that stuck out in my mind. Aric and I had papers scattered all across his office floor trying to figure out which contracts were more important than the next. We had been at it since four o'clock that afternoon with no end in sight. We had even ordered Chinese because it was apparent that the night would be later than the rest.

We had a bid to pitch to this company that specialized in mineral makeup and everything had to be packaged and ready for him to present in the morning. That's the thing about Aric, he was very hands on. So there we were in the middle of his office floor. He had kicked his shoes off and his dress shirt hung open, showing his white wife beater. I found myself staring at his chest and arms. It had become so obvious that Aric was well defined with muscle. His arms were thick and sinewy. I also noticed that he had a Kemetian tattoo that circled his right arm and he wore thin black framed reading glasses. When he inhaled and exhaled I could see the muscles in his stomach through his wife beater give a little ripple. I caught myself and looked away. Everything was going as planned until the food came and we started getting personal with our questions.

"You don't have a man you need to be getting home to Chyanne," he asked me before he put a spoonful of shrimp fried rice into his mouth. He watched me as I examined the way he licked his lips and chewed his food.

"No, and even if I did, he would have to understand that sometimes I will have to work late."

"Yeah, but you have been in here with me at least ten days straight. Don't you think that would be a problem?"

I swallowed my sweet and sour chicken before answering. "No. Which is probably why I don't have a man."

He chuckled. We sat in silence and ate a bit before I said something else to him.

"What about you? You have a girl or a wife somewhere?"

For a second and only a second his eyes clouded over and he shook his head. "Naw. Women are complicated. I fuck and keep it moving."

His bluntness caught me off guard. So much so that I damn near choked.

He continued and laughed at me. "I don't have time for a relationship or marriage. Now casual sex, a date here and there, I can do. Anything else is for the birds."

"Well okay then," was all I could answer with.

"What? You have never had casual sex Chyanne?"

"No. Not planning on it either. I view it all as a big waste of time." I took a sip of my Pepsi and moved to sit on the sofa behind me. My thick thighs and the floor were not getting along. Aric put one last spoonful of rice in his mouth and stretched out on the floor. I watched as his long body stretched and was totally thrown for a loop when he adjusted his manhood like I wasn't even in the room. My mouth was hanging open and I didn't even know it.

"Are you going to tell me why you feel it is a waste of time or is what you are staring at that fascinating to you?"

I didn't even lie. "Well, I just feel that it would be. So that's why I have never had casual sex and yes your ah . . . yes it is impressive."

He laughed a bit. "Nothing sexier than an honest woman. As for casual sex you either don't know what you are missing until you try it or you can't miss what you have never had."

"I'll take your word for it. Besides there are too many diseases out here to catch. Not to mention people get crazy after they have sex," I said as I closed my tray and stood to pick up the mess I had made. Good thing I had brought a black velour jump suit to change into. I could move around freely.

He laughed. "Especially good sex. Good sex is enough to drive most people nuts, especially women. You all get too emotional and attached."

"I wouldn't know about all of that. Are you done," I asked him before picking up his plate. He hadn't even touched his soda. I didn't realize I was standing directly over him until he quickly stood. If I had been his height we would have been standing chest to chest. That's how close we were. I felt him looking down at me and I couldn't bring myself to look up. Standing at five-seven, my head came up just about to his shoulders. I could feel the lump from his pants on my stomach. This was the place I didn't want to find myself in. I didn't want to have anything but a professional relationship with my boss, but my heart beat faster and my breathing deepened. I knew I should have stopped the conversation we were having a long time ago. I had let it get too personal. Taking his hand and placing it under my chin, he brought his eyes to meet mine. He was smiling. Pretty white teeth he had.

"You're very beautiful Chyanne. Anybody ever tell you that?"

I swallowed the lump in my throat. The cologne he had on took my senses away. "Yes."

He was still smiling a charming yet seductive smile. I watched as his eyes roamed over my face. He licked his thick lips and brought them closer to mine . . . just a bit.

"I could kiss you right now." As he talked his lips brushed up against mine and created a spark and current so strong that I started to shake a little. Whatever he was doing to me I could feel it in my bones.

"I have been watching you. The way you carry yourself. Most full figured women aren't as comfortable with themselves as you are." He ran his fingers through my fro. "There is something wild and uninhibited about you, yet there is this sweet innocence that has got me curious about you."

Both his hands caressed my face as his lips came closer to mine. His hands were warm and strong. I dropped the plates in my hand when his tongue traced my bottom lip then my top. I didn't know what to do. One part of me was screaming for me to run. The other part told me to stand right there. I inhaled and grabbed onto both his wrists when he finally brought his lips to molest mine. His lips were soft and plush. His tongue was kind of coarse and velvety. He took his time with the kiss like he was trying to decode my DNA with this kiss. I didn't even realize I was holding my breath until he released me from our dance of tongues. When it was all said and done, he left me in the middle of his office as he walked away and out of his office. I didn't know what to do or what to say so I started to clean things up. We ended up leaving the office about an hour later. Nothing was said about the kiss though. Nothing was said today either. He acted like it didn't even happen so I did the same.

April brought my attention back to the present. "By the way, what's up with you and the new boss?"

I looked at her while she sipped her drink. "What do you mean?"

She was busy bobbing her head to Wale talking about pretty girls. "I mean he promoted you and now you are always at the office working late. I have seen the man and he is finger licking fine."

That annoyed me. What she said, it annoyed me. I turned my head to people watch before asking. "When did you see him?"

"Oh the other day. I came up there to do lunch with Justin and Mr. CEO was coming off the elevator into the lobby. Sexy motherfucker. I need me one of him. And he has money too? Shit yeah. Need me one of him. Is he single?"

For some reason her saying that made me angry. I took a big swallow to finish off my drink and shrugged. "I don't know if he is single or not and there is nothing going on with us. Just work."

"Well, something needs to be going on. Shit if you don't want him, I will take him. He seems more of my type anyway."

"What does that mean?"

"I mean he just does. You don't think so?" she asked. "I may strike up a conversation if I run into him again and with the way he gave me the once over, he'd go for it and I will give it to him!"

She turned around on her stool and ordered another drink. I stared at her long and hard. I would have probably started some mess by asking her what the hell she meant by that whole he's more of her type thing again, but two brothers walked up to us and asked us to dance. Of course April immediately went for the tall mocha colored one who looked like he bathed in money. He had dark chocolate eyes with pencil thin locks that sat just above his shoulders, smooth skin, and I could tell he either visited the dentist frequently or he had brand new teeth. He had on a nice pair of dirty denim jeans that fit him loosely with a crisp white button down shirt and a black blazer. He had on a nice pair of casual white and black loafers with his attire.

April stuck her hand out to shake his and put on her mega watt hoochie-flirt smile. "Hello. I am April and this is my friend Chyanne."

He shook her hand and smiled while his chubby friend who looked like a Cedric the Entertainer reject was slobbering out of the mouth looking at her thighs. He was standing there in what looked like a three-piece baby blue suit. I shook my head and chuckled under my breath.

"Hello, my name is Jamie and this is Jamaal. We came over here to see if we could get you ladies to join us for a dance or two?"

April was off of the bar stool before he could get the words out of his mouth. "We were just about to take it to the floor anyway." She turned to me. "Chyanne this is his friend Jamaal . . . ."

"Actually," Jamie cut her off. "Jamaal came over to dance with you and I came over to keep your friend company."

"Oh," was all April could get out. Jamie removed his hand from hers and held it out for me to take. I shook his hand.

"Nice to meet you, but actually I am not in the mood to dance so if you want to go ahead and dance with my girl that's cool," I said.

"No. I am not a dancer. I can chill right here with you until they get back," he laughed and winked at me. April looked back at us like she was at a loss for words. Jamaal took her now vacant hand and was grinning like a Cheshire cat as he led her onto the dance floor. Jamie and I sat there and kept a pretty descent conversation going. He was a bookstore owner who was feeling the weight of the economy crashing around him. He owned five bookstores throughout Georgia and was in the process of shutting down one. He was thirty-two and single and had one child who he had joint custody of. He had his own place and liked to think he was drama, debt, and STD free. He was a cool dude, but I was ready to leave.

About twenty-minutes later April came storming back over and snatched up her clutch.

"Girl, let's get the hell out of here," she snapped.

"Fine with me. Nice to meet you Jamie," I said before hopping off of the bar stool and shaking his hand.

"You too Chyanne. Can I call you sometimes or maybe you can call me," he said, handing me a business card. I slid it into my purse and told him I would, knowing I really had no intentions to do so. I just wanted to get out of there and go home to my bed. It took us about another fifteen to twenty minutes to get through the crowded club. Once outside the wind had its way with my fro. I folded my arms together tightly to try and keep from shivering. I knew April was about to freeze to death. It was warm when we left the house and now this September wind was cutting deep. Nights like this I was glad I had meat on my bones. We were so stiff walking to my car. April's arms were stiff by her side and she had her head down to shield her face from the wind. It was blowing directly at us.

"Damn!" That was me. I said that as soon as my derriere hit the seat in my 650i BMW Coupe. It was black. My favorite color. "Dang! It's cold. . . ."

"You didn't have to play me like that in there," April snapped.

"What?"

I cranked the car and turned the heat on. I watched as she folded her arms and snapped her neck around at me.

"Oh, *you can dance with my friend if you want.* What the fuck? I don't need you pushing niggas off on me like I am some charity case!"

"April, what are you talking about? All I did was tell Jamie that if you two wanted to dance . . . ."

"That's the thing. I don't need you to *tell* nobody shit for me!"

"Oh, wow! Okay. But whatever."

I put the car in reverse and pulled out onto Peachtree Street.

"Don't whatever me and put me off. That shit was embarrassing!"

"Well now you know how I feel when you do it. You are always pushing somebody's raggedy friend off on me."

"So what? There's a difference between me and you. You always sit your ass there and keep the bar company. Nobody ever asks you to dance anyway."

I didn't say anything after that. I had to hold back my anger and bite my tongue so I wouldn't say something that I would regret. I put my foot on the gas and got her home quick. I almost jumped out of the car and whipped her butt for slamming my door. She was more upset because the one she had laid eyes on first didn't have eyes for her, and that really bothered me. I mean, as friends, there should be no competition for men between us. I didn't hear from April for the rest of the weekend. Not like I cared. I was tired of dealing with her mess anyway.

Chapter 3

Monday rolled around and I found myself in a board meeting with Aric. Good thing I had done those Power-Point presentations and spreadsheets because I ended up running around that boardroom and office like a chicken with its head cut off. Making copies of this, faxing that, and filing this. I found myself watching Aric way more than I should have been. He was working the all black pinstriped Armani suit. He had taken the suit jacket off and laid it on the back of his chair. The vest to match his pants and the white shirt, the black tie, and the wing tipped dress shoes all worked well on him. The thick New York accent washed over me at times and the way he said my name was working on me from the inside out. I needed to get it together. This man had messed me up with one kiss and I had absolutely no explanation for it. *It was one kiss Chyanne! Get it together. The man has barely said two words to you that had nothing to do with business.* I came back to my senses as the last of the executives were leaving and Aric clapped his big hands together.

"We are in the money baby," he said. Excitement was laced in his voice. He smiled as he bit down on his bottom lip and sat on the edge of the long conference table. I smiled and kept picking up the contracts that had been signed.

"Love when we have days like this," he continued. "I need you to get those faxed down to accounting as soon as possible though."

I shrugged. "I'll just walk them down. I have to hand deliver some things to production that I want to make sure get into the right hands anyway."

I picked up the last folder and was getting ready to walk past him when he grabbed my arm and pulled me close to him. I stood directly in between his legs as he took his hand and placed it under my chin lifting my face to his. With his glasses on his hazel brown eyes had an extra sparkle. He brought his lips to mine and gave my top lip a gentle suck before placing his lips fully against mine, letting our tongues touch just once before pulling back and letting his thumb brush across my lips. I could feel my clit swell against my boy shorts and my most delicate part felt like it had a heart beat. My body felt like it was about to float from beneath me and I didn't know what to make of that kiss. My breathing had deepened so much so that you could clearly see my chest rise and fall. I couldn't figure this man out and it was threatening to drive me mad. What is it about him that made him such a mystery?

"Why don't you have dinner with me tonight Chyanne? Me and you. You like the CheeseCake Factory?"

I nodded and he got up with his body placed right next to mine, chilling me. He walked over and gently snatched his suit jacket from the back of the chair and once again he left me standing there. Just me, my thoughts, and my wet underwear.

We never made it to dinner. April called me right after that to go to the school and pick up her boys. She would never make it from her job in time and she didn't want them to be taken to juvie hall. Apparently Jonathan, the eldest who was seventeen, was about to get jumped and the twins, Aaron and Aaden, weren't having it so it turned into a five on three brawl with April's sons being the victors. By the time I made it to the school it was two-thirty and the twins were sitting in the principal's office looking smug.

"Sexy Chy. Mom sent you to get us," Aaron called out to me. That was his name for me. I don't know why he did that.

"Yes, Aaron. What the hell happened?" I asked when I saw the bruises and cuts on their faces.

"You know how it is Auntie Chyanne," Aaden answered. "Niggas thought they were about to jump Jo-Jo and that aint happening. You dig?"

I cringed at his vernacular and looked around for Jo-Jo. "Where's Jo-Jo?"

"Coaches got the team doctor checking him," Aaron answered. Even though he and Aaden looked exactly alike, they were as different as night and day. "You know he has to play next week for the homecoming game. Are you coming Sexy Chy?"

I nodded. "I plan on it. Where do I need to go to sign you guys out?"

They both pointed to the double doors. "Go through there and ask shawty at the desk."

Aaden and I were going to have to have a talk about his language. Both of those boys looked like their father who resembled Morris Chestnut, but ten times better. Jo-Jo looked like April. I got up and made my way through the double doors as Jo-Jo was coming towards me. I almost fainted looking at the big bruise across his torso. He was holding an ice pack to his eye and what was left of his shirt in his hand.

"Dang Jo-Jo! What the hell," I said before I could stop myself. The whole office turned to look at me.

"Stop tripping Chyanne. I'm all right," he said with that dimpled smile plastered across his light, bright face. His hazel and green eyes stared at me with a sparkle. He walked over to me and hugged me. He towered over me. I could see he had a fan club. Some little big booty and big chesty girl walked over to him, handing him some water and a towel.

"You need anything else Jo-Jo," she asked him. It was clear she was infatuated.

"Naw baby girl. This is good." He kissed her forehead and she giggled before walking off. I didn't know what to say, especially when another group of young girls called the other a fat bitch and mumbled about what he wanted with her.

"Come on, Jo-Jo. Let me sign ya'll out."

I shook my head as I walked with them to check them out. April was known to act a fool when they got in trouble at school. We walked over to the front desk with Jo-Jo's arm casually thrown across my shoulders.

"You know your mother is going to act a fool right?" I asked looking up at him.

He shrugged. "Well what she want? Me to get my ass kicked?"

I cocked my head back, shocked by his choice of words.

"Sorry Chyanne. But I am not taking no as—I ain't getting beat up for nobody!"

"Did you have to get Aaron and Aaden in it?"

"Those two damn fools—"

I snapped my head around at him again.

He shamefully dropped his head. "Sorry. They came out of nowhere. One minute I was slanging niggas off of me and the next I see these two fools slamming niggas."

"Must y'all use the N word like that," I snapped.

"Sorry Chyanne. I've been working on that though. Ever since you showed us that DVD about the march on Selma and those other DVD's on Emett Till and what not."

I nodded. "Good."

I asked the principal's assistant to get me started on checking them out and waited for her to get me the proper paperwork. Aaron and Aaden came in and they along with Jo-Jo gave colorful commentary to me on the fight. I had to admit, I was happy they helped their brother and ended up winning with the odds against them. Come to find out, some little boy was mad because he thought Jo-Jo was talking to his girlfriend. I shook my head. Something stupid but they had to defend themselves.

"Come on," I said to them once the process was over. I swear it was like Jo-Jo was a celebrity. Everybody was waving and speaking to him like he was the star of a show. Being on the football team and the star wide receiver had its perks I suppose. Hell he didn't even get suspended. We stopped at McDonalds and picked them up some food for now and I took them home with me until April got off. I know she was pissed because of the way she was snapping when I called her and told her they were home with me.

"You should have let those bad motherfuckers starve," she snapped and yelled. "They get on my nerves! Their daddy needs to come and get them. I am sick of this mess Chy! Sick of going through this shit with them!"

I shut up and let her vent. Truth is, I didn't think the boys were that bad. They just needed April to listen to them and be there for them more. I helped them all with their homework until I heard April's car door slam. The laughter going on at my dining room table immediately ceased. April banged on my door. I looked at the boys and their eyes immediately focused on their homework.

"It'll be okay."

That's all I could say. I opened the door and April almost knocked me down, going right for Jo-Jo. She hit him so hard across his already bruised face that it brought tears to my eyes.

"April, why you hit him?"

She ignored me.

"You think I send your fucking ass to school to get into fights Jo-Jo?"

Jo-Jo had backed into the corner in my dining room.

"They started it Mama." Aaron said.

She reached over and smacked him too. "You shut the fuck up! I aint talking to you!" Aaden got up and moved before her hand could connect with him, but she caught him anyway. He got what his brothers got.

"I am sick of ya'll! Ya'll hear me? Every damn day it's something! I have to work all of these fucking hours and pay for shit for y'all and you ungrateful fools want to be in school fighting and acting like idiots? And I should whoop your ass Jo-Jo! You don't cause enough problems so now you want to drag them into your mess!"

I could tell by the look on Jo-Jo's face that he'd just about had it. And so had I. I had seen this mess too much for my liking. So many times April had gone after Jo-Jo in anger, especially after their father left. April's face was red and twisted with anger. All three of her sons towered over her, but right now she looked way bigger than them.

"Mama, I'm tired of you putting your hands on me," Jo-Jo said through staggered breaths and tears. Before I knew what happened, April had balled her fist up and went at Jo-Jo like he was a grown man. I jumped over my sofa and rushed over as fast as I could.

"Who the fuck you think you talking to," she yelled at him. Jo-Jo shielded his face and just stood there, but I could see that he was at his breaking point when he balled his lips and his fist. He came out of the corner and pushed April away from him. She stumbled back, but didn't fall. April picked up the vase from the table and I grabbed Jo-Jo before she could hit him. The vase crashed against my wall. Aaron and Aaden were yelling and crying for her to stop. She followed me and tried to swing over and around me to get to him.

"April stop!!!" I screamed at her because if she hit me in my head again I was going to turn around and whoop her behind. I managed to shield Jo-Jo until I got him to my bedroom and pulled the door closed.

"Chyanne get the fuck out of my way! He put his hands on me with all that I do for him. I am going to kill him!"

I stood in front of my door with my hands on the knob. April tried to get past me and I pushed her back.

"Back up April. That's your child in there—"

"Exactly! Now move out of my way—"

"Mama please . . . ." Aaron pleaded. Aaden had tears in his eyes as he stood beside his twin. "Wasn't his fault Mama. They were trying to jump him. He had to fight back Mama. He had to."

This scene broke my heart. I could feel tears burning my eyelids. April stood there with this wild look in her eyes before she looked over at her other two sons.

"Get your shit and let's go! You can keep his ass over here. Nobody I clothe and feed is going to put his hands on me," she said and pushed her way past Aaron and Aaden.

They stood there looking at me and my closed bedroom door. I don't know what the look on their faces read. Don't know if it read help, I want to stay with you, or what.

"I said let's go!"

They went to the table and grabbed their book bags quickly making their way out of the door. She slammed my door on the way out. I dropped my head and went to lock my front door when I heard her pulling out of my driveway. I started to clean my kitchen and picked up the glass from the vase that she broke. My whole front room and dining room was done in black and snow white. I shook my head and looked at the juice that had spilled on my all white carpet. I left Jo-Jo in my room until he was ready to come out. It took him a full thirty minutes to decide to do that. By then I was done scrubbing my carpet with Shout, baking soda, and Oxy-Clean. He stood in the entry way leading to the front room and the dining room looking broken.

"Why she don't like me Chyanne," he asked. It was times like this that I hated April. She had broken his spirit so many times. And when he was like this he was a big kid. He wasn't the mature young man who was in all advanced classes. He was a kid. A little boy who wasn't quite sure his mother loved him. Hell, I wasn't so sure. I do know that she made them all pay for their father's mistake. For him leaving her, she made them pay. Tears rolled down his handsome face.

"She does Jo-Jo. Your mom just has a lot on her shoulders. She loves you."

I patted the sofa beside me so he could sit down. We sat quiet for a while. We both watched Smackdown on my forty-seven inch flat screen.

"I talked to Daddy," he said.

My eyes got wide and I asked, "Say what now?" I turned the volume down and looked at him.

"I talked to daddy. Me and The Twin Towers." That's what he called his little brothers who were almost bigger and taller than him. "He came to the school last week and this week. Gave us all a thousand dollars."

"Did you tell your mom?"

He shook his head. "Daddy doesn't want us to." He stared straight ahead at the TV. "We have been talking to him since he left."

"Really? Why don't you guys tell April?"

"Because then she would be mad and we wouldn't be able to see him no more. He wants us to come and live with him."

I slightly turned towards him and propped one leg under the other on the sofa.

"Oh, wow! Where does he live?"

"Alpharetta Country Club."

"For real? Jonathan is doing it like that now?"

He smiled and looked at me while he nodded. "He came to get us last Saturday and took us to his crib while mama was at work. He's got a fiancée. She's pretty. Nothing on Mama though. They have a big ass crib Chyanne."

"Language Jo-Jo."

"Sorry. Daddy said they gave him his old job back and then promoted him to VP so he got a fat check."

I nodded. I was happy for Jonathan because I believe that was one of the reasons he and April had so many problems. He had lost his job at the architectural firm because of the economy and I was so glad he got that back and then some. Jo-Jo stayed with me the whole weekend. Aaron and Aaden came over every day and set up the PS3 or the 360 in my front room with him. Those boys loved each other. I even got in on some of the butt kicking action on Madden 2011. Aaron and Aaden shocked me with the way they joked on each other's girlfriends. Aaron said he liked them like me, thicker than a snicker and he told Aaden that the skinny chicks he dated needed to eat a couple of biscuits with gravy. I laughed so hard at those two. Jonathon called me to come over and see Jo-Jo. I didn't want to get in the middle of that so I made other arrangements. I gave Jo-Jo the keys to my car, told him to be careful and he and his brothers met their dad somewhere. I had no idea what I would tell April.

Chapter 4

The next couple of weeks were a blur. Jo-Jo went back home the following Monday after he and April's altercation. He told me he had talked to her and she said it was okay for him to come back home. I was happy about that. October was here so fast that I didn't even realize it. It had been raining and thunder storming like we were in Seattle. Work had been crazy. With the extensive media coverage on our old executives it was a wonder we could still even get clients, but they were coming left and right. I don't know what Aric was doing or saying but it was working. Although we hadn't shared one of those kisses again, the late night hours didn't let up and the flirting was undeniable. So was the sexual tension. I had been trying to stay my distance. You know keep it professional since I seemed to lose my good sense whenever he came close to me. I didn't know what it was about him that made me forget all about that rule I had of never mixing business with pleasure.

I looked at the clock as I pushed the send button on the email I was sending out to the whole office for Aric. It was just an email he asked me to send out every week thanking everyone for their hard work. This email included numbers for everyone's bonus too, which I was happy about because we hadn't gotten one in two years. He had already told me that we wouldn't be working late today so as soon as five o'clock hit I was out of there.

My phone buzzed. "Chyanne let me see you in my office for a minute."

That thick New York accent had a lot of women drooling and their panties dripping wet. There was something else mixed with it that I couldn't place.

"Sure," I answered before logging off my computer. "Do you mind if I step into the restroom first?"

"Not at all."

I clicked off the phone and quickly went to the restroom to handle my business. I gave myself the once over in the mirror. The black high waist pencil skirt and black and white collared button down shirt showed off all of my assets and then some. Truth be told I looked like a school teacher who dressed way too sexy. I laughed at myself. Even though the only skin I showed was what the skirt left of my calves, my breasts, hips, and backside would not be denied. The Spanx did a good job of pulling in all of the extra meat on my bones. I hated a muffin top look. Nothing was worse than seeing a plus-sized sister in tight fitting clothes with no extra support. My black and white head band still had my fro sitting nice and pretty and the band kept my hair out of my face. I washed my hands and then looked at my black CL pumps to make sure there wasn't a scuff on them. I was a shoe whore . . . sue me.

I made my way back to Aric's office and waited for him to end a phone call before he addressed me. He must have been talking to an old friend because of the casual conversation he had going on. I looked around his big office. A small family could live in here comfortably. Books lined the wall on a floor to ceiling bookshelf. The big window behind and on both sides of his desk kept the sun, when it was out, shining in. I sat on the burgundy Tudor style sofa after I added some water to the few plants he had. I turned around to look at him just as he bit into a peach. The way he bit down into that thing made his lips enclose around it and suck on it. That gesture made my core bud start to jump. Juice from the fruit slid down his mouth and chin. What he didn't catch with the paper napkin he had in his hand and he licked it away with his tongue. Once he hung up the phone he looked at me. I watched as he stretched his tall body before he came to join me on the couch. He smelled so damn good. He took his glasses off and stretched his arms wide as his head fell back on the sofa.

"Are you busy tonight," he asked. "Around eight?"

"No. Why? You need me to stay?"

He shook his head. "No. I was on the phone with a friend from college and business associate of mine. His bosses are having a little get together with some other business associates and he asked me to come. Think you could join me?"

"Yeah, I guess. Sure."

"Damn," he said as he sat up, leaned on his legs and looked at me as he clasped his hands together. "You don't have to sound so excited about it."

I giggled a bit and waved my hand. "No. I didn't mean it like that. It's just that I was thinking about if I had anything to wear," I lied.

"I am sure whatever it is you decide to wear you will look good in it. Should I pick you up at about seven?"

I nodded. "Sounds good."

I looked at the clock on his wall. He stood and so did I. "Oh yeah, if you don't mind, ask a friend of yours to join you. My friend is new in town and needs someone to talk to."

"I'm sure that won't be a problem."

"Good," he said, watching me as I left his office.

As soon as I got to my desk I called April. She was the only friend I had so of course she was the one I would ask. I called her at work, but she wasn't there so I called her cell.

"Yeah. What's up," she answered.

I hadn't talked to her since that incident in my dining room. "Hey. You busy?"

"On lunch."

I could hear noise in her background. "Well, I was calling to see if you wanted to go to this social event Aric invited me to tonight."

"Hold on."

I could tell she was walking away from the noise. "What time is it?"

"Well he said he would be by to pick me up at around seven."

"So we're riding with him?"

I figured she had decided she was going already. "Yeah."

"OK. I'll be at your place around six-thirty."

"OK and it's like a business social type thing, dress accordingly."

She was quiet a second. "Bitch, I know what to wear to a business gathering," she laughed. "Anyway. Got to get ready to go back to work, but I will see you at six thirty and you're the one who needs to be trying to figure out what to wear."

Before I could respond, she hung up. That's just how April was. I guess calling me the "b" word was her favorite pastime since she had been doing it since we had become friends. I let what she said slide. Although she laughed, what she said grated my nerves. I left work early and did a little shopping. First thing I did was stop by a hair salon and got a four strand French braid so my fro wouldn't be all over the place. I must say that

I was pleased with the outcome. I didn't visit the salon that much so that was a treat. I stopped by Simplicity Spa to hook up a manicure and a pedicure. I had no choice but to rush into Lenoxx Mall and ran inside of Neiman Marcus to pick up a nice evening wear gown. I didn't want anything extravagant but I wanted to be cute. So I spent way more than I should have on a black one shoulder draped Charmeuse dress that came past my knees and contoured to my body. The pair of silver Jimmy Choo six inch stiletto heels with diamond studs on the cuff that strapped around the ankle was costly too.

By the time I was done, it was five o'clock. I rushed into my house, and couldn't remember the last time I had rushed so fast to get ready for a date. I jumped in the shower so quick it was like the water barely touched me. I moisturized my skin with honey and vanilla body cream from Bath and Body Works. I quickly got dressed and hurried to the door when the doorbell rang to let April in. I must admit that she looked stunning. The bold red dress that flared over her hips and ass, stopped mid-thigh, left me speechless. The silver strap up stilettos only enhanced what God had already blessed her with. Her short hair style was freshly done and her makeup brought out the glow in her butterscotch skin complexion. The dress hugged her extra small waist and drew attention to her forty inch hips. Her C-cups were almost spilling out of the top of the dress that tied around her neck and made a V on her chest, leaving most of her back exposed.

"Damn, girl! I said we were going to a business social not the Velvet Room," I exclaimed.

She only looked at me and rolled her eyes before walking in past me.

"Whatever! Are you driving or are we being picked up?"

I looked her over once again and I felt underdressed. "You look good though," I complimented her.

"Thank you. So you driving?"

I shook my head. "No. I told you Mr. McHale is picking us up."

She smiled. "So you're back to calling him Mr. McHale now?"

I shrugged while looking in my mirror on the wall behind my loveseat and putting my diamond earrings in my ears.

"He insists that everyone calls him Aric, but I want to keep it professional."

"Yeah sure he does and I bet you do."

April made her way to my kitchen. I heard her pull my fridge open.

"So are you and Mr. Man getting y'all grown folk on?"

I frowned at her when she rounded the corner with a bottle of my Dasani water in her hand. "No. I don't mix business with pleasure."

"Bitch please! As fine as that man is I would be sucking and fucking every chance I got."

I didn't get a chance to answer. The headlights turning into my driveway let me know Aric was here.

"Speaking of the devil," April crooned. The way she smiled and the seductive look that laced her eyes gave me a sinking feeling in the pit of my stomach. I didn't know why I was tripping. All this man had ever done was kiss me twice and he hadn't said a word about us hooking up. My doorbell rang and it was like I was stuck where I was. Aric made me nervous like that. I watched as April opened my door like it was her house. I noticed the surprise register on his face and then I saw the way his eyes gave her a once over and a once over again. His face clearly showed that he liked what he saw. April's slow and easy smile clearly gave off the vibe that she approved of his approving of her. My hand went to my hair and then back down to my side. I felt my hair to make sure my edges were still lying down. You know just making sure my natural look was holding up.

Aric held his hand out for April to shake. "Hello, April. Nice to see you again," he greeted.

She bypassed his outstretched hand and went in for a hug with a giggle. "No need for all of the business and polite stuff. Save that for Chyanne. How are you this evening?"

He embraced her and I looked away.

"I'm doing fine. Thank you. You look great by the way."

She pulled away from his hold and playfully tapped him on the shoulder with another giggle. "Thank you. You know, you are not looking too bad yourself. You are making that suit look good."

He gave a chuckle. "Thank you."

April finally moved and let him in the door. He had to kind of crouch down so his head wouldn't hit the door frame. Looking at him left me speechless. I mean I had seen him done up in business suits and all at work, but he was killing this all black Armani suit. It was so well tailored to fit him that nobody else could come close to pulling that look off. The wide legged pants were cuffed to fit his tall frame perfectly. I stood there like a deaf mute until he looked over at me. When he finally did a slow and easy smile crept over his face. His pearly white teeth added even more sexiness to his smile.

"Good evening Chyanne. Wow! You look beautiful," he said, walking over to me.

"Thank you," I said to him as he grabbed me into a tight embrace. He smelled so good. Like Ivory soap mixed with a masculine fragrance. He pulled away slowly from the hug and when I thought he would kiss me my heart rate sped up. He didn't kiss me although his eyes lingered on my lips. I ran my tongue across them out of nervousness.

"You look very handsome tonight as well."

"Not as good as you do," he whispered to me so only I could hear.

I smiled. "Let me get my purse and keys."

"Do you need for me to stay with you while you lock up," he asked.

I shook my head and smiled. "No I got it."

Truth be told, I needed to get myself together. I quickly went to my room and grabbed my purse, Blackberry, and keys. Aric and April had already stepped out to his truck. I walked out to hear the end of whatever conversation they were having.

"We'll talk," I heard him say to her.

With the way she was standing close to him it made me wonder what he meant by that statement. He was standing on the passenger side of his cream colored Cadillac Escalade with the door open. When she walked around him her breast brushed across his chest. He smiled at her and looked over at me. I don't know why she felt that she automatically got to ride in the front beside him. I don't know if it was in my walk or what, but when he opened the back door for me I didn't even look at him. I am sure my attitude was visible. He tried to take my hand and help me up, but I snatched it away from him.

"You okay," he asked me.

I looked at him. He didn't have his glasses on and his light eyes shone at me. "Yeah. Shut the door."

I didn't give him a chance to say anything else. I reached over and slammed the door shut for him.

"Damn, Chyanne," April laughed.

With steam coming from my ears, I watched Aric walk around to get into the truck.

"You ain't mad, are you?" April teased me as he slid into the truck.

Something in her voice struck a nerve, but I let it go. Aric put the car in reverse and turned to back out. I don't know how he backed out without hitting anything because his eyes stayed on me the whole time. I couldn't look at him for as long as he looked at me so I turned my head in another direction.

We ended up at the Intercontinental Buckhead in one of their ballrooms with Atlanta's business elite. So much business power in one room made for a boring night for me. After we found our table Aric introduced us to his friend and business associate Gabriel. Gabriel was a sexy dark chocolate brother that should have been a carnal sin. He and Aric were the same height. Aric had a thicker build than Gabriel and a sexier smile but that didn't take away Gabriel's appeal. The brother had a nice head of neatly done locks that swayed around his shoulders and his accent was a killer. He had that deep Southern baritone that would make a woman drop all of her clothes in a matter of seconds. His goatee was perfectly aligned and his eyes made his smile more enticing.

"Hello, April," he said as he stood to greet her. She always got the greeting first and it wasn't lost on anyone that his eyes roamed over her body from head to toe then toe to head again before he even looked at me. As usual she gave a tight hug and returned the greeting.

"Nice meeting you, Gabriel," she crooned. "Chyanne never told me she worked with brothers who looked like this."

All three of them chuckled and laughed. I didn't. Gabriel took his eyes off of April long enough to turn to me.

"You must be Chyanne," he said with a smile.

"Yes I am," I said extending my hand to him. He bypassed my hand and pulled me into an embrace that made me feel some type of way. For whatever reason, I glanced over at Aric. He sipped his drink and looked away for a quick second. His smile had disappeared.

"I've heard a lot about you," he said pulling away. "I guess Aric is happy he finally found a competent assistant."

I smiled. "That's always a good thing and I hope everything is all good that he has told you about me."

Gabriel chuckled and handed his glass to a passing waitress. "All good, but he didn't tell me how beautiful you are. Guess he wants to keep you all to himself."

I didn't know what to say to that. I just laughed a bit. "With as much work that is on my desk he has me for at least . . . another ten years."

He said, "You could always come and work for me. I know how to treat my employees and with one that is as good as Aric says you are I could use you in more ways than one."

I took a quick sip of my drink and looked at April as we all took a seat at the table. She only chuckled and moved her tongue around in her mouth before sipping on her wine and giving me a side eye. Before I could think of anything to say Aric spoke up because I really didn't know how to respond.

"That's too bad now isn't it? She's not going anywhere. As a matter of fact when we get back to the office on Monday I'm going to need that in writing. This Negro is trying to take you from me. Not going to happen. Besides nobody will do her like I do. It would do you good to remember that Chyanne," he laughed.

I was glad he laughed because if I didn't know any better I would think they were serious. Especially when Gabriel looked me up and down, smirked, and made a 'hmph' sound under his breath. He folded his arms across his chest and looked at Aric then at me.

"Chyanne, everything is not always what it seems and if ever you get tired of this asshole, look me up," Gabriel finished.

I smiled. "I will keep that in mind," I said. I needed to get away for a second so I excused myself. "Excuse me. I need to visit the ladies room."

April stood as well. "I'm going to go and keep Chyanne company. You guys behave until we return."

Gabriel and Aric stood when we stood. I assumed they didn't sit back down until we had walked away. I observed as men drooled over April. She had what we liked to call the pony walk and when you threw in the stilettos she had on, it made her all the more enticing. This was a mess. My body and my nerves were jittery and shot to hell. For whatever reason, I didn't know why. I made it to the ladies room, staring at myself and tossing cold water in my face. April was standing at the counter with her arms folded looking at me.

"What," I asked her.

The smirk on her face let me know this would not be good. What I should have done was left right then and there, but I didn't.

"Why didn't you tell me Jonathan called you?"

"When?"

"When Jo-Jo was at your place?"

I exhaled and shrugged. "I didn't think it was a big deal. He called and asked to speak to the boys. I thought it would be okay."

"Why in the fuck did you think I would be okay with that bastard talking to my kids?"

"Because they are his kids too April. All he did was—"

"And you let Jo-Jo take your car to take Aaron and Aaden to see him. Why?"

Other women in the bathroom were looking at us on the sly.

"Because they asked. What's the big freaking deal April? Jonathan has a right to see his children. Just because he doesn't want anything to do with you doesn't mean he doesn't love his kids. You need to stop trying to make them choose between you and their father. He doesn't want you anymore! So what? He has moved on. Why don't you?"

I knew I had said too much before the words left my mouth. April stood to her full height and I did the same. Hell, if she was going to swing then I wasn't backing down. People were looking at us. They all had stopped doing what they had come in the bathroom to do to watch us. Over the years April and I had been through a lot. I was with her when her mom died. With her when Jonathan started coming home later and later. I was her shoulder to cry on. I stayed with her when she drank herself sick. I was with her when she and Jonathan lost the last child they conceived together. Now we had come to this and I didn't know why. We had been friends for five years. Met when we were in Georgia State together. She ended up having to quit for a while because Jonathan lost his job. Her whole attitude had changed when Jonathan actually left, but I just thought it was because she was hurt. Now I didn't know what the problem was but I was done trying to figure it out. She put her hands on her hips, clucked her tongue to the roof of her mouth, and looked me up and down before snatching the bathroom door open and walking out with the same smug smirk that she had been carrying all night

I rushed behind her. "Look, April, I'm sorry," I apologized as I tried to grab her arm and she turned and snatched away. She looked at me, the look in her eyes cold.

"It's cool," was all she said before she sashayed off. I rushed behind her and then remembered I had left my clutch in the bathroom on the sink. I quickly turned around and slammed right into somebody that was built like a brick wall. I stumbled and almost fell back. He caught me by my arm.

"Excuse me," I said. "I am so sorry."

"Chyanne?"

I finally looked up and into the face of a man who looked familiar.

He said, "It's me, Jamie. Do you remember me from a few weeks ago? We met at Club Miami."

I nodded. "Oh, yeah. I am so sorry about running into you, but let me go and get my purse. I left it in the restroom and I will be right back."

He nodded and I went into the restroom to get my purse. Thank God it was lying where I had left it. I walked back out into the lobby and Jamie was nowhere to be seen so I walked back in the direction of the table where we were all sitting. I stopped in my tracks when I spotted Aric with his arms wrapped around April and they were dancing to a slow song the live band was playing. He was looking down at her and smiling and she was so close to him she may as well have been his skin. My heart dropped when she brushed her fingers across his lips and all he did was run his tongue across his lips in return. I was so caught up in what was going on in front of me that when someone tapped my shoulders from behind I nearly jumped out of my skin.

I turned around and Jamie had an amused look on his face with his hands up like I was sticking him up. "My bad! I'm sorry!" He laughed when I smiled.

"You just scared whatever hell I had in me away," I joked.

"I am truly sorry but I came over to ask if you would like to dance. I don't know what the hell they are playing, but I think we can keep up," he smiled.

He looked different tonight. Maybe it was because his locks were pulled back nice and neat and the black suit he was wearing complimented his physique. His dark eyes held a sparkle that pulled me in and his smile was enough to charm me into the dance he asked me for. I let him lead me to the dance floor and when he pulled me close to him for some reason I laid my head on his chest and relaxed.

"So what brings you here, Ms. Chyanne? I didn't think of you as the uptight type," he said.

I lifted my head and looked up at him. "What does that mean?"

"I mean look around you." He shrugged gazing down at me with a smile on his face. "Look at all of these boring business men and women and listen to this music."

I laughed. "Hey my boss isn't boring and what does that make you since you are here?"

His head fell back a bit and he laughed before looking back down at me. "Good question. Who's your boss by the way?"

"Aric McHale . . ."

"Oh the brother who took over at B&G?"

I nodded. "That's him."

"Well I heard about what they used to do over there. You good?"

I nodded. "Oh, yeah. Aric is the best. I haven't had any problems."

"Well you can always call me if you do."

Before I could respond Aric and April were right in my view, Aric's eyes were planted on me. I looked away for a second and then back at him. He kept his eyes locked with mine.

When he mouthed the words '*I want you*' to me my heart rate increased and coochie started to leap around against my lace boy shorts. I could feel myself get so moist that I wanted to cross my legs to stave off the feeling. Jamie was saying something to me but I couldn't register it especially when Aric blew a kiss at me from where he was standing. I stopped dancing for a second and was lost.

"You okay," Jamie stopped to ask me. Luckily the music was ending.

"Yes. A little dizzy."

"Where's your table?"

"Over by the balcony, but I'm sure I can make it. I'm fine."

He gripped my right elbow and was holding me steady. Aric was still watching me.

"I'll feel better if I walk you over to your seat," Jamie said. He put his hand on the small of my back and led me over to my table where Gabriel was talking to some blonde haired golden eyed woman who had a body like that Latin singer Shakira. Gabriel looked at me when we got to the table.

He and Jamie exchanged greetings. "You okay Chyanne," Gabriel asked me.

I nodded and sat in the chair Jamie had pulled out for me.

"Yeah, I'm fine."

Gabriel stopped a passing waitress and asked for a glass of water. The Shakira look-a-like was looking at me like I had interrupted them or something. Jamie brought my attention back to him as he kneeled in front of me to make sure I was okay. I listened as he handed me his business card again and told me to call him. My attention was thwarted as I saw Aric and April walking back to the table. She was walking in front of him but his eyes stayed on me and then turned to Jamie. Jamie stood as Aric neared the table. They exchanged greetings, but there was nothing pleasant about Aric's demeanor and it wasn't lost on Jamie. He looked from me to Aric and then back to me. Aric didn't sit until Jamie said his final goodbye to me and walked off.

Aric sat down beside me as I was trying to slide Jamie's card into my clutch, but he caught my hand under the table and took it from me. I kept my cool and looked over at him, but all he did was speak to the blonde chick across from Gabriel.

"Shelley, it's good to see you again. How are Robert and the kids," he asked like he hadn't just ripped up Jamie's card and discarded it on the floor.

"Great, Aric and how's Stephanie?" Shelley responded.

I didn't know what was going on but it was something about the way Gabriel chuckled and Shelley cut her eyes at Aric that let me know something was going on there. Aric's eyes darkened when he looked at her but he didn't answer. She quickly turned her attention back to Gabriel. Aric turned his attention to April, and for some reason, I felt like I was out of place. The waitress finally came back and handed the glass of water to Gabriel and he passed it to me.

"What's wrong Chyanne," April asked. I could tell it wasn't genuine by the smirk on her face and the tone of her voice.

I shook my head. "Nothing. I'm fine."

Aric was talking to her but his hand was still on my leg. I knocked it off and his head snapped over at me. I arched a brow and stared back at him. I didn't know what kind of game he thought he was playing but I was about over it. I stood so I could go somewhere else. I wasn't about to sit there looking crazy. I grabbed my clutch and was about to walk off, until Aric grabbed my wrist and stood with me.

"Excuse us," he said to everyone at the table. I followed him, until we made it to a secluded area in the lobby. There was a black bench style sitting stool in the corner and I sat there. Aric stood in the little space across from me with one leg crossed over the other at the ankle. He slid his hands in his pockets while staring at me.

"Want to tell me what's bothering you?" He asked casually.

I looked up and caught the lick he placed across his lips.

"Nothing is bothering me."

"Could have fooled me."

I exhaled, crossed my legs, and looked around. Saw a man helping a staggering dark skinned chick to the door. It was obvious she had too much to drink. The guy didn't seem to mind as he was smiling and telling her something in her ear. She laughed loudly as they made their way out of the door.

I shrugged and looked back up at Aric. I shook my head and made a dramatic effect of pursing my lips up to say, "Nope. No problem."

He stood up straight with his hands still in his pockets and moved closer to me. "One thing you will have to learn about me Chyanne is I hate to be lied to and I hate to be bullshitted around and tried to be played like I'm stupid."

His eyes never left mine and his tone and demeanor showed the exact thing his mouth had just told me. I diverted my eyes down to his waist since his dick was now in my face. I slowly stood.

"Look, I said I'm fine. . . ."

He moved closer to me. I tried to step back but the stool only let me move back so far. His scent was like a drug and as much as I wanted to stay away from him, it kept pulling me in. I tried walking past him. Instead, he snatched me back into him and put my back against the wall before I knew what was happening.

His hands gripped my waist and he was looking down into my eyes. "What's wrong with you, Chyanne? My last time asking you. You either tell me what's wrong or I'm going to make you tell me."

"Excuse me?" My head tilted to the side and my eyes widened a bit as I moved a few inches away from the wall.

The only answer I got was his lips against mine. The kiss was so heated and primal that I lost all my senses. I didn't know what to do with my hands and when I felt his left hand raising my right leg to his waist and his hand coming around to grip my backside to pull me closer into him, I almost lost it. I could feel him getting harder against my body. The heels I had on gave me just enough height for me to feel it in the right area. My most private area was throbbing . . . aching . . . and jumping. When I felt his hand had found a way under my dress my breath hitched. I was so lost I had forgotten we were in a corner in a hotel lobby. When his hands came up and gripped my breast with a firm hold, I released his lips and almost screamed when he bit down on my neck.

"Oh God," was all I could get out as my eyes rolled to the back of my head. My body was hot. Blood rushing. . . .

"Oh, damn! My bad!"

My eyes shot open and Gabriel was there. I put my head down and covered half of my face in between

Aric's neck and shoulders, attempting to fix the top of my dress.

"Ah . . . your presence is being requested back in the banquet room," Gabriel said as his eyes caught mine.

Aric didn't turn around and he kept my body shielded with his. My leg slowly slid back down to the floor.

"OK. I'll be there," Aric said over his shoulders.

Gabriel kept his eyes on me as he said," OK. Cool."

He turned to walk away and something in his eyes bothered me. What he didn't say bothered me. I fixed myself and made myself look like I hadn't come close to having sex in a corner in the lobby of a hotel. I watched out of the corner of my eye as Aric fought to adjust his hard on.

"I'll be in. Give me a minute. Go ahead," he said to me nodding his head in the direction of the banquet room with his hand still trying to adjust himself in his pants.

I walked off, trying to look as normal as I could as I made my way back inside of the room and to the table. April and Shelley were talking like they were the best of friends until I got to the table and sat down. April looked at me and rolled her eyes before taking a sip of her wine.

"So, Chyanne," Shelley called out to me with a plastered smile on her face.

"Yes."

"April tells me that you have been at B&G for four years." Shelley took a sip of her drink, leaned forward, and smiled. "Surprised you hadn't filed a lawsuit yet. I mean it's no secret that the old execs had a thing for their employees."

"I don't, nor will I ever lay on my back to get a position," I said as I put my clutch on the table.

Shelley laughed over the soft jazz that was playing. "Girl, you never know what you can get on your back. You better try it! At least for some good dick. You feel me? It's a dog eat dog world out here in this big corporate world and as a woman you have to do what you have to do to stay one step ahead of the competition."

April chimed in. "You don't have to worry about Ms. Goody Goody doing any of that. Chyanne hasn't seen a dick since one spit her out."

April gave a little chuckle and Shelley's eyes widened as she tilted her head to the side.

April continued, "She's so busy trying to be perfect that she . . ."

"Just because I choose to keep to myself does not mean I am aiming to be perfect," I said. I sat back in my chair and folded my arms across my chest.

April had a smile on her face but the vibes coming from her were anything but friendly.

"Please! When's the last time you had a man?"

"About the last time you haven't had one."

I saw Shelley's eyes widen even more and she laughed out loud. April slowly sat her glass down on the table.

"What the hell is that supposed to mean? Since you have gotten this promotion you have been beside your fucking self. Don't think because you think Aric is sniffing behind your ass that you the shit now. You are still the same fat ass Chyanne that claims she doesn't want a man when in reality she just can't get one."

This coming from a woman who couldn't even keep a man! To say I was embarrassed would have been an understatement, but not because of what this semi-drunk hussy was saying to me. I was embarrassed because half of the whole side of this room was looking at us and Aric had introduced me to everyone as his assistant. So they knew I represented B&G Marketing and Advertising.

I slowly pushed away from the table and stood. "OK . . . you know what? I am going to leave. It's apparent that you have had too much to drink and before we both say something that we will regret . . ."

April laughed. "Trust me, Chyanne, there aint nothing you can say to me that will hurt my feelings. Okay?"

I kept my composure and smiled. I could tell Shelley didn't know what to think, but judging by the slick smile on her face, it was clear she was enjoying the scene unfolding before her. I calmly picked up my clutch and started to walk away. I made my way over to the far side of the room where they had set up a bar and copped a squat on an empty stool. I was fine just sitting there and minding my business. Although some people were still looking from me to April then back to me, I kept my cool. From where I was sitting I could see Aric walk back into the room and I was hoping he was ready to go.

Right about then I was wishing I would have driven my own car. I sat there for at least another ten minutes and people watched. Aric and Gabriel had been caught up in a conversation with a group of white men across the room from me. I saw April and Shelley still chatting it up. Maybe April was just having a bad day or something. I didn't know what her problem was. I had noticed she had been acting like this from time to time but I blamed it on stress from her own problems. I had love for April but sometimes it was hard to believe she was a thirty-five year old woman with the way she acted. I was so focused on my thoughts that I didn't even notice her walking up to me. I jumped when I felt a hand on my shoulder turning me around on the stool. April stood there with one hand on her hip and a look on her face that let me know she was pissed.

"What is your problem, Chyanne? What was up with you trying to embarrass me back there," she snapped.

"Oh. I tried to embarrass you? You are the one who started."

"Started what? What did I say? What that you hadn't seen a dick since one gave you away? And that was reason for you to try and throw shade at me?"

She had begun to wave her finger and move her neck. Once again people in the vicinity were starting to pay attention to us. Why did she want to get in here in front of all of these white people and act an ass?

"Look April. If I said something to . . ."

"If? Bitch, you know what you said was fucked up!"

"I am not about to be too many more bitches, April."

"Oh, so you bad now, huh? This job has really gone to your head. Or you really think Aric wants your ass or something. One or two men show you some attention and that goes straight to your head."

"OK April, I think it's time for me to go. When you want to talk or ask me something, I will tell you . . ."

"Oh, like you told me Jonathan tried to fuck you?"

I stood. "What?"

"Don't get stupid now. Thought I didn't know huh? You weren't going to tell me either were you? You wanted attention so bad that you would take it any way it came huh? You think I don't know about him having you against the wall in my garage. Camera's bitch. My house has cameras."

"Look, April. Nothing happened. He was drunk . . ."

"Oh, I know nothing happened. And look at youuuuu," she said with very clear dramatics using her hands. Her face carried a smile mixed with a sneer. "You making excuses for him now? You are a thirsty heifer, you know that? You let him kiss you before you pushed him away but now you want to stand up here and act like you all innocent and shit. Ever notice I don't bring any man around you now?"

She had pissed me off. "That's fine, April. Trust me I don't want anybody you have been with. So we are good on that. Now, if you will excuse me . . ."

I tried to move past her, but what happened next came as a total shock to me. April picked up a glass from the bar and threw its contents in my face. Before I could react to the shock, her opened palm connected with my face. She slapped me so hard that it knocked my head back. All I heard were the gasps and *'oh my God's'* coming from the room. I was seconds away from messing her up! When I was able to release myself from the shock of what had happened, I went to grab for her but Aric had blocked me before I could. I didn't even get much of a glimpse of her after that. Aric had grabbed my clutch from the floor and was escorting me out of the room. That didn't stop me from still trying to get around him.

Only when the cold wind pierced my eyes from outside did I allow myself to calm down. My eyes were already watering from being slapped. Add my anger to that and I was in tears. I folded my arms across my chest as he gave the valet his ticket to pull his truck around. I guess because my anger had me shaking Aric thought I was cold. He took his suit jacket off and wrapped it around my shoulders. Once they pulled his truck around, he held the passenger side door open for me to get in.

For a few seconds, I was in the truck, behind his tinted windows watching him as he tipped the valet. I quickly covered my face and let out a muted scream and an exasperated breath. No matter how I tried, I couldn't stop my nerves from making me shake and I couldn't stop the tears. I had a full frontal headache and the left side of my face stung like a thousand killer bees had attacked me. Aric climbed into the driver seat and turned left onto Peachtree Street. He adjusted the heater at the light and some jazz played on the radio. It wasn't until we got on the expressway that he interrupted my thoughts of kicking April's behind.

"Want to tell me what happened?" He asked as he turned the music down a little.

"I don't know what happened. One minute I was talking to that chick Shelley. The next minute April is talking mess. I get up and leave the table. Next thing I know she is in my face at the bar."

I made a fuss of taking my shoes off.

"I could be wrong, but I thought you two were close." I turned to look at him at the same time his eyes caught mine. We both turned back to look at the road ahead of us.

"I thought we were too," was all I responded.

I was thinking back on that day in her garage. I had stopped by to chill and talk with April but after sitting in her front room for thirty minutes and she still hadn't showed up, I got up to leave. I walked out through the garage and Jonathan was sitting on the hood of his Lexus. He was as drunk as an everyday wino. Once he saw me come out, he spoke and I spoke back. I told him I was leaving and to tell April to call me. I didn't know what he was thinking, but the next minute he was telling me how beautiful, sexy, and educated he thought I was. The closer he got to me the further I backed into the wall. The next thing I knew I was up and around his waist with his tongue in my mouth. I would be lying if I said that I didn't feel some type of way about it because I did. Some kind of way his hands had found their way under my skirt and into my underwear. His fingers had made their way inside of me all before I even knew what was going on. I broke away from the kiss and yelled for him to stop and he did. He apologized over and over, and to this day, every time he sees me he apologizes. I chalk it all up to the fact he was drunk and didn't know what he was doing. I wanted to tell April, but how do you tell your best friend that her husband had his fingers inside of you in their garage?

"You okay over there?" Aric asked.

I nodded. We pulled into my driveway a few minutes later. I didn't wait for him to open my door before I grabbed my shoes and hopped out of his truck. I pressed the button on my keys to let up my garage so I could go in through my kitchen.

"Let me see your face, Chyanne," he said to me once I turned the light on in my garage. I stopped and let him turn my face into the light. I cut my eyes at him when he laughed a bit.

"What's so funny?"

"Good thing you are chocolate. Otherwise there would be a nasty bruise on your face tomorrow."

He touched it and I winced away.

"You should put some ice on it or something because she slapped the shit out of you!"

He laughed when I pushed him away.

"Go to hell," I snapped as I turned to unlock my door. He pulled me back to him.

"Stop being so sensitive! I am only trying to make you laugh."

"Not in a laughing mood."

He pulled me closer and into him. "Well, get into one."

"Whatever."

He placed light kisses on the part of my face that had been assaulted. Those kisses then went to my ear and then down to my neck and back up to my lips. Heavy breathing and the wind blowing is all that could be heard.

"OK. I'm going to leave because you got my dick hard and I may have to put you on the hood of this car and fuck the shit out of you."

My eyes bugged out and I gasped. "Oh, wow . . ." That was all I could get out.

His smile relaxed me. "Don't be afraid of me, Chyanne. You don't ever have to be afraid of me. You just have to come to grips with the fact that I'm a man that says whatever is on his mind."

"I get that . . . now."

We both laughed. "Go ahead and unlock your door so I can make sure you get in safe. Do I need to come and check for monsters and shit," he joked.

I laughed as I pushed my door open and deactivated my alarm. "No. I'm good."

"Cool. See you tomorrow."

Once we had said goodnight and after I was in my bed I had time to think. I wondered if April had made it home safe so I picked up the phone to call her. After two rings, it went to voice mail. I tried twice more and the same thing. So I called Jo-Jo's phone a little later and he told me that she was outside talking to some guy. I assumed it was Gabriel since Aric had said he had volunteered to bring her home. As long as she was home, I could sleep.

Chapter 5

Aric and I were sitting in a part of his office that I didn't even know existed. We had gotten to the office a little early and he didn't want to be bothered before the meeting today at eleven. Needing some privacy, he had asked me to step into this room with him that looked like a very small apartment. A small stall with a shower was in the far right corner with a toilet next to it. A small desk was on the other side of it. An oversized loveseat that turned into a pull out bed sat by itself against the other wall. We had been sitting there going over the agenda for the meeting and his schedule for the day. He was dressed down in a pair of loose fitting dark denim jeans, a red polo style shirt and he was bare foot. The sexiest thing I had ever seen.

"So, tell me again how many numbers we are away from being in the black again," he asked as he typed away on his laptop.

I answered. "Over two hundred million."

"Damn!" He had been frustrated all morning. "As soon as I get one thing fixed some more shit happens! How many days have we been in the red?"

"Four hundred and seventy-two days," I answered him. I watched as he shook his head and kept typing.

"Did you send the figures down to accounting this morning?" He turned to look at me.

I stood and stretched. "I sent them last night before I went to bed and I also hand delivered the disk before I came up this morning."

"So did Katie send the report back up yet?"

I shook my head. "No, but she said she had to correct something that she had overlooked before. She said she would have them up before the meeting."

He nodded. "What about production? How are they on things?"

I moved over to the files on the desk that I had brought in earlier and pulled out the papers on production, telling him what he wanted to know. He was pleased that they had come in under budget without slacking on the quality of things, but his happy mood didn't last long when I told him that the marketing side of things was going way over budget. He moved his laptop from his lap and removed his glasses before groaning his frustrations out loud.

"These fuckers are going to kill me early!"

I didn't even know what I was doing, but I walked over to him and straddled his lap, trying to kiss away his frustrations. I caressed his bald head and then his face as I slowly and methodically intertwined his tongue with mine. I moaned into his mouth and took the kiss deeper. I didn't have on my work clothes yet. Only a white T-shirt and some sweats. My kiss became greedy and I pulled his face closer to mine and him closer to me. He had fully sat up on the couch and it didn't even seem like the kiss broke when he removed my shirt. I quickly went back in to taste his tongue and just as quick he was removing my bra and had both hands gripping and squeezing my breasts. He pushed me up to look in my eyes.

"You better tell me if you are sure this is what you want because I don't stop once I get started."

The area between my thighs felt heavy and it was throbbing . . . aching. My mind really screamed HELL NO! But my body was saying otherwise.

"It's what I want," I manage to get out.

He quickly shifted us so that I was underneath him and he made quick work of removing my sweats.

"Damn, Chyanne! You are thicker than a motherfucker," he said as he looked down at me. My hands were covering my breasts and he removed them, taking my right, then left one into his mouth.

While teasing me, he used his lips and tongue to pull on each nipple. He kissed my neck down to that area between my breasts and let his tongue trail down to my navel before slightly brushing his lips across the area hidden by my lace thong. I hissed, arched, and moaned before he came back up to kiss me. He used his hand to stroke me through the lace. I reached for him to bring him closer but he stood and my eyes opened when I heard the sound of his belt buckle clink. I watched as his jeans dropped to the floor and he stepped out of them. His body was sick. His abs contracted as he pulled his shirt off and I giggled when he made his chest jump.

Then my eyes nearly jumped out of my head when he pulled his boxer briefs down and his dick sprang forward like it had new life. It had a slight curve and it was two toned, like a chocolate and caramel mixed. The head was big like the fattest mushroom I had ever seen. He had thick veins going down the side of it and I could actually see it throb. He was blessed beyond measures. His thighs were masculine and yelled that he was all male. I closed my eyes and inhaled when he turned out the lights and brought his body back down over mine. He slid down the couch and placed his face where I had soaked my panties. His hands gripped my thighs as he spread my legs apart and pulled my thong to the side and sucked my clit into his mouth.

"Oh my God," I cried out. Against my will my back arched and made me grind into his face.

When his fingers found their way inside of me, and his tongue and lips continued to suck and dabble on my swollen clitoris I was near tears. Moaning, screaming and pulling on my own hair. He removed his fingers and stuck his tongue in and out of my body. I was so wet I could feel it running down in between my cheeks.

"Want to see what you taste like," he asked me before coming up to kiss me. His lips and tongue were wet with my juices. Reaching down, he ripped my thong away from my body. My heartbeat sped up and I got nervous. I looked up and into his eyes as he seductively smiled down at me. Those hazel brown eyes were pulling me in to his allure and seduction. He pulled my left leg up and cupped the back of my knee with the inside of his elbow. I wondered if he noticed that my body was tensed and had started to shake. I closed my eyes as he placed butterfly kisses on my lips. I could feel the head of his swollen dick right at my opening and it gave me the chills. I almost yelled out when his head first tried to break skin.

Between bated breaths I gasped out, "Ahh . . . Aric . . . Ow . . . wait . . ."

I had almost come up off that couch. I didn't know if he had caught on yet . . . but he was coming close to killing me. He inched his way inside, before he finally broke skin. I was clawing at his back and beating on his shoulders. I had started to sweat and with every inch of himself that he pushed inside of me, it was more pain than I cared to take.

"Wa. . . . Wait . . . Aric, wait! Ouch . . . shit. Damn, please wait!" I yelled out loudly as he found his way all the way inside of me.

I almost bit half of my damn tongue off, and that's when I assumed he realized what was going on.

"Damn it Chyanne! Why didn't you tell me you were a fucking virgin?!"

I tell you no lie when I tell you me, a grown woman, was crying right now.

"Aric, it hurts. . . ."

"Fuck," he yelled out. I could feel his dick flexing inside of me and that made it worse. I cringed when he punched the arm of the couch. I didn't care. I was in so much pain that I wasn't able to think straight and found myself trying to push him off of me.

"Wait Chyanne! Shit, I can't just snatch my dick out. Relax baby please. Just calm down."

"Just hurry up and . . . come out. Please!"

I cringed, groaned, and bit down on my lips as he started to slowly pull out of me. It hurt so badly that it made my stomach hurt, made me dizzy, and gave me a headache. I could hear him groan and cursing under his breath. When I thought he was coming out he slid back in and slipped deep into me. I screamed out and jerked myself forward to bite down between his neck and his shoulder. He growled and roughly stroked inside of me, making it hurt me worse.

I backed away from his neck and loudly called his name. "Aric!"

He said nothing.

"Aric . . . this hurts," I cried.

Yes, I was in tears. He leaned into me and kissed my tears.

"I know, but you really should have told me this before now . . ."

He relaxed into me and wrapped his arms around me almost like cupping my shoulders in his hands. My body tensed even more and I tried to squirm away from him.

"Do me a favor, baby, and calm . . ."

"This hurts, Aric . . ."

"I know, but you have to calm down so I can fix it."

I was still squirming and praying that he would get up as we both just laid there. I could still feel him flexing inside of me. My walls and muscles were contracting. Felt like my vagina was inhaling and exhaling. Aric placed his mouth on mine and began to slowly move in and out of me. I moaned into his mouth and still tried to move away but he kept me locked in place. He moved slowly with a disciplined motioned that broke through the pain and introduced me to pleasure . . . and then pain . . . and then pleasure again. He would pull out a couple of inches and go deep again, but when he brought my knees up to my shoulders, I literally backed away as far as I could, which wasn't far on that loveseat. I backed away enough to make him come out of me. I was aching and throbbing like jumping beans down below. He caged me in between his arms and hovered over me, while we stared into each other's eyes. No lie, I was scared . . . .nervous.

"You started this, Chyanne," he said to me. His eyes held me hostage. "Now you running? It's your first time, baby. Let me take you where you need to be. You got me chasing you like a junkie right now. You gave me a taste and now I want it all."

He brought his face closer to mine and moved my head to the side so he could nibble on my ear. A soft moan escaped from within, as chills shivered up and down my spine.

"Can I taste that fat pussy again?" he whispered in my ear.

That same feeling in my spine was shivering down amid my thighs.

"Tell me, Chyanne. Tell me I can taste your pussy."

All I could do was squirm around under him when I felt his hand cup my pussy and stroke me.

"Tell me Chyanne . . . tell me what you want me to do."

That baritone in his voice was messing me up. Mix that with the fact that his fingers were making my insides quake and sucking on my breasts at the same time—if I had the secret of the Nile I would have given it to him. I told him to take what he asked for and he went down south, taking me to a whole other level. My back arched and I felt like I was free falling. There was this aching feeling like I had to pee and then the urge to scream out and clamp my legs around his head.

"Oh my God . . . oh my God . . . oh shit! Oh. . . ." I panted over and over again.

Before I could come down from such an overwhelming feeling, Aric quickly came back up and slid so deep into me that even he moaned and growled out. He had pulled me close to him so that I couldn't run away and although the mixture of pain and pleasure was new to me, I wasn't sure if I wanted to get away. The way he moaned out my name on top of that thick New York accent, and the way he was hitting that one spot as he systematically stroked and grinded his hips into me, it was enough to bring water to my eyes. He had control of my ample hips, moving them to the speed and tune that he wanted them. As he pumped harder into me, I felt him swell and get harder inside of my sugar walls. I bit down on my bottom lip and dug my nails into his back until he let out a primal groan, giving one last hard push into me. Exhausted we lay sprawled out on the couch for a long while. I thought he had fallen asleep while he was still inside of me. I actually fell asleep with him resting between my legs.

The sound of an alarm woke me. It took a while for me to gather my thoughts. The soreness in between my thighs and legs surprised me. I looked around and realized that I was in my boss's hide-a-way office at work and we had just had sex. I looked around for Aric and did not see him. I noticed his gym bag was on top of the desk and his suit was gone. It was thirty minutes past twelve and I had missed more than half of the meeting. I sat up on the couch and then tried to stand but I was dizzy. My legs were wobbly but I somehow managed. As I was walking to the shower, the door opened and Aric walked in with bags in his hand. I smelled food. It was obvious he had been to the meeting and it was over with. I realized I was naked and moved back over to the floor near the sofa and reached for my T-shirt to pull it on. At the moment, I wasn't sure how I was feeling. I was nervous. I had just had sex with my boss. How was I supposed to feel? I heard him maneuvering around behind me.

"You OK," he asked as he stepped closer to me and enclosed one arm around my waist.

I lied nervously as I nodded. "Yeah, I'm good." I smiled and peeked back at him.

He kissed my neck before answering his ringing phone and I listened to him threaten to fire half of the accounting department if they didn't get numbers that made sense by the end of the day. He handed me a Target bag and I looked inside to find a pair of red cotton boy shorts and a pack of Maxi panty liners.

"Thank you," I said in a whisper to him.

He nodded and pointed to the Red Lobster bag on the desk and mouthed for me to eat. I was starving and had already opened the bag and pulled out two containers. They both had the same thing, lobster tails with shrimp scampi and brown and wild rice with those biscuits that were going to go right to my thighs. I gave one of the containers to him and I sat down next to him to eat. We didn't say much to each other since he was still on the phone cursing people out.

After eating, I jumped in for a quick shower noticing that I was bleeding a little. I was thankful for the panty liners and the black wide leg pant suit I would be wearing today. I hid behind the curtain that separated the couch from the rest of room and put my suit on. It was the shortest work day I have ever had. I gathered the rest of my things back into my bag. As I was about to leave, Aric put the caller on hold long enough to stand and hug and kiss me. I didn't know how to feel and what to expect, but I was glad that he had put my mind at ease. My heels clicked against the hardwood floor as I left Aric. I hid my bag on the side of the leather sofa in Aric's main office before walking out to my desk. My head and the spot between my legs were still hurting a bit so I popped a few Tylenols. The rest of the day went by uneventfully. It was back to work as usual. Although for the rest of the day my mind played back this being my first time having sex and I was still in a state of shock. The lower half of my body kept reminding me that she had been pried open. The throbbing never left and every time Aric walked past me, my lower region jumped. A nervous feeling took over and I wondered how he would look at me now. Wondered if his image of me would change? By the end of the day, my stomach was in knots and I had a migraine that just wouldn't quit.

That same night, at about ten o'clock, Aric was at my door. He had knocked on the door in my kitchen and as soon as I opened it he pulled me into his arms. All I had on was a T-shirt. The wind was attacking me left and right, but when Aric put me on top of the hood of my car, pulled my T-shirt off, and spread my legs, heat rushed all over my insides. I clawed at the car when his lips enclosed around my lower set of lips and he sucked, licked, and ate all around my wetness. All you could hear was heavy breathing, me moaning, Aric smacking, and the wind howling. It was like the wind was a voyeur and I didn't mind one bit. Aric and the wind were taking turns fondling my body. My hand grabbed a hold to both sides of his face and tugged at his ears. I pulled his face closer to my pussy. I guess I was trying to either saturate his face in my juices or smother the man. He didn't seem to mind though. He kept right on fingering and licking. Licking and eating. Eating and drinking. I looked down and saw my juices had his face shining. It made me come harder, especially when he used his fingers to spread my lips and suck down on my clit. I moaned so loud. . . . I knew the old man across the street could hear me. I could feel and hear Aric going for his belt buckle and I was scared, but antsy. I wanted it . . . but I knew I couldn't handle it. His belt buckle clinking alerted me to when his pants were down. As he came up to kiss me, he pulled me to the edge of the car, and I braced myself for impact. I let out a startled moan when his head broke skin.

"My fucking . . . God . . ." he roared out with his eyes closed with his head thrown back.

I was panting and trying to catch my breath as he slid in and out of me with precise motion. I was clawing at his back so hard, I heard his shirt rip. I was literally on the verge of slobbering out of the mouth if I wasn't already slobbering. Once he got the position that he wanted, his rhythm changed to a steady beat. One minute his mouth was open and the next he was biting down on his bottom lip. I pulled his shirt over his head revealing nothing but muscles. My ankles were placed on his shoulders and he pulled me closer to him without breaking a stroke. The coldness of the hood gave me chills, but the feel of him inside of me, hugging my walls warmed me all over.

"Damn, Chyanne . . . umph . . . good pussy," he said to me with one hand on my breasts and the other massaging my clit. My back was arched, head back, and my body was convulsing at the way he entered me. I knew when he was about to come. The harder he pumped and the fatter he swelled on the inside of me let me know he was nearing the edge. I placed my hand against the panel of his stomach to try and push him back a bit, but to no avail. He simply moved my hand and rode me deeper . . . harder . . . and faster. I yelled . . . no scratch that . . . I screamed his name out and it seemed as if it stilled the night with my orgasm. The wind stopped blowing and with one last push Aric fell against my breasts. I was already sore from earlier. Now my inner vaginal walls were twisting and shouting in pain, but the feeling that I had just experienced was well worth it.

Chapter 6

What was left of October went by at a speed that I couldn't keep up with. Between me and Aric having sex, at the drop of a dime, anywhere at any time, my body was becoming addicted to him. I had gotten cocky and decided that I wanted to have my first oral sex session and I'd like to think I got an A plus being that I made him come the first time around. He could look at me and my boy shorts or thong would drop in an instant. At work we had little conversations here and there. He would leave me notes telling me how much he wanted to be inside of me and how much he missed me.

We had been at each other's houses quite a lot too. His house could sit ten of mine in it and still have room to comfortably live. His home was in a private Buckhead Estate. I remember listening as he told me about the whole house including the layered stucco and custom cut limestone finishes. He told me about the imported mahogany doors and windows, elevator, smart home, wine cellar, media room, custom master closets and outside had an incredible 2.95 plus acre lot overlooking a lake. The landscaping was immaculate. I had become accustomed to his California king sized bed.

He had become accustomed to my cooking. I would find myself shopping and filling my fridge and his with the stuff he liked most. Chicken, salmon, steaks, fresh veggies, and lots of apple juice, just to name a few. Was there a title on what we had? No. Why? Because Aric said it would be better this way. No title. No drama was what he said. I guess. And to be honest it was all good at first because he was being receptive to me and we both liked the same things. He was easy to talk to but as of late he had been distant. Not that it was a big deal because he was known to get very quiet when work was stressing him. So I was trying not to make a big deal of nothing, but you know that feeling you get when you just know something . . . something just doesn't feel right? Well . . . yeah, I was feeling that way.

I hadn't talked to Justin in a while and he called me up today, filling me in on the happenings down on the first floor. Lola was still busy slandering my name. Justin said she was pissed about being down there, especially seeing how Aric was making progress with the company, but whatever. Right now I had other things to worry about, like why in the hell April kept calling for Aric. Each time she called she seemed more impatient than before. She never spoke to me at all.

The phone ringing was what snapped me out of my thoughts. "Good afternoon. Aric McHale's office," I answered with the energetic tone that Gabriel had started to tease me about every time he called.

"I need to speak to Aric again please and thank you." It was April.

"Hey, April," I spoke. I was trying to keep it together. We hadn't spoken to each other since she showed her tail at that business function.

"Chyanne, may I speak with Aric, please? Thank you."

I put her on hold and transferred her call to Aric. His office door was open and although I couldn't quite hear what he was saying to her, I knew it was brief. When he was off the phone I walked into his office and closed the door behind me. I knew April didn't know the first thing about marketing or advertising and I wanted to know what she wanted. He looked up at me from behind his desk before taking his glasses off. I gave a semi-curt smile and stood at the door with my arms folded.

"So why is April calling you?"

He put the paper down and his right eyebrow arched a bit.

"So April can't call me now?"

That struck a nerve since I didn't know they had become close enough for her to be calling him at all. I unfolded my arms and moved toward his desk. The sun was shining but I knew for a fact that it was cold outside. It was about as cold out there as it had turned in here.

"I know it's not about business being that she doesn't know a thing about what we do. . . ."

"Oh, so the only time I can talk to somebody is when it's business?"

His face frowned and he stood up. He moved past me and toward his file cabinet. I felt like I had just been brushed off.

"When it's April, yes," I answered. My anger meter was through the roof.

He stopped messing with the file cabinet and turned to me. The look on his face said he was either annoyed or pissed or both.

"Chyanne, I am a grown ass man. You don't get to tell me who I can talk to and who I can't. Get that?"

I don't know. I guess I was just expecting some type of common courtesy or something. I mean knowing that April is . . . was my friend and he saw the mess she had done. We stared at each other for a while before I turned and walked back out to my desk. I wanted to cry I was so mad, but what would I be crying for? I plopped back down at my desk and I could hear my phone vibrating in my purse. I didn't bother to answer it though. I had let my mind drift off, until I saw April strut around the corner. She had on tighter than tight denim skinny jeans, a red sweater so tight it showed the complete outline of her nipples, and red Chanel caged booties. Her makeup was flawless as was her spiked pixie hair cut. She walked right past me and into Aric's office. She didn't even acknowledge me. My leg started to shake and I could feel my blood pressure rise. It didn't help me any when I turned to see her give him a tight hug and he embraced her back. It really hurt when he walked out of his office with her.

"Hold my calls for me," he said to me as he slid his arms into his leather jacket. "I'll be right back."

He looked at me and I didn't nod or acknowledge that I had even heard him. I rolled my eyes and looked away. I didn't even bother to look at April. When they rounded the corner and I heard the elevator chime, I blew out a breath like it was steam. No more than ten minutes later the elevator chimed again and I was hoping it was Aric, but no such luck. It was Gabriel. I must admit even though my feelings were hurt, Gabriel's sexiness wasn't lost on me.

Hello, Ms. Chy," he said, greeting me with a gentle, yet magnetic smile. "Your boss around here anywhere?"

His teeth were the same size and perfectly white. Those dark coffee colored eyes beckoned to me.

"No, he stepped out for a second," I answered him back with a smile.

He nodded "Must have been a woman. Only a woman can take Aric away from work. Any idea when he will be back? We were supposed to do lunch. Had some things we were supposed to discuss."

Part of his statement bothered me, but I answered anyway. "Nope. No idea when he will return."

He sat down in the chair across from my desk as I answered the ringing phone and sent someone to Aric's voicemail. I looked up to find Gabriel watching me. He was casually dressed in tailored black dress slacks and a royal blue long sleeved crisp dress shirt. No tie. Black square toed dress shoes that set off his whole attire.

"What," I asked when he kept staring. "Is my fro lop-sided or something?"

He chuckled. "No not at all. In fact, it really looks good on you. Matches your personality perfectly. Wild and untamed yet innocent and got it all together. You look good too. Black suits you. It's just that you have this new glow about you is all. I've noticed you had that extra something in your voice lately as well and who-ever has put that smile on your face has to be one hell of a lucky man!"

I blushed. "Thank you."

I had on an all black skirt suit with white accessories and black and white spiked Gucci heels.

"Have you had lunch today?" He asked as he crossed one leg over the other.

"No. Aric and I usually . . ." I caught myself. "Mr. McHale and I usually . . . well I usually go and get lunch for the both of us."

I could tell he had already caught on to my mistake. He only smiled a knowing smile. He didn't say any-thing though.

"Well, can I take you to lunch? After all, seems like you will be doing it alone today anyway right?"

I thought about it and I know I made the decision out of spite, but I said yes. Aric must be out of his mind if he thought I was about to sit there and cry and brood over him. I grabbed my purse and my jacket after setting the phone to office "out mode" and we left for lunch. We ended up at Maggiano's. It was an authentic Italian restaurant. I had been to a lot of places, but never here before. We sat silently as I looked over the menu. It was apparent that he had been here plenty of times because it didn't take him long to look at the menu and decide what he wanted. I finally made up my mind and ordered the spinach and chicken manicotti, a small glass of Moscato D'asti and a glass of water.

"So Chy, tell me something about you," Gabriel asked of me.

I shrugged. "Nothing to tell. I am twenty four with three degrees. Graduated high school when I was seventeen. Don't have much family and no friends at all it seems."

"Where's your family?"

I looked up at him and stared before answering him. "Long story and if you don't mind, I would rather not talk about that."

He chuckled and nodded. "I can respect that. Why no friends?"

I shrugged again and watched him take a swallow of water before answering. "It is what it is you know? Keep your friends close and your enemies closer and it seems I do a bang up job on that last part."

I could tell by his amused facial expression that he knew I was referring to the incident with April.

"By the way, thank you for making sure she made it home safely," I added after taking a sip of my wine.

He nodded and took a piece of the bread the waiter had sat on the table.

"No problem at all. All I had to do was drop her off and keep it moving."

The bottom of my stomach fell out at that. Did that mean that the man Jo-Jo saw April talking to was Aric? Did he leave my house and go to April's? As if Gabriel had read my mind. . . .

"Aric told me he stopped by her place to make sure she had gotten in as well," he told me.

I didn't respond. Just turned and look at the ongoing traffic on Peachtree Road and listened to the noise of the old Italian music and the muttering of the patrons at the restaurant.

"Did I say something wrong," he spoke up and asked after a while.

I shook my head. "No. I just have a lot on my mind is all."

Gabriel exhaled. "I hope it doesn't have anything to do with Aric. If that's the case, then I wouldn't worry. I wouldn't let him get to me. Aric will be Aric and he has been since I have known him."

"Who said it had anything to do with him?"

He leaned forward and clasped his hands together, looking me in my eyes. "Chyanne, sometimes we have to listen to what's not being said."

His eyes studied mine and it was like he could see past the whole facade I was putting up. I was so thankful that the food came at that moment. I don't understand how I let these unseen feelings for Aric sneak up on me, but this man had embedded himself into my DNA in more ways than one. Over the last month or so, everything he had done had deepened my feelings for him. The trips to the movies, the shopping, the sneaking away for lunch at work together, the spending the night at each other's places, and the sex! Lord the sex! Thinking about it right now had me squeezing my legs together and silently moaning.

This was something that I wasn't used to. I wasn't used to getting lost in a man. I never wanted to be there. I never wanted to be the woman who couldn't see past a man's smile. Yet, here I was. I barely touched my food. My appetite had been lost. I was tempted to sneak to the restroom and call to see if Aric had made it back to the office, but there was no need. Aric was texting me in the middle of lunch asking me where I was.

Gabriel and I made small talk for what time I had left of lunch. I liked talking to Gabriel. He was fun and his deep baritone and Southern accent sent chills through me especially when he called my name. I asked him questions about his LX 11 truck just to keep the conversation flowing until we made it back to the office. Gabriel was a comedian too. He kept me laughing, almost making me forget that Aric had left with April . . . almost.

Gabriel was a gentleman through and through. I hadn't had to open a door for myself this entire time with him. It was funny to see chicks gawking at him as he passed with me. He opened the door for me when we made it back to the office and hugged me. There was something in his hug. Something I didn't care to dwell on because that would require me to admit that I was sexually attracted to him. I didn't want to go there so when he leaned in for a kiss, I politely moved my head to the side and declined.

"I . . . I can't. . . . Not right now," I said to him as we stood hidden from the cameras in the parking deck.

"I understand," was all he said. He kissed me on my cheek, handed me my doggy bag from lunch, and walked me to the elevator. I stepped onto the elevator a little embarrassed.

"Chyanne," he called out to me and I had to rush to stop the elevator doors from closing.

"Yeah," I answered.

"I'm always around."

I watched as he walked off towards his truck. I let the elevator doors close and finally let the breath I had been holding out. Lord what had I gotten myself into? I stepped off the elevator and made my way to my desk. Aric was in his office and I hated to admit it but I was glad he was there. I was still pissed. However, he was not with April so I was good. I dropped my purse in the bottom drawer of my desk and switched the phone back on. I left my doggy bag on the desk. It was no more than five minutes later before Aric's office door swung open.

"Where have you been?" He asked me.

Something about the tone of his voice startled me.

"I went to lunch." I said sarcastically pointing at the bag on my desk.

"With who? Your car was still in the parking deck."

I wasn't so sure I wanted to answer that question. So I tried not to.

"Look I went to lunch. Is that a problem?"

I was sitting in my chair looking up at him in the doorway of his office with his arms folded across his broad chest.

"Don't play with me Chyanne!" he said through gritted teeth. "Who did you go to lunch with? Don't think I won't fu . . . mess you up because we are in this office."

My brows furrowed and I looked at him like he had lost his mind!

"I am a grown woman and I go to lunch with whomever I choose. Get that?"

The way he was looking at me had me feeling some type of way and I don't mean anything good about that either. He had bit down on his bottom lip and was nodding his head like he was keeping from saying what he really wanted to say. He turned and went back into his office, slamming the door so hard other assistants were sticking their heads around the corner to see what was going on. I put on a fake smile whenever someone asked if everything was okay and hyperventilated when no one could see me. I picked up the phone and pressed one.

Aric picked up. "What?"

"I went to lunch with Gabriel."

"Who?"

I could hear something akin to disbelief and anger in his voice.

"Your friend Gabriel who was at the. . . ."

Before I could get the last part out I heard a click in my ear. I heard when he moved into his hide-a-way office a few minutes later. A few minutes after that, he called me to meet him in there. I slowly stood and walked into his office, locking the door behind me. I was not in the mood to fight with this man, especially when he was the one who didn't want to put a "title" on our relationship. I pushed the button on the wall to his hide-a-way office and stepped in. He was sitting on the couch, arms wide, legs spread with a mean mug on his face.

"So you fucking Gabriel?" he asked.

I answered with my face bunched in disbelief. "What? No!" I chuckled a bit. "I only went to lunch with the man. Since you decided that you wanted to go do "whatever" with April. . . ."

He stood and walked over to me cutting me off and making me back up against the desk that was on the wall by the door.

"You think I'm stupid, Chyanne?"

He was right up on me and had cupped my chin to make me look up at him.

"No."

"Are you fucking Gabriel?"

He asked that with clenched teeth.

"No. How am I having sex with Gabriel when I have been with you every day all day until today? Are sleeping with April?"

His grip tightened on my face and his eyes watered, becoming red. "Don't play with me Chyanne! Tell me the truth."

"Who's playing? I'm telling you the truth." The attitude I had copped was laced in my voice.

I tensed because he snatched my face closer to his and his grip tightened causing pain in my jaw. He picked me up and sat me on top of the desk. Snatching me close to him, his right hand found its way under my skirt and his lips roughly enclosed around mine. I felt my thong rip on one side and he used his knee to push my legs further apart. He kept kissing me and pushing his tongue in and out of my mouth. I felt the split in the back of my skirt rip. It was all going in slow motion. I heard his zipper come down, and seconds later, I screamed inside of his mouth when he shoved his way inside of me. I was scratching and clawing at his back. I tried to push him off of me, but he grabbed both wrists and slammed them into the wall before removing his mouth from mine.

Looking me dead in my teary eyes he said, "Your pussy had better always feel like this. I'll know if somebody has touched my pussy," he said before pushing hard and so deep inside of me that my legs started to shake uncontrollably.

I bit down on my lips to keep from screaming. His mood, the tension in the room, the way he was treating me, all caused tears to fall from my eyes. I tried calling his name to get his attention to let him know he was hurting me.

"Aric," I called out to him again. "You are hurting me! Aric, stop!"

I squirmed and moved around, letting out silent screams and clamping my legs around his waist to try and get him to ease up and slow down. No such luck. I was forced to ask myself what was happening here, but I didn't really want to know what was happening. Aric was like an animal that couldn't be tamed. I didn't know where the moisture between my legs was coming from because this hurt. Aric's thrusts were so fast and hard that I didn't know where the pain ended or where it began. After a while I couldn't hold in my sobs any longer and I began to cry out loud. When he heard me he abruptly stopped and looked intently at me.

"I'm sorry," he repeated over and over to me in a near whisper, kissing my tears while they slid down my face. I didn't know how I felt. I was numb. I felt nothing. The pain inside hurt way worse than what he had done to me. I sat silent as he kissed his way down to my thighs. I hissed out and tensed when his lips touched my now swollen and hurting lips down below.

He planted butterfly kisses there and gently licked, trying to kiss away what he had done. I hated to admit it but he made me come. I didn't want to, but I couldn't help it. When he was done, he laid there with his head on my lap for a long while. I didn't touch him. I couldn't bring myself to touch him. After a while, I pushed him away from me. It hurt for me to walk so I stopped for a second to get myself together.

After a moment I cried my way to the shower and got in with all of my clothes on. While in there I peeled my clothes off and sat there. I could hear him moving around. Did I want a man so bad that I would let him do this kind of thing to me? Was I no better than April or all of the other women that I had called stupid? I rocked back and forth as I cried and thought. After trying to wash away what Aric had done to me, I stepped out of the shower slowly and steadied myself. I didn't even look up when his naked body came closer to me. I let him pull me up and let him pull me into his embrace.

"I'm sorry baby. I never. . . . Forgive me. Please forgive me. . . ."

His voice sounded as if he was weak, but I didn't care. I had no words for him at the moment. I let him reach down and pull me up around his waist.

"Look at me baby," he called out, shaking me a bit.

I looked away and didn't say a word.

"Chyanne look at me."

Finally, I looked at him. I listened to him apologize to me again. At that moment he wasn't even sexy to me anymore. He could do nothing for me. Within an hour, I went home. I crawled into my queen-sized bed, thinking about my relationship with Aric. What had I gotten myself into and how would I ever be able to get out of it?

I didn't talk to Aric for the next week or so. He would call but I wouldn't answer. I took a sick week from work. Justin told me Lola had been all too happy to fill my seat. I had been moping around my house all week. It did a little winter cleaning and I had been helping Jo-Jo with a PowerPoint Presentation for school. One particular day I was cleaning my room and my purse fell from the dresser. It was a clutch that I often carried with me when going to clubs. Jamie's business card fell out. It was the one he gave me when we were at Club Miami. I felt better that day, but a little lonely, so I went against the grain and called him. I was happy I did. He brought my spirits up. I let him take me to dinner and a movie and we hung out for a couple of days after that. He came to my house to watch a movie or two. I had taken all of Aric's belongings and put them away in a plastic tote until I could get them back to him.

As for Jamie and I, we decided to take it up a notch. I let him eat the coochie because he wanted to. Let me tell you I don't know who could do it better Jamie or Aric, but Jamie's tongue was long enough for him to reach the depths of my soul through the opening between my legs. And that man licked everywhere, missing not one nook or cranny. He did it so good it had me fanning myself down below trying to calm her down. Basically, he had me running from his tongue, but the feel of it was so good—a pussy monster for real. I enjoyed his company and was looking forward to spending more time with him.

My phone was vibrating like crazy. I stopped dressing long enough to see who was trying so hard to contact me. I picked up my BlackBerry after I pulled my fro back into a big puffball. Five texts from Aric and two from Jamie. I erased all of Aric's texts without looking at them and went to Jaime's texts. He and I were supposed to catch a live outdoor jazz show tonight. I was actually pretty excited. Friday night and I was on my way out. In Atlanta, live outdoor jazz festivals were the best. Vendors served the best food and drinks and it was mostly an older mature crowd so there was not a lot of mess to put up with. I texted Jaime back and told him I was getting dressed. Jamie was cool . . . laid back even. Very artistic I had learned. I dropped my phone back on the bed and finished dressing. I tugged on some wide legged high waist jeans and buttoned up my black collared shirt that flared over my hips and back side. Around my waist I put on a wide chocolate brown corset type belt, threw on some big brown feathered earrings, and threw on my brown caged Chanel booties. I stood in the mirror turning from side to side to make sure I had no muffin tops. Then I took a picture of myself and sent it to Jamie. We were supposed to meet up on Piedmont so I was leaving a little early. I picked up my bag and dropped my vibrating phone over into it. Again, it was Aric.

I had slipped up and told Jaime about me and Aric. Didn't tell him about that last incident, but gave him enough details to let him know we weren't seeing each other anymore. I wasn't going to lie, I missed Aric like crazy. I did. Hell, don't ask me why. I guess I had let myself fall in love with the man. As much as I hated to admit it, I couldn't fool myself any longer. From the moment I stepped foot into his office he had worked some kind of magic on me. Still, I would be damned if I let a man do what he had done to me and still be running after him. I may be young, but stupid I was not. I hummed and grabbed my keys as I strutted to the door with a smile on my face. I was actually looking forward to seeing Jamie. I opened my door and stepped outside into the brisk breeze. My coat was already in the car. I noticed a movement out the side of my eye and turned to find Aric casually leaning against the grill of his truck. I stopped in my tracks.

"I have called you, texted, left messages . . . whatever. Trying to get in contact with you," he said to me.

No threat was detected in his voice. The leather jacket, black jeans, black D&G turtle neck sweater, and even the D&G white perforated leather lace up sneakers made the appeal of this man much more lethal.

"I've been busy," I said, turning to lock my door. With my purse hanging in the crease of my elbow, I walked towards my car which he had parked his truck behind and was blocking me in.

"Too busy for me, Chyanne?"

I stopped walking and looked over at him. "Apparently so."

He chuckled and stood straight up folding his arms and standing in his signature wide legged stance.

"Got a date?" he asked me. My body turned hot at the way he looked me over. It's like his eyes had x-ray vision or something.

"Why? Is there something you wanted? I'll be back to work on Monday. I have a doctor's excuse which I'll turn in to HR on Monday. . . ."

"I miss you, Chyanne."

I stepped back when he moved closer to me. I exhaled loudly and shook my head.

"You don't get to do this Aric. You don't get to pull what you did and then say you miss me. You don't get away with that and think you can come over here and butter me up . . ."

I was annoyed. I had been easily annoyed a lot lately. My blood pressure was going up again. I could feel myself getting jittery.

"Listen to me." He moved closer to me and put his finger to my lips to quiet me. "I fucked up. I fucked up bad and I know that, but at least give me a chance to make it right."

I pushed off and away from him. He caught my wrist and pulled me back into him. I could see my old neighbor eyeing us and tried not to create a scene.

"You don't miss me, Chyanne?"

His scent was making me dizzy or maybe it was because he had driven my blood pressure up. I looked up at him with a frown on my face and snatched my arm away from him.

"No, I don't. Now if you will excuse me, I have some place I need to be."

"I miss you," he called out to me.

I stopped and turned back around to him. I hated to admit it to myself but I missed this man. Why did I have to miss him? I had thought about him every day. We stood there watching each other and his eyes burned a hole through me.

"What do you want, Aric?" I said impatiently.

"Let me show you I'm sorry. Look, why in hell you got me begging you to tell you I'm sorry?" He was using his hands to talk. "I don't like to repeat myself and I am not the one to beg."

It was my turn to fold my arms.

"First of all I didn't ask for your apology. Second of all you can't. . . . How do you apologize for using your dick as a weapon? What? You think that you can roll up here, flash that dimpled smile, and everything will be cool again? Some stuff you do you just can't take it back once it's done. What you did was one of them."

I quickly turned and made my way to the driver side of my car. I hit the automated button and unlocked the door. I threw my purse on the passenger side and was prepared to get in.

"I admit it, I was wrong. I keep saying that shit over and over Chyanne, but why do you always have to make a nigga beg?"

I had never heard him use the "N" word before and that was the second thing out of his mouth that shocked me. He stood with his arms wide. "Damn! What in hell do I have to do?"

I got nervous and looked around as some of my nosey neighbors had come outside. Some pretending to be doing something in their yard and others just plain out looking and listening.

"You see me face to face. You can see I am for real. Why make me do this shit out here? I messed up! I said it again. Now what? A nigga got to stand on his head and do tricks? Come on, baby! Don't make me do this out here like this."

I sighed and looked away from him as he approached me. When his hands touched my waist I nibbled on my bottom lip and folded my arms when he pulled me close to him.

With his voice low and baritone deep he said, "You don't know what it has been like with you not around me every day. I messed up, baby. I know that, but I won't do it again. I can guarantee you that. I lost it. I don't know. I guess the thought of you with another man fucked me up."

I finally looked up at him. "Oh and I'm supposed to be okay with you leaving the office with my best friend?"

"She asked to buy me lunch . . ."

"And you said yes?"

My voice was a little louder than I intended. He shook his head and answered.

"Look, baby. April has been trying to get my attention since she met me. I went with her that day to tell her that I was with you . . ."

I gave a faux chuckle and shook my head. "And you couldn't do that over the phone? What about that whole *I'm a grown ass man* thing?"

He smiled. "I was already annoyed and I lashed out at you. I was wrong for that."

"So what did you and April do that day when you left the office with her?"

"Nothing. I came back into the office about twenty, thirty minutes later and you were gone."

I turned my head again and looked elsewhere. I tried to be stubborn when he gently cupped my chin and tried to kiss me. I moved my face and he did it again, this time connecting his lips with mine. I had missed these thick chocolate lips. Heat settled in between my legs and my resolve slowly faded. He gripped my backside and pulled me closer to him as our tongues touched. I don't know. It was like a different feeling washed over me as he kissed me. My mind quickly went to Jamie. I didn't know if I was going to make our date. I stood there as Aric pulled my purse from my car and locked my doors back. I followed him to my front door, but before I unlocked it, he captured my attention. After a lengthy kiss, we both walked into my house hand in hand.

It was two hours later when I got to my phone to text Jamie. I rolled out of Aric's arms and took my phone to the bathroom with me. I texted Jamie that an emergency came up and told him I was sorry I couldn't make it. After I had finished using the restroom, he texted me back.

It's cool. Maybe some other time we can hook up. BTW I drove to your house to make sure nothing had happened since it wasn't like you not to call or show up.

I sighed. I felt so bad all I could type back was, I'm sorry.

It's cool. Don't worry about it.

I could detect the sarcasm and nonchalant tone. I heard Aric moving around in my room and quickly put my phone on the counter. I washed my hands, dried them, and walked out of the bathroom. My body was sore. Aric and I had made love forever it seemed. I still had to get used the stamina that he possessed. He took his time and took me to places that I didn't think I could go. I had missed him and my body showed it. I was dripping wet before he even had my clothes all the way off. I loved it when he got behind me. I liked the way he let his head lay at my opening and let my muscles pull him in. Aric's magic stick was way too big for me, but I loved the hell out of it. Loved the way he moved in and out of me like he was looking to hit that one spot and create another one. Loved the way he gripped my cheeks and spread them so he could fall deeper inside of me. And it turned me on more when he would tell me to *throw it back*. I had learned what he liked. I listened to his moans and paid attention to the way his grip tightened when I moved a certain way.

I walked over to the bed. He was sitting up looking at his phone. He had a frown on his face.

"Everything OK," I asked.

He nodded and yawned. "Family issues." He threw his phone back on the night stand beside my bed. "I'm hungry baby."

My eyes washed over his naked frame as he laid back and propped his left arm behind his head as the other rubbed his stomach. His baby maker never seemed to go all the way soft after we would finish making love, I thought to myself as I pulled on my pink terry cloth robe.

"What do you want to eat," I asked.

That was the normal for him. After sex, he always wanted food.

"I don't care. I'm just hungry." He yawned again. "Will you pass me the remote behind you?"

I grabbed the remote from my dresser and tossed it to him. I went to the kitchen and looked around my fridge. It was going on ten-thirty. I pulled out the ingredients for sandwiches and small salads. I made sure I had all of the toppings that he liked. He probably wouldn't want tomatoes in his salad, especially if I put them on his sandwich. I put the late night snack together and set the table. I could hear him laughing in the room. He had this habit of watching Sanford and Son. I called out to him when I was done. A few seconds later he emerged from the room and after he blessed the food, we ate. It was hard to focus on eating when Aric was sitting across from me in nothing but black boxer briefs. He had a healthy appetite which was probably why he worked out the way he did. After we finished eating we sat outside on my back patio and talked about what had happened in his office. After telling him that I was still not feeling that whole thing because it took me somewhere I didn't want to be, he assured me that it wouldn't happen again. The love I felt for him made me believe him.

Chapter 7

I guess you can say the relationship between Aric and I was growing and all that, but we still didn't have a title and it didn't seem if he had any intentions of giving us one. Every time I said something about it, we ended up arguing or not saying anything to each other for a while. We were back to our old routine of spending the night with each other, although he had been at my house most of the time, which was cool because anytime I wanted a change of scenery we would go to his place.

I had tried to call Jaime back a few times and got no response. I just wanted to apologize face to face, but he wasn't answering my calls. I guess I wanted more so to apologize because Aric and I were arguing again. Little things he kept doing raised my suspicions of him doing other things. Sometimes he was warm and affectionate. Other times it was like his mind was somewhere else with somebody else and it was starting to annoy me. Like at that moment his phone kept ringing. All other times his phone vibrated, but then it was ringing to the tune of a Trey Songz hit. He had ignored the call about five times. Whoever she was, she was not letting up. We were sitting on my couch watching a re-run of NCIS on USA. I had been putting the finishing touches on Jo-Jo's PowerPoint presentation and after Aric and I had eaten dinner, we decided to stay in and watch TV. His head had been lying on my lap until his phone rang again. He had on no shirt and a pair of black sweats. I watched the muscles in his chest and arms flex as he annoyingly answered his phone. You know my eyes and ears were on alert.

"What?" He answered.

He didn't look over at me as he moved past me to the dining room area.

"What?" He snapped again. "Why in hell do you keep calling me? What the fuck do you want?"

I watched his body language between looking back and forth at the TV. I stood and tightened my robe, making my way to the kitchen as if I wanted to get some water.

"You want something to drink," I asked. I said it loud enough so my voice could carry. He ignored me.

I guess the person on the other end of the phone asked who I was, because he answered 'nobody' and my blood spiked.

I pulled a bottle of water from the fridge and slowly walked near him.

"Who are you talking to," I asked him.

He looked at me but it was like there was nothing in his eyes. He ignored me again. With the phone to his ear he tried to leave the dining room, but I blocked him.

"Aric, who are you talking to?"

I just knew damn well he was not doing what I thought he was doing! Again, I was ignored but he answered the woman on the other end of the phone. I knew it was a woman because I could hear her asking the same thing I was. He brushed past me and out of the dining room. I slammed the bottle of water down on the table and followed him back into the front room. As he yelled and talked to the woman on the other end of the phone, I stepped in front of him again.

I waved my hands in his face. "Hello, earth to Aric!! Who in the hell are you talking to?"

He inhaled and cut his eyes at me. "Not now!"

His tone backed me up a bit. That was all he said to me and he had the nerve to move me to the side and walk toward the front door. All I saw was red and I slapped him and the phone from his hand. His phone went flying across the room under my couch. Hell, I shocked myself! So imagine the look on his face. After the initial shock wore off for him, and it was quick, I found myself slammed against the wall so hard that it knocked the air out of me. I didn't even have time to get over the surprise of what he had done before his hand came up and around my neck.

The look in his eyes scared whatever boldness I had in me out. "Don't you ever in your fucking life put your hands in my face again, Chyanne. I will beat your ass! You hear me?"

All I could do was try and grab at his hand around my neck. His lips were twisted in anger and he was talking through clenched teeth. Tears started to fall from my eyes more so because I couldn't breathe. He moved his hand and I slid down the wall and watched through tears as he went for his phone. He snatched the door opened and stormed out. I knew he wasn't leaving because his keys, watch, and wallet were still on my nightstand in my room. I sat there in disbelief for a while before getting up and turning my TV off. I could hear him outside still talking to whoever she was on the phone. He had just shown me my importance to him. How in hell could he tell me he cared so much about me when he knew damn well he didn't? He couldn't care like he said and do the things that he did to me. I went into my room and crawled into my bed. My head was pounding and before I knew it, I had fallen asleep. What seemed like a few minutes later, I jerked awake when I felt him climb into the bed with me. I moved away from him when he tried to wrap his arms around me.

"Chyanne." He called my name slightly above a whisper. I didn't answer. He turned me over on my back. He was leaning on his right arm with his body semi covering mine. I looked up at him. It was dark in my room but the moonlight gave enough light for us to see each other. All I did was look at him.

"You mad?" he asked me.

Was this man crazy? How in hell did he think I was feeling? I didn't answer him. Only looked at him.

"So you're not going to say anything to me now, huh?"

I still didn't answer. He leaned down to kiss me and I turned my head away from him. He moved fully on top of me and urged my legs open with his. I tensed. He tried to kiss me again and I turned my head again. He pushed my robe up and around my waist. Then I spoke up.

"What? Are you going to take it like you did when we were in your office," I asked him.

That stopped him dead in his tracks. His facial expression looked as if he was about to say something but he caught himself and got up. I watched as he turned the light on and found his white T-shirt. He gathered his watch, wallet, and keys then pulled on his Nike Air Force Ones. Once he was dressed, he turned the light back out. He kissed my forehead and then left. I didn't have to get up because he had the key to my door so he could lock it on his way out. As I lay there, my mind kept wondering who was on the other end of his phone. I couldn't believe he would disrespect me, in my house, like that! I guess you could say I was confused right now. Part of me wanted to get up and run behind him, beg him to come back. Aric had some kind of hold on me and as much as I wanted to break it at times, I just couldn't. I stood, quickly walking to my front room window to see if he had gone. It was good he was gone because I probably would have gone after him.

I woke up the next morning with the same headache I had gone to sleep with. I looked at my alarm clock after doing my morning hygiene thing and it was almost seven thirty. Dang it! I needed to get Jo-Jo his Power-Point project. I pulled on a terry cloth sweat suit I had and some sneakers and ran for my door. His bus would be there soon and I was trying to get it to him before I missed it. Instead of jumping in my car, since April lived only two streets over, I ran through a pathway the kids in the neighborhood had made. As soon as I hit their street his bus was pulling off. My heart fell out of my chest. Not because I had missed his bus either. I kept walking towards April's house. I looked at the cream colored Escalade parked in her driveway as I pulled my cell from my pocket.

"Yeah," Aric answered when I called him.

"Where are you," I asked him.

"Home?"

"Really? You went right home after you left my house last night?"

"Yeah. Why?"

I jogged over to the Escalade sitting in April's driveway and pounded on the hood. The alarm went off. I looked up towards her bedroom and saw someone peek out of her blinds.

"Shit," is all I heard him say before his phone hung up.

A few seconds later he was coming out of her front door. She was not too far behind him, only she closed her screen door and stood behind it in nothing but her green bra and panties. There was that smug look of hers on her face again. I tried to move past Aric towards her, but he grabbed me. I pushed and swung at him, screaming for him to let me go. My mind didn't want to wrap around the fact that I knew he had sex with April. I could just feel it in the pit of my stomach. I could look at her body language and tell.

I bit down on my lip while shaking my head and asked, "Really, Aric? This is what you do?" I was talking with my hands and was so mad that I couldn't think straight.

He walked closer to me. "Chyanne, come on. We can talk at your place. Don't do this out here," he said while trying to grab my hands and pull me away.

Once again Aric and I were putting on a show for the neighborhood. I could tell he was annoyed by the way he was cutting his eyes at me and sighing. That pissed me off even more because he didn't have a right to be angry or annoyed.

"Why, Aric? Why would you do this to me and with her?" I screamed at him using my right hand to point towards April.

"It's not what you think, Chyanne," he countered. I could tell he was lying because he kept avoiding eye contact with me and he kept running his hands up and down his face.

"Well please tell me what it is!" I snapped at him trying to keep the tears at bay that were threatening to fall.

"Let's just go back to your place and talk."

"No, we don't have to go back to my place and talk. You can tell me all I need to know right here."

Standing there like he hadn't done a thing wrong with his arms folded across his chest, he sighed loudly and responded. "Look either we go back to your place or I'm going home. I'm not going to do this shit out here!"

My body was trembling and my mind was racing a thousand thoughts per second. April's screen door opened and she stepped out onto the front steps of her house. We stared each other down for a minute before my attention turned back to Aric. I would deal with her later. I didn't have it in me to stand in front of the neighborhood, let alone April, and have this conversation with him. So I gave in to his demands. No more than five minutes later we were back at my house. I didn't say anything to him. I jumped out of the truck and slammed the door so hard it shook! I knew he was following me into my house so I tried to slam the door in his face, but he caught it and shoved it back open. Almost immediately, I started with the questions. I barely gave him time to close the door.

"Why? Is that who was on the phone last night?"

He casually sat down before answering, "No."

"How long?" I was trying hard to keep my anger in check.

"How long what?" He arched one eyebrow, giving me a look that implied he really didn't feel as if he had to answer what I had asked.

"How long have you been having sex with her?"

He sighed. "Do you really want me to answer that, Chyanne.?

I knew steam had to be coming from my ears, eyes had to be throwing daggers and I had to be foaming from the mouth! "Yes, Aric! Why would you do some mess like that? And then you act like you don't even care that this is hurting me."

I wanted to scream. I wanted to yell, but . . . I just didn't have it in me. I was weak. He had weakened me.

My love for him made me weak. "I . . . I cannot believe you would leave my bed and go straight to hers."

"It wasn't like that, Chyanne. You're assuming shit!"

"You keep saying that, but yet, you have been lying and were going to lie to me about it. So what is it like?"

"It was a spur of the moment thing. She called me when I was on my way home and . . ."

"Oh, so you gave her your cell number too? I guess that's why the no title thing works for you, huh? Got me walking around her looking as stupid as I want to be. Did you at least use protection?"

He frowned. "Yes, Chyanne. You don't ever have to worry about catching anything. I wouldn't do that to you."

"But it's okay to screw my best friend and all of this other mess you have been doing as long as you don't give me anything right?"

I could tell I was annoying him because he only stared at me. I shook my head and walked off towards my bedroom. I didn't even know why I was wasting my time with questioning him. It was clear that he didn't feel he had done anything worth being questioned about. To be disrespected by this man, not once, but twice in less than twenty-four hours had me ready to kill somebody. I grabbed my car keys so I could get Jo-Jo his work at school. I noticed I had missed his call as I grabbed my purse.

"Where are you going," he asked me.

He saw the disk in my hand so that gave him his answer.

"It was just sex. Nothing else. April was a quick fuck that's it! She doesn't mean to me what you do. She doesn't mean anything to me at all."

"I guess the woman on the other end of the phone last night means a lot to you too, huh?"

His expression was unreadable. "It's not what you are thinking."

"Then explain it."

He walked over to me, bringing me closer to him and caressing my arms. "Listen to me. I have some things going on right now that I need to fix. Some things that I can't explain right now, but you are the only woman that I care this much about. These other women don't mean shit to me. I need you to always remember that, no matter what. Just chill and let me do what I have to do. In due time, everything will come together."

"And I guess I am supposed to accept that there are other women," I asked looking into his hazel brown eyes.

"Just accept the fact that I care enough about you to tell you the truth."

I don't know why, but at that moment Gabriel's voice was in my head. *Sometimes you have to listen to what's not being said.*

Chapter 8

For Thanksgiving the office was closed for a week. Aric and I spent that holiday together. It was just me and him for the day. Jo-Jo, Aaden, and Aaron came over and kept us company for a little bit then they were off to their dad's. Jo-Jo wanted to thank me for helping to get an A on his project. Yes, Aric and I had worked through that whole April fiasco. Don't get me wrong, I was still pissed that he had sex with her, of all people, but what was done was done. One reason I was not about to give up on him and let him go was because I didn't want April to think she had gotten to me. I was pissed enough to let him go, but I didn't want her to have him. I mean what exactly are the odds that I would even meet another man like Aric? A man like him could have a model type chick or a video vixen type, but he chose me.

He had kept his promise with leaving April alone, but other things were still bothering me. Like who that other woman was on the other end of his phone that night. He still hadn't told me the deal with her, leaving me puzzled. Later on that night Aric and I had been invited to one of his boss's house for a holiday gala. I didn't mind going, but I never expected to see Jamie there. I would find Jaime watching me from time to time or maybe I am the one who had been checking for him. I hadn't seen him since the last time he was at my house, but we had a few phone conversations. He and

I had established a nice friendship from our conversations over the phone. Maybe he kept looking because I looked different. Aric had talked me into straightening my hair. No perm, but I had gotten it pressed. My hair flowed down to the middle of my back once the stylist was done styling it. I had on very little makeup and my red dress had caused a lot of people to compliment me. It was a long red dress that complimented my full figured shape and the platinum accessories and shoes set it off.

When Gabriel complimented me I noticed Aric pulled me closer to him. I had caught Gabriel staring at me quite a few times as well. The look in his eyes was readable. There was no doubt what he would do to me if I would allow him to. Once Aric had been pulled into a conversation on target markets and what not, I snuck away and followed Jamie into the secluded area of the backyard.

I lost sight of him when he rounded the corner. I called out to him twice and got no response. I cut my losses and turned back for the house. That's when he scared the hell out of me. He was standing right behind me. I stumbled back and twisted my right ankle a bit. He caught me before I fell.

"Jamie, why didn't you answer me?" I snapped. "You scared the crap out of me."

We could still hear the music and the chatter coming from inside of the massive structure the owners called a house.

"My bad. You okay?"

He helped me to the bench that sat by a flowing angel fountain. "Yeah. I hurt my ankle though."

He kneeled down and unhooked the strap around my ankle and took my foot into his hand. "Damn, Chyanne! Why do you wear these tall heels?"

"Because I like them and I have never hurt myself in them until now."

I looked at him when he smiled. It warmed me. His locks were pulled back into a nice neat ponytail and he looked GQ ready in the black tux he was sporting. Those dark chocolate eyes were pulling me in. I started to feel bad about standing him up. I tried to apologize and he stopped me.

"I said it's cool. I'm good. You should be too," he said as he kept massaging my foot.

I could feel my foot swelling.

"You may have to get a doctor to look at this."

I nodded. "Probably so."

"You look out of this world sexy tonight. What made you straighten your hair?"

I smiled and thanked him. I didn't want him to know Aric had talked me into it so I shrugged. Over the last couple of weeks he had darn near changed my whole wardrobe. "Just wanted to try something different. You like it?"

It was his turn to shrug now. "It's beautiful. I mean you have beautiful hair, but I loved the way your fro looked on you."

I laughed because I missed my fro too and this hair was too much to keep in check. I told him as much. He laughed with me.

"I miss hanging with you, Chyanne," he said out of the blue.

I smiled and looked out over the vast expansion of the green landscape.

"I actually miss that too," I admitted when I looked back down at him.

We continued to gaze at each other until the noise from the house got louder. I looked up the surplus of stone stairs and Aric and Gabriel were standing there. Aric's face was as hard as the stone steps he was standing on. Jamie placed my foot gently down on the ground and helped me to stand when it was clear I couldn't stand on my own. My heart rate picked up a beat or two when I noticed Aric coming down the stairs towards us. Jaime picked up my shoe and handed it to me just as Aric was nearing us. Gabriel was still standing at the top of the stairs looking on with a drink in his hand.

"Hey, baby," I said nervously to Aric. "I twisted my ankle and Jamie helped me out a bit."

I was trying to ease the obvious tension.

"What are you doing back here anyway," he asked me looking at my arm still around Jamie's neck. I quickly removed it and hobbled over to Aric.

"I came out to get some air. It was kind of stuffy in there."

I knew Aric could smell bull a mile away and I knew he was calling mine. Jamie didn't move. I wished he would.

"Maybe you should be worried about her ankle instead of why she is outside, don't you think," Jamie casually asked.

My eyes got as wide as saucers. Aric glared over at Jamie. "Maybe you should mind your own business don't you think?"

"Maybe she is my business," Jamie snapped back. The cold look in his eyes chilled the already cold night.

If I could have been taken up in the Rapture right now, I wouldn't even care. I couldn't believe Jamie just said that!

Aric stepped forward a bit and said, "Say what?"

I could tell by the look on his face that this was not going in the best direction.

"Baby, please," I begged Aric as I limped in front of him to try and stop him. "Not here. Not in front of your bosses," I said so only he could hear me.

By now Gabriel had come down to give me a helping hand.

"Come on, Aric, man. It's not worth it," he said to Aric. "Chyanne needs to get to the doctor."

I was so thankful for that. Aric gave Jamie another hard stare before picking me up and carrying me around the house to the front area where the cars were waiting. A valet quickly took his ticket and brought his truck around. We were in the black Navigator tonight. Once in the car and on the highway Aric didn't say much to me and he didn't say much as we sat in the ER getting my ankle wrapped. But when we got back to his place, that was when he let me know exactly what he was thinking. After we had gotten undressed and had showered, we were lying in his bed when he broke his silence.

"You fuck that nigga?" he asked.

"No. I have never done anything with him," I lied because Jamie and I did have oral sex.

"He seemed too sure of that shit he said to me for ya'll to have never done anything."

"I went on a few dates with him. That's it."

He was quiet after that. To be honest, I was scared that I had said the wrong thing. You never knew what would set him off. My head would not stop hurting. I could hear the rustle of the covers as he moved around. He pulled me close to him and wrapped his arms around me. I could feel him hardening on my back. He loved to sleep naked.

"Chyanne."

"Yeah."

"I will hurt you up if you even think about fucking that nigga. Don't make me go there."

I didn't respond. I was just happy that was all he said. It wasn't long after that we made love. It was like heaven of course. Not the usual aggressive Aric. He made love to me slow and long. He had me climbing the walls and snatching sheets off the bed. Our bodies were wrapped so tight I didn't know where mine ended and where his began.

I was looking forward to spending the Christmas holiday with Aric. I had been making arrangements and preparations for the last couple of weeks or so. I had bought food and a couple of new outfits and we both had helped to decorate each other's houses, inside and out. I was falling behind on my Christmas shopping because I had gotten sick for about three days. Somehow I caught a stomach virus. But Aric took care of me. He had made me come home with him and he took two days off just so it wouldn't look suspicious with us both being out, but I was better now.

I parked my car in Aric's garage and pulled out the bags of food I had with me. As I unlocked the door and walked into the kitchen I could hear him on the phone. Whoever he was talking to had pissed him off. As soon as he heard me come into the kitchen he stopped talking and walked into his office. I heard him lock the door. I shook my head. He had been doing that a lot lately. I popped three Tylenol to help my headache and scratched my nipples. He didn't come back out of his office for another thirty minutes and I was too tired to argue with him. Instead, I cooked. We ate and we went to bed shortly thereafter. I could barely keep my eyes open and I didn't understand why I was so sleepy because I had basically slept all day and the night before. While in the bed that night he told me that he had decided to go home, to New York, to see his parents for Christmas. At first, I put up a fuss and I actually shed some tears. I had been doing a lot of that lately. It wasn't because he wasn't going to be here for Christmas. It was because I knew he was lying. I knew a woman had been on the other end of those secret phone calls, but what could I do? I had heard him tell her he loved her tonight and that bothered me more than anything. I was weak for this man and I hated myself for being so weak. He knew that I knew he was lying.

I could tell by the way he was looking at me when I was cursing and yelling at him and we were standing across from each other like opponents in a fight. I could tell when he pulled me close to him and tried to get me to calm down. I could tell when he stripped me of my clothes and placed kisses that ignited my insides all over my body. I could tell he knew when he spread my lips and sucked on that most sensitive part of me and when he licked, kissed, and sucked on my wet oasis. I could tell when he long stroked in and out of me. I could tell. . . .

For a week, I didn't see Aric. I didn't hear from him. Seven whole days. Seven whole nights. It broke me. I'm not going to lie. For the first few days I was sick about it. I stayed in bed crying myself stupid, but after a while I found myself calling Jamie. I needed someone to talk to and he had been that person for a while now. I had found that whenever I had problems concerning me and Aric, I called Jamie. Most times, all he did was listen, and only when I asked did he give me his opinion.

That night, he invited me to his house for dinner. He lived in Atlanta and I had to admit I was excited to see him as I knocked on his door. From the outside his place looked like an old firehouse or police station. You saw that a lot in Atlanta. Old buildings would be turned into lofts. I had on a Polo red velour sweat suit that Aric had bought me with a pair of Polo Brenly Leather sneakers. My hair was flowing down my back and around my shoulders. I was shocked when he opened the door. His locs were in disarray and he was only in a pair of cream linen draw string pants. He had on no shirt and that was the first time I had seen the tribal tattoos surrounding his upper chest. Jamie's body was the business. His upper body had the cut of a cobra head. Broad chest that fanned out and then curved down into the perfect V that had a nice package hanging beneath it. I could hear light mood music playing in the background.

"Hey, how are you," I asked him as he embraced me.

"Good, come in."

He moved to the side and ushered me in. The smell of vanilla and peppermint hit my nose as soon as I stepped inside. The inside of his place was like a wide open space. This place was so huge I believed if I would have yelled there would have been an echo. He had stained cement floors and his sofas and art work were all earth toned colors. He gave me a quick tour of the place and I must say I was impressed. Everything was in place minus a few pair of his jeans lying around. After dinner, after everything had been put away, Jamie and I lay on his oversized sofa talking about nothing and everything all at the same time.

"So I take it Aric is not around? That would be the only reason you are here right now. Am I right?" He asked.

I looked at him. "No, he's not around, but that's not the only reason I'm here."

He chuckled. "Yeah, OK Chyanne. I was born at night, but not last night."

The only luminosity we had was by candlelight but I could still make out the offhand smirk on his face. I was about to try and defend my actions, but he stopped me.

"Don't play games with me, Chyanne. I am not going to be the man you can run to when you and ole boy have problems. I am not a toy. You can't put me down and pick me up when you feel like it."

His voice was raspy and deep as he looked at me through hooded lenses. It was eleven-thirty at night Christmas Eve and here I was with Jamie. I wouldn't have thought I would be here, but here I was.

"I understand that," I said back to him. "I am not trying to hurt you Jamie, but to be honest, I don't know where he and I are going to go. I haven't heard from him in a week. I'm lonely and I just needed someone to talk to."

Neither one of us said anything for a while. I knew I had probably made him feel some type of way about what I had said, but I hated to be lied to. So I was not about to lie to him. We laid with each other well into the night, sometimes talking, at times touching. The later it got into the night, the more intense our touches became. My mind wandered to Aric. I wondered what he was doing . . . wondered who he was doing. A few times I got this feeling that I couldn't shake along with images of Aric in between another woman's thighs, sexing her like he sexed me. I wanted to call him, but couldn't bring myself to hear another call going to voicemail or another text going unanswered. That's probably what made me turn to Jamie and place his hand between my thighs once more.

Only this time, he didn't stop at just touching. Before I knew it all of my clothes were on the floor and I was about to give to Jamie what only one other man had gotten. As Jamie worked magic between my thighs, images of Aric flashed through my head. Not to say that Jamie was lacking because he definitely was not. Jamie had skills that had me salivating from the mouth. He gave me what I needed to take my mind off of Aric for a while. Not just tonight but the next night and the next one too. Jamie didn't celebrate Christmas so I helped him to set up for Kwanza. I learned that he was a freelance photographer on the side too and I let him take snap shots of me that I thought I would never do. During one of our slow sexing sessions, I let him set the camera in front of his bed and snap pictures of us.

Although I was having fun with Jamie, I found a way to send Aric a text. Simply because . . . I was missing him like crazy. I knew he was probably with whoever that woman was on the other end of the phone, but I just needed to hear something from him. He had asked me to trust him, so that's what I was doing.

I love you, I sent to him. I stayed in the bathroom for about ten minutes, hoping he would text me back. I got nothing. My feelings were hurt. I wanted to cry until I was walking out of the bathroom and my phone buzzed.

Ditto was all he replied, but that was enough for me. He may have been with whomever, and as crazy as it sounds, in my heart I knew he was thinking about me.

Chapter 9

The New Year found me back to my usual routine. There was work and there was Aric. I took it upon myself to question him on his whereabouts over the Christmas holiday. We had a knock down drag out fight about that.

"Why are you always questioning me like I am your damn child," I remembered him yelling at me.

I just shook my head and answered, "Whatever Aric. This coming from the man who will mess me up if I even think about being with another man right? Last time I checked, I was a grown woman too!"

I knew I was pushing the limit with that, but to hell with it. Yeah I had to endure him yelling and telling me, of course, not to try him, but I was not holding my tongue anymore. Forget that. He could kiss my whole entire juicy behind. So yeah I got hemmed up in a corner and I got him in my face, but he got a piece of me too. That was about a week or two ago. It is now the thirteenth of January, my birthday. Yesterday was his birthday. Yes, our birthdays fell one day after the other one. We celebrated his birthday yesterday and all he wanted to do was be inside of me all day. Not that I was complaining, but it was already a bit much to handle. He said he was making up for what he missed during the Christmas week. We went out for a while but all we could do was think about getting back home to his bed. Sambuca was a great place to celebrate with the live jazz and all, but with the romantic atmosphere and dim lighting, it didn't help our horny mood any.

While sitting at my desk, I was working on a memo to send to all of the executives. I opened my top desk drawer and noticed there was a small maroon velvet box. My heart raced and then skipped a beat. It was from Aric. I slowly picked up the box and opened it. The sight of the tear drop diamond ring set in platinum gave my heart a conniption. I almost jumped out of my skin. I calmed myself quickly, picked up the box, and walked into Aric's office.

He looked up at me and gave a smile when he saw it in my hand. "What does this mean?" I asked him. I needed to know because he was the one insisting we have no official title. "What finger do I put this on?" I asked before he could answer the first question.

I waited impatiently for his answer.

"You can put it on whatever finger you want. I don't care as long as you put it on," he answered."

Whatever thoughts and hopes I had went right out of the window. I was so sick of crying, especially over him. He walked around to the front of his desk.

He sighed before asking, "What are you crying for, Chyanne?"

I closed the box and looked up at him. "For a minute I thought maybe you actually cared about my feelings like you say . . ."

He cut me off. "I do. . . ."

"But we don't need the title right? Just as long as you can mark and tag your territory."

He frowned and walked over to me. "Why do you keep doing this, Chyanne? I keep telling you how much I care about you. My feelings won't change just because we don't have a title or just because you feel you need more to be secure. I told you there is some shit that I have to take care of first. You have to let me do that. Don't try to pressure this or try to force this into what you want it to be. The ring is not about me marking my territory. This ring is just another way to show you how deep my feelings are and how much I really do care about you."

I wiped the tears from my face and looked down at the box in my hand then back up at him. "What do you want from me Aric? You don't want us to have a title, but we do all the things that people in committed relationships do from the arguing to the love making. Is there even any future in me doing this with you?"

He pulled me into him and hugged me. "You're thinking too much about this and getting yourself all worked up over nothing. We'll talk later okay? It's your birthday, don't do this today."

I wrapped my arms back around him and we stood there until we heard the elevator ding. He removed the ring and quickly slid it on my left ring finger and then gave me a quick peck on the lips. A few minutes later we were in the break room where Justin had set up a surprise party for me. It did surprise me and we all were in for a surprise when Jamie was escorted in by security with a big flower arrangement of carnations and roses. He had about six balloons that all read happy birthday. He also had about three different gift bags. He had on dark denim loose fitting jeans, a red scoop neck sweater, and black Tims. His locks were braided back into two braids.

"Damn, bitch," Justin whispered to me. "You ain't tell me you were pulling them like that!"

The mouth of every woman in the break room had dropped to the floor. I could hear the whispers and the *'damns'* traveling around the room. My eyes diverted to Aric and the smile he was carrying only a few seconds before had disappeared. If looks could kill, Jamie would be road kill. Jamie smiled and walked over to me and pulled me into a tight hug and Lord help me, but I was not prepared for the kiss he planted on my lips. And I could have died a thousand deaths when he kept the kiss going so long that Justin started hissing and making cat calls with the other women in the room.

"I want one of him for my birthday," I heard someone say and a few other ladies laughed loudly and agreed.

When Jamie was done kissing me he handed me the gift bags and looked over to Aric. He gave a head nod and asked, "What's up Aric?"

I now knew how a person having a heart attack felt. Of course Aric gave a head nod back, since no one knew about what we had going on and now all of the rumors may stop since Jamie had pulled this stunt.

"Can I speak to you outside?" Jamie asked.

I didn't know what else to say so I nodded and let him lead me out into the hall.

"Did you get the pictures?" he asked.

I nodded. He had sent me the pictures he had taken of us and he made a few into artistic nudes.

"Yeah. I checked the mail this morning and they were there."

"You like them?"

"Love them. Didn't know they would come out so perfect." We were quiet for a minute before I asked, "Why did you do that, Jamie?"

He shrugged. "Because I could. What is he going to do? Let everyone know he's having sex with his assistant?"

I cut my eyes at him.

He held his hands up like he was being robbed. "Well, hey. You said you guys weren't in a relationship. Not me, but look I have to go. I'll get at you a little later."

We said our good-bye and he was gone. When I walked back into the room Aric was gone and a few of the other executives were as well. We finished up the party and then it was back to business. Aric didn't come back to his office for the rest of the day, and I didn't get to finish all of my work until about six. I tried calling him a few times but got no answer. I already knew what would happen as soon as he laid eyes on me and I was preparing myself for the fight. I stopped and picked up a few items for my house before going home. As soon as I saw his platinum colored 7 series BMW in my driveway my head started to hurt. I quickly got all of my bags out of the car and made my way inside. I headed for the kitchen and started putting away the items I had purchased. I was shaking and my nerves were on end. So much so that I knocked over the three glasses sitting on my counter.

"Damn!" I felt as if I was about to pass out.

I rushed out of the kitchen to get the broom from the small closet in my dining room. I didn't see or hear Aric, but I knew he was here. I could feel his anger. I swept the glass up and was going to go to my bedroom until I walked out of the kitchen and saw Aric was sitting on my sofa. I already knew it was about to be some mess. I could tell by the way he was sitting and by the way his eyes cast a despondent glance at me. Once again his arms were thrown across the back of the couch and he was sitting with his legs spread wide. He had changed into some gray sweats with a white thermal shirt and all white Nike Air Force Ones.

"Aric I don't feel like fighting . . ."

"You fuck him?"

Something in his voice unnerved me.

I lied. "No."

He stood and his eyes told me to try again.

"Don't lie to me."

I was balling and un-balling my fists trying to get my nerves together.

"I said no."

I panicked when he slowly began to walk over to me. I wasn't prepared for him to pull the brown envelope with the pictures of me and Jamie out and throw them in my face. I turned my head and put my hands to my face to avoid impact. I had left them on my dresser this morning because I was in a hurry leaving. I didn't think to put them away. I looked down at the pictures of me and Jaime having sex . . . Jamie's face between my thighs . . . me with my head thrown back enjoying it . . . me on top of Jamie . . . Jamie on top of me . . . and so on . . . and so on. The pictures had flown all around my living room. Before I could fix my mouth to say anything Aric was in my face. He looked like a mad man. His eyes were red and his breathing was rampant. With his hand gripping the back of my neck and my hair, he pulled me to him. I don't know but a certain level of defiance arose in me.

"Let me go, Aric," I screamed and struggled with him.

He nearly lifted me off of the floor and threw me across the room. I got up to try and run for my room but slipped on one of the pictures and twisted my ankle again. I didn't have time to relive that pain because Aric had snatched me up by my shirt and yanked me to him. With the way he had me I had no choice but to look up at him.

"So did you fuck him?" he asked me again. His voice was deep, low, and lethal.

I was still trying to snatch away from him to no avail. So I stood very still and gazed at him.

"I did with him whatever you did with whomever you were with in New York!"

He pushed me back into the sofa so hard my back hit the base of it and it caused nerve wracking pain in my lower back. I didn't even have time to recover from the flashing lights behind my eye lids because he grabbed me again and started dragging me towards my room. I kicked, screamed, swung wildly. I was scared. One of my kicks connected with his thigh and I got up and tried to run for my front door. Before I even made it he grabbed me from behind by my hair and then picked me up by my waist. Once we made it to my room, he slammed my door, locked it, and slammed me against the wall.

"Aric please stop! It meant nothing," I cried. "He meant nothing."

My body was hurting and my ankle was burning. My breaths were coming out in spurts and I had become nauseous.

"You thought I was playing when I told you I would fuck you up . . ."

"I'm sorry, Aric! Damn! I don't even know what you were doing in New York and you want to be mad at me for being with somebody else," I screamed at him cutting him off.

I tried to duck when he went to snatch me up by my hair again. Images of my childhood flashed before my eyes and before I knew it my fist had balled and I was fighting back. Images of my father dragging my mother through the halls of our house by her hair haunted me. I could see my mother kicking and screaming, fighting for her life. My hand connected with his face and I guess that pissed him off even more because that's when he backhanded me. My head snapped back as I went flying across my bed. My jaw felt like it would come unhinged and I was so dizzy that the room was spinning. I saw him coming toward me and I moved so fast getting off the bed and trying to get away from him that I fell onto the floor on the side of my bed. It felt like I fractured my hip I fell so hard, but I crawled to my bathroom and quickly locked the door.

"Open the door, Chyanne!"

I slid down to the floor and rocked back and forth. My whole body was hurting. My head was pounding and so was my heart. I could not believe this mess. My breathing was labored and I felt as if I was about to throw up any minute. I ignored Aric's banging on the door demanding that I open it. I ignored his pleading that he didn't mean to hit me. I turned my light on and looked at myself in the mirror. My eye was already swelling and they both were blood shot red. I touched my jaw and winched at the pain. I could barely stand on my ankle and my hair made me look like a mad woman. I turned the water on to take a sip and as soon as I did I had to throw up. I made it to the toilet just in time. I threw up so much that all I could do was dry heave for a minute. Aric was still knocking on the door and threatened to kick it down if I didn't open it up. I loved this man, yes I did, but not more than I loved myself. He would not be putting his hands on me another time because this was it! I was done! This was too much to be putting up with for me not to even be in a relationship with him. I was a lot of things, but stupid I would not continue to be. I wanted to be mad at my mother right now. All I saw her do was get her behind kicked, sometimes just because my daddy was having a bad day. I saw her fight with woman after woman because my father just didn't give a damn and I always wondered why she never left. I promised myself that

I would not be my mother. I was startled out of my thoughts when Aric beat on the door again.

"Aric, please," I screamed at the door. "Just leave!! Leave me alone and get out of my house!"

"Chyanne, just open the damn door," he yelled.

"No, Aric. I'm done. I . . . cannot do this . . . .This is too much. You put your hands on me too much!"

"Don't act like you haven't done that shit too! But that's how you are going to do me? You fuck that nigga and have him mail the pictures to your house! That shit ain't cool. . . ."

"But it was cool when you where screwing April right? And who ever . . ."

He kicked the door and I jumped. "Get out of my house, Aric!"

"Come make me get the fuck out," he snapped.

I never left my bathroom because Aric didn't leave my room. I pulled my suit off and looked at dark, purple, and red bruises on my side and back. My hip and thigh were hurting and caused me to limp. I was happy that my linen closet was in my bathroom. I pulled down a pillow and two comforters and made myself a pallet in my oversized garden tub. That is where I slept. Throughout the night I could hear Aric moving beside the bathroom door. Every so often he would twist the knob or ask for me to let him in. Each time I ignored him.

I woke up at about seven the next morning. I heard him yelling at someone on his phone. I heard when he slammed my front door and left. I called out to him to see if he was still there and when I got no answer, I finally left my bathroom. He was gone. I sat down and wrapped my ankle and popped some Tylenol for the rest of my body aches. I would go see a doctor later about my ankle. I was having sharp pains in my stomach and hoping the Tylenol would hurry up and kick in. I sat down at my computer and typed up my resignation letter after picking up all of the photos. No way was I going to keep working there with him either. He could have it all. I showered and put on a purple velour jogging suit with my white DK sneakers. Once I got to my job, I stopped by HR to drop off a resignation letter. When people kept asking why I was leaving, I just told them that I had family issues. I made sure to keep on my glasses so my eye and face could stay hidden. I knew half of the bruise on my jaw still showed, but oh well. I hopped on the elevator and made my way to the seventh floor so I could leave Aric the same letter and clean out my desk. I waited for the elevator to stop and was surprised to see Lola talking to Gabriel.

"Hey, Chyanne," Lola spoke to me. Although I found it strange that she spoke to me, I was prepared to speak back.

Before I could speak out of nowhere somebody punched me so hard, I heard bells ringing. I heard half of the office gasp as I stumbled back. I only had a few seconds to see it was an exotic looking dark skinned chick. She was a tall skinny woman and she had long wavy black hair. She came for me again and I caught her before she got to me again. I threw a punch that knocked her backwards. She looked stunned but I didn't give her time to think about it. I had no idea who she was or why she'd hit me, but I caught that broad by her hair and slung her to the floor.

I was quite sure it looked like something off of a YouTube fight video, but I didn't care. I kept her down by the hair and beat her like she had threatened my life. Every slap, punch, stomp, and kick I gave her was from the pent-up anger I had held inside of me. I beat her for the slap I never paid April back for. I stomped her for the mess Aric had put me through. Through her screams and yells for me to let her go, I imagined she was April and Aric and beat her like she stole something from me! Gabriel had run and tried to get me off of her giving her a chance to get up and kick me in my stomach. I maneuvered around him and punched her in the face as many times as I could before he was finally able to get some help in pulling us apart. One of the security officers had pulled whoever she was to one end of the office and Gabriel was dragging me kicking and screaming to get back to her. He had picked up my purse and shades, and by now, everyone had seen the big bruise on my face. Gabriel escorted me to the elevator and he pushed the buttons for the door to close. Once the doors closed, I let out a frustrated scream.

"Calm down, Chyanne," he said to me.

"Who in hell was that?" I yelled at him. I hadn't meant to. It just came out that way.

"That was my sister," he said to me.

I was confused. "OK, and what did she come after me for? I don't even know her."

Gabriel looked as if he was about to say something that I didn't want to hear. "She's my sister and . . . Aric's wife."

Even though the elevator was moving, my world stopped.

"No . . . no . . . no . . ." I kept repeating that myself.

I was so tired of crying, but I couldn't help it. I leaned forward and rested my hands on my knees then came back up to look at Gabriel.

"What . . . what do you mean his wife?"

Gabriel exhaled and held his hand to steady me. I guess I looked how I felt. Faint.

"She's his wife, Chyanne," he answered.

I looked up and squeezed my eyes shut as I tried to catch my breath. I don't know why . . . wait . . . yes I do. I know why my hand connected with Gabriel's face. He could have told me the truth.

He must have known what I was thinking because he absorbed the slap and said, "It wasn't my place to tell you, Chyanne."

"Like hell it wasn't! If not for me, then at least for your sister!"

"Not everything is always black and white."

"You are so full of it and you know it," I snapped at him.

That was the last thing I said to him. I stepped off into the parking deck and limped to my car with Gabriel calling out to me, trying to get my attention. I drove like a bat out of hell trying to get away from that place and all things Aric. Through tears I barreled through traffic. Lord, please let this be a lie! Please tell me the man that I had fallen in love with was not a married man! I was so hurt. The physical pain bombarding my body had nothing on what I was feeling on the inside right now. I wondered how long his wife had known about me. Where had she been all this time? Was it her that he had been talking to on the phone? Was she who he was with in New York? All of these questions attacked my mind at one time. I felt deceived in a sense. Now I knew what he meant when he said he had something that he needed to take care of. It all made sense now, but it still hurt like hell! I had been an unwilling mistress, but at least now I knew that he was not just treating me like crap because of my weight. His wife was the complete opposite of me and it looked like he was giving her hell too!

***

I didn't hear from Aric for two days. My body was aching and my stomach wouldn't stop hurting. The pain had crippled me. I grabbed my stomach and toppled over in pain as I tried to make my way to the bathroom. The pain was so bad that my knees hit the floor hard and I yelled out. I was tempted to call the police and have her arrested. Just thinking about being sucker punched had me wanting to whoop that trick again.

My mind kept going back to that night that Shelley had asked Aric about 'Stephanie'. I wanted to kick myself for being so stupid and naïve. But the pain in my stomach wouldn't allow me time to think about it. I crawled to the bathroom as I heard my front door open. Through the throbbing pain in my ankle and the gut clenching pain in my stomach, I stood and limped back into my bedroom. Aric stopped at my bedroom door when he saw me. I guess the scratches all over my face and neck and the bruise he had left on my face stopped him. I knew by now that it was no secret what had happened.

Justin had already called me and told me the talk had started. I was so mad at the man standing in front of me all I could do was struggle to take the ring off my finger, and when I did, I threw it at his head. He easily dodged it and it traveled into the hall, hitting the floor. I heard it bounce a few times.

"You are a lying . . . I don't even have words for you right now. So why not just leave and do both of us a favor?"

My eyes were filled with tears and my throat already hurt from crying all night before. It felt like somebody had fisted the lower half of my stomach and was twisting it for dear life, but I refused to flinch in pain. I wouldn't let him see me in any more pain than he had already caused. He tried to come near me and I quickly picked up the thick glass vase on my dresser. He stopped.

"I know you are mad, Chyanne, but you are going to put that damn vase down so I can talk to you," he snapped at me.

I looked him over. He was still in business attire and what usually turned me on about him, his eyes, dimples, lips, build, accent, it now revolted me.

"Forget you, Aric! I hate the day I walked into your office. Curse the day I let you kiss me, the day I let you touch me! I hate you so much right now!"

I was screaming and yelling. I knew by now I was the talk of the neighborhood.

"Watch how the hell you speak to me first of all and don't act like I am not hurt by this shit too," he started.

I looked at this man like he had lost his ever loving mind.

"Hurt! You hurt? You lying son of a bitch!"

I yelled that in disbelief and before I knew it I had stepped forward and launched the vase at him. He ducked.

"Chyanne, you had better calm the hell down! Let me explain . . ."

"You don't have to explain a damn thing," I said through bated breaths.

The pain had me sweating, I was hurting so badly. I squeezed my eyes shut and then quickly opened them.

"Keep . . . your damn explanation . . ."

My vision was becoming blurry . . .

"Chyanne," I heard him call out to me as he inched his way closer to me.

"Don't . . . don't come near me, Aric. . . ."

My legs felt unsteady as if they were crumbling underneath me and all I remember is hearing Aric call my name and rushing to catch me as I hit the floor.

When I woke up it was to the beeps of the machines surrounding me. I looked around and saw I was in a hospital room. I saw Aric sitting to the left of me.

Although I was still mad at him I asked, "What happened?"

He leaned forward looking at me. "You passed out."

There was an expression on his face that I couldn't read and I didn't really care to try and figure it out. I was more concerned with what was wrong with me. I wanted to page a nurse or something but was too weak to move my arms.

"Will you page a nurse for me and then leave?"

I was so serious with him.

"I will call you a nurse, but I am not going anywhere."

He stood and I rolled my eyes. I was not in the mood to fight.

"They will be back soon anyway. They said they were running some tests," he told me before standing and walking over to the table where a pitcher of water was sitting.

"Tests for what?"

"You need to drink some water," he said to me before answering. "They said you were dehydrated."

Come to think about I hadn't eaten or drunk anything in two days. I tried to snatch the Styrofoam cup from him but he must have known I would have because he had a tight grip on the cup. I rolled my eyes again and eased the cup from his grip. He cut his eyes at me and pressed the button to let the bed up to angle it so I could drink. He removed his watch as he always did when he was going to play in my hair. I moved my head and side eyed him hard. He only adjusted my pillow. I tried to bring the cup to my mouth and my hand was shaking like I had Parkinson's. He watched me as I tried twice to drink from the cup, but wasted more on me than I did the first time. He removed the cup from my hands, poured more water into it, and then held it to my mouth. I didn't want to take anything from him. I kept my lips tight.

"Drink the damn water, Chyanne! Stop . . ."

Before he could finish, I mustered up enough strength and knocked the cup from his hand to the floor. Water splashed all over his expensive suit. I would die of thirst before I took anything from him again.

Before he could retaliate or before I could finish my thoughts a tall black woman in a white lab coat entered the room. She introduced herself as Dr. St. Simeon. I listened as she explained that they had run a few tests and asked when my last menstrual cycle was. I had to think back and told her it was in October. I also told her that my cycle had a mind of its own and came and went as it pleased. She nodded and I waited for her to say more.

"Well that explains it," she said as she scribbled notes.

"Explains what?"

She looked at me and smiled. "Why you are twelve to thirteen weeks pregnant and don't know it."

"Excuse me!" I shouted that at her. She looked taken aback and I apologized. I calmed myself enough for her to repeat what she had said.

"Your body shut down on you because you haven't been getting the proper prenatal care and it looks like you have been in a fight or two. Do you need me to call the police? Is anyone physically harming you at home, Ms. Johnson? There are laws in the state of Georgia that protects a woman with child against any kind of domestic violence. Once again, is anyone physically harming you Ms. Johnson?"

She looked over at Aric like she cared even less for his presence than I did. She slowly rolled her eyes from him back over to me.

I shook my head. "No." Although I wanted to have him and his wife arrested, I was more concerned with the life that was or was still inside of me. "Did I lose the baby?"

"No, but you were very close to it. We are going to keep you here overnight to keep an eye on you to determine if you get to go home or if we keep you in here until you have this baby. It is possible that you may still miscarry and just to be sure that we are out of trouble and in the clear we will run more tests. Your cervix is thin and your progesterone levels are low, and for that reason, it may be a possibility that you may have to either stay in here until you deliver or we may seek other solutions like the P17 shot. If it comes down to any of those things, I will explain everything to you thoroughly at that time. Cool?"

It took me a minute to register what she was saying to me, but I nodded. She gave Aric the once over again and walked out of the room. If I was twelve to thirteen weeks pregnant that meant I got pregnant around the first time we had sex. I fiddled with my fingers and held my head down. Here I was twenty five years old; I had quit my job, and was pregnant by a married man. How in the hell did I find myself here? I wanted to ask Aric so many questions, but my mind could only think about this life that was inside of me. Tears started to slowly fall down my face. I looked over at Aric and he was standing there with his arms folded across his wide chest.

I was about to ask him about this wife of his and what we were going to do about this baby, but before I could open my mouth, he asked "Is it my baby?"

I frowned and looked at him. "Are you really asking me that?"

He shrugged with a nonchalant look on his face. "I'm just saying, I did see pictures of you fucking another. . . ."

"Oh Lord! Here we go! Really Aric? So what do you want? A DNA test?"

"I don't care what you get as long as it's something to let me know this baby is mine," he said before wiping his hand down his face and exhaling loudly. "But, if it is mine, then I guess you will be having this *lying son of a bitch's* baby, huh?

I rolled my eyes, shook my head, and folded my arms over my ample breasts and sarcastically remarked, "Tell me about it."

LAILA LALAMI

· *Morocco* ·

❖

THE POLITICS OF READING

I GREW UP in a house full of books. One of my earliest and fondest memories is of my parents curled up on opposite corners of the divan, with a novel or a memoir in their hands. I suppose it was only natural that I became a voracious reader myself. Yet I didn't begin to read the literature of my own country until later in life—not because of lack of taste or laziness, but because of the vagaries of history.

When the French colonized Morocco in 1912, they did not simply engage in the systematic plunder of its natural and human resources, they also renamed towns and villages, replaced the symbol on the national flag, and imposed French as the language of business and administration. A small number of Moroccans were trained in French schools, and groomed to become clerks, people who could help run the empire without threatening it. After independence in 1956, the Moroccan government embarked on a large-scale effort to open up education to everyone, but it failed to smoothly, or completely, replace French with Arabic and Berber. By the mid-1970s, nearly all the children's books available in my hometown of Rabat were still in French. So it was that, while an American child might start her reading life with E. B. White and Beverly Cleary, and a British child might be given the stories of Roald Dahl and Enid Blyton, I, though a Moroccan, was weaned on Hergé and Jules Verne, Théophile Gautier and Alexandre Dumas.

Over time, the school curriculum began to include novels, stories, and poems from North Africa. Starting in the sixth grade, we were assigned works such as *Le Fils du Pauvre* (*The Poor Man's Son*) by the Algerian Mouloud Feraoun, *Iradat Al-Hayat* (*The Will to Live*) by the Tunisian Aboul-Qacem Echchebi, *Al-Ayyam* (*The Days*) by the Egyptian Taha Hussein, and many of Naguib Mahfouz's novels, including *Bayn Al-Qasrayn* (*Palace Walk*). These books hit me with a strange, revelatory power, so deeply did I identify with the characters. Their names, their languages, their customs were recognizable to me; their families' concerns were similar to mine; their society's troubles were those of mine. As a small child, literature had been exclusively the realm of the foreign and the unusual, but in my adolescence I discovered that it also included the close and the mundane. There were many people, many lives, many stories in books—things were delightfully more complicated.

With a few exceptions, the school curriculum stayed away from contemporary Moroccan authors. This might have had something to do with the fact that some of our writers were directly or indirectly critical of the government, and had occasionally been censored. Driss Chraïbi's *Le Passé Simple* (*The Simple Past*) was banned for a few years, presumably because the tale of an angry, French-educated young man constantly at odds with his traditionalist Moroccan father (who is referred to only as "Le Seigneur" or "The Lord" in the book) was deemed transgressive in a country still reeling from the struggle and sacrifices that led to independence from France. Mohamed Choukri's powerful and autobiographical *Al-Khubz Al-Hafi* (*For Bread Alone*) was also censored for many years, while the English-language translation, by Paul Bowles, sold more than 100,000 copies in America. Abdellatif Laabi, the poet who founded the seminal literary magazine *Anfas/Souffles,* spent time in a Kenitra prison for his political activities. Tahar Ben Jelloun's frank treatment of sexual identity in novels such as *L'Enfant de Sable* (*The Sand Child*) and its sequel, *La Nuit Sacrée* (*The Sacred Night*), ensured he would never be assigned at the junior or high school level.

But, through recommendations from teachers, parents, or older siblings, my friends and I read all these writers. I remember how we passed around copies of Choukri's book to each other (the authorities were, thankfully, never very good at enforcing their own bans, and *Al-Khubz Al-Hafi* could still be found at used-book stores, or in French translation). I remember reading Tahar Ben Jelloun's *Harrouda* with as much trepidation as I had felt when I first laid my hands on a copy of *Lady Chatterley's Lover.* I remember falling in love with the mother in *La Civilisation, Ma Mère,* because I had at last met a Muslim heroine who was more than a sad, helpless victim. So I managed.

Later, when I went to college to study English, I was fortunate enough to take an African literature class that introduced me to African novelists who write in English, among whom were Chinua Achebe, Wole Soyinka, and Ngũgĩ wa Thiong'o. I remember reading *A Man of the People* and thinking that Chief the Honorable M.A. Nanga, M.P., would have fit right into our Parliament in Rabat, and that Odili could have been one of our teachers. I was struck by the fact that, even though these characters lived in a culture that was as different in terms of language and religion as any European culture, we shared a common experience.

I had not come across Achebe's work before, because of the terrible lack of translations into Arabic on the one hand, and the paucity of French translations of English-language African authors on the other. One legacy of colonialism is an artificial division of Africa between Francophone, Lusophone, and Anglophone regions, which is unfortunately carried through in publishing, distribution, and translation. Too often, readers have access only to writers from their own region, which is very limiting. Too often, Western critics who have read in one linguistic tradition make claims about all of Africa. I remember reading in more than one American newspaper that the magnificent *Things Fall Apart* was the first African novel—an absurd claim. We need more reading across regions.

If my experience is any indication, colonialism—and its love child, dictatorship—have had quite a bit to do with the way in which North African literature was read and taught from the mid-1970s to the late 1980s. Of course, things have changed somewhat since then, and nowadays these writers' works, as well as children's books in Arabic and Berber, are more widely available in bookstores. But now we are experiencing another great upheaval that is likely to affect our literature—globalization.

Large numbers of immigrants from Mauritania, Morocco, Algeria, Tunisia, Libya, Egypt and the Sudan now live abroad. Fleeing civil wars or dictatorship, or seeking greater economic opportunity, they have settled in Western Europe, America and even as far as Australia. The writers among them have begun to produce work written in the language of their host countries. Ahdaf Soueif, Hisham Matar, and Leila Aboulela write in English; Fouad Laroui and Edmond Amran el Maleh write in French; Abdelkader Benali and Hafid Bouazza write in Dutch; Amara Lakhouss writes in Italian; and the list goes on. Meanwhile, writers like Leila Abouzeid, Alaa Al-Aswany, Bahaa Taher, and Mohammed Berrada continue to live in their native countries and write in Arabic.

By and large, writers who live in North Africa have to be mindful of state censors, while those in the diaspora need not fear being thrown in jail for their work. But diaspora writers face another cost: being viewed suspiciously by the representation mafia. At a reading in Kenitra last year, a Moroccan reader of my first book asked me whether it had been published in America because it depicted the corruption of Moroccan society. During the back and forth of the discussion, the argument was soon turned into its opposite: that I had depicted corruption *in order* to be published. Although I am frustrated by such comments, I also understand that they are rooted in a certain reality. It is infinitely easier for a North African novel to be published in Europe or America if it trades in clichés rather than in complex fictional realities.

In addition, diaspora writers, particularly those who work in English, have greater access to translations and to large audiences, while those who live in North Africa have a hard time finding a wider readership. There are also great differences in setting, style, and literary influences. I sometimes feel I can hear echoes of George Eliot and Jane Austen in Ahdaf Soueif's work. Abdelkader Benali seems to me to owe a greater debt to Gabriel García Márquez than to his countryman Mohamed Choukri. Some of the younger writers, like Hafid Bouazza, might even resent being labeled as North African writers, rather than Dutch writers, or writers *tout court.*

Because of this huge diversity, I think it is quite difficult to speak of one North African literature. It is even harder to speak of one African literature. Africa is made up of 40 nations, whose people speak a multitude of languages and belong to many different religious traditions and ethnic groups. The continent is larger than China, Europe and the United States put together. Just as world maps often shrink the size of

Africa to that of South America for representational purposes, speaking of *one* African literature risks giving the impression that it is a monolithic literature. It risks pointing to a unique literary tradition. It risks equating Africanness with blackness. I think, therefore, that it is more proper to speak of North African and African *literatures.*

It is, of course, possible to organize these literatures along certain lines, whether genre, temporal, stylistic, or thematic. For instance, because nearly all of the continent was under colonial rule in the 19th and 20th centuries, many novels originating in Africa share certain themes: the struggle for freedom, the pain of exile, the plight of immigrants and asylum-seekers. I can see many similarities between the French-educated Driss Ferdi in Driss Chraïbi's *The Simple Past,* and the British-educated Mustafa Sa'eed in Tayib Salih's *Season of Migration to the North.* In Muslim African literature, whether from Morocco, Egypt or Senegal, the foibles of a religious society have provided inspiration to many writers. Leila Abouzeid's *Year of the Elephant,* Alifa Rifaat's *Distant View of a Minaret* and Mariama Ba's *So Long a Letter* could easily be read together.

"All novels belong to a family," the late Edward Said once wrote, "and any reader of novels is a reader of this complex family to which they all belong." Whereas I was initially exposed to only a few members of this family when I was a child, my hope is that today's children will get to meet as many relatives as possible.

NAWAL EL SAADAWI

· *Egypt* ·

✤

from WOMAN AT POINT ZERO

"HOW CAN YOU be one of the masters? A woman on her own cannot be a master, let alone a woman who's a prostitute. Can't you see you're asking for the impossible?"

"The word impossible does not exist for me," I said.

I tried to slip through the door, but he pushed me back and shut it. I looked him in the eye and said, "I intend to leave."

He stared back at me. I heard him mutter, "You will never leave."

I continued to look straight at him without blinking. I knew I hated him as only a woman can hate a man, as only a slave can hate his master. I saw from the expression in his eyes that he feared me as only a master can fear his slave, as only a man can fear a woman. But it lasted for only a second. Then the arrogant expression of the master, the aggressive look of the male who fears nothing, returned. I caught hold of the latch of the door to open it, but he lifted his arm up in the air and slapped me. I raised my hand even higher than he had done, and brought it down violently on his face. The whites of his eyes went red. His hand started to reach for the knife he carried in his pocket, but my hand was quicker than his. I raised the knife and buried it deep in his neck, pulled it out of his neck and then thrust it deep into his chest, pulled it out of his chest and plunged it deep into his belly. I stuck the knife into almost every part of his body. I was astonished to find how easily my hand moved as I thrust the knife into his flesh, and pulled it out almost without effort. My surprise was all the greater since I had never done what I was doing before. A question flashed through my mind. Why was it that I had never stabbed a man before? I realized that I had been afraid, and that the fear had been within me all the time, until the fleeting moment when I read fear in his eyes.

I opened the door and walked down the stairs into the street. My body was as light as a feather, as though its weight had been nothing more than the accumulation of fear over the years. The night was silent, the darkness filled me with wonder, as though light had only been one illusion after another dropping like veils over my eyes. The Nile had something almost magical about it. The air was fresh, invigorating. I walked down the street, my head held high to the heavens, with the pride of having destroyed all masks to reveal what is hidden behind. My footsteps broke the silence with their steady rhythmic beat on the pavement. They were neither fast as though I was hurrying away from something in fear, nor were they slow. They were the footsteps of a woman who believed in herself, knew where she was going, and could see her goal. They were the footsteps of a woman wearing expensive leather shoes, with strong high heels, her feet arched in a feminine curve, rising up to full rounded legs, with a smooth, taut skin and not a single hair.

No one would have easily recognized me. I looked no different from respectable, upper-class women. My hair had been done by a stylist who catered only to the rich. My lips were painted in the natural tone preferred by respectable women because it neither completely hides nor completely exposes their lust. My eyes were penciled in perfect lines drawn to suggest a seductive appeal, or a provocative withdrawal. I looked no different from the wife of an upper-class government official occupying a high position of authority. But my firm, confident steps resounding on the pavement proved that I was nobody's wife.

I crossed by a number of men working in the police force, but none of them realized who I was. Perhaps they thought I was a princess, or a queen, or a goddess. For who else would hold her head so high as she walked? And who else's footsteps could resound in this way as they struck the ground? They watched me as I passed by, and I kept my head high like a challenge to their lascivious eyes. I moved along as calm as ice, my steps beating down with a steady unfaltering sound. For I knew that they stood there waiting for a woman like me to stumble, so that they could throw themselves on her like birds of prey.

At the corner of the street I spotted a luxurious car, with the head of a man protruding from the window, its tongue almost hanging out. He opened the door of the car and said,

"Come with me."

I held back and said, "No."

"I will pay whatever you ask for."

"No," I repeated.

"Believe me, I will pay you anything you want."

"You cannot pay my price, it's very high."

"I can pay any price. I'm an Arab prince."

"And I am a princess."

"I'll pay a thousand."

"No."

"Two thousand, then."

I looked deep into his eyes. I could tell he was a prince or from the ruling family, for there was a lurking fear in their depths. "Three thousand," I said. "I accept."

In the soft luxurious bed, I closed my eyes, and let my body slip away from me. It was still young and vigorous, strong enough to retreat, powerful enough to resist. I felt his body bearing down on my breast, heavy with long untold years of his life, swollen with stagnant sweat. A body full of flesh from years of eating beyond his needs, beyond his greed. With every movement he kept repeating the same stupid question:

"Do you feel pleasure?"

And I would close my eyes and say, "Yes."

Each time he rejoiced like a happy fool, and repeated his question with a gasping breath and each time I gave the same answer: "Yes."

With the passing moments his foolishness grew, and with it his assurance that my repeated affirmations of pleasure were true. Every time I said "yes" he beamed at me like an idiot, and an instant later I could feel the weight of his body bear down on me, more heavily than before. I could stand no more, and just when he was on the point of repeating the same stupid question again, I snapped out angrily,

"No!"

When he held out his hand with the money, I was still wildly angry with him. I snatched the notes from his hand and tore them up into little pieces with a pent-up fury.

The feel of the notes under my fingers was the same as that of the first piastre ever held between them. The movement of my hands as I tore the money to pieces, tore off the veil, the last, remaining veil from before my eyes, to reveal the whole enigma which had puzzled me throughout, the true enigma of my life. I rediscovered the truth I had already discovered many years before when my father held out his hand to me with the first piastre he had ever given me. I returned to the money in my hand and with a redoubled fury tore the remaining bank notes into shreds. It was as though I was destroying all the money I had ever held, my father's piastre, my uncle's piastre, all the piastres I had ever known, and at the same time destroying all the men I had ever known, one after the other in a row: my uncle, my husband, my father, Marzouk and Bayoumi, Di'aa, Ibrahim, and tearing them all to pieces one after the other, ridding myself of them once and for all, removing every trace their piastres had left on my fingers, tearing away the very flesh of my fingers to leave nothing but bone, ensuring that not a single vestige of these men would remain at all.

His eyes opened wide in amazement as he watched me tear up the whole sheaf of bank notes. I heard him say:

"You are verily a princess. How did I not believe you right from the start?"

"I'm not a princess," I said angrily.

"At first I thought you were a prostitute."

"I am not a prostitute. But right from my early days my father, my uncle, my husband, all of them, taught me to grow up as a prostitute."

The prince laughed as he eyed me again and then said, "You are not telling the truth. From your face, I can see you are the daughter of a king."

"My father was no different from a king except for one thing."

"And what is that?"

"He never taught me to kill. He left me to learn it alone as I went through life."

"Did life teach you to kill?"

"Of course it did."

"And have you killed anybody yet?"

"Yes, I have."

He stared at me for a brief moment, laughed, and then said, "I can't believe that someone like you can kill."

"Why not?"

"Because you are too gentle."

"And who said that to kill does not require gentleness?"

He looked into my eyes again, laughed, and said, "I cannot believe that you are capable of killing anything, even a mosquito."

"I might not kill a mosquito, but I can kill a man."

He stared at me once more, but this time only very quickly, then said, "I do not believe it."

"How can I convince you that what I say is true?"

"I do not really know how you can do that."

So I lifted my hand high up above my head and landed it violently on his face.

"Now you can believe that I have slapped you. Burying a knife in your neck is just as easy and requires exactly the same movement."

This time, when he looked at me, his eyes were full of fear.

I said, "Perhaps now you will believe that I am perfectly capable of killing you, for you are no better than an insect, and all you do is to spend the thousands you take from your starving people on prostitutes."

Before I had time to raise my hand high up in the air once more, he screamed in panic like a woman in trouble. He did not stop screaming until the police arrived on the scene.

He said to the police, "Don't let her go. She's a criminal, a killer."

And they asked me, "Is what he says true?"

"I am a killer, but I've committed no crime. Like you, I kill only criminals."

"But he is a prince, and a hero. He's not a criminal."

"For me the feats of kings and princes are no more than crimes, for I do not see things the way you do."

"You are a criminal," they said, "and your mother is a criminal."

"My mother was not a criminal. No woman can be a criminal. To be a criminal one must be a man."

"Now look here, what is this that you are saying?"

"I am saying that you are criminals, all of you: the fathers, the uncles, the husbands, the pimps, the lawyers, the doctors, the journalists, and all men of all professions."

They said, "You are a savage and dangerous woman."

"I am speaking the truth. And truth is savage and dangerous."

MOHAMED MAGANI

· *Algiers* ·

❖

from THE BUTCHER'S AESTHETIC

Translated from the French by Lulu Norman

THE TWO FRIENDS' meetings resembled a ritual that went back to the years of holy struggle when they would drink more cups of coffee than they could count to give them energy, a small vice Laid Touhami had picked up in the mountains and the mayor at a young age, since his father considered coffee an aphrodisiac and permanently wore a necklace of coffee beans round his neck.

In fact, coffee had been behind Zineddine Ayachi's flight into the Ouarsenis and his joining the ranks of the Front. One day an enemy unit invaded his house on the false tip-off that he'd been helping the rebels, supplied by a local collaborator who was operating on a large scale for lack of specific names. His information targeted blocks of houses demarcated by roads and alleyways and numbered in sections. The soldiers surrounded Zineddine Ayachi's house; some of them climbed onto the roof while others kicked in the door with their boots. Four men suddenly landed in front of him as he sat in the yard. He stared in terror at the black jaws of the submachine guns. A finger pointed to the coffeepot beside him and a voice screamed: "Who's been here? Where are the others?" The soldier seized the single cup and the coffeepot, which he overturned. The black sand of coffee grounds fell on Zineddine Ayachi's foot, and drips of coffee stained his white shirt in damp zigzags.

"It was me! It was me!" he said.

"This coffeepot is empty," said the soldier.

"I drank it all, it was me," said Zineddine Ayachi.

"It must hold at least ten cups. You weren't alone! Where are the others?"

"There's only my family. I drink a lot of coffee. I can't help it."

"You Arab donkey! You're going to show us what you can do."

Zineddine Ayachi's wife put the coffeepot on the fire, half full of water. The soldier giving the orders filled it to the brim, then poured a packet of coffee into the boiling water. "A man that fond of coffee must like it strong," he said to Zineddine Ayachi's wife, who sensed her husband's imminent ordeal. All the soldiers gathered in the yard. None of them wanted to miss the spectacle of the man undergoing the torture of the strong coffee dose. They cleared out all there was to eat in the tiny kitchen. Zineddine Ayachi started on the first cup and answered questions about his amazing capacity to absorb an entire coffeepot with no damage to his physical and mental health. He was supposed to sip the thick black liquid slowly; disobeying orders cost him a rifle butt across the shoulders. His wife and children were shut, sobbing, in a room. He tried downing the third cup in two gulps. The soldiers were in no hurry, they were just sorry they hadn't found any wine in the house—one of them said he thought grape juice flowed from the taps in a hot country, this paradise where vines were the only crop. The gulps of coffee fell heavily on Zineddine Ayachi's stomach, like tar soup. On the fifth cup a nauseating saliva filled his mouth, a gurgle rose from his guts, he tried to speed up the forced tasting, then a blow from the rifle butt across his back caused a retching that momentarily relieved his stomach.

"Swallow it," said one of the soldiers, "you can't waste all that coffee."

Zineddine Ayachi seized the coffeepot, lifted it into the air like a goatskin and let the contents pour into his wide-open mouth. A coffee hemorrhage immediately spurted from his nose, prompted by the heavy punch of a gun right in the stomach. Then the soldiers took him to the Lattifia barracks, where the torture continued: they made him drink saucepan after saucepan of coffee prepared with soapy water, this time with the aid of a funnel. His denials did little to alter Zineddine Ayachi's fate; the soldiers set about ridding him of his taste for coffee so long as he would not deliver the names of the men who had shared it with him in his home. A possible way out of his ordeal crept into his mind in the brief moments of prayer afforded him by his executioners, for he sensed the end was near. The faces of those he loved, his friends and family, passed before his eyes; invoked silently, he asked each of them for forgiveness, forgiveness for his mistakes and his faults, his aberrations on this earth. In the end, Zineddine Ayachi arrived at the last name, his dead father's. Helped by the combination of circumstances or the irony of fate, his thoughts returned by a curious path to the cause of his misfortune, and he remembered the coffee bean necklace his father used to wear round his neck.

"I'll tell you the truth," he said. "My coffee isn't really coffee at all. It's a mixture of burnt chickpeas, black pepper, paprika and coffee. My father loved this drink, it was his secret recipe. It's an excellent aphrodisiac. A man becomes a bull with that coffee! The more cups, the more thrusts."

Every time they met in the mountains, Laid Touhami would laugh at his friend's story. Neither he nor the other resistance fighters had any need of the magic potion Zineddine Ayachi had invented in a torture chamber; without women it would be a disaster. The enemy soldiers sent Zineddine Ayachi back to his house. He was to prepare five liters of his special coffee, which would multiply their orgasms with the fatmas. The future mayor of Lattifia owed his salvation to a psychological trick: he instinctively knew that these foreigners, the masters of his country, would follow their orders but also their lust. A very short time sufficed to say good-bye to his family; the torturers' credulity would not last long. Zineddine Ayachi had no illusions about the effect of his concoction, yet he was tempted to add a few fluid ounces of piss from his belly, swollen with the soapy coffee ingurgitated through the funnel. On the Ouarsenis paths, he urinated symbolically on the enemy he'd be fighting for years to come.

AZIZ CHOUAKI

· *Algiers* ·

from THE STAR OF ALGIERS

Four

A WEEK LATER, 12 June, the municipal elections. The first free elections since Independence. Dozens of parties are contending, the walls of Algiers are dripping with posters. It's a bitter, anarchic struggle between all the parties except the FFS, which has called for a boycott.

Moussa, of course, didn't vote, convinced it would be rigged as always, 99.99 percent for the FLN, the famous "Continuity within Change."

At 8 p.m. the entire family gathers in front of the TV for the results of the polls. Visibly ill at ease, the female news anchor announces that the FIS has won a landslide victory taking three-quarters of Algeria's municipal councils. Even in the affluent districts, the well-heeled having spent the day at the beach.

Then a breakdown of the results by constituency. It's one long death knell, the FIS emerges triumphant almost everywhere, even in Kabylia.

The hydra's been legitimised.

At first Moussa laughs nervously, his knees tremble. No, it's not true . . . They're bound to say it's a joke.

Is this Iran?

Nacéra and Kahina start to cry, that's it, we're done for, they're going to force us to wear the hijab. Pa bawls at them to be quiet. Slimane's inwardly jubilant, Ma groans, her diabetes. Sahnoun's with his thriller.

Through the window, a mighty clamour echoes from every corner of the city. Moussa goes out onto the balcony and sees a dense moving throng, a vast black ocean. Hordes of bearded young men in kamis, thousands of them, in the grip of hysteria. Koran in hand, they chant verses and slogans: "Sharia now! There is no God but Allah."

Behind them, kids parading behind a barefoot, snotty-nosed self-appointed leader waving a makeshift flag, a torn plastic milk sachet on the end of a long reed.

All around, cars honking, ululations, traffic jams. The FIS stewards zealously direct the cars. Moussa recognises familiar faces: Spartacus, Baiza, Mustapha, Fatiha's brother. Look, even Slimane's down there, for God's sake. Going to have to sort him out, give him an earful, he deserves it.

Moussa doesn't want to see or hear any more. He goes back to his room to calm down and breaks out in a sweat. This isn't really happening?

What to do?

A chill runs down his spine. His mind's frozen, his limbs numb, his blood pressure plummets, he paces up and down. It can't be true? Better off sticking with the FLN in that case . . .

His mouth's dry, he goes to the kitchen and pours himself a glass of water. His grandma, wearing a yellow and bright pink Kabyle dress, asks him what's going on.

"This is it, the FIS has won, we're dead."

"Dead? The FIS, who's the FIS?"

Moussa goes back to his room and stares at the Michael Jackson poster and his own, side by side. Calm down, dammit. Yeah the FIS'll be buggered. Carry on, work, work, work, hang in there. Music . . .

The following Thursday, there's a wedding at Frais-Vallon. Late afternoon, usual briefing with the band. Sort out the set.

Djelloul's taking care of the transport. Pick-up truck for the gear and the musicians.

Moussa rides in front, of course.

Djelloul's the band's official driver. He charges 100 dinars for each musician and has a good night out. Djelloul's never had a car of his own, he always drives the ones he's repairing.

Rashid should be coming. When Rashid comes, it's important, it's not the same.

Forgotten anything? No, set of strings for the mandola, found them at the last minute, black market. Stage outfit chosen with care, and the posters. Rashid's given him three, first proofs. He told him to put one on a display stand, clearly visible. Visibility is crucial.

Djelloul reverses into a parking space, puts on the hand brake, and turns off the engine. Everyone gets out, loads of people, cars parked haphazardly, kids. They're shown into a kind of dressing room—big cushions on the floor, smell of perfume, cakes.

On a side table is some Muslim whisky—in a teapot, in other words. They roll joints, take slugs of whisky, buff their shoes to a shine, tune their instruments.

Rashid chats to Moussa as he dresses in front of a huge mirror. He tells him about a video he saw on MTV and suggests ideas for Moussa's look. Moussa feels good when Rashid's there. Rashid knows his shit, fuck yeah, solid.

Dazzling in his green-spangled suit and leather tie, and fragrant with perfume, Moussa gives the band last-minute instructions, the order of the songs. Final adjustment to his bow tie, everyone looks immaculate.

Sound check, then launch into the first number. Vibe tense at first, audience on edge, the elections, shadow of the FIS?

Pouring all his rage into his mandola, Moussa goes straight for the gut, no pissing about. Let's do it!

From the first song, the audience goes wild, men and women. They invade the dance floor. Moussa's on a high, he tries out different styles of song, different moves.

By the fourth number, he's Hendrix: he plays the mandola behind his head, on his knees, the crowd's ecstatic.

Then it's the break, Moussa's in front of the mirror, checking his kohl, his teeth, his tie, his make-up. Everyone's congratulating him, that was amazing, thank you.

The bridegroom, wearing a tuxedo and white burnous, comes over in person to thank him. Moussa wishes him joy and lots of children.

In the mirror, Moussa looks himself in the eye. He can see into the far distance, a faint green glimmer at the back of the cave. The smell of certain, early fame. Yesss, he's away.

Where's that joint got to, anyway? The bassist.

Moussa:

"Hey, don't bogart that joint."

Bassist, doesn't quite catch what he says:

"Huh, what?"

Moussa, cool velvet:

"Bogart, Humphrey Bogart, you heard of him?"

Bassist, "Er . . ."

Moussa:

"You know, the '50s, Bogart, always had a cigarette in his mouth, he never passed the joint, get it? Don't bogart the joint."

Bassist, no reaction . . . Rashid chuckles quietly.

He got that one from Rashid, apparently it's an American thing, "don't bogart the joint," pass it on. Good old Rashid.

At last the bass player passes him the joint, Moussa takes two drags, passes it to Rashid, and signals to the band. They're on again. Come on, boys!

He begins with a very gentle ballad, an old lullaby about mothers separated from their babies. Muted bass, light cymbals, bit of synth in the background, that's it. Moussa pitches his voice quite low, very ethereal, just on the verge of tears.

The emotion's overwhelming. All the mothers are dabbing at their eyes, wailing rises from the balconies. It gives Moussa goose bumps.

At the end, old women come on the stage to kiss him, to wish him long life, health, and happiness.

Now for the real deal . . . two, three, four, he gives the signal. "Ayadho," beautiful melody, lively, haunting chorus. It's going well, Moussa watches the bassist, the off-beat rhythm, gets the audience to clap their hands.

The second half's going better, the PA system's pretty much OK. Moussa has the audience eating out of his hand, he's ruling the stage, he makes love to the mike, plays all his trump cards. The party goes on till the sun's already high, the first heat of the day. Moussa's tired but happy. He feels free, it does a guy good.

✤

Two weeks later, all the posters are printed, Rashid drove over to pick them up himself. Moussa on tenterhooks, meet up at Rashid's at 5 p.m. He's promised him some spliff to celebrate.

No problem, Moussa goes downstairs in his flip-flops and, from the entrance to his building, hails the first kid he sees, literally the first, and asks him to bring back 200 dinars' worth of gear.

Spartacus, leaning against the wall, beard and kamis, overhears. He walks up to Moussa:

"Brother, you looking for spliff? Listen, Dahmane got busted by the police, but they didn't find the stuff, his wife had hidden it. Now she's selling it to pay for a lawyer for him. If you want to do a good deed, in the name of God, she's got three kids, she's on her own . . ."

Feeling charitable, Moussa takes pity. OK then, he'll take 400 dinars' worth. Braiding his goatee, Spartacus runs off to get him the gear.

On reaching Rashid's place, Moussa already feels plural: five hundred posters, just think!

Rashid's spread them all over the living room. MOUSSA MASSY, MOUSSA MASSY, MOUSSA MASSY everywhere.

"Take fifty or so for yourself, your friends, events, parties. We'll keep the rest for the day you release a cassette, and we'll add a sticker to promote it. By the way, have you thought about the title for the album?"

Moussa, excited:

"I thought of 'Zombretto.' You know, the kids are all out of their skulls on *zombretto*. It's mother's milk to them. It's a title that reflects their world, their deprivation."

"Perfect, yeah, 'Zombretto.' That's pretty cool. OK, let's go for it. 'Zombretto, an album by Moussa Massy!' Yeah, and it sounds quite salsa, too. Great!"

After two joints, a beer, they've got a plan of action. Rashid takes notes, turns on his computer, yeah, technology. Program, file, that's it, Moussa's knocked out by the computer, the mouse, it's a different planet. Rashid does projections, simulations, clicks on the mouse. Moussa watches his name come up on the screen, it's like NASA or something.

Shit, really got to make this work . . .

The plan's put together at last, Rashid's thought of everything, distribution, flyposting . . .

Moussa gave Spartacus three posters to put up around the neighbourhood. At Bouhar the baker's, in front of the bus stop, on the wall of his apartment building.

Djelloul wanted one for his garage, Kahina for her supermarket, and Saliha, yeah, even Saliha, for her high school.

Moussa's put up four in his bedroom, plus another stuck on cardboard backing. Now he's a pro, he can start talking career a little, just a little.

And he'll have to up the rate for weddings.

At last, it's all beginning to come together. Little by little, not quite how he'd like it, but it's coming.

Moussa knows deep down he's not there yet, he's well aware it'll take more, a lot more. TV, mega concerts at La Coupole or Ryadh El Feth, on the esplanade, yeah, 50,000 people with at least a 60,000-watt PA. That means you've really taken off.

And then, the ultimate, of course: recording in a studio, releasing a cassette like everyone else. Don't settle for less, aim for the sky, beyond the horizon.

LEILA ABOULELA

· *Sudan* ·

✤

SOUVENIRS

THEY SET OUT early, before sunset. Not the right time for visiting, but it was going to be a long drive and his sister Manaal said she would not be able to recognize the painter's house in the dark. The car slipped from the shaded car-port into the white sunlight of the afternoon, the streets were empty, their silence reminiscent of dawn.

Since he had come on the plane from Scotland two weeks ago, Yassir had not gone out at this time of day. Instead he had rested after lunch wearing his old jellabia. He would lie on one of the beds that were against the walls of the sitting room, playing with a toothpick in his mouth and talking to Manaal without looking at her. On the bed perpendicular to his, she would lie with her feet near his head so that had they been children she might have reached out and pulled his hair with her toes. And the child Yassir would have let his heels graze the white wall leaving brown stains for which he would be punished later. Now they talked slowly, probing for common interests and so remembering things past, gossiping lightly about others, while all the time the air cooler blew the edges of the bedsheets just a little, intermittently, and the smells of lunch receded. Then the air cooler's sound would take over, dominate the room, blowing their thoughts away, and they would sleep until the time came when all the garden was in shade.

In this respect, Yassir had slotted easily into the life of Khartoum, after five years on the North Sea oil-rigs, noisy helicopter flights to and from Dyce airport, a grey sea with waves as crazy as the sky. Five years of two weeks off-shore, two weeks on with Emma in Aberdeen. No naps after lunch there and yet he could here lie and know that the rhythms the air cooler whispered into his heart were familiar, well known. When he had first arrived he had put fresh straw into the air cooler's box. Standing outdoors on an upturned Pepsi crate, he had wedged open the grimy perforated frame with a screwdriver, unleashed cobwebs and plenty of dust: fresh powdery dust and solid fluffs that had lost all resemblance to sand. The old bale of straw had shrunk over the years, gone dark and rigid from the constant exposure to water. He oiled the water pump and put in the new bale of straw. Its smell filled the house for days, the air that blew out was cooler. For this his mother had thanked him and like other times before, prayed that he would only find good people in his path. It was true, he was always fortunate in the connections he made, in the people who held the ability to further his interests. In the past teachers, now his boss, his colleagues, Emma.

But "Your wife—what's her name?" was how his mother referred to Emma. She would not say Emma's name. She would not "remember" it. It would have been the same if Emma had been Jane, Alison or Susan, any woman from "outside." Outside that large pool of names his mother knew and could relate to. That was his punishment, nothing more, nothing less. He accepted it as the nomad bears the times of drought which come to starve his cattle, biding time, waiting for the tightness to run its course and the rain that must eventually fall. Manaal would smile in an embarrassed way when their mother said that. And as if time had dissolved the age gap between them, she would attempt a faint defence. "Leave him alone, Mama," she would say, in a whisper, avoiding their eyes, wary, lest her words, instead of calming, provoked the much feared outburst. Manaal had met Emma two years ago in Aberdeen. What she had told his mother about Emma, what she had said to try to drive away the rejection that gripped her, he didn't know.

For Yassir, Emma was Aberdeen. Unbroken land after the sea. Real life after the straight lines of the oil-rig. A kind of freedom. Before Emma his leave on-shore had floated, never living up to his expectations. And it was essential for those who worked on the rigs that those on-shore days were fulfilling enough to justify the hardship of the rigs.

A certain formula was needed, a certain balance which evaded him. Until one day he visited the dentist for two fillings and, with lips frozen with procaine, read out loud the name, Emma, written in Arabic, on a golden necklace that hung around the receptionist's throat.

"Your wife—what's her name?" his mother says as if clumsily smudging out a fact, hurting it. A fact, a history: three years ago he drove Emma to the maternity ward in Foresterhill, in the middle of a summer's night that looked like twilight, to deliver a daughter who did not make her appearance until the afternoon of the following day. Samia changed in the two weeks that he did not see her. Her growth marked time like nothing else did. Two weeks off-shore, two weeks with Emma and Samia, two weeks off-shore again, Emma driving him to the heliport, the child in her own seat at the back. A fact, a history. Yet here, when Manaal's friends visited, some with toddlers, some with good jobs, careers, there was a "see what you've missed" atmosphere around the house. An atmosphere that was neither jocular nor of regret. So that he had come to realise, with the sick bleakness that accompanies truth, that his mother imagined that he could just leave Emma and leave the child, come home, and those five years would have been just an aberration, time forgotten. He could marry one of Manaal's friends, one who would not mind that he had been married before, that he had left behind a child somewhere in Europe. A bride who would regard all that as a man's experience. When talking to her friends she would say the word "experienced" in a certain way, smiling secretly.

Because the streets were silent, Yassir and Manaal were silent too, as if by talking they would disturb those who were resting indoors. Yassir drove slowly, pebbles spat out from under the wheels, he was careful to avoid the potholes. The windows wide open let in dust but closing them would be suffocating. From their house in Safia they crossed the bridge into Khartoum and it was busier there, more cars, more people walking in the streets. That part of the journey, the entry into Khartoum, reminded him of the Blue Nile Cinema, which was a little way under the bridge. He remembered as a student walking back from the cinema, late at night to the Barracks, as his hostel was called, because it was once army barracks. He used to walk with his friends in a kind of swollen high, full of the film he had just seen. Films like *A Man for All Seasons, Educating Rita, Chariots of Fire.*

There was still a long way for them to go, past the Extension, beyond the airport, past Riyadh to the newly built areas of Taif and El-Ma'moura. Not a very practical idea, a drain of the week's ration of petrol, and there was the possibility that the painter would not be in and the whole journey would have been wasted. Manaal was optimistic though. "They'll be in," she said, "*Insha Allah.* Especially if we get there early enough before they go out anywhere." There were no telephones in El-Ma'moura, it was a newly built area with no street numbers, no addresses.

That morning, he had mentioned buying a painting or two to take back to Aberdeen and Manaal had suggested Ronan K. He was English; his wife gave private English lessons (Manaal was once her student). Now in the car when he asked more about him she said, "For years he sat doing nothing, he had no job, maybe he was painting. I didn't know about that until the Hilton commissioned him to do some paintings for the cafeteria. No one knows why this couple live here. They are either crazy or they are spies. Everyone thinks they are spies."

"You all like to think these sensational things," he said. "What is there to spy on anyway?"

"They're nice though," she said. "I hope they are not spies." Yassir shook his head, thinking it was hopeless to talk sense to her.

The paintings were not his idea, they were Emma's. Emma was good with ideas, new suggestions, it was one of the things he admired about her. Yassir didn't know much about painting. If he walked into a room he would not notice the paintings on the wall and he secretly thought they were an extravagance. But then he felt like that about many of the things Emma bought. What he considered luxuries, she considered necessities. Like the Bambi wallpaper in Samia's room must be bought to match the curtains, which match the bedspread, which match Thumper on the pillowcase. And there was a Bambi video, a Ladybird book, a pop-up book. He would grumble but she would persuade him. She would say that as a child she had cried in the cinema when Bambi's mother was shot. Popcorn could not stop the tears, the nasal flood. Of pop-up books and Halloween costumes, she would say, as a child I had these things. He would think, "I didn't."

This time Emma had asked, "What can you get from Khartoum for the house?" They were eating muesli and watching Mr. Motivator on GMTV. Mr. M. had a litre and a half of bottled mineral water in each hand. He was using them as weights while he squatted down and up, down and up, *Knees over your toes.* The labels on the bottles had been slyly removed.

"Nothing. There's nothing there," Yassir said.

"What do tourists get when they go there?"

"Tourists don't go there," he said. "It's not a touristy place. The only foreigners there are working." Once when Yassir was in University he had met a British journalist. The journalist was wearing shorts which looked comical because no one else wore shorts unless they were playing sports. He had chatted to Yassir and some of his friends.

"There must be something you can get," Emma said. "Things carved in wood, baskets . . ."

"There's a shop which sell ivory things. Elephants made of ivory and things like that."

"No. Not ivory."

"I could get you a handbag made of crocodile skin?"

"No, yuck."

"Snake skin?"

"Stop it, I'm serious."

"Ostrich feathers?"

"NO DEAD ANIMALS. Think of something else."

"There's a bead market. Someone once told me about that. I don't know where it is though. I'll have to find out."

"If you get me beads I can have them made here into a necklace." Emma liked necklaces but not bracelets or earrings. The golden necklace with her name in Arabic was from an ex-boyfriend, a mud-logger who had been working rotational from the oil-rigs in Oman.

"Change your mind and come with me. You can take the Malaria pills, Samia can take the syrup and it's just a few vaccines . . ."

"A few jabs! Typhoid, yellow fever, cholera, TB! And Samia might get bitten by this sandfly Manaal told us about when she came here. She is only three. It's not worth it—maybe when she's older . . ."

"You're not curious to see where I grew up?"

"I am interested a bit but—I don't know—I've never heard anything good about that place."

"This is just a two-week holiday, that's all. My mother will get to see you and Samia, you'll have a look around . . ." he said switching Mr. Motivator off.

"Paintings," she said, "that's what you should get. You can bring back paintings of all those things you think I should be curious about. Or just take lots of photographs and bring the beads."

He bought the beads but did not take any photographs. He had shied away from that, as if unable to click a camera at his house, his old school, the cinemas that brought the sparkle of life abroad. So when Manaal said she knew this English painter, he was enthusiastic about the idea even though it was his last evening in Khartoum. Tomorrow his flight would leave for home. He hoped he would have with him some paintings for Emma. She would care about where each one went, on this wall or that. She cared about things more than he did. She even cared about Samia more than he did. Emma was in tune with the child's every burp and whimper. In comparison to Emma, Yassir's feelings for Samia were jammed up, unable to flow. Sometimes with the two of them he felt himself dispensable, he thought they could manage without him. They did just that when he was off-shore. They had a life together: playgroup, kindergym, Duthie Park. When Manaal came to Aberdeen she said many times, "Emma is so good with the child. She talks to her as if she is an adult."

Yassir now wondered, as they drove down Airport Road, if Manaal had said such positive things to his mother. Or if she had only told of the first day of her visit to Aberdeen. The day she reached out to hold the sleeping child and Emma said, "No, I'd rather you didn't. She'll be frightened if she wakes up and finds a stranger holding her." The expression on Manaal's face had lingered throughout the whole visit as she cringed in Emma's jumpers that were too loose, too big for her. Then, as if lost in the cold, his sister hibernated, slept and slept through the nights and large parts of the days. So that Emma began to say, she must be ill, there must be something wrong with her, some disease, why does she sleep so much, Yassir, why?

Possessive of Manaal, he had shrugged, Aberdeen's fresh air, and not explained that his sister had always been like that, easily tired, that she reacted to life's confusions by digging herself into sleep.

When they left the airport behind them and began to pass Riyadh, Manaal suddenly said that to make sure they get to the right house, she had better drop in on her friend Zahra. Zahra's mother, a Bulgarian, was a good friend of Mrs. K. and they would know where the house was.

"I thought you knew where it is?"

"I do—but it's better to be sure. It's on our way anyway."

"Isn't it too early to go banging on people's doors?"

"No, it's nearly five. Anyway her parents are away—they've gone to Hajj."

"Who? The Bulgarian woman? You're joking."

"No, *wallahi*." Manaal seemed amused by his surprise. "Zahra's mother prays and fasts Ramadan. We were teasing her the last time I went there, telling her that when she comes back from Hajj, she'll start covering her hair and wearing long sleeves. And she said, 'No never, your country is too hot; it's an oven.'" Manaal did an impersonation of grammatically incorrect Arabic with a Bulgarian accent which made Yassir laugh. He thought of Zahra's father, a man who was able to draw his foreign wife to Islam, and Yassir attributed to him qualities of strength and confidence.

The house, in front of which Manaal told him to stop, had a high wall around it. The tops of the trees, that grew inside, fell over the wall shading the pavement. Manaal banged on the metal door—there was no bell. She banged with her palms, and peered through the chink in the door to see if anyone was coming.

Yassir opened the car door to let in some air but there was hardly any breeze. There were tears in the plastic of Manaal's seat from which bits of yellow foam protruded. There was a crack in the window, fine and long, like a map of the Nile, and one of the doors in the back was stuck and could never be opened. This car, he thought, would not pass its MOT in Aberdeen; it would not be deemed Road Worthy. What keeps it going here is *baraka*. The car had seen finer days in his father's lifetime. Then it was solid and tinged with prestige. Now more than anything else, its decay was proof of the passing away of time, the years of Yassir's absence. He had suggested to his mother and Manaal that he should buy them a new one. Indeed this had been one of the topics of his stay—A new car— The house needs fixing—Parts of the garden wall are crumbling away— Why don't you get out of this dump and move to a new house? But his mother and sister tended to put up with things. Like with Manaal recently losing her job. She had worked since graduation with a Danish aid agency, writing reports in their main office in Souk Two. When they had reduced their operations in the South, staff cuts followed. "Start looking for a new job," he told her, "or have you got certain plans that I don't know of yet?" She laughed and said, "When you leave I'll start looking for a job and no, there are no certain plans. There is no one on the horizon yet."

It was a joke between them. There is no one on the horizon yet. She wrote this at the bottom of letters, letters in Arabic that Emma could not read. Year after year. She was twenty-six now and could feel the words touched by the frizzle of anxiety. "Every university graduate is abroad, making money so that he can come back and marry a pretty girl like you," he had said recently to her. "Really?" she replied with a sarcasm that was not characteristic of her.

From the door of Zahra's house, Manaal looked at Yassir in the car and shrugged, then banged again with both hands. But she must have heard someone coming for she raised her hand to him and nodded.

The girl who opened the door had a towel wrapped around her hair like a turban. She kissed Manaal and he could hear, amidst their greetings, the words "shower" and "sorry." They walked towards him, something he was not expecting and before he could get out of the car the girl leaned, and through the open window of the seat next to his, extended her hand. The car filled up with the smell of soap and shampoo; he thought his hand would later smell of her soap. She had the same colouring as his daughter Samia, the froth of cappuccino, dark-grey eyes, thick eyebrows. Her face was dotted with pink spots, round and raised like little sweets. He imagined those grey eyes soft with sadness when she examined her acne in the bathroom mirror, running her fingertips over the bumps.

With a twig and some pebbles, Zahra drew them a map of the painter's house in the dust of the pavement. She sat on her heels rather primly, careful not to get dust on her jellabia. She marked the main road and where they should turn left. When you see a house with no garden walls, no fence, she said, that's where you should turn left.

She stood up, dusted off her hands and, when Manaal got into the car, she waved to them until they turned and were out of sight. Yassir drove back on to the main road, from the dust to the asphalt. The asphalt road was raised and because it had no pavements, its sides were continually being eroded, eaten away. They looked jagged, crumbly. The afternoon was beginning to mellow; sunset was drawing near.

"I imagine that when Samia grows up she will look like your friend," he said.

"Maybe, yes. I haven't thought of it before," Manaal said. "Did you like the earrings for Samia?"

He nodded. His mother had given him a pair of earrings for Samia. He had thanked her and not said that his daughter's ears were not pierced.

"She's beginning to accept the situation." His voice had a tingle of bravado about it. He was talking about his mother and Manaal knew. She was looking out of the window. She turned to him and said, "She likes the photographs that you send. She shows them to everyone."

Yassir had been sending photographs from Aberdeen. Photographs of Emma and Samia. Some were in the snow, some taken in the Winter Gardens at Duthie Park, some at home.

"So why doesn't she tell me that? Instead of 'What's her name?' or whatever she keeps saying?"

"You should have given her some idea very early on, you should have . . . consulted her." Manaal spoke slowly, with caution, like she was afraid or just tired.

"And what would she have said if I had asked her? Tell me, what do you think she would have said?"

"I don't know."

"You do know."

"How can I?"

"She would have said no and then what?"

"I don't know. I just know that it was wrong to suddenly write a letter and say 'I got married'—in the past tense. Nobody does that."

He didn't answer her. He did not like the hurt in her voice, like it was her own hurt not their mother's.

As if his silence disturbed her and she wanted the conversation to continue she said, "It wasn't kind."

"It was honest."

"But it was hard. She was like someone ill when she read your letter. Defeated and ill . . ."

"She'll come to accept it."

"Of course she'll come to accept it. That's the whole point. It's inevitable but you could have made it easier for her, that's all." Then in a lighter tone she said, "Do something theatrical. Get down on your knees and beg for forgiveness."

They laughed at this together, somewhat deliberately to ease the tension. What he wanted to do was explain, speak about Emma and say, She welcomed me, I was on the periphery and she let me in. Do people get tortured to death in that dentist's chair or was I going to be the first? he had asked Emma that day, and made her smile, when he stumbled out of pain and spoke to her with lips numb with procaine.

"It would have been good if Emma and Samia had come with you," Manaal was saying.

"I wanted that too."

"Why didn't they?" She had asked that question before as had others. He gave different reasons to different people. Now in the car he felt that Manaal was asking deliberately, wanting him to tell her the truth. Could he say that from this part of the world Emma wanted malleable pieces, not the random whole? She desired frankincense from the Body Shop, tahina safe in a supermarket container.

"She has fears," he said.

"What fears?"

"I don't know. The sandfly, malaria . . . Some rubbish like that." He felt embarrassed and disloyal.

They heard the sunset azan when they began to look for the house without a garden wall which Zahra had told them about. But there were many houses like that; people built their homes and ran out of money by the time it came to build the garden wall. So they turned left off the asphalt road anyway when they reached El-Ma'moura, hoping that Manaal would be able to recognise the street or the house.

"Nothing looks familiar to you?" he asked.

"But everything looks different than the last time I was here," she said. "All those new houses, it's confusing."

There were no roads, just tracks made by previous cars, hardly any pavements. They drove through dust and stones. The houses in various stages of construction stood in straight lines. In some parts the houses formed a square around a large empty area, as if marking a place which would always be empty, where houses would not be allowed to be built.

"Maybe it's this house," Manaal said. He parked, they rang the bell, but it was the wrong house.

Back in the car they drove through the different tracks and decided to ask around. How many foreigners were living in this area anyway? People were bound to know them.

Yassir asked a man sitting in front of his house, one knee against his chest, picking his toenails. Near him an elderly man was praying, using a newspaper as a mat. The man didn't seem to know but he gave Yassir several elaborate suggestions.

Yassir asked some people who were walking past but again they didn't know. This was taking a long time as everyone he asked seemed willing to engage him in conversation.

"It's your turn," he said to Manaal when they saw a woman coming out of her house.

She went towards the woman and stood talking to her. Sunset was nearly over by then, the western sky, the houses, the dusty roads were all one colour, like the flare that burns off the rig, he thought. Manaal stood, a dark silhouette against red and brick. One hand reached out to hold her hair from blowing and her thin elbows made an angle with her head and neck from which the light came through. This is what I would paint, Yassir thought, if I knew how, I would paint Manaal like this, with her elbows sticking out against the setting sun.

When she came back she seemed pleased. "We're nearly there," she said, "that woman knew them. First right, and it's the second house."

As soon as they turned right, Manaal recognised the one-storey house with the blue gate. She got out before him and rang the bell.

Ronan K. was older than Yassir had imagined. He looked like a football coach, overweight yet light in his movements. The light from the lamp near the gate made him look slightly bald. He recognised Manaal, and as they stepped into a large bare courtyard while he closed the gate behind them, she launched into a long explanation of why they had come and how they had nearly got lost on the way.

The house inside had no tiles on the floors, its surface was of uneven textured stone, giving it the appearance that it was unfinished, still in the process of being built. Yet the furniture was arranged in an orderly way, and there were carpets on the floor. Birds rustled in a cage near the kitchen door. On one of the walls there was a painting of the back of a woman in a *tobe,* balancing a basket on her head.

"One of yours?" Yassir asked but Ronan said no, he did not like to hang his own paintings in the house.

"All of my work is on the roof," he said and from the kitchen he got a tray with a plastic jug full of *kerkadeh* and ice and three glasses. Some of the ice splashed into the glasses as he began to pour, and a pool of redness gathered in the tray, sliding slowly around in large patterns.

"You have a room on the roof?" Yassir asked.

"That's where I paint," Ronan said. "I lock it though, we've had many *haramiah* in the area. Not that they would steal my paintings but it's better to be careful. I'm in there most nights though, the *kahrabah* permitting."

Hearing the Arabic words for thieves and electricity made Yassir smile. He remembered Manaal copying the way Zahra's mother spoke. He wondered how well Ronan K. knew Arabic.

"My wife has the key. But she is right next door. The neighbour's daughter had a baby last week. There's a party of some kind there," and he looked at Manaal as if for an explanation.

"A *simayah*," she said.

"That's right," said Ronan, "a *simayah*. Maybe you could go over and get the key from her? It's right next door."

"Is it Amna and her people?" Manaal asked him. "I've seen them here before."

"Yes, that's them."

"Last time I was here, Amna walked in with chickens to put in your freezer. There wasn't enough room in theirs."

"Chickens with their heads still on them and all the insides," said Ronan. "Terrible . . . This morning she brought over a leg of lamb," and he gestured vaguely towards the kitchen.

"So who had the baby?" Manaal asked.

"Let's see if I can get this one right," he said. "The sister of Amna's husband, who happens to be—just to get things complicated—married to the cousin of Amna's mother."

They laughed because Ronan gave an exaggerated sigh as if he had done a lot of hard work.

"I thought you said it was the neighbours' daughter," said Yassir.

"Well this Amna character," he said and Manaal laughed and nodded at the word "character," "she is living with her in-laws, so it is really the in-laws' house."

Manaal got up to go and Ronan said, "I'll tell you what. Just throw the keys up to us on the roof. We'll wait for you in there. It will save time."

The roof was dark and cool, its floor more uneven than that of the house had been. The ledge all around it was low, only knee-high. El-Ma'moura lay spread out before them, the half-built houses surrounded by scaffolding, the piles of sand and discarded bricks. Shadows of stray dogs made their way through the rubble. Domes of cardboard marked the places where the caretakers of the houses and their families lived. Their job was to guard the bags of cement, the toilets, the tiles that came for the new houses. Once the houses were built they would linger, drawing water from the pipes that splashed on the embryonic streets, until they were eventually sent away.

From the house next door came the sounds of children playing football, scuffling, names called out loud. A woman's voice shrieked from indoors. Yassir and Ronan sat on the ledge. He offered Yassir a cigarette and Yassir accepted though he hadn't smoked for several years. Ronan put his box of matches between them. It had a picture of a crocodile on it, mouth wide open, tail arched up in the air. Yassir had forgotten how good it felt to strike a match, flick grey ash away. It was one of the things he and Emma had done together—given up smoking.

"A long way from Aberdeen, or rather Aberdeen is a long way from here," Ronan said.

"Have you been there before?"

"I know it well, my mother originally came from Elgin. They can be a bit parochial up there, don't you think?"

At the back of Yassir's mind questions formed themselves, rose out of a sense of habit, but dropped languidly as if there was no fuel to vocalise them. What was this man doing here, in a place where even the nights were hot and alcohol was forbidden? Where there was little comfort and little material gain? The painter sat on his roof and like the raised spots on the girl's face did not arouse in Yassir derision, only passive wonder.

"If you look this way," Ronan said, "you can see the airport where the red and blue lights are. Sometimes I see the aeroplanes circling and landing. They pass right over me when they take off. I see the fat bellies of planes full of people going away."

"Last August we had so much rain. This whole area was flooded— we couldn't drive to the main road. The Nile rose and I could see it with my telescope—even though it is far from here."

"How long have you been here?" Yassir asked.

"Fifteen years."

"That's a long time."

Giant wisps of white brushed the sky as if the smoke from their cigarettes had risen high, expanded and stood still. Stars were pushing their way into view, gathering around them the darkest dregs of night.

On the roof, speaking Emma's language for the first time in two weeks, Yassir missed her, not with the light eagerness he had known on the rigs but with something else, something plain and unwanted: the grim awareness of distance. He knew why he had wanted her to come with him, not to "see," but so that Africa would move her, startle her, touch her in some irreversible way.

Manaal threw up the keys, Ronan opened the locked room and put the light on. It was a single bulb which dangled from the ceiling, speckled with the still bodies of black insects. The room smelt of paint, a large fan stood in the corner. Conscious of his ignorance, Yassir was silent as Ronan, cigarette drooping from his mouth, showed him one painting after the other. "I like them," he said and it was true. They were clear and uncluttered, the colours light, giving an impression of sunlight. Most were of village scenes, mud houses, one of children playing with a goat, one of a tree that had fallen into the river.

"Paper is my biggest problem," said Ronan. "The brushes and paints last for quite some time. But if I know someone who is going abroad I always ask them for paper."

"Is it special paper that you need?"

"Yes, thicker for water colours."

"I like the one of the donkey in front of the mud house," said Yassir.

"The Hilton don't seem to want mud houses."

"Did they tell you that?"

"No, I just got this feeling."

"That means I could get them at a discount?"

"Maybe . . . How many were you thinking of taking?"

Yassir chose three, one of them the children with the goat because he thought Samia might like that. He paid after some haggling. Downstairs the birds were asleep in their cage, there was no longer any ice in the jug of *kerkadeh*. Manaal was waiting for him by the gate. She had a handful of dates from next door which she offered to Ronan and Yassir. The dates were dry and cracked uncomfortably under Yassir's teeth before softening into sweetness. It was now time to leave. He shook hands with Ronan; the visit was a success; he had achieved what he came for.

❖

Manaal slept in the car on the way home. Yassir drove through streets busier than the ones he had found in the afternoon. This was his last day in Khartoum. Tomorrow night a plane would take him to Paris, another plane to Glasgow, then the train to Aberdeen. Perhaps Ronan K. would be on his roof tomorrow night, watching Air France rise up over the new houses of El-Ma'moura.

The city was acknowledging his departure, recognising his need for a farewell. Headlamps of cars jerked in the badly lit streets, thin people in white floated like clouds. Voices, rumbling lorries, trucks leaning to one side snorting fumes. On a junction with a busier road, a small bus went past carrying a wedding party. It was lit inside, an orange light that caught the singing faces, the clapping hands. Ululations, the sound of a drum, lines from a song. Yassir drove on and gathered around him what he would take back with him, the things he could not deliver. Not the beads, not the paintings, but other things. Things devoid of the sense of their own worth. Manaal's silhouette against the rig's flare, against a sky dyed with *kerkadeh*. The scent of soap and shampoo in his car, a man picking his toenails, a page from a newspaper spread out as a mat. A voice that said, I see the planes circling at night, I see their lights . . . all the people going away. Manaal saying, you could have made it easier for her, you could have been more kind.

• *East Africa* •

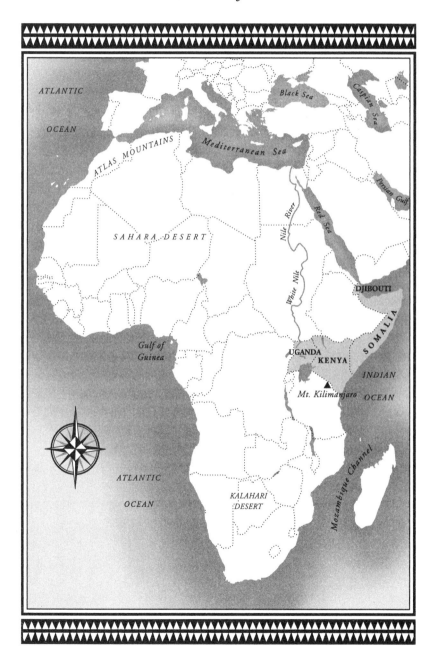

BINYAVANGA WAINAINA

· *Kenya* ·

❖

from DISCOVERING HOME

I AM VISITING home, from South Africa. I take the dawn Nissan matatu from Nairobi to Nakuru, a two hour drive. It is 1995 and it has been three years since I saw my parents, my brother Jim, and my sister Chiqy. I have been working as a journalist in South Africa for the last three years.

The Kikuyu-grass by the side of the road is crying silver tears the colour of remembered light; Nairobi is a smoggy haze in the distance. Soon, the innocence that dresses itself in mist will be shoved aside by a confident sun, and the chase for money will reach its crescendo.

A man wearing a Yale University sweatshirt and tattered trousers staggers behind his enormous mkokoteni, stacked high with bags of potatoes moving so slowly it seems he will never get to his destination. He is transporting. No vehicle gives him room to move. The barrow is so full that it seems that some bags will fall off onto the road. Already, he is sweating. He smiles and waves at a friend on the side of the road, they chat briefly, laughing as if they had no care in the world. Then the mkokoteni man proceeds to move the impossible.

Why, when all odds are against our thriving, do we move with so much resolution? Kenya's economy is on the brink of collapse, but we march on like safari ants, waving our pincers as if we will win.

Years ago, a guy, outside a theatre in Nairobi, told me he found Kenya strange. He was from the Caribbean.

"It is as if it is a country that has not thought itself into being."

Maybe motion is necessary even when it produces nothing.

I sit next to the driver, who wears a Stetson hat, and has been playing an upcountry matatu classic on the cassette player: Kenny Rogers' *The Gambler.* There are two women behind me talking. I can't hear what they are saying, but it seems very animated. I catch snatches, when exclamations send their voices higher than they would like.

"Eh! Apana! I don't believe!".

"Haki!"

"I swear!"

"Me I heard ati . . ."

Aha. Members of the Me-I-Heard-Ati society.

I construct their conversation in my mind:

"Eee-heeee! Even me I've heard that one! Ati you know, they are mining oil in Lake Victoria, together with Biwott."

"Really!"

"Yah!"

"And they are exporting the ka-plant to Australia. They use it to feed sheep."

"Nooo! Really? What plant?"

"You knooow, that plant—Water-hyak haycy . . . haia. Argh! That ka-plant that is covering the lake!"

"Hyacinth?"

"Yah! That hya-thing was planted by Moi and Biwott and them in Lake Victoria. They want to finish the Luos!"

And the Illuminati, the Free Masons—where Biwott, a short man who is said to run everything, is supposed to be the hooded Masonic overlord, higher there even, we hear, than the president.

The Nissan drones on, we are in a narrow tunnel made of star-stitched black felt, all fifteen of us lost in our own thoughts. Outside, in the valley below, all I can see is thousands of sepia paraffin lamps, flickering dots, each carrying wriggling dreams—hidden behind stoic faces, and sturdy mud and wood homes, muffled behind the shrieking silence of night.

I know in these red fertile hills, where my own ancestors come from, and where pyrethrum and potatoes are grown, strange cults thrive, hundreds of charismatic churches, tens of apocalyptic churches, and in the dark, tongues flutter and throb, eyes roll; and in the morning, faces are stoic.

At seven, the taxi goes somber as the music is turned off, and the news comes on, and we discover that today President Daniel Toroitich Arap Moi lifted an eyebrow, shut one eye, examined a pimple, drank tea. There are funeral announcements on the radio, then a song comes on that takes me straight back to a childhood memory. *Charonye ni Wasi.*

It must have been a Sunday, and I was standing outside *KukuDen* restaurant in Nakuru, as my mother chatted away with an old friend. It was quite hot, and my Sunday clothes itched, the clean lines of colonial Nakuru met the raw and seemingly inarticulate noise of something else.

Then this song came on . . . Congo music, with voices as thick as hot honey, and wayward in a way Christian school tunes and English nursery melodies hadn't prepared me for. The music was familiar enough, there is no way to avoid rhumba in Kenya, but I *heard* the music for the first time today. Guitar and trumpet, parched like before the rains, dived into the honey and out again. The voices pleaded in a strange language, men sending their voices higher than men should, and letting go of control, letting their voices flow, slow and phlegmy, like the honey. There was a lorry outside, and the men unloading the maize were singing to the music, pleading with the honey. The song burst out with the odd Swahili phrase, then forgot itself and started on its gibberish again. Maroon Commandos.

It disturbed me, demanding too much of my attention, derailing my daydreams. I lean back, and close my eyes. Those were good days.

• • •

I am maybe seven.

A flamingo woman, her stick-like legs in cloggy high heels, handbag in her beak. Flying away. We are sitting on a patch of some tough nylony grass next to the verandah. I used to love that flamingo book, it came with a carton of books my mum got from some American missionary neighbours who were going back home. Sun is hot. I close my eyes and let the sun shine on my eyelids. Red tongues and beasts flutter, aureoles of red and burning blue. The colours of dizzy.

Mum is shelling peas and humming; Ciru is running around, with a yo-yo, from the same American carton of goodies. When Ciru laughs, everybody laughs, and when she is running and laughing, everybody is warm and smiling.

Yellow dahlias hang their heads, like they are sad. Jimmy is making a kite. Take a newspaper. Baba will beat you if you use the Sunday paper. Cut one page off its twin. Use a knife to split a stick of old bamboo from the fence. Tape sticks, diagonally, with cellotape. Three holes in a triangle, in the right place. Make a long long newspaper tail. Run. Run. Run.

There are two old kites stuck on the electricity wire.

I don't laugh a lot, my laugh is far away inside, like the morning car not starting when the key turns. It is Ciru number one in school, blue and red and yellow stars on every page. When I laugh it is when Ciru laughs and I find myself inside her laugh, and we fall down holding each other. She is seventeen months younger than me. It is Ciru in a white dress giving flowers to Mr. Ben Methu in school. If I am in the bath alone, I will sink inside and see the thick colours of things outside from inside the water, until my eyes are numb. If I am washing with Ciru, we are splashing and laughing and fighting and soon we are in a fever of tears or giggles.

From here we can see my whole home town, stretched springs of smoke, the silos, one a clump of four tall, glued together concrete cylinders, UNGA (Flour) LTD., and two separate metallic blue tubes where Baba works, at Pyrethrum Board of Kenya. PieBoard. Behind, Menengai Crater; to the left, Lena Moi Primary School, sitting under Nakuru Golf Club. Everywhere, there are purple, puffed up cabbages of jacaranda. Past the silos, green maize and paler wheat stretch out. All around, in the distance, are mountains, we are at the bottom of the Rift Valley.

Brown is near. Green far. Blue farthest.

From here you can see Nairobi road, and often there are long long lines of tanks and trucks and tanks and trucks and lorries going to the Lanet barracks.

President Kenyatta is going to beat Idi Amin.

President Kenyatta is a bull.

I look at pink and blue Lake Nakuru below me, watch the flamingoes rise up like leaves in the wind, our dog Juma grinning, mouth open and panting, and I have this *feeling*.

It is a pink and blue feeling, as sharp as clear sky; a slight breeze, and the edges of Lake Nakuru would rise like the ruffle at the edge of a skirt; and I am pockmarked with whole-body pinpricks of potentiality. A stretch of my body would surely stretch as far as the sky. The whole universe poised, and I am the agent of any movement.

These are the maps; you dig your hand deep into the bag and extract them for use later, when your body is sluggish and awkward, and it seems you are wading through thick mud in the dark.

Nakuru. I am at home. The past eight hours are already receding into the forgotten; I was in Cape Town yesterday morning, I am in Nakuru, Kenya, now.

Blink.

Mum looks tired and her eyes are sleepier than usual. She has never seemed frail, but does so now. I decide that it is I who am growing, changing, and my attempts at maturity make her seem more human.

We sit, in the dining room, and talk from breakfast to lunch, congealing eggs around us. Every so often she will grab my hand and check my nails; a hand will reach into her mouth to lick a spot off my forehead.

We wander and chat, and things gather to some invisible assessment inside her, and she turns, sharp and certain, and says, "You smoke."

I nod, eyes tap-dancing awkwardly, waiting for it to come: the full blow of power. It does not come: there is restraint.

They are worried about me, and for the first time in my life, worried enough not to bring it up.

I make my way around the house. My mother's voice, talking to my dad, echoes in the corridor. None of us has her voice: if crystal was water solidified, her voice would be the last splash of water before it sets.

Light from the kitchen brings the Nandi woman to life. A painting.

I was terrified of her when I was a kid. Her eyes seemed so alive and the red bits growled at me. Her broad face announced an immobility that really scared me; I was stuck there, fenced into a tribal reserve by her features: *rings on her ankles and bells on her nose, she will make music wherever she goes.*

Two sorts of people: those on one side of the line will wear third-hand clothing till it rots. They will eat dirt, but school fees will be paid. On the other side of the line live people some see in coffee-table books, we see in weekend trips to the village to visit family, on market days in small towns, and on television, translated back to us by a foreign man with a deep voice that has come to represent timeless days and bygone ways and an Africa ten metres away from us in the living room, and a million light-years from any reality we can process: this Africa is the same as Disney World, and Woody Woodpecker and Groovy Ghoulies and the Boomtown Rats. We are maybe less ironical about it because it comes from too far away from us for us to see into its motives, we can only try to seem familiar with a television language that is the Way the World Works.

So, in Nature Televisionese, these people are like an old and lush jungle that continues to flourish its leaves and unfurl extravagant blooms, refusing to realise that somebody cut off the water.

Often, somebody from the other side of the line.

We, the modern ones, are fascinated by the completeness of the old ones. To us, it seems that everything is mapped out and defined for them, and everybody is fluent in those definitions. In televisionspeak, they are a different species: they are spoken of in hushed reverential tones, like when the naturalist is showing us the birthing albino dragon-fly. We are interested only in their general bygones.

The old ones are not much impressed with our society, or manners—what catches their attention is our tools: the cars and medicines and telephones and wind-up dolls and guns and anthropologists and Funding and International Indigenous Peoples' networks.

In my teens, set alight by the poems of Senghor and Okot p'Bitek, the Nandi woman became my Tigritude. I pronounced her beautiful, marvelled at her cheekbones and mourned the lost wisdom in her eyes, but I still would have preferred to sleep with Pam Ewing or Iman.

It was a source of terrible fear for me that I could never love her. I covered that betrayal with a complicated imagery that had no connection to my gut: O Nubian Princess, and other bad poetry. She moved to my bedroom for a while, next to the faux-Kente wall hanging, but my mother took her back to her pulpit.

Over the years, I learned to look at her amiably. She filled me with a fake nostalgia that was exactly what I felt I should be feeling because a lot of poetry-loving black people seemed to be spontaneously feeling this. I never again attempted to look beyond her costume.

She is younger than me now; I can see that she has girlishness about her. Her eyes are the artist's only real success: they suggest mischief, serenity, vulnerability and a weary wisdom.

I find myself desiring her. And I am willing to admit that this could be too because she has started to look like it is funky to look somewhere in this new Zap Mama, Erykah Badu, Alek Wek, polenta and sushi world.

I look up at the picture again.

Then I see it.

Ha!

Everything: the slight smile, the angle of her head and shoulders, the mild flirtation with the artist. I know you want me, I know something you don't.

Mona Lisa: nothing says otherwise. The truth is that I never saw the smile. Her thick lips were such a war between my intellect and emotion. I never noticed the smile. The artist was painting "An African Mona Lisa."

The woman's expression is odd. In Kenya, you will only see such an expression in girls who went to private schools, or were brought up in the richer suburbs of the larger towns.

That look, that slight toying smile, could not have happened with an actual Nandi woman. The lips too. The mouth strives too hard for symmetry, to apologise for its thickness. That mouth is meant to break open like the flesh of a clapping Sunday.

The eyes are enormous: Oxfam eyes, urging the viewer to care.

· · ·

Later I wander behind the garage, which smells of old oil and rat nest and childhood, and light a cigarette, pocket-radio rhumba in the sound of an afternoon breeze, as clothes flutter on a childhood clothesline I once perched on, batlike, and entered a bestial world of naked gums, flailing laughter, and snarling toenails on orange Bata flip-flops, this world-stopping surge of fear always brought back to sanity by my radar, my big brother Jimmy, as certain as my bed, as sure as a ceiling.

There is a line of old cedars to my left, nappy and grey-furred, they refused to look like television Christmas trees, stooping and bowed, never arranging to rise sharply to a peak, where a star would sit, the twinkling graph points of television life, like washed pine forests in Canada. One of our cedars once had a woodpecker, and its hole, long abandoned, was a place to hide meaningful nothings, the woodpecker mattered most because it helped us map out a world of similarity with a thing from television: *Woody Woodpecker.*

My young uncle Kadogo lived with us once, during the Amin years—when my mother's family was starting to scatter in Uganda, they would eventually spread to Kenya, Rwanda, Lesotho, South Africa, New York and Europe. I was maybe five the year that Kadogo killed one cedar by loping its head off for a Christmas tree, cheered on by us, happy to find a possible and symmetric tree. It still stands, creaking and threatening, brown and naked.

When I was seven, in 1978, Kenyatta died, and school was closed for months it seemed, and all there was on television was Kenyatta, Kenyatta, songs, dirges and the stench of fear everywhere you lifted your mental nostrils—powerful instruments when you are seven. Idi Amin was a subject of horror in our household, so much of my mother's family remained in Uganda, and we were always primed to expect the worst. One of my father's best friends traveled there on a business trip and disappeared. His remains were found buried in a mass grave, years later, after Amin's government fell. After Kenyatta died, Amin loomed in my mind for years, a man of squirming intestine laughter.

But that long long holiday, with its whispers and frissons, was the sweet and tart and memorable. Parents were distracted; and the fear made us seek fun with some aggression.

There were some sparkling days: my mother was at work, and we would sneak through the hedge to play with the neighbours, Georgie and Antonina, whose parents worked for Kenya Co-operative Creameries, and who had a Kiwashili sex manual in their bedroom drawer, which we often browsed.

A whole quarter acre of ripe maize filled the back of their garden. One day, we ran, leaves crackling and breaking, and played, sun hot and sure, soft feathers and grass in an abandoned bird's nest, smelling rotting and feathery; rats' nests and mongrel puppies; yellow and brown bumble bees which we tied with string and let fly. Hot syrup sweat dripped into eyes and stung, and I was lost in this wheat coloured world of flapping leaves and bare feet digging into hot soil, familiar things now had some momentum.

We forgot to sneak back in time, and as we came out of the fence, there was mum, a belt in hand, face stony and silent. When she gets angry she does not talk.

At the corner of this fence, there was a dead log, an old eucalyptus tree, and an abandoned car we had mutilated. We had turned it into a clubhouse of sorts. A friend of my father's had left it in his care—a year or so later, my father would nearly kill us, when he saw the condition we had left it, our names scrawled all over the paintwork.

As we followed mum, pleading, I stopped for a moment to perform the ritual of this place—every time we knocked on the old log, ants would come streaming out—the idea of this, this sprawl of chaotic black squiggles, immeasurable, and as reliable as a clock, is still a marker for me, of nature's invisible precisions. Every time, we pounded on them, to kill as many as possible, and lo and behold, they would stream out the next time we came. Here it was: the hidden order of the floppy head of an incorrect cedar Christmas tree, shaking a drooping and bearded head, in a wind that resonated with pungent choices discarded, for the glitter of a shallow and powerful thing.

. . .

I wake up early the next morning, and walk out of the gate, and up the hill to catch a view of the lake and town.

We live in a house on the slopes of Menengai Crater.

Ten miles above us, on this hill is Africa's second largest caldera, after Ngorongoro. There is a road to the summit, and from there you can see the massive saucer-shaped crater—twelve by eight kilometres wide, five hundred metres deep, on its sheer cliffs. It was formed eight thousand years ago—after its last major eruption.

Over a hundred and twenty years ago, one of the decisive battles of a great war is said to have taken place here. For centuries the Maa military complex—a cattle keeping civilization—had dominated much of Kenya's hinterland. As the cattle were the currency of trade for many Kenyan societies, including my own, the Gikuyu, the Masai's great herds made them the wealthiest society in the Rift Valley. They were our bank of protein. Because of this, most of Kenya's towns are named by the Masai. Nakuru means *Dusty Place.* Menengai is said to mean *Place of Corpses.*

In the nineteenth century, there was a series of civil wars among the Masai; a great Rinderpest plague; and the famine of 1870—this significantly weakened the Masai, and they have never recovered their power: especially after their Laibon, Lenana, was tricked by the British, and they gave up much of their lands. It is said one of the decisive Masai battles was fought at Menengai Crater. Ilaikipiak Morans (warriors) were thrown in the calderas. Most people in this area refuse to go down the crater.

There are stories about the rising jets of steam; that they are the ghosts of old Masai warriors trying to make their way up to heaven while being pulled back by the gravity of hell. For years there were stories about a giant fog-coloured umbrella that rises above the floor when it rains, and covers the crater, so the ground below remains dry. There are also stories, lots of them, about people who disappeared down the crater for days, and were found later, disoriented; they could not remember what happened. When I was a child, there was much talk of a humming sound—like a distant diesel engine, some say, that throbs and disappears after a few minutes. I have heard it many times—a muffled rotor blade—as if some underground helicopter is stirring the bowels of the earth. Many Christians come to the caves just below the cliffs, to pray and fast.

Every decade or so, when drought hits, Masai elders call out to their youth, some in school, some even in college, and they send them out to the towns to look for pasture. For some of these young men, this is the first and maybe the only time they will get to walk through the old grazing routes; through the barbed wire fences and industrial areas, and small farms and leafy suburbs that were once a part of their vast lands.

This year, towns all over Kenya are flooded with Masai cattle—this area was once Masai lands. Everybody is talking about it—there are some battles. The Morans always lose—the pattern has reversed: power was in the hands of the cattle-keepers two hundred years ago—now it is in the hands of former peasants. They adapted to the changing world faster. A hundred years ago, any surplus of grain would buy cattle: the Gikuyu would buy cattle from the Masai. By 1920, surpluses were converted into cash, and the economy of the Masai foundered.

Our new home, five hundred metres from the house I was brought up in, is on the last line before the blue gum forest that extends all the way to the rim of Menengai Crater.

I heard them come in last night, the Morans with their cattle. The strong smell of urine and dung flooded our house; and old throaty songs, and the cow bells. They sang the whole night, and for a while I could pretend that time had rolled back, and I sat among them, as a biblical nomad, or much as my great-grandparents would have.

The two ideas are mixed up in my head.

Throughout my childhood: this view, of flamingos, lake and town in front of us, of the loom and shadow of Menengai and rain clouds gathering and rumbling behind us, the bible, a smoky memory of a time before that.

· · ·

Some Masai proverbs:

Hold respect like a club. A thing flawed within is unmaintainable.

Quiet, young man! You are not like firewood, which can be burnt. The tongue is not straight, it will say anything. The tongue has no joint. A monkey does not see itself. Impetuosity cannot jump a hedge. Tomorrow praises itself.

Never take two paths, the pelvis will collapse. Don't kneel down when water is far away.

Remember that a worm can destroy a whole plain. Home is to be alive, it is not a place. Never let wanderers lead you to bottle-necked places. The ear penetrates darkness. Zig-zag is the way to success. The well-fed belly does not know the unfed belly. Never tempt warriors with cattle.

· · ·

After breakfast, I set off to walk all the way down to town. I will take, instead of coins for change, a bunch of tropical mints.

I know this road very well. At the Provincial Commissioner's houses, where there is a triangular roundabout, is the boundary of rain. If it is raining in town, down below, this rain stops right here. We get our rain from the Subukia hills, beyond the crater behind my back. From this roundabout you can see Hyrax Hill to the left—a Prehistoric Site. The jacaranda lined road begins—old colonial homes from the 1930s in large one acre plots line the street all the way to St. Christopher's church. Rain from town will stop right here.

You swoop downhill, past Waterworks, stop at the small kiosk for a cold Coke, in a tray in front of the kiosk, there are three rows of round red tomatoes and several bunches of kale, as there have been for years. There is a small gathering of Maragoli speakers on the bench drinking tea and chatting.

I turn into the vacant plot, for the short cut that is not really shorter, to your left an open stream—rainwater drains. And rocky paths. Some aloe and sisal plants. Grass. Goats.

There is a small faded house here, right at the corner, with a large rocky garden that stretches downhill to border State House. It has a swimming pool, now grey and green and empty.

It is one of several houses that were given to the children of Old Man Bomett—whose sister was married to the President.

A short gnarled old tree, that has twisted around and back on itself like a dog leaning to nibble an itch in its back; it has a rich brown bark, few leaves and orange flowers that look like anemones. It must have been common in this area before memories of Surrey and Anglo-Bangalore changed the landscape in the 1930s: jacaranda and eucalyptus and straight stems, in straight lines. You can find this tree all over the wild parts of the crater forest. Its pretty red seeds are used to make jewellery. I don't know its name.

Here are the elements of power and influence: here, small memories of old old people, the Sirikwa live at Hyrax Hill, they built irrigation canals at the escarpment I can see from here.

Then there is the rumble of the Masai—more recent, all feared, and who dominated all the landscape I can see—and whose power now mostly rests in names—most of the towns and rivers and lakes were named by the Masai.

Then, this century, squat and awkward comes the stone and railway lines, the jacarandas and rockeries, the single-room dorm houses for cheap African labour; the red-faced discomforts of large colonial homes with small windows and geometrical gardens—all fading now, but still dominant. The solid matter of this town, beaten and stretched. Rusting and rearranged and built upon.

And now, streaming down the wires the British built their roads, and satellites; and the ones we built in the last forty years, somewhat shoddily, but based on their model.

In the 1970s, America arrives, gum chewing America—a colour, a tone, an attitude, slouching and grinning.

And brewing inside this space are sixty languages and as many micro-nations, angling into this young Nation, twisting and turning and asking to be Kenyan—a thing still unclear, picking here, choosing there; stealing here, and there—disembowelling that which came before, remaking it. Being Kenyan is not yet a commitment, not enough forces have gathered within us to remake the space we occupy.

In January, dry wind would blow into town, a fan shaped blowtorch; and grass would singe; and life claw backwards and backwards and summersault into the horizon, in the escarpment in the distance we could see springs of dust rise.

Reading all those distant English books as a child, the idea of spring made its way into my picture of this place. We have no real spring—we are on the equator. But for me, spring was every morning, dew and soft mists, and the lake still and blue in the distance, sometimes all pink with flamingoes rippling with a breeze, and rising like leaves to whirl against the sky. Summer is midday, the sun above your head, and you have no shadow. Autumn is September, when the jacaranda trees shed all their purple flowers and the short rains began—and the idea of an autumn, of a spring was resident in the imagination of the English Settlers who planned this suburb, and thought of blooms and bees and White highlands made into a new English countryside.

So, in a way, spring has come to be a real thing in Milimani. You read about it in English books, and you experience it with your senses here. But—here is the curse of the Post Colonial: it means nothing here, you can do nothing meaningful with it. All it does is allow you to have false ambitions, to place yourself in a fake middle-class future.

Sometimes you catch a glimpse of what this all was before. On the slopes of this giant caldera, the soil is a flat brown, no red at all in it; and this place was full of light rocks. You can still see them in gardens, piled up into rockeries and stashed away in little forgotten patches. A curse lingers in what was rock and wheat coloured grass and sharp thorny bushes, all now lawn and spring and hedge and red brick homes in two acre plots.

You can see it all laid bare in dry January.

I walk. Small maize, beans and kale plots; and to your left, you stare down at the bowels of State House, Nakuru: sleeping plainclothes policemen—red socks and grey shoes for all to see; scurrying servants, and Mercedes-Benzes—of every kind and length and colour.

When the path levels, there are all manner of ferns and small wild flowers—you step across the stream and cut through the fallen *kei* apple hedge, and into the grand mossy and old buildings of the Medical Training Centre at the War Memorial Hospital—where all the Wainaina children were born.

The hospital has white picket fences, thick lawns and a thick silence that makes me think of silent screams.

I was circumcised here, at thirteen. Became a man.

My father hemmed-hawed at the parking lot at 2 p.m. on a Monday afternoon. Talking about—uh—sexual intercourse—and the, uh—responsibilities of . . . uh . . . man. A bored nurse laughed when I told her that I would not take off my clothes in front of her. The doctor, an Iranian, kept fussing and telling me I should have done the operation when I was a baby. I watched, my cock swelling like a balloon, then fascinated as he cut and I felt nothing.

I bounced out of the room in half an hour ready to tell the world I was pain-free and manly. My mother found me, an hour later, leaning against a jacaranda tree and moaning in pain, after fainting.

At the main building, I turn back into the main road, a dead straight road that starts at the gates of State House, Nakuru, goes past the hospital and meets the newspaper sellers, the bougainvillea range of mountains, the tarmacked walkway, through the bougainvillea, to the cemetery, some churches, the louder and more chaotic Provincial General Hospital. The path branches, at some point, into town—all this area is a boundary between the leafier sections of town—broken cleanly by the railway; and the old African and Indian sections of the town—now a widely spread and messy city of nearly a million.

I walk down the straight road. When I was in high school, I once saw President Moi driving out on this road on his own in a VW combi. He had a jaunty hat on—and nobody by his side. It did not seem possible.

I cross the road, an old house at the corner, on stilts, the sellers of young plants for gardens, the giant bougainvillea that lines the entrance to town, that borders the railway, which cuts the town in half—leafy suburbs and jacarandas, the Colonial old Nakuru on one side, and on the other the town centre—a mix of many things: old Masailand; pioneer Gikuyuland; Gujarat; Punjaab; the Kalenjin Highlands—now Kenya's power centre; food processing; Norfolk, England; the Provincial Headquarters; zebra-patterned curio shops; paleontologists in town from the hills to buy goods; tourvans and flamingoes; a refuge for orphans from ethnic clashes; hundreds of churches; schools; games; NGO people in huge SUVs; our New Kenya; corrugated iron; farmers coming to buy groceries, feed and seed; traffic from the Port of Mombasa, to Kisumu, Uganda, Rwanda and even Congo.

Fuel for growth, and tinder for conflict. Depends on how you look at it.

NGŪGĪ WA THIONG'O

· *Kenya* ·

❖

from WIZARD OF THE CROW

Bearded Daemons

NOW EVERYBODY IN the country knew something or other about the Ruler's Birthday because, before it was firmly set in the national calendar, the date of his birth and the manner of its celebration had been the subject of a heated debate in Parliament that went on for seven months, seven days, seven hours, and seven minutes, and even then the honorable members could not arrive at a consensus mainly because nobody knew for sure the actual date of the Ruler's birth and when they failed to break the impasse, the honorable members sent a formal delegation to the very seat of power to seek wise guidance, after which they passed a motion of gratitude to the Ruler for helping the chamber find a solution to a problem that had completely defeated their combined knowledge and experience. The birthday celebrations would always start at the seventh hour of the seventh day of the seventh month, seven being the Ruler's sacred number, and precisely because in Aburĩria the Ruler controlled how the months followed each other—January for instance trading places with July—he therefore had the power to declare any month in the year the seventh month, and any day within that seventh month the seventh day and therefore the Ruler's Birthday. The same applied to time, and any hour, depending on the wishes of the Ruler, could be the seventh hour.

The attendance at these annual assemblies always varied, but that particular year the stadium was almost full because the curiosity of the citizens had been aroused by a special announcement, repeated over and over in the media, that there would be a special birthday cake, which the entire country had made for the Ruler and which he might make multiply and feed the multitude the way Jesus Christ once did with just five loaves and two fishes. The prospect of cakes for the multitude may explain the more than usual presence of victims of kwashiorkor.

The celebration started at noon, and late in the afternoon it was still going strong. The sun dried people's throats. The Ruler, his ministers, and the leaders of the Ruler's Party, all under a shade, kept cooling their tongues with cold water. The citizens without shade or water distracted themselves from the hot darts of the sun by observing and commenting on what was happening on the platform: the clothes the dignitaries wore, the way they walked, or even where each sat relative to the seat of might.

Immediately behind the Ruler was a man who held a pen the width of an inch water pipe in his right hand and a huge leather-bound book in his left, and since he was always writing people assumed that he was a member of the press, although there were some who wondered why he was not at the press gallery. Beside him sat the four sons of the Ruler—Kucera, Moya, Soi, and Runyenje—studiously drinking from bottles labeled Diet.

Near the sons sat Dr. Wilfred Kaboca, the Ruler's personal physician, and next to him, the only woman on the platform, who was also conspicuous in her silence. Some assumed that she was one of the Ruler's daughters, but then, they wondered, why was she not speaking to her brothers? Others thought that she was Dr. Kaboca's wife, but then why this silence between them?

To the Ruler's right sat the Minister of Foreign Affairs in a dark striped suit and a red tie with a picture of the Ruler, the emblem of the Ruler's Party.

The story goes that Markus used to be an ordinary member of Parliament. Then one day he flew to England, where under the glare of publicity he entered a major London hospital not because he was ill but because he wanted to have his eyes enlarged, to make them ferociously sharp, or as he put it in Kiswahili, *Yawe Macho Kali,* so that they would be able to spot the enemies of the Ruler no matter how far their hiding places. Enlarged to the size of electric bulbs, his eyes were now the most prominent feature of his face, dwarfing his nose, cheeks, and forehead. The Ruler was so touched by his devotion and public expression of loyalty that even before the MP returned home from England the Ruler had given him the Ministry of Foreign Affairs, an important Cabinet post, so that Machokali would be his representative eye wherever, in whatever corner of the globe lay the Ruler's interests. And so Machokali he became, and later he even forgot the name given at his birth.

To the left of the Ruler sat another Cabinet minister, the Minister of State in the Ruler's office, dressed in a white silk suit, a red handkerchief in his breast pocket, and of course the Party tie. He too had started as a not particularly distinguished member of Parliament, and he probably would have remained thus, except that when he heard of the good fortune that had befallen Machokali he decided to follow suit. He did not have much money, so he secretly sold his father's plot and borrowed the rest to buy himself a flight to France and a hospital bed in Paris, where he had his ears enlarged so that, as he also put it in a press statement, he would be able to hear better and therefore be privy to the most private of conversations between husband and wife, children and their parents, students and teachers, priests and their flock, psychiatrists and their patients—all in the service of the Ruler. His ears were larger than a rabbit's and always primed to detect danger at any time and from any direction. His devotion did not go unnoticed, and he was made Minister of State in charge of spying on the citizenry. The secret police machine known as M5 was now under his direction. And so Silver Sikiokuu he became, jettisoning his earlier names.

The success of the two erstwhile members of Parliament was, ironically, the beginning of their rivalry: one considered himself the Ruler's Eye and the other his Ear. People at the stadium kept comparing their different expressions, particularly the movements of their eyes and ears, for it had long been known that the two were always in a mortal struggle to establish which organ was more powerful: the Eye or the Ear of the Ruler. Machokali always swore by his eyes: May these turn against me if I am not telling the truth. Sikiokuu invoked his ears: May these be my witness that what I am saying is true—and in mentioning them, he would tug at the earlobes. The gesture, rehearsed and perfected over time, gave him a slight edge in their rivalry for attention, because Machokali could never match it by tugging at his eyelids and he was reduced to doing the second best thing, pointing at his eyes for emphasis.

Other members of Parliament would have followed suit and had their bodies altered depending on what services they wanted to render the Ruler except for what befell Benjamin Mambo. As a young man Mambo had failed to get into the army because he was small, but the fire for a military life never died, and now, with the new avenues of power opened by Machokali and Sikiokuu, he thought this his best chance to realize his dream, and he agonized over the best bodily change to land him the Defense Minister portfolio. He chose to have his tongue elongated so that in echoing the Ruler's command his words would reach every soldier in the country and his threats to his enemies before they could reach the Aburīrian borders. He first emulated Sikiokuu and went to Paris, but there was some misunderstanding about the required size, and the tongue, like a dog's, now hung out way beyond his lips, rendering speech impossible. Machokali came to his aid by arranging for him to go to a clinic in Berlin, where the lips were pulled and elongated to cover the tongue, but even then not completely and the tongue protruded now just a little. But the Ruler misread the signified and gave him the Ministry of Information. This was not bad, and Mambo marked his elevation to a Cabinet post by changing his forenames and called himself Big Ben, inspired by the clock at the British Houses of Parliament. His full name was now Big Ben Mambo. He did not forget the help that Machokali had rendered him, and in the political struggle between Markus and Silver, he often took Machokali's side.

The idea of a special national gift had come from Machokali—though of course he had gotten strong hints from high above—and it was with the pride of the inventor that he signaled the military, the police, and the prison brass bands to get themselves ready to strike the birthday tune. The moment had come.

There was great curiosity among the crowd as Machokali, aided by members of the Birthday Committee and some police officers, dramatically unfolded and held aloft a huge cloth! Shoving one another aside, people tried to position themselves to see, and they were puzzled when they saw, on the cloth, a huge drawing of something that looked like a building. A drawing on a white cloth for the Ruler's birthday gift?

Taking full advantage of the curiosity and raised expectations, Machokali first appealed to the people to calm themselves because not only was he going to describe everything that was on that cloth, but he was going to make sure that copies of what the English call *an artist's impression* would be distributed to the entire country. He would in fact take that opportunity to thank the teacher who had volunteered his services to do the impression, but regretted that he could not reveal the teacher's name because the artist had forbidden him.

Teaching was a noble profession and its practitioners were modest, driven not by self-glory but selfless service, an ideal for all citizens.

At the far end of the congregation a man raised his hand and waved it frantically while shouting a contradiction, *It's okay, you can mention my name,* and even when told to shut up by those around him, he continued, *I am here—you can reveal my identity.* He was too far back to be heard on the platform but he was near some policemen, and one of them asked him, What is your name? Kaniũrũ, John Kaniũrũ, the man said, and I am the teacher the speaker is referring to. Turn your pockets inside out, the police officer ordered him. After he had made sure that Kaniũrũ was not carrying a weapon, the police officer, pointing at his own gun, asked him, Do you see this? If you continue disrupting the meeting, as sure as my name is Askari Arigaigai Gathere and my boss Inspector Wonderful Tumbo, I will relieve you of that nose. The man Kaniũrũ sat back. Not many people noticed this little commotion because all their eyes and ears were riveted on the bigger drama on the platform.

The whole country, the Minister for Foreign Affairs was saying, the entire Aburĩrian populace, had decided unanimously to erect a building such as had never been attempted in history except once by the children of Israel, and even they had failed miserably to complete the House of Babel. Aburĩria would now do what the Israelites could not do: raise a building to the very gates of Heaven so that the Ruler could call on God daily to say good morning or good evening or simply how was your day today, God? The Ruler would be the daily recipient of God's advice, resulting in a rapid growth of Aburĩria to heights never before dreamt by humans. The entire project, Heavenscrape or simply Marching to Heaven, would be run by a National Building Committee, the chair of which would be announced in good time.

As these wonderful ideas had come from the Birthday Gift Committee, Machokali went on to say, he would like to acknowledge their good work by introducing each of them to the Ruler. The committee members were mostly parliamentarians but there were two or three private citizens, one of whom, Titus Tajirika, almost fell to the ground as he jumped up when his name was called out. Tajirika had never shaken hands with the Ruler, and the thought that this was actually happening in front of thousands was so overwhelming that his whole body trembled in sheer wonderment at his good fortune. Even when he returned to his seat, Tajirika kept on looking at his hands in disbelief, wondering what he could do to avoid using his right hand to shake hands with others or to avoid washing it for some time. He detested gloves but now he wished he had some in his pockets. He would certainly rectify this, but in the meantime he would wrap the lucky hand with his handkerchief so that when he shook hands with his left, people would assume that it was because of an injury to the other. Tajirika was so absorbed in bandaging his right hand that he missed some of the story of Marching to Heaven, but now he tried to catch up with Machokali's narrative.

Minister Machokali was waxing ecstatic about how the benefits of the project could trickle down to all citizens. Once the project was completed, no historian would ever again talk about any other wonders in the world, for the fame of this Modern House of Babel would dwarf the Hanging Gardens of Babylon, the Egyptian pyramids, the Aztecan Tenochtitlán, or the Great Wall of China. And who would ever talk of the Taj Mahal? Our project will be the first and only superwonder in the history of the world. In short, Machokali declared, Marching to Heaven was the special birthday cake the citizens had decided to bake for their one and only leader, the eternal Ruler of the Free Republic of Aburĩria.

Here Machokali paused dramatically to allow time for an ovation.

Except for members of Parliament, Cabinet ministers, officials of the Ruler's Party, and representatives of the armed forces, nobody clapped, but nevertheless Machokali thanked the entire assembly for their overwhelming support and he invited any citizen eager to say a word in praise of Marching to Heaven to step forward. People stared at one another and at the platform in stony silence. The only hands raised were those of the ministers, members of Parliament, and officials of the Ruler's Party, but the minister ignored them and appealed to the citizenry. Are you so overwhelmed by happiness that you are lost for words? Is there no one able to express his joy in words?

A man raised his hand and Machokali quickly beckoned him to come over to the microphone. The man, clearly advanced in years, leaned on a walking stick as he pushed through the crowd. Two police officers ran to him and helped him toward the microphone near the platform. Age was still revered in Aburĩria, and the multitude waited for his words as if from an oracle. But when the old man began to speak it was clear that he had difficulty in pronouncing Swahili words for the Ruler, *Mtukufu Rais,* calling out instead, *Mtukutu Rahisi.* Horrified at the Ruler's being called a Cheap Excellency, one of the policemen quickly whispered in the old man's ear that the phrase was *Mtukufu Rais* or *Rais Mtukufu,* which confused him even more. Coughing and clearing his throat to still himself, he called out into the microphone, *Rahisi Mkundu.* Oh, no, it is not Cheap Arsehole, the other policeman whispered in the other ear, no, no, it is His Holy Mightiness, *Mtukufu Mtakatifu,* which did not help matters because the old man now said, with what the old man thought was confidence, *Mkundu Takatifu.* At the mention of "His Holy Arsehole," the multitude broke out in hilarious laughter, which made the old man forget what he had wanted to say, and he stuck religiously to the phrase *Rahisi Mkundu,* which made Machokali quickly signal that he be removed from the microphone. The old man did not understand why he was not being allowed to speak, and, as he was led back into the crowd, he let out a stream of *Rahisi Mkundu, Mtukutu Takatifu Mkundu, Mtukutu,* any combination of cheap and holy arseholes he thought might work, gesturing toward the Ruler as if begging for his divine intervention.

In order to distract people from the embarrassing scene, Machokali took the microphone and thanked the old man for saying that the entire enterprise was easy and cheap if only the people put their minds and pockets to it. But no matter what spin he put on it, the words *cheap* and *holy arsehole* remained in the air, an embarrassment that clearly left the minister lost in a quandary of inarticulateness.

Minister Sikiokuu seized the moment to deepen the confusion. Claiming that he was actually speaking on behalf of all the others who had raised their hands but had been ignored in favor of the old man, who Machokali was still showering with praise, Sikiokuu asked, Did "brother" Machokali and his committee not realize that the Ruler would get very tired climbing up the staircase to Heaven's gate on foot or riding in a modern elevator, no matter how swift?

He suggested that another committee under his chairmanship be set up to explore possibilities for the construction of a space luxury liner called the Ruler's Angel, and with it a land vehicle, something slightly bigger than the one the Americans had once launched to Mars, to be called Star Rover or simply Rock Rover in Heaven. Armed with the personal spaceship, the only leader in the world to possess one, the Ruler would make pleasure trips wherever and whenever he fancied, hopping from planet to planet, and once on the surface of each star he would simply use the Rock Rover in Heaven to move and pick up gold and diamonds in the sky. As Sikiokuu concluded, he dramatically tugged at his two earlobes as witness and sat down, shouting: A space luxury liner!

Having reclaimed the microphone, Machokali, after thanking his fellow minister for his support of the chosen gift and for his brilliant idea about the Ruler's travel needs in Heaven, quickly pointed out that if the minister had bothered to look at the drawing on the cloth he would have seen that the existing committee had already thought through the problem of heavenly travel. At the very top of Marching to Heaven was a spaceport where such a vehicle could land and take off on journeys to other stars. Machokali now swore a couple of times, pointing at his own eyes as a confirmation of his claim that the committee had been very farsighted.

But it was also obvious from the smile that hovered around the edges of his mouth as he countered Sikiokuu's challenge that he had something else up his sleeve, and when Machokali announced it, it took even the other ministers by surprise. The Global Bank would soon send a mission to the country to discuss Marching to Heaven and see if the bank could loan Aburĩria the money for its completion.

After a dramatic pause to let the news sink in properly, Machokali now called upon the Ruler to accept Marching to Heaven as the gift of a grateful nation to its Ruler.

The brass bands struck up the tune:

Happy Birthday to You
Happy Birthday to You
Happy Birthday, Dear Ruler
Happy Birthday to You

The Ruler, a staff and a fly whisk in his left hand, stood up. His dark suit was almost identical to that worn by Machokali, but on careful examination one could see that the stripes were made of tiny letters that read MIGHT IS RIGHT. Rumor had it that all his clothes were made to measure in Europe, that his London, Paris, and Rome tailors did nothing else but make his clothes. What distinguished his clothes from all imitations by all political fawns were the patches on the shoulders and elbows of his jackets, because they were made from skins of the big cats, mainly leopards, tigers, and lions. In short, no politician was allowed to wear clothes with patches made from the skin of His Mighty Cats. This special feature had inspired the children to sing how their Lord:

Walks the earth like a leopard
Lights the path with the eyes of a tiger
And roars with a lion's fury

With his height and his custom suits, the Ruler cut quite an imposing figure, and that is why the holders of the fifth theory keep going back to how he looked that day. He had been the very picture of good health as he cleared his throat and declaimed, "I am deeply moved by the tremendous love that you have shown me today . . ." adding that before speaking further, he would like to show his appreciation of their love with an act of mercy by announcing the release of hundreds of political prisoners, among them a few authors and journalists all held without trial including one historian who had been in prison for ten years for crimes that included writing a book called *People Make History, Then a Ruler Makes It His Story.* The alleged literary sins of the historian still consumed the Ruler, because even now he came back to the case of the historian. Professor Materu, he called him, sarcastically referring to the fact that on his arrival in prison the professor's long beard had been the first thing to go under a blunt knife. This terrorist of the intellect has spent ten years in jail, said the Ruler, but because of this historic occasion, I have let him out early. But Professor Materu would not be allowed to grow his beard a length more than half an inch, and if he transgressed, he would be reimprisoned. He was to report once a month to a police station to have the length of his beard measured. All the other dissidents had to swear that never again would they collect and pass on rumors as history, literature, or journalism. If they mended their ways, they would know him as Lord Generosity who rewarded the truly repentant, he said, before turning to the sole woman on the platform.

"Dr. Yunice Immaculate Mgenzi," he called out.

Slowly and deliberately, the silent woman stood up; she was truly striking in poise and general appearance.

"Do you see this woman?" he continued. "In the days of the cold war this one you now see was a revolutionary. Very radical. Her name said it all. Dr. Yunity Mgeuzi-Bila-Shaka. You see? A revolutionary without a doubt. Maoist. *Alikuwa mtu ya* Beijing. But in the final days of the cold war, she gave up this revolutionary foolishness, repented, and pledged faithful service to me. Did I jail her? No. I even asked Big Ben Mambo to give her a job as an information officer, and now I am happy to announce that I have appointed Dr. Yunice Immaculate Mgenzi as the next deputy to my ambassador in Washington. The first woman in the history of Aburĩria to hold such a post."

Dr. Mgenzi acknowledged the thunderous applause from the crowd with a bow and a wave of the hand, and then sat down.

"And now," continued the Ruler when the applause subsided, "I want to talk about another radical who used to breathe fire and brimstone at imperialism, capitalism, colonialism, neocolonialism, the whole lot. He used to go by the name of Dr. Luminous Karamu-Mbuya-Ituĩka. You see, calling on luminous pens to scrawl revolution? An agitator. A Moscow man. Educated in East Germany's Institute of Marxist Revolutionary Journalism. There was even a time when some of our neighbors, drunk with the foolishness of African socialism, had hired his services to write radical articles calling for class struggle in Africa. As soon as it was clear that communism was a spent force, he too wisely repented and hastened to remove the word *revolution* from his name. What did I do? Jail him? No. I forgave him. And he has proven himself worthy of my forgiveness with his work. In the *Eternal Patriot,* the underground leaflet he used to edit, he used to denounce me as a creator of a nation of sheep. Now in the *Daily Parrot* he helps me shepherd the sheep with his literary lashes."

To protect the country against malicious rumormongers, so-called historians, and novelists, and to counter their lies and distortions, the Ruler appointed him to be his official biographer, and as everyone knows his biography was really the story of the country, and the true history. "My Devoted and Trusted Historian," roared the Ruler, "I want you to stand up that they may behold you and learn."

The biographer obliged, and it was then that everybody realized that the man with the leather-bound notebook and a pen the size of a water pipe was the Ruler's official biographer. My beloved children, the Ruler now called out, turning to the multitude, I want to say, may you all be blessed for your superwonder gift to me. Not least of what made it so endearing, he said, was that it came as a complete surprise: not in his wildest dreams had he thought that Aburĩria would show its gratitude by attempting something that had never been done in the history of the world. He had never expected any rewards; doing what he had done had been its own reward, and he would continue to do so out of a fatherly love. He stopped, for suddenly near the center of the multitude issued a bloodcurdling scream. A snake! A snake! came the cry taken up by others. Soon there was pandemonium. People shoved and shouted in every direction to escape a snake unseen by many. It was enough that others had; the cry was now not about one but several snakes. Unable to believe what was happening and with none wanting to be first to show fear, the Cabinet ministers cast surreptitious glances at one another, waiting for someone to make the first move.

Part of the crowd started pushing its way toward the platform, shouting, Snake! Snake! Some police officers and soldiers were about to run away but when they saw the Ruler's guard ready their guns to shoot into the crowd, they stood their ground. The chaos continued unabated.

To calm things down, the police chief shot his gun into the air, but this only made matters worse and the melee turned into a riot of self-preservation as people took to their heels in every direction; after a few minutes, only the Ruler and his entourage of ministers, soldiers, and policemen were left in the park. The head of the secret police woke up from a stupor and whispered to the Ruler, This might be the beginning of a coup d'état, and within seconds the Ruler was on his way to the State House.

DOREEN BAINGANA

· *Uganda* ·

✦

CHRISTIANITY KILLED THE CAT

MY FATHER WAS fierce sometimes, a coward otherwise, and that is why he married my mother. One day, he was the worst sinner ever, three wives, overdrinking, you name it, and the next, he switched to his father's religion, Christianity, but exaggerated it to the point of obsession, that is, he became born-again. When he saw the light he chased away all the family except my mother and me, and married her in his new church that week. Why her? Because it was her kiosk and garden we lived on, and because she threatened him all the way to the altar. Why him? I can't answer that. He was already married to booze, and perhaps she was stimulated by competition. His excuse for his love for the bottle was that his father was a gifted and true medicine man from a long family of *basezi*, but he had not passed on his secret and powerful knowledge because the whites came and confused him into Christianity. And so my poor father, with nothing to inherit but a borrowed religion, drowned his sorrows. No son too, was his other excuse, pointing at whomever of us girls were nearby, as if it was our fault. I was as frightened and confused as my sisters were by the babble of tongues of all the church people who came to the house to help him clear out the evil of polygamy. I was jealous too, because I thought my sisters were packing for a long trip, until I discovered I would have my father all to myself.

The conversion stopped his sorrowful drowning for about a month, and then he took to wading into it now and then. After school, it was I who went and secretly bought crude Waragi for him from Obama's bar. We understood that a saint should not be seen in bars, especially a brand new one. Obama knew whose it was, but you couldn't expect him to refuse money. I got there early enough, five o'clock, before the regular drinkers came, and he filled my plastic bottle of Orangina with the clear firewater. We would sit outside, my father and I, leaning on the far wall of the house, away from both the main road and the kitchen, me on my little bamboo stool now the shape of my small bum, he on a worn smooth wooden one. I scratched the dust with a stick while he sipped in silence, or murmured to himself, mostly about good and evil. "The demon's got me." "Ah, just a little won't hurt." "All gods may be one." As the evening wore on, there was less murmur and more silence, and he relaxed into himself, the ropes of religion loosening off him.

From the other side of the house, I could see and smell wisps of smoke from the *sigiri* rising into the air, mixing with my mother's complaining conversation with our neighbor Lidiya. Maama went on about my father being at home the whole day, doing nothing but praying and reading his Bible, just sitting there and calling it The Work of the Lord. Lidiya would take over with wails about her man who she never saw the whole day; work, work, work, he said, but who knew what he was doing? They sighed heavily, sinking comfortably into their womanly burdens, while my father and I sighed with more important weight.

One evening, the air heavy with smoke from many houses' suppers, my father interrupted his silence by shuffling into the house, and I heard him move their metal bed, and pull and shift around something heavy. I guessed he was rummaging in those old baskets he kept under the bed. Maama had threatened to throw them all out, but my father growled, "I'll throw you out first," but of course he had not. Instead, he stopped talking to her, and to me too, which I thought was unfair. He retreated into himself, and not just physically. Hunched over and brooding, he became a cold ghost at the table, one that moved from room to room in our three-room house, filling it with a bitter smell. But after a week, he suddenly smiled at her when she silently put food on the table. "For all your faults, you are a good cook," he said, as he shaped a small white lump of *posho* in his thin fingers, rolling and rolling it before dipping it in the bean sauce. Our mouths formed wide white smiles, and we wouldn't have stopped even if we had been slapped. I would have fought my mother over those smelly bags.

Taata came back out with a tattered, gray, long hairy sack. It was a cow's leg, the dark hoof weighing it down at the bottom, the long sack of dry old skin had most of its hair missing. He sat down and put his arm deep inside, searched around in it, and came out with crumbs that looked like soil and lint. From his coat pocket, he pulled out a pipe that seemed just as old, and sprinkled the particles into the pipe, hardly filling it. "Nothing," he murmured. "Nothing, that's all." He lit the pipe as I stared; I knew he wanted me to watch. He must have smoked the skin itself. The smoke curled up and disappeared into the thin air with a faint but somehow familiar scent.

"I'm not giving you any," he said, not looking at me, but out at the blue-black shadows that had been trees and houses a moment ago. The dark made the known shapes mysterious. When I looked back at him, tears glinted faintly on his face, perhaps from the smoke.

"Okay—I'll teach you to kill, at least."

I was jerked out of an almost trance-like silence. "What?"

"Don't eat anything tomorrow. At least I was taught that."

"Kill what?"

"For your size, a bird. But you have to be hungry for it."

I kept quiet. My father didn't make much sense on these evenings of ours, but this was worse. I sometimes wished he wouldn't talk at all.

My mother came round the corner of the house. "Have you Christians drank enough? Come and eat," she called, cheerfully.

We could not bask in silence forever. My father got up wearily, and I got up like him, pretending weary. "Women," we both muttered under our breath, but followed her, her huge swaying buttocks an affront to our spirit.

The next day, Saturday, was a good day not to eat because there was no school. Mother was the fussy one. "What? Not eating? It's fish for lunch."

"No. Taata said so." He was always my way out. But today of all days, when fish was so rare, obeying him was painful.

"What is your fool of a father up to now?"

"He is teaching me things." I didn't want to get into it. "Haven't you heard of fasting?"

She stared at me for a long moment, her large eyes like two drills, then let it go. Perhaps she believed in my father a little bit. She brushed her hand over my head. "You still have to open your hair and wash it, wash your school uniform. Don't think I'm doing that for you."

The morning was easy, but by afternoon, there was nothing I wanted to do but just sit still. I went over to the shade of the mango tree near Maama's garden, its thick green leaves a solid shade. It was not too far from the rubbish heap that was high, huge; Taata was supposed to have burnt it up last week. I couldn't ignore the mountain of yellow and white milk cartons, gray torn packets for *posho* flour, dark green and black curling wet banana peels, yellow and black ones too, some slimy orangey liquidy stuff, grayish fruit, torn bits of paper fluttering pink, blue and white, dust, old mattress stuffing of mildewed cotton, red sweet potato peels, hard brown cassava ones, mango leaves scattered all over like garnish, and on top of it all, fish bones that smelt as sweet as, as, what? As sharp as pineapple cutting your tongue pleasurably. I could only stare, smell and suffer.

This thin stray cat that was a dirty white all over, that always hung around our neighborhood, crept up and over the rubbish heap. It jerked to a stop and turned to me, its red eyes sharp and unblinking. I had held this cat before when it was a scrawny slip of a kitten. It used to wander into our kitchen to steal scraps, and I had the job of chasing it away. But it would claw into the weaving of my mother's faded blue and green sisal mat and cling fast. I tugged at it by its thin neck, feeling sinewy muscle and fur only, no bone, as it squealed and squirmed in my hands. Finally, its tiny claws tore out of the mat, and it hung limp in my hand. I would rush out and fling it away as forcefully and fiercely and as far away as I could, out into the garden, where it landed so gracefully, like water flung and forming a pattern in the air before landing. The kitten would shake itself and skip away, leaving me jealous. And it would always return.

Now grown, the cat dismissed me quickly, and continued its slow crawl over the refuse, bones under the thin patchy fur moving gracefully, menacingly. It found the fish bones, picked and played with them with small teeth, dropping precious bits of whitish-gray skin and flesh. My fish. The wish to grab that small skeleton from the cat's claws was as sharp as the need to pee. Like when you have diarrhea and you are running to the toilet, holding it, holding it. The smell of near rot intensified, wafts of it killing me, like moonflowers whose scent whispered at you at dusk, then disappeared with faint promises. The cat took its time cracking the soft bones. My stomach lurched loudly. Did it hear it? The cat shot its small head up and glared at me, its red eyes flaring for one long moment, tiny pieces of flesh hanging from its mouth. I could easily have shouted it away, thrown a stone at it, anything, if I had not seen a person in its eyes. I mean a demon. I swear. It snarled a laugh, tempting me, just like Jesus was tempted. Then it gobbled up the rest of the carcass, sending only more smells my way, before it crawled over and away from the heap, satisfied. But it didn't go away. I kept my eyes on it as it sat a little distance from me and licked itself clean, its long pink tongue working out and in quickly, like a pale darting flame. It yawned, showing me its tiny yellow fangs, pink eyes still leering, and there we sat, staring at each other, it, languid; I, mad and afraid.

Hunger crawled through my whole body, stomach, arms and legs, like how that cat had swarmed over the heap of refuse. But hunger made my mind stark and clear, emptied it of all but one idea: I would kill this cat, not shoot some silly bird. It was a demon that sensed the saint in me. My father's drunken murmurs of good and evil begun to make sense.

I told him so later that evening as we sat by our wall. His eyes widened and he looked at me strangely. Was he scared, or pleased? I couldn't tell.

"You? A cat?"

"Yes. It ate my fish."

My father just kept on staring at me.

"It isn't afraid of me. It thinks I am weak." Then I whispered, half-hoping he wouldn't hear. "That cat is a demon."

My father turned away from me, as if to hide a grin that had sprung out of his severe, squarish face. The smile turned into chuckles that came out in short painful spurts, and he held his chest as if to stop them, but couldn't. I had pleased him, I think. Now he was coughing, so I got up and rubbed his back over his frayed brown coat as he bent over, weak, but warm. He said I could eat that night.

My father said we used to get poison from snakes, but there are hardly any snakes left; they had all been killed or are hiding in the forest. So the next day we went up the main road to Auntie Sukuma's store. Everyone called her Auntie; who wouldn't want to be related to someone whose store had everything under the sun, including black sticky sweets that tasted of shoe polish mixed with bananas. They were from China. If I had a chance to move there, I would eat only sweets. Taata did not waste time with long greetings, like most people, but Auntie was used to this.

"Rat poison?"

"How are you, Namuli?" She looked only at me.

"I am fine, thank you, Auntie. Do you have any rat poison? We are suffering with too many rats." I was used to talking for my father.

She scanned her eyes over shelves upon shelves of blue soap, cartons of matchboxes, petroleum jelly, instant coffee, hot sauce, plastic cups, plates and jugs, and on and on. It would have taken a whole day to list all the things packed together on the shelves.

"I had it here somewhere, hmmm . . . but why don't you get a cat?"

"Do you want money or not?"

I cringed. Taata should have had a drink first before coming here. She turned and gave him a stern look. She was not scared of him. If I had a store like hers, I wouldn't have been either.

"Ah yes, I put it far up there to keep it from the wrong hands." She glanced back at my father, then got a stool, moved to a dark corner stuffed with tins and boxes and swollen blue plastic bags, climbed up, pulling her bulky frame up with effort, and got a jar from a row of colorful squashed packages. She clambered down, dusted it off with a rag, and peered at the label.

"Be careful with this, eh? This poison is strong, eh, it's not a joke."

"Who's laughing? We can read the instructions just as well as you. How much?"

"I was talking to Namuli. My dear, give it to your mother to use, okay? Don't touch it. Five thousand only."

I took the jar wrapped in a thin black plastic bag as my father searched his pockets. For some reason Maama gave him money. She was like me; we did what he wanted, eventually.

As we turned away, Auntie said, "*Kale,* Namuli, greet your mother, okay? Such a nice woman." She shook her head at my father, but he was already gone. I rushed to follow, pulling my skirt down over my knees.

Back home, my father got busy. We moved to our side of the compound, and using a stick, he mixed the thick poison paste with a little water on the cracked half of an old plate.

"Go get some of yesterday's supper."

My mother was not in the kitchen, thank God. I found some groundnut sauce and posho, which was now as hard as a brick. Taata broke it up into powdery pieces, and mixed it with the pink sauce and grayish poison. Wasn't I relieved; I had thought I had to kill the cat with my bare hands. This was going to be easy.

"Okay, don't touch it, you hear?"

I nodded, and he went indoors and began rummaging around in his old bags again. He came out of the house brandishing a decrepit looking bow and arrows. The bow's string was frayed and sagging, the bow worn smooth with age. The arrows were as long as my arm, with rusty metal pointed tips. *Me,* use those?

"Isn't the poison enough?" I tried.

"E-eh, Namuli, that's not killing, that's cheating. We're using it just to make it easier for you. Maybe later, a gun, why not?" His eyes glinted, and he chuckled as if the demon had entered him too.

All I had to do was tell my mother so that I could get out of this. It was getting to be too much.

"Ah-ha, you want to run back to the skirts, I can tell. Go then." Of course I couldn't. I knelt in the dust next to him as he fidgeted with the small skin sack he had brought out the other day. His fingers trembled as he struggled to undo the strings tied around the top of the sack. I knew what he needed, and went off to get him his bottle. He took a swig, head leaning back, then sputtered and coughed. It didn't help right away; I still had to help him open the bag, pulling at the tight knots first with my fingers then with my teeth. "There you go," he muttered. "Use whatever you can." Again, he scraped the bottom of the sack and came out with whitish dust. "Now I remember," he said. "A rooster's crown, dried and crushed," and sprinkled it on the mash we had prepared for the cat. He continued, "This is not easy, not simple, but necessary, you understand? Can you be—you must be dedicated, slow, methodical, mechanical. Don't think too much. Act." I would. I would.

My mother knew how to choose the worst times to appear. "Taata, are you—what are you two playing at now?"

"Cat and kid." My father giggled, and took a sip of his drink.

"What?"

"Why ask when you won't understand?" He was busy tightening the bowstring.

"He—we are going to, um, practice hunting," I said.

"*Katonda wange*, Chalisi, when will you grow up?"

"Ee-h, you hear her. You think killing is a child's game? I am trying to show her what is real: death after life."

Her eyes turned a boiling red. "Rubbish. If you want to play, play with fire. What about that heap of rubbish you were supposed to burn? That's why dirty cats are here all the time—"

"And I am trying to get rid of them. Fire? You want fire, yes, okay, we'll burn it. Don't worry. Just go. Go see Lidiya."

I hid a small grin behind my hand as Maama chewed her teeth and turned away. She knew by now that you could not reason with Taata. She stalked off, her big hips saying back off as they rolled away like a cement-mixing machine. Her backside could say come hug, or I'm sick of you, or I could be your pillow. My father smiled, his lips curling over his scattered moustache.

We moved to the garden, not too far from the huge mango tree. Taata stood poised, one leg in front of the other, steady. He took aim, one eye almost closed, and in a blink, the arrow whizzed through the air and got stuck in the trunk. It sounded like a big fat bee racing past.

"Now you."

He stood beside me, slightly bent, and held the bow in my hands, his fingers over my own. He stretched the string taut with me, aimed for me. My beating heart was soothed by his warm hands. "Steady, steady, pull, now . . . let go!"

Out of my hands it flew, fast and sure, but then curved away and hit the ground beside the tree. "Not bad. Try again, pull harder, use more force."

I did so again and again, wiping the sweat off my palms onto my dress, wiping my forehead with my hands. This was my favorite tree. I struck it on the fifth attempt, screamed and jumped high. Taata laughed. "See!?" The direct hit, aiming for something and getting it, my mind controlling my eyes, hands, the air, the bow and the arrow, that was power. A quick shot of pleasure swarmed through my arms and legs, I found myself trembling. I had to do it again.

I picked up the scattered arrows and handed them to my father. We could not stop grinning. As I squatted beside him and watched, excited, he dipped the arrow tips into a thick mix of rat poison and a few drops of water, adding some muttered words into the mix. I swear I heard some Latin from the priest at church. The other words I didn't know, but yes, we needed God to help us with the demon.

To be frank, the exhilaration of could-I-hit-or-not was sharper now than the evil that had gleamed out of the cat, despite a dream I had the night before. The cat had come up to me, eyes glowing like hell, and rubbed its dirty gray damp fur against my legs, its fish smell trying to suffocate me. I pulled and pulled at it, but it clung to my legs tighter, whining, not snarling, as if it needed me, like a baby starved of milk, while I struggled against it. The crying thing would not let go, its body stretching long like thick slippery elastic. As it wailed, I begun moaning with it until finally, thankfully, my whimpers woke me up. Relief gushed through and out of me like sweat. I sat up in bed and vowed not to sleep again that night, but of course I did.

But now, now the dream was mere shadow, as the bow and arrows became a potent extension of my arms. More than fear, I wanted to see if I could aim accurately again, and hit and hit and hit.

The cat had kept away while we were practicing, but now all was quiet. It slunk back to the rubbish heap, which was still nice and high and colorful with fresh refuse, the cracked plate of food and poison balanced on the top where I placed it. A few flies that landed on it failed to fly off. My father had told me not to eat again to help me focus. "Sit in the sun and wait," he said, and I did, closer to the heap, its smell stinging my nostrils. My father sat a little way off under the shade of the mango tree, sipping as usual, watching and waiting with me. My mother was not even a thought in my mind.

As the sun struck my forehead, and my father drank more spirit, he began his mutterings again. "Sacrifice. For my father's father's gods, a chicken was enough. A goat, maybe, a cow even. But what better sacrifice than a *man?* The Son of God, who is God also. What my father could have done, but many *many* times over. For the past, the present and the future, even for those not yet born. Yes, that is the essential thing: sacrifice."

Taata's monotone became an incessant hum in my ears as the sun bore down. I watched the cat sniff at the plate then gobble up the food quickly. It licked its lips and face with that agile pink darting tongue, then sniffed around for more. I kept my eyes on it as it moved down the heap, heading towards me. It stopped abruptly and started coughing, its little white head jerking up and down. I had to act before it got away. A part of me coughed with it, a strange echo of the wails in my dream. Another part of me was also the cat, rising up slowly, body taut with resolve, all arms and shoulder and muscle and aim and stretching; all with the cat's sure grace. Tight, tight, I pulled and stretched the bowstring, hungry for the cat's narrow body, hungry not to miss.

With all my will I let the poisoned arrow go, and its swift zing was joined in the very same second by a devilish screech, and I felt it, I did, the sharp metal point plunging through soft fur and skin, the second of resistance, then the impossibility of it. My mind shot back to when my mother had passed a needle through fire then stabbed my ear lobes, one after the other, while I, all fright, felt my flesh from the inside, deeply. Now, as sweat fell into my eyes, I saw red bursting bright like a flower out of the grayish-white. A bubbling flower that I had made.

The cat scrambled and slipped, desperately trying to crawl away, but I scrambled too, quickly, my mind sharp and clear. I aimed and shot again, and again felt that sweet sharp invasion of hard cold metal meeting, tearing and entering soft hot skin and flesh. I grabbed yet another poisoned arrow, but from somewhere far away, heard my father shouting, "Stop!" I staggered back, and like the writhing cat, could not escape. I was its body; the poison gained life as it took it, seeking veins and sneaking through, racing quickly throughout the dirty little hot body. Now the flesh itself became thirsty for it, begged for it, like how after my fast, I had drunk water so frantically I almost choked, and felt it flush cold down my throat and spread, tingling, even to the tips of my fingers and toes.

The cat had to stop writhing, and it did, slumping down dead. Still, blood moved out and over it, covering the once white fur with blotches of crimson. Its red eyes remained open. I had chased out its sleek and tawny grace and was left with a limp nothing. I would have to throw it on the rubbish heap, and I wanted to throw myself there too.

Instead, I turned away and ran to my father who, with his arms raised, filled the air with shouts of praise. He stopped long enough to give me a small precious sip of his almost empty bottle, for the very first time, then he went on hollering to the sun. What could I do but try to shout like him, even adding a dance on trembling legs, until I could dance and shout for real. I waved the bow and arrows over my head and screamed, "I did it! I did it!" My father was full of loud hallelujahs, so I danced for him, and he laughed. But he had not seen the cat's red eyes. Though they had stopped glowing, they were not defeated.

I swiveled round and round, my skirt flying, then threw the bow and arrows down as if in victory, not disgust. I can end a life, I Namuli. The dancing finally, finally took hold, and I jumped and screamed higher.

My mother, hearing all the commotion, rushed out of the house. "Have you gone mad?" She shrieked like the dying cat, like me, only louder.

"I killed a cat! I killed—"

She came right up, and with all the weight of her wonderful body, shook me by the shoulders until my cheeks wobbled and I shut up. When she let go, I fell down still. Finally, like the cat, I let go. Something warm oozed out of me, streamed down my leg. Blood? Pee. Warm, tangy pee. What had I done? Then came the tears, and I let them.

Mother continued to scream, her cries filling the air like a swarm of crickets as she tried to put the up-side-down world straight again, tried to make us sane, but it was too late. My father tugged at me. "Come on, you're too old for this now." But I couldn't stop. "You won," he pleaded, and I turned away from him. The soil making me dirty seemed right. He shrugged, let his arms fall to his sides, turned and strode off, mumbling and grumbling, he couldn't stay and listen to women crying and cursing. This time, I wanted him to go, go get his own drink.

My mother got quiet, now that Taata was no longer there to scream at. "Typical! The fool causes trouble, then runs away."

She turned to me. "Namuli?" Although I now felt stupid, lying there wet and dirty on the ground, I didn't want what she would do: pull me up gently, wipe my face with her wrapper, dust my dress, try and fold me back into her. Couldn't she see I now had claws like a cat?

"Leave me alone. Just leave me, okay?" I got myself up and moved away. I would wash myself, and go sit on my stool by our wall for a while. I wanted to sit alone.

NURUDDIN FARAH

· *Somalia* ·

❖

from KNOTS

CAMBARA TEARS DOWN the stairway, as though on a warpath, and strides over to the toolshed in the backyard, which has been converted to the *qaat*-chewers' retreat. There, the driver and several youths are busy munching away, their cheeks bulging with the stuff, slurping very sweet tea and sipping Coca-Cola. From where she is eavesdropping on their conversation, barely a few meters from the door to the shed, she can hear them chatting lazily about cutthroat civil war politics and also debating about which warlord controls which of the most lucrative thoroughfares in the city and how much money he collects daily from his tax-levying ventures. Speculating, they move on to another related topic, mentioning the name of an upstart clansman of the same warlord, formerly a deputy to him, most likely to unseat said warlord with a view to laying his hands on the thriving business.

Having heard enough about warlords and their presumptive, empty jabbering, she decides it is time she barged in without announcing either her presence or motive. First, she takes her position in the doorway, blocking it—arms akimbo, her feet spread wide apart—and fuming at their conjectural politics and their slovenly behavior. Some of the men look appalled; others appear amused; yet others shake their heads in surprise, as they all unfailingly turn their heads in her direction and then toward each other. To a man, they stop whatever they have been doing, maybe because they were unprepared for her entry.

They are baffled, because it is unclear to them under whose authority she is acting, and because they have no idea where Zaak is on this or what part he is playing. One of them whispers to his mate that she is like a headmistress at a convent school who is disciplining her charges. His mate, in riposte, compares her to a parent waking his truant teenagers from a late lie-in, shaking them awake. When a couple of the others resume talking in their normal voices and some go back to their chewing or tea sipping, Cambara embarks on a more startling undertaking: She confiscates their *qaat*. The whisperer now says, "How incredibly fearless!" His mate remarks that it is not enough for her to barge in on them as if she owned the place; she must show us she is the boss. Another wonders where it will all end.

As if to prove the whisperer's mate right, she gathers the bundles of *qaat* that they have not so far consumed from in front of them—they are too gobsmacked to challenge her—and she dumps the sheaves in a waste bin crawling with noxious vermin. Turning and seeing the shock on their faces, she does not ease off. She shouts, "This is a sight worse than I've ever imagined. How can you stand living so close to the fetid odor coming from the waste bin, which none of you has bothered to empty for a very long time?" And before the driver or any of the youths has recovered from her relentless barrage, she tells them, "It is time to be up."

No one speaks. They are all eyes, fixed on her. After a brief pause, however, the driver gathers his things and joins her; several others do likewise. One might wonder why the driver or the youths act out of character and remain biddably unassertive when it is very common among the class of men to which the armed vigilantes and the driver belong to take recourse to the use of guns at the slightest provocation. Cambara puts their compliant mood down to the fact that her behavior has taken them by surprise and that many of the armed militiamen hardly know how to respond to the instructions of women.

She orders the driver to supervise the two youths who earlier had bullied SilkHair, whom she tells to wash the inside and outside of the truck, vacuum, and make sure they rid it of the execrable odor. When the driver retorts that he does not have a Hoover or any of the other sanitizers about which she is speaking, she suggests that they use a house disinfectant. Still, when each of them, except for the driver, picks up his gun—for they seem naked without one, now that they are upright, their hands uselessly hanging down—and they argue that they do not know where they can find any deodorizers, Cambara eyes them unkindly. Then she takes one of them by the hand, dragging him into the kitchen; she provides him with an assortment of these cleaning items from a stack of household goods, mostly for cleaning, which presumably Zaak bought and locked away in one of the cupboards. She returns with the youth bearing the stuff and breathing unevenly. She gets them down to work, on occasion swearing at them under her breath. On top of being amused, she watches them for a few minutes with keen interest. Good heavens, how clumsy they appear now that they are missing their weapons, which over the years have become extensions of themselves; they appear wretched without them. With their bodily movements uncoordinated, they are as ungainly as left-handers employing their right hands to lift something off the ground. For their part, the guns have an abandoned look about them, to all intents and purposes, just pieces of metal worked into pieces of wood and no more menacing than a child's toy.

When the driver and the other youths have washed the outside and the inside of the truck, she sets them to work in the living room: sweeping, dusting, and cleaning it. Watching them as they shift the settees and other furniture, she wonders if they have ever lifted anything heavier than their AK-47s. To while away the time pleasantly as they work, she puts on the CD player, and out comes blaring some Somali music, actually a song of her own composition, the CD cut privately in a back-alley studio in Toronto. The words and the voice-over are both hers, set to music by a Jamaican friend of Maimouna's. Maybe they recognize the voice, because they all stop working and stare at her in doe-eyed fascination. She becomes self-conscious, realizing that this is the first time she is listening to her own words and voice on a CD. In the context, she thinks that maybe she needs to do more work on it, tightening it here and there, strengthening the weaker parts, in short re-recording everything before releasing it. Thinking, "Not too bad, though," she lets them hear it several times.

In the song, a boy—the voice is that of Dalmar—says, "When is a man a man?"

A woman's voice, Cambara's, replies, "A man is a man when he can work like a man, hardy, dedicated, mindful that he uses his strength to serve the good of the community."

Eerily, her heart almost misses a beat, as she assumes that she has had a distinct glimpse of a boy wearing familiar clothes, a boy who reminds her of her son, and who is now standing in the entrance to the living room, dressed in *his* trousers and shirt. For an instant, Cambara feels dislocated from her surroundings, and then she remembers that she is the one who has presented SilkHair with the clothes, which fit him perfectly. When it dawns on her that she does not like the song anymore, she turns the CD off, then walks over to where SilkHair is and, beaming with delight, says to him, "Well done." Then things begin to take a bad turn.

Call it what you like: jealousy, because one of their number, the youngest, whom they could bully with impunity until earlier today, has been luckier than they, having charmed The Woman; call it in character or reverting to type, because you could not expect the youths to act as normally as others might. Whatever the case, one of the youths, bearing the nickname LongEars, who earlier bullied SilkHair, has found his tongue. He speaks loud enough for everyone to hear, now that the music is off, and everyone is invidiously focusing on Cambara hugging and welcoming SilkHair.

"We are not servants," LongEars announces. "We are Security." LongEars mispronounces the word, replacing the *c* in "Security" with a *g*. He continues, "We don't carry settees, we don't mop floors; we are Segurity. Not only that, we are men, and cleaning is a woman's job, and we won't do it."

In the uneasy silence that follows, Cambara and SilkHair stand apart, watching, warily waiting. She looks around, not knowing what to do and wondering whether to say something that will put things in perspective. She feels there is time yet for someone to calm things down. She also senses that if any of the other youths come forward and talk in support of LongEars, then you can be sure the mutineers will win the day. She prays that someone older and with more authority—she can mean only the driver, and she looks hopefully in his direction—might gamble on shoring up her plans, propping them with his own words of endorsement. But the driver remains not only silent but also noncommittal in his body language. She is about ready to take a walk away from it all when the driver clears his throat to attract attention and then enters the fray.

He addresses his words to LongEars, his voice level, calm, unafraid. The driver says, "I am older, and I remember the years when everybody had a job. I was a driver; someone was a cleaner; another was a clerk; another was a head of department; whether he qualified for the job or not, there was a president of the country; and we had a government. Most important, we had peace. You have no memories of any of this; I do. You are not Security; you know it, and I know it. We are members of a nation of losers, of clans warring, of youths without schooling, of women continuously harangued. We are a people living in abnormal times."

In the silence, Cambara, her heart warmed, can now see the sun boldly shining through. SilkHair and almost all the other youths stand motionless, listening attentively to the driver's words with more attentiveness than they have ever imagined possible. LongEars seems alone, as lifeless as the tongue of a mute.

"If you think of it the way I do, this lady is a godsend," the driver goes on. "She has been with us for a couple of hours, and look at what she has achieved. In less than a day. Look at Agoon," he says, and they all turn to SilkHair, several of the youths nodding in agreement with the driver. "If she can bring about such positive change in the short time she has had with us, imagine what it will be like when she has been with us for much longer. My brothers, let's all resume working, for there is time yet for us to save ourselves. There is hope yet for us to regain peace."

A youth known to be an ally of LongEars has something to say. The driver encourages him to get it off his chest. "But this has always been a woman's job, cleaning, not a man's job."

The driver has an answer. "Because women are doing men's jobs. That is why. They are raising the young family and keeping the house and keeping it united, protected from hunger and death. And since women are doing our jobs, it follows that we must do theirs, doesn't it?"

She hears someone clapping and then sees the heads of several of the youths turning toward her, then away to the driver. LongEars storms out in anger. Cambara wonders if he may have gone to join forces with Zaak. Pray, what is Zaak up to?

To set an example, the driver is the first to get back on his knees, mopping, washing, and assisting another youth. She works together with SilkHair to remove the accumulated grit from a corner where two walls meet and where someone spilled a drink with high sugar content. It's just as well, she observes to herself, that they've dislodged a clan of ants that have set up their base of operation for several months. They all join in the general banter, teasing each other amicably. She takes the opportunity to remind them that even though they are half her age, they cannot haul the furniture back and forth without fuss or complaint. She challenges the remaining two bullies who were nasty to Silk-Hair to help her pick up the two two-seater settees. She discovers that neither has any idea how to lift his side of a settee off the floor without doing his back in. Then she tells them, "Forget it," and does it with SilkHair after explaining to him how to position his body.

All eyes swarm to her, as if she were a bee soon after the season's flowers have blossomed into pollen of welcome seeds. Thanks to the driver, she has stung every one of them, and they are besotted not so much with her as they are with the idea of her or the idea of what she can do for them. She hopes that the driver has helped them relax into what they are doing and into relishing the sweetness of their labor. Her skin bristling, her body serves her as a radar trap in which she catches their admiring eyes as they stray away from the work they are engaged in and zoom in on her. She is relieved that the driver has spoken, saving her from caving in under the pressure of making difficult choices. Now she has two allies, SilkHair and the driver: the one because she has stuck her neck out for him and then presented him with clothes; the other because he has gone out on a limb for her and set a precedent.

She believes that the youths have gotten to know her far better than they have Zaak, with whom they chew *qaat* and whom they see as a boss, because he never dirties his hands, never bothers about house cleaning or cooking. She reasons that since all her involvements with men have been on a one-to-one basis and since this has proven to be unsuccessful, it is her wish to build a bridge of some kind of rapport with so many men all at the same time, something that she hopes she is going to be good at, as an artist. There is no pleasure like the pleasure of watching audiences lapping up the heartfelt intimacies of an actor at her best, when the audience might confuse who she is in real life and what makes her tick, move, love, and hate with the character she is just portraying.

She thinks that SilkHair looks more grown-up than when he went into the bathroom. No longer in tatters, smelly, or dirty, he has become the envy of every youth who is there. Cambara assumes that in their eyes she deserves their high praise, especially after the driver has added his word to support her action. She hopes she will have become a person to befriend, not the new boss on the block. This nervy awareness puts a proud spring in her stride and a grin blemishing the corner of her mouth.

Someone asks, "Where is Zaak?"

Cambara couldn't care less where he is and does not want to talk about him. Instead, she wraps her arms around SilkHair, and together they walk to where the driver is giving the final touches to a spot he has just cleaned.

She asks, "What about lunch?"

"Chicken," SilkHair announces.

He strikes her as a poseur, and she is amused.

"A good idea," the driver comments.

A door in Cambara's head opens. She puts her hand in her slacks pockets, bringing out five U.S. dollars in singles, which she hands over to the driver, whom she asks to take two or three youths, including SilkHair, to the open-air market and to buy chicken and vegetables sufficient to feed everybody. SilkHair's eyes anchor their new cast in the bay of self-confidence.

The driver picks up the trace of worry entering Cambara's eyes when she notices that the kitchen is not clean enough to cook in. The driver takes three of the youths, whom she presumes to be closer to him, aside, and they speak in low voices. They volunteer to finish the job, mop the floor, clean out the cupboards and the surfaces, as Cambara goes up to have a shower.

Then the driver says, "Let's go get the food."

After yet another cold shower, for which she is better prepared, Cambara comes down to ready the kitchen in time for the youths' imminent return from the errand to the open-air market. In her effort to do so, she opens the lower and upper cupboards, the storeroom, the pantry, and every drawer with functioning runners and, to her great dismay, finds the shelves not dusted as well as she might like. Moreover, she can see that although the youths have washed the cooking implements, they have not rinsed them in hot water, or properly. Not a single utensil or piece of crockery is of top quality. The wood of the cupboards is cracked, damaged, or warped; the soap too dry to be of use, or moldy. The more she gets to know of the state of disrepair of the kitchen and of the foul condition that it is in, despite the attempt on the part of the youths to clean it, the more she thinks of herself as a frontierswoman come to reclaim these men from their primitive condition. But she decides to keep her vow to the youths and cook for them in appreciation of their collaboration, certain that it will make a good impression on their thinking. She wants to leave the scene of their encounter in a more improved fettle than the one in which she has found it. Maybe then she may win over their hearts and minds—even if only briefly—to her triad of society: work, honest living, and peace. She is aware that in the views of someone like Zaak, she is being naive. So be it.

Like a rodent nosing an edible bit of food out of a spot difficult to access, she prises open the cupboards, the drawers, and the sideboards in order to ascertain what is in them. There is, overall, a basic lack: of cooking oil, of sharp knives or knife sharpeners, cutting boards, of butter that has not gone rancid, of sieves and swabs, of detergents, disinfectants, and serviceable sponges; of mops with enough pieces of string or cloth attached to the handle. Nor are there washing-up facilities, clean dishcloths, usable hand or paper towels, or wooden spoons and other implements necessary to provide a decent meal for a dozen persons. The pots are of the wrong shape or are of midget size, too small for her purposes.

What there is in the way of cutlery points to the house's multiple occupancy through the years: comparable to the cutlery of variously married households, the plates not matching, the forks and the spoons likewise.

She tries to make do with what there is. She mixes soap powder with water, lathering it up, and eventually decides to use the facecloths as dishcloths. It takes her a long time to wash and then wipe the drain board, on which she plans to dry the pots and dishes.

Scarcely has she done that when she hears a sound, which, at first, she mistakes for a door with creaky hinges being forcibly opened. She is waiting for evidence of Zaak's presence nearby when she identifies the noise as being that of a chicken clucking. She cranes her head to have a glimpse of the scene before her and sees SilkHair carrying three live chickens, their heads down, their necks stretched and struggling, wings opening outward and wrestling, their legs tied together with string. Trailing behind him are a couple of the other youths, nerves strained. They are bearing baskets on their heads, their steps hesitant, slow, and exhausted.

She thinks disaster, remembering that she has never killed a chicken in all her years. Neither before she left the country, when there were servants who performed those chores, nor in Toronto, where she bought them ready to go into the oven. She wonders what she must do if the men are too untutored in the art of slaughtering chickens. After all, it does require some training or at least a type of guts to kill to eat. It will be no problem to boil their feathers off and then cook them, if someone hands them over, dead. Her mind is running fast through these and her other inadequacies when SilkHair joins her in the kitchen. He puts down the chickens in a corner on the floor and instructs the others to deposit their basket loads likewise. Just as the other youths make themselves scarce—returning, most likely, to their *qaat*-chewing—SilkHair crowns his sense of achievement by consulting a piece of paper, his tongue running off the price of potatoes, tomatoes, garlic, carrots, live chickens, washing-up liquid, metal brush, et cetera, first in Somali shillings, then in their dollar equivalent. Then he gives her wads of change in the local currency.

"Well done," she says. "I am impressed." Moved, she ruffles his silky hair, almost taking the liberty to hug him and then kiss him.

Expansive joy shines in his eyes. As he gazes into hers, her pupils are set ablaze with memories of her son. She turns her head away as though in obedience to a secret command that tells her not to weep but to rejoice.

Then something happens for which no one is ready. One of the birds kicks one leg free, and when SilkHair rushes to hold her, she kicks harder and harder until she releases her second leg and jumps out of his grasp, clucking, screeching, and crying, as chickens that know that their time has come, do. Cambara watches, determined not to intervene or help him in any way, because she wants to know what stuff he is made of, how patient and resourceful he is, and whether he will tire easily and give up, throwing his hands up in the air.

He makes a wise move. He stands in the doorway, blocking the exit, then bends down, almost crouching, clucking over the bird's attempts to flee, admonishing her for embarrassing him, now snapping his fingers to go to him, now keeping his hands ahead of him, in readiness to accept her into his grasp, if not to pounce on her and take a good hold of her. He is silent; everything still, everything serious. Cambara watches as SilkHair waits, the sound he is making putting her in mind of the noise that some of the men who ply water in plastic jerry cans on the backs of donkeys utter in part to encourage their beasts of burden to move at a faster speed. No sooner has he turned round, seeking Cambara's approval, than the hen slips past his outstretched hands, out of the kitchen, and through his splayed legs.

Whereupon he chases the chicken into the living room and out, then past the kitchen, the bird half flying, half trotting, body atilt because of half-folded wings. Suddenly the chicken stops to look over a shoulder, eyes alert, and he pursues her into a corner to trap her. The chicken lifts her scrawny body up in time to fly above his head, mischievously clucking but only after securing safe escape.

The footloose chicken and the clamor in the kitchen in addition to the hubbub created by the youths who join SilkHair in the chase draw the driver out of the toolshed and bring Zaak out of his sulk, or is it sleep—Cambara cannot tell when she sees him.

"Have you gone mad?" Zaak asks her.

She runs past Zaak without bothering to answer his question. She tells herself that the youths stalking their lunch is, to her mind, more of a welcome relief than the thought of them running after their human victims to shoot or kill them. Excited by the chase, SilkHair is shouting loudly as he continues to pursue the chicken. Once the din reaches the back garden, LongEars comes out of the shed, cheeks swollen with his chewing and gun at the ready. Cambara has the calm to notice what LongEars wants to do, and she shouts to him, "Don't shoot."

The words have barely traveled the distance separating her from SilkHair and the chicken he is going after with fervor and is about to catch, having already bent down to do so, when she hears the gunshot, two bullets on the trot, the second one hitting its target and wounding it, feathers flying zigzag toward the ground. A hoarse cry emerges from the depth of SilkHair's viscera. Cambara has a tenuous comprehension of what it means to be powerless in the face of brute force. She stands stock still, feeling like someone opening her eyes to the engulfing darkness and coming to see an indescribable betrayal in the action of those around her. She goes over to where SilkHair is crouched, furiously weeping, as though mourning the death of a beloved pet. She lets him leave the chicken where it has fallen and walks past Zaak and the youths, who are all staring, into the kitchen—to prepare the other chickens.

Alone with SilkHair, she suggests that he swing each of the remaining birds as disc throwers do, making several full circles. Just when the first one has become disoriented and he is about to put it on the draining board in the kitchen, LongEars presents himself and offers to slaughter both birds, which he does with the efficiency of an assistant chef whose primary job it is to do so. One sudden swat, and the chicken is as good as dead and Cambara is ready to pour boiling water over it to help remove its feathers. She uses her Swiss penknife to quiet the thrashing of the second chicken, which is struggling animatedly. The rest proves to be as easy as one, two, three.

When she has prepared the meal and Zaak deigns to eat with them, Cambara requests that as soon as they have finished eating they ask the driver to take them in the truck so that Zaak can show her the family's expropriated property. To her great relief, he agrees to her demand.

ABDOURAHMAN A. WABERI

Djibouti

❖

from THE UNITED STATES OF AFRICA

I. A Voyage to Asmara, the Federal Capital.

I

In which the author gives a brief account of the origins of our prosperity and the reasons why the Caucasians were thrown onto the paths of exile.

HE'S THERE, EXHAUSTED. Silent. The wavering glow of a candle barely lights the carpenter's bedroom in this shelter for immigrant workers. This ethnically Swiss Caucasian speaks a Germanic dialect, and in this age of the jet and the Internet, claims he has fled violence and famine. Yet he still has all of the aura that fascinated our nurses and aid workers.

Let's call him Yacuba, first to protect his identity and second because he has an impossible family name. He was born outside Zurich in an unhealthy favela, where infant mortality and the rate of infection by the AIDS virus remain the highest in the world today. The figures are drawn from studies of the World Health Organization (WHO) based in our country in the fine peaceful city of Banjul, as everyone knows. AIDS first appeared some two decades ago in the shady underworld of prostitution, drugs and promiscuity in Greece and is now endemic worldwide, according to the high priests of world science at the Mascate meeting in the noble kingdom of Oman.

The cream of international diplomacy also meets in Banjul; they are supposedly settling the fate of millions of Caucasian refugees of various ethnic groups (Austrian, Canadian, American, Norwegian, Belgian,

Bulgarian, Hungarian, British, Icelandic, Swedish, Portuguese . . .) not to mention the skeletal boat people from the northern Mediterranean, at the end of their rope from dodging all the mortar-shells and missiles that darken the unfortunate lands of Euramerica.

Some of them cut and run, wander around, get exhausted and then brusquely give up, until they are sucked into the void. Prostitutes of every sex, Monte Carlians or Vaticanians but others too, wash up on the Djerba beaches and the cobalt blue bay of Algiers. These poor devils are looking for the bread, rice or flour distributed by Afghan, Haitian, Laotian or Sahelian aid organizations. Ever since our world has been what it is, little French, Spanish, Batavian or Luxembourgian schoolchildren, hit hard by kwashiorkor, leprosy, glaucoma and poliomyelitis, only survive with food surpluses from Vietnamese, North Korean or Ethiopian farmers.

These warlike tribes with their barbaric customs and deceitful, uncontrollable moves keep raiding the scorched lands of the Auvergne, Tuscany or Flanders, when they're not shedding the blood of their atavistic enemies—Teutons, Gascons or backward Iberians—for the slightest little thing, for rifles or trifles, because they recognize a prisoner or because they don't. They're all waiting for a peace that has yet to come.

But let us return to the shack of our flea-ridden Germanic or Alemannic carpenter. Take a furtive look into the darkness of his dwelling. A mud floor scantily strewn with wood shavings, no furniture or utensils. No electricity or running water, of course. This individual, poor as Job on his dung heap, has never seen a trace of soap, cannot imagine the flavor of yogurt, has no conception of the sweetness of a fruit salad. He is a thousand miles from our most basic Sahelian conveniences. Which is further from us, the moon, polished by Malian and Liberian astronauts, or this creature?

Let us cross what we might call the threshold: swarms of flies block your view and a sour smell immediately grabs you by the throat. You try to move forward nonetheless, but you can't. You stand there, dumbstruck.

Your eyes are beginning to get used to the darkness. You can make out the contours of what seems to be a painting with crude patterns.

One of those daubs called primitive: clueless tourists are crazy about them. Two crossed zebu horns and a Protestant sword decorate the other side of the wall, a sign of the religious zeal that pervades this shelter for foreign workers in our rich, dynamic Eritrean state.

Let us say in passing that our values of solidarity, conviviality and morality are now threatened by rapid social transformations and the violent unleashing of the unbridled free market, as the Afrigeltcard has replaced our ancestral traditions of mutual aid. The ancient country of Eritrea, governed for centuries by a long line of Muslim puritans, deeply influenced by the rigorism of the Senegalese Mourides, was able to prosper by combining good business sense with the virtues of parliamentary democracy. From its business center in Massawa or its online stock market on Lumumba Street, not to mention the very *high-tech Keren Valley Project*[1] and the military-industrial complexes in Assab, everything here works together for success and prosperity. This is what attracts the hundreds of thousands of wretched Euramericans subjected to a host of calamities and a deprivation of hope.

Our carpenter is muttering in his beard. What can he possibly be saying with his tongue rolled up at the back of his throat? God alone could decipher his white pidgin dialect. He is racked by the desire to leave the cotton fields of his slavery—quite understandable, but let's get back to the subject.

Still more dizzying is the flow of capital between Eritrea and its dynamic neighbors, who are all members of the federation of the United States of Africa, as is the former Hamitic kingdom of Chad, rich in oil; and also the ex-Sultanate of Djibouti that handles millions of guineas and surfs on its gas boom; or the Madagascar archipelago, birthplace of the conquest of space and tourism for the *enfants terribles* of the new high finance. The golden boys of Tananarive are light-years away from the black wretchedness of the white Helvetian carpenter.

You're still standing? Ah, okay! Now you recognize a familiar sound. You try a risky maneuver, taking one, then two steps into the darkness.

---

1 In English in the original—Translator's note.

You walk through the tiny door. You can make out the first measures of some mumbo-jumbo full of shouts and strangled sounds. An antediluvian black and white TV, made in Albania, dominates the living room of this shelter for destitute Caucasians, with their straight hair and infected lungs. After an insipid soap opera, a professor from the *Kenyatta School of European and American Studies,*[2] an eminent specialist in Africanization—the latest fad in our universities, now setting the tone for the whole planet—claims that the United States of Africa can no longer accommodate all the world's poor. You might be taken in by his unctuous voice as you listen to him, but in fact his polished statements, all cheap lace and silk rhetoric, fool nobody—certainly not the immigrants from outside Africa. His idea can be summed up in one sentence: the federal authorities must face up to their responsibilities firmly but humanely by escorting all foreign nationals back to the border, by force if necessary—first the illegal immigrants, then the semilegal, then the paralegal, and so on.

Alternative voices have arisen, all or almost all from liberal circles which hardly needed the TV talks of Professor Emeritus Garba Huntingwabe to react against "the irrational fear of the Other, of 'undesirable aliens,' that continues to be the greatest threat to African unity" (www.foreign -policy.afr, editorial, last March). Assembled under the aegis of the World Academy of Gorean Cultures, which includes all the enlightened minds in the world from Rangoon to Lomé and from Madras to Lusaka, these voices remind us that the millions of starving Japanese kept alive on the food surpluses from central Africa could be adequately taken care of with what that region spends on defense in just three days. You may recall that the face of this network—reviled by all the ulemas, nabobs, Neguses, Rais and Mwamis—is none other than Arafat Peace Prize winner Ms. Dunya Daher of Langston Hughes University in Harar. In September, the young ecologist put 15,800,000 guineas granted her by the austere Society of Sciences of Botswana into the kitty of many humanitarian aid organizations. The learned society's announcement stated

---

2   In English in the original—Translator's note.

that this prestigious prize was unanimously awarded to her for "her struggle against the corrupt dictatorship of New Zealand, her fight against AIDS [whereas] the ecclesiastical authorities of Uganda are still preaching abstinence, and her promotion of Nebraska bananas by vaunting their native merits in the supermarkets of Abidjan . . . [and finally] Ms. Daher made the world aware of the tangible facts that Dean Mamadou Diouf of the University of Gao had set forth long ago in a satirical tract that has remained famous to this day." (*Invisible Borders: The Challenge of Alaskan Immigration,* Rwanda University Press/Free Press, Kigali, 1994. 820 pp. 35 guineas.)

Dean Diouf, Ms. Daher, Ahmed Baba XV, Sophia Marley, Thomas Sankara Jr., the rappers King Cain and Queen Sheba, Hakim Bey, Siwela Nkosi and company were never in favor with the big turbans of the world. Ms. Daher deplored the silence of the political leaders of the first continent about questions crucial to the future of our planet. His Excellency El Hadj Saidou Touré, United States of Africa Press Secretary, had accustomed us to a different chant. He stated that our first priority remains keeping peace in Western Europe; and then he was relatively optimistic about signing a cease-fire in the American Midwest and Quebec, where French-speaking warlords have reiterated their firm intention of going to war with the uncontrollable English-speaking militias in the Hull region near Ottawa, the former capital, now under a curfew enforced by UN peacekeeping forces from Nigeria, Cyprus, Zimbabwe, Malawi and Bangladesh. The federal councilor (highest political authority of what remains of Canada)—the proud aborigine William Neville Attawag—has remained extremely vague on the question of a time frame for relaxing the emergency laws now in place. Sir Attawag has violently rejected the term "apartheid" used by newspapers completely ignorant of the conditions of life for Whites in the Canada of his ancestors. And yet Human Rights Watch and El Hombre, with their long experience in this North American quagmire, relentlessly keep sounding the alarm.

Yacuba has just left his shelter. He dashed into Ray Charles Avenue, caught his breath at the corner of Habib Bourguiba Street and is now walking towards Abebe-Bikila Square. He is wearing a shirt the same color as his chronic cold; an indigo boubou floats around his body. People turn around as he walks by, more intrigued than an ethnologist taken in by a primitive tribe in the remotest parts of Bavaria. Have no fear, our long-distance cameras are recording his every move. In less than fifteen minutes, he'll be back in his den. Which won't prevent him from getting into trouble again.

Surely you are aware that our media have been digging up their most scornful, odious stereotypes again, which go back at least as far as Methusuleiman! Like, the new migrants propagate their soaring birth-rate, their centuries-old soot, their lack of ambition, their ancestral machismo, their reactionary religions like Protestantism, Judaism or Catholicism, their endemic diseases. In short, they are introducing the Third World right up the anus of the United States of Africa. The least scrupulous of our newspapers have abandoned all restraint for decades and fan the flames of fear of what has been called—hastily, to be sure—the "White Peril." Isn't form, after all, the very flesh of thought, to paraphrase the great Sahelian writer Naguib Wolegorzee? Thus, a popular daily in N'Djamena, *Bilad el Sudan,* periodically goes back to its favorite headline: "Back Across the Mediterranean, Clodhoppers!" From Tripoli, *El Ard,* owned by the magnate Hannibal Cabral, shouts "Go Johnny, Go!" Which the *Lagos Herald* echoes with an ultimatum: "White Trash, Back Home!" More laconic is the *Messager des Seychelles,* in two English words: "Apocalypse Now!"

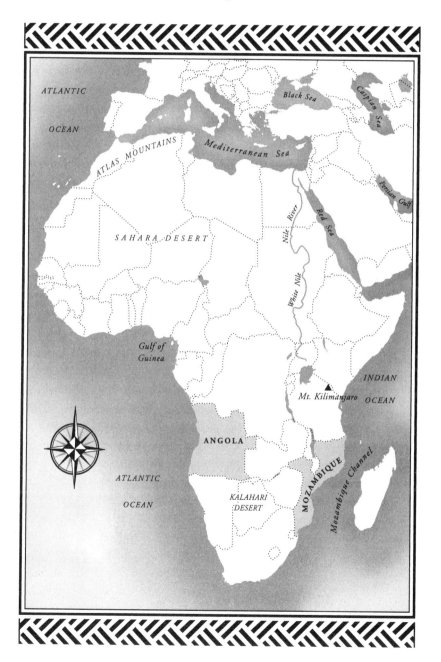

MIA COUTO

Mozambique

❖

LANGUAGES WE DON'T KNOW WE KNOW

IN AN AS yet unpublished short story of mine, the action is as follows: a terminally ill woman asks her husband to tell her a story so as to alleviate her unbearable pains. No sooner does he begin his tale than she stops him:

> —*No, not like that. I want you to speak to me in an unknown language.*
> —*Unknown? he asks.*
> —*A language that doesn't exist. For I have such a need not to understand anything at all.*

The husband asks himself: how can you speak a language that doesn't exist? He starts off by mumbling some strange words and feels like a fool, as if he were establishing his inability to be human. But gradually, he begins to feel more at ease with this language that is devoid of rules. And he no longer knows whether he's speaking, singing, or praying. When he pauses, he notices his wife has fallen asleep, with the most peaceful smile on her face. Later, she confesses to him: those sounds had brought back memories of a time before she even had a memory! And they had given her the solace of that same sleep which provides the link between us and what was here before we were alive.

When we were children, all of us experienced that first language, the language of chaos, all of us enjoyed that divine moment when our life was capable of being all lives, and the world still awaited a destiny. James Joyce called this relationship with an unformed, chaotic world "chaosmology." This relationship, my friends, is what breathes life into writing, whatever the continent, whatever the nation, whatever the language or the literary genre.

I believe that all of us, whether poets or fiction writers, never stop seeking this seminal chaos. All of us aspire to return to that state in which we were so removed from a particular language that all languages were ours. To put it another way, we are all the impossible translators of dreams. In truth, dreams speak within us what no word is capable of saying.

Our purpose, as producers of dreams, is to gain access to that other language no one can speak, that hidden language in which all things can have all names. What the sick woman was asking was what we all wish for: to annul time and send death to sleep.

Maybe you expected me, coming as I do from Africa, to use this platform to lament, to accuse others, while absolving my immediate fellows from guilt. But I prefer to talk about something of which we are all victims and guilty at the same time, about how the process that has impoverished my continent is in fact devitalizing our common, universal position as creators of stories.

In a congress that celebrates the value of words, the theme of my intervention is the way dominant criteria are devaluing good literature in the name of easy and immediate profitability. I am talking about a commercial rationale that is closed to other cultures, other languages, other ways of thinking. The words of today are increasingly those that are shorn of any poetic dimension, that do not convey to us any utopian vision of a different world.

What has ensured human survival is not just our intelligence but our capacity to produce diversity. This diversity is nowadays being denied us by a system that makes its choice solely on the grounds of profit and easy success. Africans have become the "others" once again, those who have little to sell, and who can buy even less. African authors (and especially those who write in Portuguese) live on the periphery of the periphery, there where words have to struggle in order not to be silence.

✧

My dear friends

Languages serve to communicate. But they don't just "serve." They transcend that practical dimension. Languages cause us to *be*. And sometimes, just as in the story I mentioned, they cause us to *stop being*. We are born and we die inside speech, we are beholden to language even after we lose our body. Even those who were never born, even they exist within us as the desire for a word and as a yearning for a silence.

Our lives are dominated by a reductive and utilitarian perception that converts languages into the business of linguists and their technical skills. Yet the languages we know—and even those we are not aware that we knew—are multiple and not always possible to grasp by the rationalist logic that governs our conscious mind. Something exists that escapes norms and codes. This elusive dimension is what fascinates me as a writer. What motivates me is the divine vocation of the word, which not only names but also invents and produces enchantment.

We are all bound by the collective codes with which we communicate in our everyday lives. But the writer seeks to convey things that are beyond everyday life. Never before has our world had at its disposal so many means of communication. Yet our solitude has never been so extreme. Never before have we had so many highways. And yet never before have we visited each other so little.

I am a biologist and I travel a lot through my country's savanna. In these regions, I meet people who don't know how to read books. But they know how to read their world. In such a universe where other wisdoms prevail, I am the one who is illiterate. I don't know how to read the signs in the soil, the trees, the animals. I can't read clouds and the likelihood of rain. I don't know how to talk to the dead, I've lost all contact with ancestors who give us our sense of the eternal. In these visits to the savanna, I learn sensitivities that help me to come out of myself and remove me from my certainties. In this type of territory, I don't just have dreams. I am dreamable.

Mozambique is a huge country, as huge as it is new. More than twenty-five languages are spoken within it. Ever since independence, which was achieved in 1975, Portuguese has been the official language. Thirty years ago, only a tiny minority spoke this language, ironically borrowed from the colonizer in order to disaffirm the country's colonial past. Thirty years ago, almost no Mozambicans had Portuguese as their mother tongue. Now, more than 12 percent of Mozambicans have Portuguese as their first language. And the great majority understands and speaks Portuguese, stamping standard Portuguese with the imprimatur of African cultures.

This tendency towards change places worlds that are not only distinguished by language in confrontation with each other. Languages exist as part of culturally much vaster universes. There are those who fight to keep alive languages that are at risk of extinction. Such a fight is an utterly worthy one and recalls our own struggle as biologists to save animals and plants from disappearance. But languages can only be saved if the culture that harbours them can remain dynamic. In the same way, biological species can only be saved if their habitats and natural life patterns can be preserved.

Cultures survive for as long as they remain productive, as long as they are subject to change and can dialogue and mingle with other cultures. Languages and cultures do what living organisms do: they exchange genes and invent symbioses in response to the challenges of time and environment.

In Mozambique, we are living in an age when encounters and disencounters are occurring within a melting-pot full of exuberance and paradox. Words do not always serve as a bridge between these diverse worlds. For example, concepts that seem to us to be universal, such as Nature, Culture, and Society, are sometimes difficult to reconcile. There are often no words in local languages to express these ideas. Sometimes, the opposite is true: European languages do not possess expressions that may translate the values and concepts contained in Mozambican cultures.

I remember something that really happened to me. In 1989, I was doing research on the island of Inhaca when a team of United Nations technicians arrived there. They had come to carry out what is generally known as "environmental education." I don't want to comment here on how this concept of environmental education often conceals a type of messianic arrogance. The truth of the matter is that these scientists, brimming with good faith, had brought with them cases containing slide projectors and films. In a word, they had brought with them educational kits, in the naïve expectation that technology would prove the solution to problems of understanding and communication.

During the first meeting with the local population, some curious misunderstandings emerged that illustrate the difficulty of translating not so much words but thoughts. On the podium were the scientists who spoke in English, myself, who translated this into Portuguese, and a fisherman who translated the Portuguese into Chidindinhe, the local language. It all began when the visitors introduced themselves (I should mention here that most of them happened to be Swedish). We are "scientists," they said. But the word "scientist" doesn't exist in the local language. The term chosen by the translator was "inguetlha," which means "witchdoctor." In those folks' eyes therefore, the visitors were white witchdoctors. The Swedish leader of the delegation (unaware of the status conferred upon him) then announced: "we have come here to work on the environment." Now, in that culture, the idea of the environment has no autonomous meaning and there is no word that exactly describes such a concept. The translator hesitated and eventually chose the word "ntumbuluku," which has various meanings, but refers above all to a sort of Big Bang, the moment when humanity was created. As you can imagine, these island folk were fascinated: their little island had been chosen to study a matter of the highest, most noble metaphysical importance.

During the course of the dialogue, the same Swedish member of the delegation asked his audience to identify the environmental problems that were of greatest concern to the islanders. The crowd looked at each other, perplexed: "environmental problems"? After consulting among themselves, the people chose their greatest problem: the invasion of their plantations by the "tinguluve," or bush pigs. Interestingly, the term "tinguluve" also describes the spirits of the dead who fell ill after they had stopped living. Whether they were spirits or pigs, the foreign expert didn't understand very well what these "tinguluve" were. He had never seen such an animal. His audience explained: the pigs had appeared mysteriously on the island and had begun to multiply in the forest. Now, they were destroying the plantations.

— *They're destroying the plantations? Well, that's easy: we can shoot them!*

The crowd's reaction was one of fearful silence. Shoot spirits? No one wanted to talk or listen anymore, no matter what the subject. And the meeting came to an abrupt end, damaged by a tacit loss of trust.

That night, a group of elders knocked on my door. They asked me to summon the foreigners so that they could better explain the problem of the pigs. The experts appeared, astonished by this interruption to their sleep.

> —*It's because of the wild pigs.*
> —*What about the pigs?*
> —*It's because they're not quite pigs . . .*
> —*So what are they, then? they asked, certain that a creature couldn't exist and at the same time not exist.*
> —*They are almost pigs. But they're not* complete *pigs.*

Their explanation was going from bad to worse. The pigs were defined in ever more vague terms: "convertible creatures," "temporary animals" or "visitors who had been sent by someone." Eventually, the zoologist, who was by now getting tired, took out his manual and showed them the photograph of a wild pig. The locals looked and exclaimed: "Yes, that's the one." The scientists smiled, satisfied, but their victory was short lived, for one of the elders added: *Yes, this is the animal, but only at night time.* I have few doubts that by this time, the experts doubted my ability as a translator. In this way, they didn't need to question what they were saying or query how they had arrived in an unknown locality.

Whatever the correct translation might be, the truth is that the relationship between the experts and the local community was never good and no manner of modern PowerPoint presentation could make up for the initial misunderstanding.

On another occasion, I was accompanying a presidential delegation on a visit to a province in the North of Mozambique. The President of the Republic was introducing his ministers. When it came to the Minister of Culture, the translator, after a brief pause, then announced: "This is the Minister of Tomfoolery."

In some languages in Mozambique, there isn't a word for "poor." A poor person is designated by the term "chisiwana," which means "orphan." In these cultures, a poor person isn't just someone who doesn't possess assets, but above all it is someone who has lost the network of family relationships, which, in rural society, are a support mechanism for survival. The individual is considered poor when he or she doesn't have relatives. Poverty is loneliness, family rupture. It is possible that international experts, specialists in writing reports on destitution, don't take sufficient account of the dramatic impact of destroyed family links and social mutual help networks. Whole nations are becoming "orphans" and begging seems to be the only route to torturous survival.

By recounting these episodes, I wish to reinforce what we already know: the systems of thought in rural Africa are not easily reducible to European processes of logic. Some who seek to understand Africa plunge into analyses of political, social and cultural phenomena. To understand the diversity of Africa, however, we need to get to know systems of thought and religious universes that often don't even have a name. Such systems are curious because they are often rooted in actually negating the gods they invoke. For most of the peasantry in my country, the issues surrounding the origin of the world just don't exist: the universe quite simply has always existed. What is the role of God in a world that never had a beginning? This is why, in some religions in Mozambique, the gods are always referred to in the plural, and have the same names as living people. The problem with God, according to a Makwa proverb, is the same as the one with the egg: if we don't hold it properly we drop it; if we hold it too hard, we break it.

In the same way, the idea of the "environment" presupposes that we humans are at the centre and things dwell in orbit to us. In reality, things don't revolve around us, but along with them we form one same world, people and things dwell within one indivisible body. This diversity of thought suggests that it may be necessary to storm one last bastion of racism, which is the arrogance of assuming that there is only one system of knowledge, and of being unable to accept philosophies originating in impoverished nations.

I have been talking about the various cosmovisions found in rural areas of Mozambique. But I wouldn't want you to look at them as if they were essentialities, resistant to time and the dynamics of exchange. Today, when I revisit the island of Inhaca, I see that campaigns have been mounted to kill the wild pigs that invade plantations. And local chiefs prepare for the visits of foreign scientists, using their mobile phones. Throughout the country, millions of Mozambicans have appropriated the words "culture" and "nature" and have absorbed them into their cultural universes. These new words are working on top of the original cultures, in the same way that certain trees invent the ground out of which they appear to be growing.

In short, cultural phenomena aren't stopped in time, waiting for an anthropologist to turn up and record them as some proof of an exotic world, outside modernity. Africa has been subject to successive processes of essentialization and folklorization, and much of what is proclaimed as being authentically African is the result of inventions made outside the continent. For decades, African writers had to undergo the so-called test of authenticity: their texts were required to translate that which was understood to be their true ethnicity. Nowadays, young African writers are freeing themselves from "Africanness." They are what they are without any need for proclamation. African writers seek to be as universal as any other writer in the world.

It is true that many writers in Africa face specific problems, but I prefer not to subscribe to the idea that Africa is a unique, singular and homogeneous place. There are as many Africas as there are writers and all of them are reinventing continents that lie inside their very selves. It is true that a high proportion of African writers face challenges in order to adjust their work to different languages and cultures. But this is not a problem that is exclusively ours, those of us who are African. There isn't a writer in the world who doesn't have to seek out his or her own identity among multiple and elusive identities. In every continent, each person is a nation made up of different nations. One of these nations lives submerged and made secondary by the universe of writing. This hidden nation is called orality. Then again, orality is not a typically African phenomenon, nor is it a characteristic that is exclusive to those who are erroneously called "native peoples." Orality is a universal territory, a treasure rich in thoughts and sensibilities that is reclaimed by poetry.

The idea persists that only African writers suffer what is called the drama of language. It is true that colonization induced traumas over identity and alienation. But the truth, my friends, is that no writer has at his disposal a consummated language. We all have to find our own language in order to demonstrate our uniqueness and unrepeatability.

The Indian sociologist André Breteille wrote: "Knowing a language makes us human; fluency in more than one language makes us civilized." If this is true, Africans—assumed down the ages to be uncivilized—may be better suited to modernity than even they themselves think. A high proportion of Africans know more than one African language and, apart from these, speak a European language. That which is generally seen as problematic may after all represent considerable potential for the future. For this ability to be polyglot may provide us Africans with a passport to something that has become perilously rare nowadays: the ability to travel between different identities and to visit the intimacy of others.

Whatever the case, a civilized future implies sweeping and radical changes in this world that could be ever more our world. It implies the eradication of hunger, war and poverty. But it also implies a predisposition to deal with the material of dreams. And this has everything to do with the language that lulled the sick woman to sleep at the beginning of my talk. The man of the future should surely be a type of bilingual nation. Speaking a finished language, capable of dealing with visible, everyday matters. But fluent too in another language to express that which belongs to the invisible, dreamlike order of existence.

What I am advocating is a plural man, equipped with a plural language. Alongside a language that makes us part of the world, there should be another that makes us leave it. On the one hand, a language that creates roots and a sense of place. On the other, a language that is a wing upon which to travel.

Alongside a language that gives us our sense of humanity, there should be another that can elevate us to the divine.

Thank you very much.

ONDJAKI

· *Angola* ·

✤

DRAGONFLY

for Dr. Carvalho

if from these stones one
announced
what creates silence:
here, close by,
[. . .] this would open, like a wound
you would have to plunge into
　　　　—*Paul Celan, "The Power of Light"*

A FLUID SOUND ran through the house, brushed against the dust on the garden vines, swayed the mangoes and the papayas as they ripened, terrified a drunken dragonfly that was dozing there, made the sun diminish, and settled still strong, still distinct, at the woman's ear. Followed by a smile.

From the stereo the sound flowed continuously, without interruption. The doctor was locked into this Sunday habit of sitting outdoors on his veranda listening for long periods to the Brazilian singer Adriana Calcanhoto. Now he slept, now he read, now he wrote, now he simply lay back with teary eyes contemplating the fat clouds fleeing the sky. For him nothing more anointed a Sunday than his own peace. "Sunday" was, for the doctor, a deeply personal word, a wellspring.

Knowing this—that the doctor appeared deep in his Sunday routine—the woman hesitated. She lay her head against the iron gate and wanted to believe the impossible: that she was not thirsty. Her head throbbed; her eyes truly wanted to close, to forget the world, to stop rendering their visual services. The cold gate brought pleasure to the fingers and the heart. The music invaded her pores. Right then she and the doctor shared a common sensation. At the same moment he thought: This voice, yes, it can be shared. The voice of Adriana, purring into the afternoon: "People will be crazy, or sane . . . when they want everything to become music."

When the voice fell quiet, the dragonfly decided to wake up, moving in an open zigzag and landing near the doctor's notes. Scratchings, denied memories, fragments of more sensitive times that he did not need to accept as his own. "I forget the ground, I don't find the words," the voice sang on. It had been years since he settled accounts with the animals and settled into a balanced relationship with them. He maintained a still-conflicted relationship with the cockroaches and the lizards, but he was no killer. Instead, he used to smile. In the morning he often yearned to see Angolan antelope running like he used to see as a child in the southwestern province of Namibe; sometimes at the beach he found sweaty horses and was held back by eyes that wanted to shut, savoring the strong scent of lathering horse flesh. He was happy only on the eve of a trip, when he dreamt of white or delicately yellow butterflies, and never got an interpretation of the dream. It had been years since he made peace with the animals, including the Dengue cat that he had dealt a mortal wound. The cats, mainly cats, brought the insects back to mind.

It was after the dragonfly that he noticed the woman resting at his gate with closed eyes, listening, it seemed to him, to the music of Adriana: "On principle I never close doors, but . . . keep them open at all times . . ."

He uncrossed his legs and slowly released them from the other chair: he slipped into his sandals. Walking, he was looking at the tranquil dragonfly strolling over his letters, over the smell of his Violet #971 ink. The ink was so sticky that he had to write at a furious pace, since it dried quickly once it met the air. But the dragonfly, not particularly curious, couldn't reach the bottle and couldn't drink. One step, two. He was near the gate and the woman, despite his wishes, didn't open her eyes. But she did speak.

—Forgive the interruption . . .

It was neither a shock nor anything really describable. The doctor simply hadn't counted on that feeling of closeness.

—I recognize the smell of the ink . . . Sir, do you write with a quill?

—No . . . It's . . . Well, OK, it's a kind of quill.

The gate was unlocked. He mentioned opening it; she opened her eyes, taking her eyes off the grillwork.

—Forgive the interruption, but I'm so thirsty—maybe hoping that the doctor would reveal whether or not he forgave the disturbance, she shifted tone.

The gate was opened by the doctor's precise hand, while his other offered a friendly gesture. He was not easily ruffled. "Right there I forgot that destiny always wanted me alone," sang Adriana.

—Water or soft drink?—the doctor.

—Water, please.

The woman noticed the still dragonfly. Its heart was too alive for it to be dead or embalmed, but it was totally immune to the wind that ruffled the sheets of paper. The woman approached the table but didn't sit down. Out of curiosity she looked at the inky letters against the whiteness without intending to read the message, but more in appreciation of the beauty of the masculine handwriting. It was, she later saw, a "type of quill," as the doctor told her, that had produced those enchanting scratches. It offered no resistance and came to her nearby hand; it seemed crystalline.

—It's glass. Yes, glass. Isn't it lovely?—the doctor.

—Very . . . It's a very special quill—the woman.

He brought the water, in a normal glass, to her hands. The doctor still kept the pitcher on a long side of the table, without disturbing the dragonfly. He invited the woman to sit down.

—Thank you. You must be surprised, hmm?

—Surprised?

—Asking for water. No one has rung the bells to ask for water, right?

—That's right. You're not from here, no?

—No.

The woman served herself again. She drank slowly, as suited her.

—I remember one of my grandmothers in Silva Porto who once had a man come into her house dying of thirst and asking her for water. My grandmother returned to the room with a jug of very cold water and he chugged three glasses without stopping.

—He did?

—He did. The man only had time to return the jug to her before he dropped the glass to the floor. He died right there, you know? Ever since, my grandmother lived to tell this story, and my grandfather swore that it was true—the doctor concluded.

—That doesn't scare me.

—Sorry, it wasn't meant to scare you.

—And what was it that your grandfather said?

—Mind you, my grandfather was a man of refined temperament and sensibility. When I was little he confirmed the whole story and at the end he said: That man never thanked your grandmother for the water.

The woman held the glass and inhaled deeply.

—Do you know why I asked for water here in your house?

—No.

—Because of the music . . . This sweet voice.

—Adriana.

—Huh?

—Adriana Calcanhoto, a Brazilian singer.

—Is she a poet too?

—Yes.

—No . . . Sir . . . Sir, are you a poet?

—Ah, me! No, I'm a doctor. And you?

—I'm here on vacation.

The dragonfly made its way to the ground. At last it moved, walking.

In the expression of both of them one could see the fear of two children who, with grave open-mouthed attention, watched the sudden graceful movement of a stone. The dragonfly walked toward the object. In a short shake of its wings it jumped and became quiet—a warrior marking its conquered territory. "And the grievance of the stars is for me alone" wafted toward the porch in the afternoon.

The object was a thick glass dome, certainly expensive, that covered a small ordinary gray stone. The most that could be said of it was that it was a tiny stone, neither charming, nor unusual, nor exotic or attractive. It was a crudely common stone. The glass enclosure, however, raised its value.

—I think that the value of this stone can't be measured by its looks. Do you agree?

—Yes.

—But this dome is beautifully made . . .

The doctor, in a confident gesture, shook the dragonfly—a surprise for both the woman and the dragonfly. The insect returned to rest on the letters. The stone and its glass dome were hurled to the floor. The woman didn't have time to be scared. The object noisily hit the floor twice and, after rolling a while, ended its journey. The doctor caught the object and returned to put it on the table at the foot of the letters, the papers, the dragonfly. The insect, in a short sprinkling of wings, returned to its post.

—All glass is fragile, my grandfather said. This glass dome is very good at protecting valuable objects.

The woman started to feel thirsty but she didn't want to inconvenience him.

—A gift?

—Yes, a very special gift, very sincere.

—Do doctors receive many gifts?

—Some; it's a way for people to express thanks and affection.

And he fell silent.

The woman didn't want to leave, but she thought she was forcing the moment. The doctor stayed quiet for more than five minutes. The woman thought it was time to leave. The music seemed to stop and the voice, the voice was difficult to record in memory's ear.

—Adriana, you say?

—Adriana Calcanhoto. She's Brazilian.

—Thank you very much for the water.

—You're welcome. You know, always drink slowly.

—And thanks before I die!

The doctor sort of smiled. His lips contorted; only an attempt at a smile. Maybe.

The gate was open. The woman, grabbing the iron grates purposefully, recognized the sensation of that coldness of skin.

—You know, it was on Sunday—the doctor started. —I was called to the battlefront and no one wanted to operate on the man: he had some kind of explosive lodged in his leg. It was a very delicate operation; I still think about it today. I had to do everything very slowly so that he wouldn't be in any pain, and both of us had to be patient. Near the end, the soldier said to me: Let me die; I'm already so tired. I answered: I'll let you die, but first let me save you.

—So he died?

—No. The operation went well. In the end, he wanted to offer me a gift. As if nothing had happened, he took off the boot and said: Now I know why the stone kept bothering me for two days. Take it, doctor, just so we don't forget our conversation today. You keep the stone, I'll keep the scar.

The gate closed. The thirst had passed. The woman, walking slowly down the sidewalk, understood that it was the stone that gave value to the enclosure. She heard footsteps. The music started again: "My music wants to transcend taste, it doesn't want to have a face, it doesn't want to be culture."

Between two sepia pages—in a window of dust—the woman watched the dragonfly stop, undulating. It was a dance. At its feet lay the crudely common stone. Between the memory of the man and the unbreakable dome of glass.

JOSÉ EDUARDO AGUALUSA

Angola

❖

from THE BOOK OF CHAMELEONS

FÉLIX VENTURA STUDIES the newspapers as he has his dinner, leafing through them carefully, and if an article catches his eye he marks it with his pen, in lilac-colored ink. Once he's done eating he cuts it out and stores it carefully away in a file. On one of the shelves in the library he has dozens of these files. Another is where his hundreds of videocassettes lie. Félix likes to record news bulletins, important political happenings, anything that might one day be useful to him. The tapes are lined up in alphabetical order, by the name of the person or the event they're about. His dinner consists of a bowl of vegetable broth, a specialty of Old Esperança's, a cup of mint tea, and a thick slice of papaya, dressed with lemon and a dash of port wine. In his room, before going to bed, he puts on his pajamas with such an air of formality that I'm always half-expecting him to tie a somber-looking tie around his neck. But on this particular night, the shrill ring of the doorbell interrupted him as he ate his soup. This irritated him. He folded up his paper, got up with some effort and went to open the door. I saw a tall man come in, distinguished looking, a hooked nose, prominent cheekbones, and a generous moustache, curved and gleaming, the kind people haven't had these past hundred years. His eyes were small and bright, and seemed to take possession of everything they saw. He was wearing a blue suit, in an old-fashioned cut but which suited him, and in his left hand he was holding a document case. The room darkened. It was as though night—

or something even more grief-stricken than night—had come in with him. He took out a calling card, and read aloud:

"*Félix Ventura. Guarantee your children a better past.*" And he laughed. A sad laugh, but not unpleasant. "That would be you, I presume? A friend of mine gave me your card."

I couldn't place his accent. He spoke softly, with a mix of different pronunciations, a faint Slavic roughness, tempered by the honeyed softness of the Portuguese from Brazil. Félix Ventura took a step back: "And who are you?"

The foreigner closed the door. He walked around the room, his hands clasped behind his back, pausing for a long moment in front of the beautiful oil portrait of Frederick Douglass. Then he sat down, at last, in one of the armchairs, and with an elegant gesture invited the albino to do the same. It was as though he were the owner of the house. Certain common friends, he said—his voice becoming even gentler—had given him this address. They'd told him of a man who dealt in memories, a man who sold the past, clandestinely, the way other people deal in cocaine. Félix looked at him with mistrust. Everything about this strange man annoyed him—his manners that were both gentle and authoritative, his ironic way of speaking, the antiquated moustache. He sat himself down in a grand wickerwork chair, at the opposite end of the room, as though afraid the other man's delicacy might be contagious.

"And might I know who you are?"

Again his question received no reply. The foreigner asked permission to smoke. He took a silver cigarette case from the pocket of his jacket, opened it, and rolled a cigarette. His eyes skipped one way and another, his attention distracted, like a chicken pecking around in the dust. And then he smiled with unexpected brilliance:

"But do tell me, my dear man—who are your clients?"

Félix Ventura gave in. There was a whole class, he explained, a whole new bourgeoisie, who sought him out. They were businessmen, ministers, landowners, diamond smugglers, generals—people, in other words, whose futures are secure. But what these people lack is a good past, a distinguished ancestry, diplomas. In sum, a name that resonates with nobility and culture. He sells them a brand new past. He draws up their family tree. He provides them with photographs of their grand-parents and great-grandparents, gentlemen of elegant bearing and old-fashioned ladies. The businessmen, the ministers, would like to have women like that as their aunts, he went on, pointing to the por-traits on the walls—old ladies swathed in fabrics, authentic bourgeois *bessanganas*—they'd like to have a grandfather with the distinguished bearing of a Machado de Assis, of a Cruz e Souza, of an Alexandre Dumas. And he sells them this simple dream.

"Perfect, perfect." The foreigner smoothed his moustache. "That's what they told me. I require your services. But I'm afraid it may be rather a lot of work . . ."

"Work makes you free . . . ," Félix muttered. It may be that he was just saying this to try and get a rise out of him, to test out the intruder's identity, but if that was his intention it failed—the foreigner merely nodded. The albino got up and disappeared in the direction of the kitchen. A moment later he returned with a bottle of good Portuguese wine that he held with both hands. He showed it to the foreigner, and offered him a glass. And he asked:

"And might I know your name?"

The foreigner examined the wine by the light of the lamp. He low-ered his eyelids and drank slowly, attentively, happily, like someone fol-lowing the flight of a Bach fugue. He put the glass down on a small table right in front of him, a piece of mahogany furniture with a glass cover; then finally straightened himself up and replied:

"I've had many names, but I mean to forget them all. I'd rather you were the one to baptize me."

Félix insisted. He had to know—at the very least—what his clients' professions were. The foreigner raised his right hand—a broad hand, with long, bony fingers—in a vague gesture of refusal. But then he low-ered it again, and sighed:

"You're right. I'm a photojournalist. I collect images of wars, of hunger and its ghosts, of natural disasters and terrible misfortunes. You can think of me as a witness."

He explained that he was planning to settle in the country. He wanted more than just a decent past, a large family, uncles, aunts and cousins, nephews and nieces, grandfathers and grandmothers, including two or three *bessanganas,* now dead, of course (or perhaps living in exile somewhere?); he wanted more than just portraits and anecdotes. He needed a new name, authentic official documents that bore out this identity. The albino listened, horrified:

"No!" he managed to blurt out. "I don't do things like that. I invent dreams for people, I'm not a forger . . . And besides, if you'll pardon my bluntness, wouldn't it be a bit difficult to invent a completely African genealogy for you?"

"Indeed! And why is that?! . . ."

"Well—sir— . . . you're white."

"And what of it? You're whiter than I am . . ."

"White? Me?!" The albino choked. He took a handkerchief from his pocket and wiped his forehead. "No, no! I'm black. Pure black. I'm a native. Can't you tell that I'm black? . . ."

From my usual post at the window I couldn't help giving a little chuckle at this point. The foreigner looked upward as though he were sniffing the air. Tense—alert:

"Did you hear that? Who laughed just then?"

"Nobody," the albino replied, and pointed at me. "It was the gecko."

The man stood up. He came up closer and I could feel his eyes on me. It was as though he were looking directly into my soul—my old soul. He shook his head slowly, in a baffled silence.

"Do you know what this is?"

"What?!"

"It's a gecko, yes, but a very rare species. See these stripes? It's a tiger gecko—a shy creature, we still know very little about them. They were first discovered half a dozen years ago in Namibia. We think they can live for twenty years—even longer, perhaps. They have this amazing laugh—doesn't it sound like a human laugh?"

Félix agreed. Yes, to begin with he'd also been disturbed by it. But then having consulted a few books about reptiles—he had them right there in the house, he had books about everything, thousands of them, inherited from his adopted father, a secondhand book dealer who'd exchanged Luanda for Lisbon a few months after independence—he'd discovered that there were certain species of gecko that produce sounds that are strikingly like laughter. They spent some time discussing me, which I found annoying—talking as if I weren't there!—and yet at the same time it felt as though they were talking not about me but about some alien being, some vague and distant biological anomaly. Men know almost nothing of the little creatures that share their homes. Mice, bats, ants, ticks, fleas, flies, mosquitoes, spiders, worms, silverfish, termites, weevils, snails, beetles. I decided that I might as well simply get on with my life. At that sort of time the albino's bedroom used to fill up with mosquitoes, and I was beginning to feel hungry. The foreigner stood up again, went over to the chair where he'd put the briefcase, opened it, and took out a thick envelope. He handed it to Félix, said his good-byes, and went to the door. He opened it himself. He nodded, and was gone.

"A Ship Filled with Voices"

Five thousand dollars in large-denomination bills.

Félix Ventura tore open the envelope quickly, nervously, and the notes burst out like green butterflies—fluttered for a moment in the night air, then spread themselves all over the floor, the books, the chairs and sofas. The albino was getting anxious. He even went to open the door, meaning to chase after the foreigner, but out in the vast still night there was no sign of anyone.

"Have you seen this?!" He was talking to me. "So now what am I supposed to do?"

He gathered the notes up one by one, counted them and put them back in the envelope—it was only then that he noticed that inside the envelope there was also a note; he read aloud:

"Dear Sir, I will be giving you another five thousand when I receive the material. I'm leaving you a few passport-style photos of myself for you to use on the documents. I'll come by again in three weeks."

Félix lay down and tried to read a book—it was Nicholas Shakespeare's biography of Bruce Chatwin, in the Portuguese Quetzal edition. After ten minutes he put it down on the bedside table and got up again. He wandered round and round the house, muttering incoherent phrases, until dawn broke. His little widow's hands, tender and tiny, fluttered randomly about, independently, as he spoke. The tightly curled hair, trimmed down now, glowed around him with a miraculous aura. If someone had seen him from out on the road, seen him through the window, they would have thought they were looking at a ghost.

"No, what rubbish! I won't do it . . ."

[. . .]

"The passport wouldn't be hard to get, it wouldn't even be that risky, and it would only take a few days—cheap, too. I could do that— why not? I'll have to do it one day—it's the inevitable extension of what I'm doing anyway . . ."

[. . .]

"Take care, my friend, take care with the paths you choose to follow. You're no forger. Be patient. Invent some sort of excuse, return the money, and tell him it's not going to happen."

[. . .]

"But you don't just turn down ten thousand dollars. I could spend two or three months in New York. I could visit the secondhand book dealers in Lisbon. I'll go to Rio, watch the samba dancers, go to the dance halls, to the secondhand bookshops, or I'll go to Paris to buy records and books. How long has it been since I last went to Paris?"

[. . .]

Félix Ventura's anxiety disturbed my cynegetic activity. I'm a creature that hunts by night. Once I've tracked down my prey I chase them, forcing them up toward the ceiling. Once they're up there mosquitoes never come back down. I run around them, in ever decreasing circles, corral them into a corner and devour them. The dawn was already beginning to break when the albino—now sprawled on one of the living room sofas—began to tell me his life story.

"I used to think of this house as being a bit like a ship. An old steamship heaving itself through the heavy river mud. A vast forest, and night all around." Félix spoke quietly, and pointed vaguely at the outlines of his books. "It's full of voices, this ship of mine."

Out there I could hear the night slipping by. Something barking. Claws scratching at the glass. Looking through the window I could easily make out the river, the stars spinning across its back, skittish birds disappearing into the foliage. The mulatto Fausto Bendito Ventura, secondhand book collector, son and grandson of secondhand book collectors, awoke one Sunday morning to find a box outside his front door. Inside, stretched out on several copies of Eça de Queiroz's *The Relic*, was a little naked creature, skinny and shameless, with a glowing fuzz of hair, and a limpid smile of triumph. A widower with no children, the book collector brought the child into his home, raised him and schooled him, absolutely certain that there was some superior purpose that was plotting out this unlikely story. He kept the box, and the books that were in it too. The albino told me of it with pride.

"Eça," he said, "was my first crib."

Fausto Bendito Ventura became a secondhand book collector quite without meaning to. He took pride in never having worked in his life. He'd go out early in the morning to walk downtown, *malembe-malembe*—slowly-slowly—all elegant in his linen suit, straw hat, bow tie and cane, greeting friends and acquaintances with a light touch of his index finger on the brim of his hat. If by chance he came across a woman of his generation he'd dazzle her with a gallant smile. He'd whisper: *Good day to you, poetry . . .* He'd throw spicy compliments to the girls who worked in the bars. It's said (Félix told me) that one day some jealous man provoked him:

"So what exactly is it that you do on working days?"

Fausto Bendito's reply—*all my days, my dear sir, are days off, I amble through them at my leisure*—still provokes applause and laughter among the slim circle of old colonial functionaries who in the lifeless evenings of the wonderful Biker Beer-House still manage to cheat death, playing cards and exchanging stories. Fausto would lunch at home, have a siesta, and then sit on the veranda to enjoy the cool evening breeze. In those days, before independence, there wasn't yet the high wall separating the garden from the pavement, and the gate was always open. His clients needed only to climb a flight of stairs to have free access to his books, piles and piles of them, laid out at random on the strong living room floor.

Félix Ventura and I share a love (in my case a hopeless love) for old words. Félix Ventura was originally schooled in this by his father, Fausto Bendito, and then by an old teacher, for the first years of high school, a man subject to melancholic ways, and so slender that he seemed always to be walking in profile, like an old Egyptian engraving. Gaspar—that was the teacher's name—was moved by the helplessness of certain words. He saw them as down on their luck, abandoned in some desolate place in the language, and he sought to recover them. He used them ostentatiously, and persistently, which annoyed some people and unsettled others. I think he succeeded. His students started using these words too, to begin with merely in jest, but later like a private dialect, a tribal marking, which set them apart from their peers. Nowadays, Félix Ventura assured me, his students are still quite capable of recognizing one another, even if they've never met before, on hearing just a few words . . .

"I still shudder each time I hear someone say 'duvet,' a repulsive Gallicism, rather than 'eiderdown,' which to me (and I'm sure you'll agree with me on this) seems to be a very lovely, rather novel word. But I've resigned myself to 'brassiere.' 'Strophium' has a sort of historical dignity about it, but it still sounds a little odd—don't you think?"

· Southern Africa ·

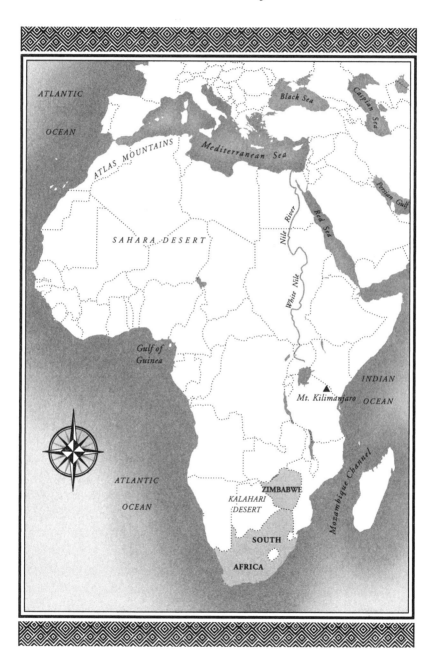

J. M. COETZEE

South Africa

❖

THE MEMOIRS OF BREYTEN BREYTENBACH

I

BREYTEN BREYTENBACH FIRST came to public attention when, from Paris, where he worked as a painter and poet, he sought permission from the South African authorities to bring his Vietnamese-born wife home on a visit, and was informed that as a couple they would not be welcome. The embarrassment of this cause célèbre persuaded the authorities, in 1973, to relent and issue limited visas. In Cape Town Breytenbach addressed a packed audience at a literary symposium. "We [Afrikaners]," he said, "are a bastard people with a bastard language. Our nature is one of bastardy. It is good and beautiful thus . . . [But] like all bastards—uncertain of their identity—we began to adhere to the concept of *purity*. That is apartheid. *Apartheid is the law of the bastard.*"[1]

A record of that visit appeared, first in the Netherlands, then in the English-speaking world, in *A Season in Paradise,* a memoir interspersed with poems, reminiscences and reflections on the South African situation; it included the text of the address.

In 1975 Breytenbach was back, but in a new role: on a clandestine mission to recruit saboteurs on behalf of the African National Congress. He was soon picked up by the security police, and spent seven years in jail. Returning to France, he publicly cut ties with his people: "I do not

---

1 *A Season in Paradise,* trans. Rike Vaughan (New York: Persea Books, 1980), p. 156.

consider myself to be an Afrikaner."[2] Nevertheless, during the 1980s he paid for further private visits, under police supervision. A 1991 visit gave rise to *Return to Paradise,* the narrative of a journey through the "reformed" South Africa of F. W. de Klerk. As he explained, the book was meant to be read together with *A Season in Paradise* and his prison memoir *The True Confessions of an Albino Terrorist* as an autobiographical triptych.

The titles of the *Paradise* books cast an ironical glance at Rimbaud's *Une Saison en enfer.* "This region of damnation," he calls South Africa in *Return to Paradise.* "I am looking at the future and it chills me to the bone." The revolution has been betrayed; cliques of middle-aged men are bargaining for their slice of the cake while on the ground their followers fight on mindlessly. The new order on the point of emerging—"more broadly based hegemony but [the] same mechanisms and same sadness"— is not what he fought for. If his own "whimpers for an impossible revolution" are utopian, it remains the right of the poet to imagine a future beyond the dreams of politicians, to have his prophetic say in the future. He even has the right to bite the hand that has fed him.[3]

At a more down-to-earth level, the story of the 1991 visit includes poetry readings in noisy halls where the audience does not understand the language and comes only to inspect the oddity named Breytenbach; perplexed reactions from old comrades-in-arms ("But aren't you *ever* happy? Now that we've won, can't you *rejoice?*"); incomprehension and hostility when he asserts that his role in the future will be, as in the past, "to be against the norm, orthodoxy, the canon, hegemony, politics, the State, power." These are sentiments which do not go down well in a country that has, as he observes dryly, slid straight from pre-humanity to post-humanity.[4]

He uses the book to lash out, in anguish and bitterness, in all directions: against white liberals, against the South African Communist

2 *The True Confessions of an Albino Terrorist* (New York: Farrar, Straus & Giroux, 1985), p. 280.

3 *Return to Paradise* (New York: Harcourt Brace, 1993), pp. 31, 201, 214, 215. The book appeared in Dutch before it appeared in English. The Dutch text is considerably longer. Passages cut include reminiscences of bohemian life in the Cape Town of the 1950s and of Breytenbach's travels in Africa.

4 Ibid., pp. 158, 160, 196.

Party and "more-doctrinaire-than-thou" bourgeois leftists, against former associates like Wole Soyinka and Jesse Jackson, and particularly, for their treatment of him when he was in jail, against the ANC itself:

> Not only did the ANC withhold assistance from my dependants, not only did they disavow me, but the London clique of bitter exiles intervened to stop any manifestation of international or local support for my cause. They blackballed and maligned me, abetted by well-meaning "old friends" inside the country. Even Amnesty International was prevailed upon not to "adopt" me as a prisoner of conscience.[5]

The plague that Breytenbach pronounces upon all parties—a condemnation in which, despite the pungency of the language, there is something wild and out of control—makes up the less interesting half of the book. Its best pages address a more intimate and more fundamental concern: what it means to him to be rooted in a landscape, to be African-born. For though he has spent almost all his adult life in Europe, Breytenbach does not feel himself to be a European:

> To be an African is not a choice, it is a condition . . . To be [an African] is not through lack of being integrated in Europe . . . neither is it from regret of the crimes perpetrated by "my people" . . . No, it is simply the only opening I have for making use of all my senses and capabilities . . . The [African] earth was the first to speak. I have been pronounced once and for all.[6]

What he means by saying that Africa allows him to use his senses and his capabilities fully is revealed in page after magical page as he responds to the sights and sounds of "the primordial continent." As a writer, Breytenbach has the gift of being able to descend effortlessly into the Africa of the poetic unconscious and return with the rhythm and

---

5 Ibid., p. 123.

6 Ibid., p. 75.

the words, the words in the rhythm, that give life. He is aware of the gift. It is not an individual matter, he insists, but is inherited from his ancestors, "forefathers with the deep eyes of injured baboons," whose lives were spent in intimate relation with their native landscape, so that when he speaks that landscape he is speaking in their voice as much as his own.[7]

It is this very traditional, very African realization—that his deepest creative being is not his own but belongs to an ancestral consciousness— that gives rise to some of the pain and confusion recorded in *Return to Paradise*. For though Breytenbach may recognize how marginal he has become in what is nowadays on all sides, with varying degrees of irony, called "the new South Africa," and may even enjoy dramatizing himself as the one without a self, the bastard, the "nomadic nobody," or, in his favorite postmodern figure, the face in the mirror, a textual shadow without substance, he knows that ultimately he owes his strength to his native earth and his ancestors.[8] Thus the most moving passages in the book tell of visiting his father's deathbed, renewing friendships, making peace with his brothers, taking his wife to the old places of Africa.

II

Dog Heart, Breytenbach's 1999 memoir, confines itself to a tiny area of South Africa, a region of the Western Cape province dubbed by him "Heartland," and within it to the town of Montagu, not far from his birthplace, where, as he records, he and his wife buy and restore a house for their own use. The economy of this area is based on viticulture and fruit farming; but in recent years Montagu itself (pop. 23,000), a town of some charm, blessed with hot springs and a spectacular setting, has become a haven for retired people, artists, and craft-workers. Demographically it is unrepresentative of the country as a whole. Whereas

---

7   Ibid., pp. 4, 27.

8   Ibid., p. 74.

two thirds of the national population is black (we will brave the mine-field of racial terminology in a moment), the people of Breytenbach's Montagu are overwhelmingly brown or white; though nationwide Afri-kaans is the mother tongue of only one person in seven, in Montagu it predominates; and, in a country whose population is skewed towards youth (nearly half of it is under the age of twenty-one), Montagu is a town of aging people: the young have migrated to the cities in search of work.

Crude though they may be, these statistics should alert us against taking *Dog Heart* for what it is not and does not pretend to be: a report on the state of the South African nation in the 1990s. Breytenbach's Heartland is not a microcosm of South Africa; *Dog Heart* has little to say about politics or black-white relations on a national scale. What it does report on, with intimate attention, is power relations between white and brown in the countryside.

Who are Breytenbach's so-called brown people? The seeming in-nocence of the appellation conceals problems not only of anthropology (culture, genetics) and history (who holds the power to call whom what, and how was that power won?), but of a conceptual nature too: what does it mean to be neither black nor white, to be defined in negative terms, as, in effect, a person without qualities?

For that is how brown (or coloured or Coloured—with a *C* the term still carries apartheid echoes; with a *c* it is more or less neutral) people were defined under apartheid legislation. The category *Coloured* was meant to pick out the descendants of unions between people (usu-ally men) of European (so-called Caucasian) descent and people (usually women) of indigenous African (usually Khoi—the term "Hottentot" is no longer polite) or Asian (usually Indonesian slave) birth. But in practice it captured many others besides, of genetically diverse origins: people of "pure" Khoi—or indeed of "pure" "African" descent—whom circumstance had led to adopt a European or European-derived name and language and lifestyle; people who through endogamy had retained a "purely" Asian, Islamic identity; "Europeans" who for one reason or another had dropped through the net of "whiteness" and were leading "mixed" lives.

Though apartheid legislation assumed a system of classification watertight enough to allocate each individual South African to one of four categories (white, Coloured, African, Indian), the basis of the system was ultimately tautological: a white was defined as a person of white appearance whom the white community accepted as white, and so forth.

The most conceptually sophisticated resistance to classification came from "coloured" quarters: if there was no "Coloured" community prepared to concede that it had pre-existed its creation by apartheid, then, logically, there could be no community criterion of "Colouredness." Throughout the apartheid years the status "Coloured" was, across almost the entire range of people whom it implicated, accepted, so to speak, under protest, as an identity forced upon them. Insofar as there is or was a "Coloured" community, it was a community created by the common fate of being forced to behave, in the face of authority, as "Coloured."

It is this history of contestation that Breytenbach calls up when he writes of "brown" people: a history of two or three million South Africans of highly diverse ethnic and social origins first compelled to conceive of themselves as a community, even (in one of the loftier predictions of apartheid historiography) as "a nation in the making"; then, in 1994, entering into a dispensation in which, while the old race laws were abolished, racial distinctions had nevertheless to be kept alive to make possible the social-engineering measures known in English as "affirmative action" and in Afrikaans, more bluntly, as "putting-right." "First not white enough, then not black enough," they complained, not without reason.

The issue of whether there is or ought to be a category between black and white is not unique to South Africa. The rights of ethnic or cultural minorities in the multi-ethnic nation-state constitute a critical issue worldwide; debate is rife in Latin America and other corners of the postcolonial world on the politics of *mestizo* identity. In South Africa this ferment has prompted people excluded from the "natural" identities of black and white to explore cultural identities for themselves entirely divorced from the set of options offered by apartheid—identities that link them to a precolonial past and even to a history older than that of "black" South Africans. Archaeological researches push the date of the migration of "black" Africans, speakers of Bantu languages, into the territory of the present South Africa further and further back in time, but no one proposes they have been there as long as the primeval hunter-gatherers of the dry southwest, the mythical heartland of Breytenbach's "brown" people.

III

Being called, in 1973, "a bastard people with a bastard language" jolted even those Afrikaners sympathetic to Breytenbach. But in the years that have passed since then, *bastardy*—or, more politely, *hybridity*—has become a fashionable term in cultural history and cultural politics.

Revisionist historians are busy rewriting the story of the Southern African colonial frontier as a zone of barter and exchange where old cultural baggage was shed and new baggage taken aboard, and where new identities—even new racial identities—were tried on like clothing. For adventurously-minded Afrikaners, laying claim to a dark ancestor now holds considerable cachet (Breytenbach himself is not immune to such self-fashioning).

Thus, half a century after the National Party came to power vowing to preserve at whatever cost the Christian Aryan identity of the Afrikaner, the wheel has come full circle: the intellectual vanguard of the Afrikaans-speaking sector, nervous of the name "Afrikaner" so long as it carries its old historical freight of racial exclusivity, yet unable to offer a better one, claim that they represent instead an embryonic, genetically hybrid, culturally syncretic, religiously diverse, non-exclusive, as yet unnamed group ("people" remains too loaded a term) defined (loosely) by attachment to a language—Afrikaans—of mixed provenance (Dutch, Khoi, Malay) but rooted in the African continent.

Breytenbach makes a large historical claim for his Heartland region: that during the time when it was part of the colonial frontier it bred a restless, nomadic, mongrel type of Afrikaner, without the social pretensions of farmers from the neighboring, more settled Boland region, where the economy had been built on slave labor—a being, in fact, not unlike the alternative Afrikaner just described.

It is a claim that will probably not stand up to scholarly scrutiny, but it does enable Breytenbach to advance his revisionist version of the

Afrikaner pioneer. Whereas in the establishment version these pioneers were white-skinned farmers who, Bible in one hand and gun in the other, trekked into the interior of Africa to found republics where they would govern themselves free of British interference, in Breytenbach's version they become people of inextricably mixed genetic origin who followed their herds and flocks into the interior because they had learned a wandering lifestyle from the Khoi pastoralists. And (Breytenbach's argument goes), the sooner the modern Afrikaner discards the illusion of himself as the bearer of light in the African darkness, and accepts himself as merely one of Africa's nomads—that is to say, as a rootless and unsettled being, with no claim of proprietorship over the earth—the better his chance of survival.

But bastardy, Breytenbach warns, is not an easy fate. It entails a continual making and unmaking of the self; it is necessarily dogged by a sense of loss. "[Yet] it is good to travel to become poor."[9] Thus Breytenbach links the two themes of his ethical philosophy: bastardy and nomadism. Just as the bastard sheds his self and enters into an unpredictable mixture with the other, so the nomad uproots himself from the old, comfortable dwelling place to follow the animals, or the smells of the wind, or the figures of his imagination, into an uncertain future.

It is against such a background that one must read the gruesome reports in *Dog Heart* of attacks on whites in the countryside of the new South Africa. These stories make disturbing reading not only because of the psychopathic violence of the attacks themselves, but because they are being repeated at all. For the circulation of horror stories is the very mechanism that drives white paranoia about being chased off the land and ultimately into the sea. Why does Breytenbach lend himself to the process?

His response is that rural violence is by no means a new phenomenon. From the old days he resurrects stories of men like Koos Sas and Gert April and Dirk Ligter, "Hottentots" or "Bushmen" who flitted like ghosts from farm to farm sowing death and destruction before at last being tracked down and killed. In the folk memory of brown people, he

---

9 *Dog Heart: A Memoir* (New York: Harcourt Brace, 1999), p. 180.

suggests, these men are not criminal bandits but "resistance fighters."[10] In other words, farm murders, and crimes in general against whites— even the crime directed against the Breytenbachs when their home in Montagu is broken into and vandalized—are indeed part of a larger historical plot which has everything to do with the arrogation of the land by whites in colonial times.

The land, says Breytenbach, belongs to no one, and the correct relation to the land is the nomad's: live on it, live off it, move on; find ways of loving it without becoming bound to it. This is the lesson he teaches his French-born daughter, a child clearly drawn to the wildness and freedom of the country, as he takes her around the sacred sites of memory. Do not become too attached, he warns. "We are painted in the colours of disappearance here . . . We are only visiting . . . It must die away."[11]

The elegiac tone that suffuses much of *Dog Heart* and distinguishes it from the previous memoirs comes in part from Breytenbach's sense of growing old and needing to begin to make farewells, in part from a Buddhist outlook in which worldly attachments retard the progress of the soul (this is the religious side of his ethics of nomadism), but also in part from a sense that the world into which he was born cannot survive. *Dog Heart* is the first of his prose works in which Breytenbach allows himself to articulate what emerges with intense feeling in the more private world of his poetry: that he comes out of a rural way of life which, despite being based on a colonial dispensation with all its manifold injustices, had become autochthonously African to a remarkable extent; and that in the same moment that the head condemns this way of life and judges it must perish, the heart must mourn its passing. (In this respect Breytenbach is suddenly and strikingly reminiscent of William Faulkner.)

In the tentative and ambivalent reconciliation that has taken place between Breytenbach and Afrikaners of the old breed, it is the Afrikaners who have had to make the greater shift. In losing political power, including control over the public media, the people from whom Breytenbach dissociated himself in 1983 have lost their power to dictate what an

---

10 Ibid., p. 136.
11 Ibid., p. 145.

Afrikaner has to be, namely, a "white" of North-European descent, an ethnic nationalist, a Calvinist, a patriarchalist. *Dog Heart* speaks for a countercurrent in which fragments of groups in disarray begin to define themselves, and perhaps even to assert themselves, in a new way, cohering this time not around a political philosophy but around a shared language larger and wiser than the sum of its speakers, and a shared history, bitter and divided though that history may be.

IV

Sharing a language, a feel for the land, a history, perhaps even blood, with "my people,"[12] the people of his Heartland, Breytenbach exchanges words with men and women of all states and conditions. Some of these exchanges disconcert him. The (brown) men who renovate his house treat him (the most celebrated poet in their language!) as a foreigner. Accompanying his brother—who stands as an independent candidate in the 1994 elections—on his canvassing rounds, he hears at first hand the level of brown prejudice against blacks. (His informants may of course be playing games with him: they are as much—or as little—Afrikaner as he, and of the Afrikaner, "stupid but sly," he himself writes, "my morning prattle and my night tattle are cut from the cloth which suits my interlocutor."[13]

At the dark heart of the memoir lies an event that Breytenbach alludes to several times but never explains. It would appear that at the age of seven he had a choking fit and stopped breathing, that in a sense he died and was reborn as a second Breyten (his very name, he points out, is like an echo; one of his poetic identities is Lazarus). "When I look into the mirror I know that the child born here is dead. It has been devoured by the dog."[14] So returning to the land of the dog is in a sense a search for the grave of the dead child, the child dead within him.

---

12 Ibid., p.60.

13 Ibid., p. 175.

14 Ibid., p. 1.

In the town museum—where the bust of D. F. Malan, Prime Minister of South Africa from 1948 to 1954, has been discreetly relegated to a storeroom—Breytenbach comes upon a photograph of his great-grandmother Rachel Susanna Keet (d. 1915). From the archives he learns that as a midwife she brought most of the children of Montagu, brown and white, into the world; that she lived unconventionally, adopting and raising a brown child who was not her own. He and his wife search for Rachel Susanna's grave but cannot find it. So they take over one of the old unmarked graves in the graveyard, adopting it, so to speak, in her name. The book ends on this emblematic note, with Breytenbach marking out, in the name of his dead ancestor rather than of his living child, the most humble of family stakes in Africa.

V

Citizen of France, most untranslatable of Afrikaans poets, Breytenbach has published this account of his re-exploration of his African roots in English, a language of which his mastery is by now almost complete. In this respect he follows his countryman André Brink and a host of other writers (including black African writers) from small language communities.

The reason for his step is, one would guess, practical: the market for books in Afrikaans is small and dwindling. Breytenbach certainly does not resort to English as a gesture of fellowship with English-speaking South African whites, for whom he has never had much time. Nevertheless, it is odd to be faced with a book in English that is so much a celebration of the folksy earthiness of Afrikaans nomenclature, that follows with such attention the nuances of Afrikaans social dialect, and that entertains without reserve the notion that there is a sensibility attuned to the South African natural world which is uniquely fostered by the Afrikaans language.

There is a wider body of what I would call sentimental orthodoxy that Breytenbach seems to accept without much reserve. Much of this orthodoxy relates to what present-day cultural politics calls "first peoples" and South African folk idiom "the old people": the San and the

Khoi. In two widely-read and influential books, *The Lost World of the Kalahari* (1958) and *The Heart of the Hunter* (1961), Laurens van der Post presented the San ("Bushmen") as the original Africans, bearers of archaic wisdom, on the brink of extinction in a world for which their gentle culture rendered them tragically unfit. Breytenbach records moving twilight utterances of nineteenth-century San, while sometimes lapsing into van der Post–like romanticizing as well ("small sinewy men [with] an inbred knowledge of the drift of clouds and the lay of mountains").[15] But his main aim is to suggest that the old San and Khoi myths live on today in unconscious re-enactments: a woman who bites off her rapist's penis, for instance, is repeating the trick of the Khoi mantis-god. Passages of *Dog Heart* carry a whiff of hand-me-down Latin American magic realism. The case for an unarticulated psychic continuity between old and new brown people is similarly unpersuasive, while the recounting of the myths has an obligatory air about it, as if they are being copied over from other books.

Breytenbach's current political beliefs are spelled out in the essays collected in *The Memory of Birds in Times of Revolution* (1996). Insofar as he is still a political animal, his program can be summed up as "fighting for revolution against politics."[16] In *Dog Heart*, however, his politics is implied rather than explained. Quarrels and antipathies emerge in the form of casual side-swipes: at white liberals, at the Communist Party colony within the ANC, at the Coloured middle class that has found a home for itself in the old National Party (rebaptized the New National Party, and still, after the 1999 elections, holding on to power in places like Montagu), at the "dogs of God" (Desmond Tutu and Alex Boraine) of the Truth and Reconciliation Commission, at the new artistic and academic establishment with its stifling political correctness. A brief brush with Nelson Mandela is recounted, from which Mandela emerges in none too favorable a light. Thus Breytenbach keeps the promise he made in *Return to Paradise:* to be a maverick, "against the norm."

---

15 Ibid., p. 84.

16 *The Memory of Birds in Times of Revolution* (London: Faber, 1996), p. 105.

Like Breytenbach's other memoirs, *Dog Heart* is loose, almost miscellaneous, in its structure. Part journal, part essay on autobiography, part book of the dead, part what one might call speculative history, it also contains searching meditations on the elusiveness of memory and passages of virtuoso writing—a description of a thunderstorm, for instance—breathtaking in the immediacy of their evocation of Africa.

YVONNE VERA

· *Zimbabwe* ·

❖

DEAD SWIMMERS

SHE LOOKS UP. Smiles. I reach for her.

The jacket my grandmother wears is no longer as red as when my mother first bought it. Then, in those days, when my mother was the age I am at now, we used to stare at my mother as though she was possessed. She would wear it and listen to Bob Marley singing "No Woman No Cry." Now she says this song is "no longer relevant." My mother is a school teacher. She uses words like "pedantic." She can look at Grandmother in the eye and say "pedantic." At this Gogo just curls her legs further under her and waits for my mother to be sensible. We call my grandmother Gogo. She speaks only one language. Shona. Sometimes, like today, she says "Good morning." Then she throws her head back and you can see her give you all the luck in the world.

My mother does not mind listening to a remake of "Furuwa." This is a song we both liked in 1979. It is the story of two lovers sitting on the crest of a wave. The music of the waves is their music, and they are swallowed by crystal showers and the clearest sand where water meets land. Then a deep foam surrounds them. They disappear, beneath it, in the music of their love. They die a happy death. They die like stars falling from the sky. They have been accepted by the great water spirit which blows upon the shimmering fabric of the sea and makes the water ripple in a violent whiteness, then wave follows wave. Neither my mother nor I have ever been to the sea. However, we have no doubt that "Furuwa" is a good song.

When we bought "Furuwa" in 1979 there were many copies of it at Anand Brothers along 6th Avenue and Fort Street in Bulawayo. Now there is nothing like it. We think this is due to independence, which arrived in 1980. Instead, the record seller looks at us blankly and offers us the new music called Di Gong. In a fit of maternal love my mother had placed the only copy of the record in an envelope and sent it to me when I was in boarding school. By the time it arrived it was broken in two. I threw it quickly in the bin and wrote to my mother. My mother says "if something hurts you then move quickly from it. It is like the sun. It is foolish to stare at the sun all day with the eyes wide open." I threw the record away without looking at it a second time. I wrote to her "Thank you for the waves. The waves have been broken." I could hear my mother's cry as I wrote that. Her sound was louder than that of the waves. I thought perhaps if I have a child I will call her Furuwa.

When she wants to pay the greatest tribute to Gogo my mother often says "your grandmother taught me to hate lightning." My mother will not even answer a telephone when there is rain outside. She goes to her bed at the first sign of lightning and covers her body with a thick blanket. If you talk to her she will not raise her head from the pillow but answer in a muffled voice which tells you not to disturb her peace. We all wait for the lightning to go away.

Today Gogo has a green clothes peg pinned to her red jacket. She tries to get up when I arrive but fails. She staggers back to the floor, beside the blue door where she has been sitting. I rush through the gate, past the lemons, the pawpaw trees, the guava tree. The guava tree which has never given birth to anything but green leaves. I rush through the tears which are always welling at the bottom of Gogo's eyes. Gogo calls me a small wind which you can only feel on the tip of your ear. She says I started walking before I could crawl.

"A woman who cannot forgive her husband's infidelity can climb the highest tree in her village and drop her infant to the ground," I hear Gogo say in her old red coat which used to belong to my mother. When it starts raining Gogo removes the coat quickly and hides it in a large black trunk. She pushes the trunk under her bed. "Red must be placed in darkness when it rains. Otherwise the lightning will burn all of us." So when I see her sitting at her doorway, leaning forward, listening to her past, I know that there is no lightning and her heart is free.

"How is your mother?" Gogo says. "Now that I have finished wiping all the mucus from your nose your mother says you are her child? Is that so?" I do not answer this invitation for a quarrel with my mother, who is not even here with me. Gogo prefers to quarrel with someone who is absent. When Gogo and my mother are together, they agree on everything. They offer each other innumerable embraces. "Your mother left you with me when you were a week old, then she went to train to be a school teacher. Now you are a woman who wears high heels and she says you belong to her." My foot hits the cracked cement block that is her stoep. I collapse beside her like a wave.

The door is wide open. I can see the darkness inside. Gogo has photographs all over her walls. Directly ahead there is a certificate given to my grandfather after he had spent twenty-five years at Lever Brothers, where he worked as a clerk. On it are all my grandfather's names—Enos Mtambeni Mugadzaweta. He was also given a silver watch. It represents time. Grandfather died in 1986. This was the first certificate ever to be received in my family.

I like the picture of Gogo and me in front of the Victoria Falls in 1995. We have our back to a large cataract with cascading waters. When we arrived at the Victoria Falls after a bus ride which lasted half a day, Gogo said this was not land she could inhabit. She turned away from the falling river. There was too much flowing water. Where would one build a shelter, she asked accusingly. I tried to explain that she was on "holiday." I had tried to remove her from the sight of a bed-ridden son whom she had watched dying slowly for over a year. Her voice struggles against the sound of crushing water. There was no place to grow a crop on this river. We turned away from the falls, and, as per our family tradition, left quickly the thing which could hurt us. It is the shortest time I have ever spent at the Victoria Falls.

On the left, just near the light switch which I could not reach till I was seven, there is a happy picture of us hugging tightly. Behind us are two small wooden elephants. Gogo is laughing and spreading luck to everybody, especially Zanele. On that day, my sister Zanele got married. We were all very happy except Zanele. Her mother-in-law had spent the morning pushing an egg between her thighs to see if she had already slept with a man. Zanele emerged looking furious, her new mother triumphant. Throughout the wedding Gogo is busy trying to give Zanele luck.

My mother is hugging Zanele, calling her Furuwa and spreading rose petals in her hair. When the official pictures are being taken outside in the small garden with only a single struggling Petrea bush in it Zanele hisses to me that she will never eat an egg again in her life. Her husband Zenzo asks me what Zanele is saying and I say that she says I should move to the end of the row. So I move away even though I would have liked to remain with Zanele. Her new mother stands next to her and holds her by the elbow. Mother apologizes, saying that her garden is drought-stricken. She holds an umbrella over Zanele's head. The soil beneath us is cracking.

One girl is enough, my father said, and walked out of the door. I was the first girl and was named the most beautiful one—Ntombehhle. Then Zanele was born and my father cursed again and said two girls are enough. He left and never returned. Since our mother now had no husband it was best to spend time with Gogo, who had a grandfather. By independence my mother had enough money to buy a house in an area where black people had not been allowed to live before. Our country was renamed Zimbabwe-Rhodesia. All of us were Zimbabwe-Rhodesians. She immediately planted a petrea bush which refused to release its petals. She kept saying that the flowers on it could turn out to be purple or white. Now we are Zimbabweans. The petrea bush is still bare.

"I have come to collect you, Gogo," I say softly over her shoulder. Gogo never wants to leave her stoep unless there is a death in the family, or a wedding. "You know that Zanele had the twins last week." Gogo shifts her weight to one arm. "Of course I know Zanele had twins last week. Where did she get the twins? There are no twins from our side of the family," she says thoughtfully. She is searching through the past she knows so well. "The children are beautiful, Gogo, but Zanele does not want them. She is refusing to look at them. She has not fed them since they were born and the clinic has had to ask other nursing mothers to feed them."

Silence. I wonder if she had heard me. She rises, without hesitation or staggering. She walks firmly into the house. She has heard me. I feel two years old to see her walking solidly like that. The past thirty years of my life vanish. I wait outside where she has left me. She closes the blue door. Another door opens and closes. Another closes. Then a silence in which I can see foam mounting where land meets water. I hear a sound more quiet than waves. I know that Gogo has turned away from the thing which will hurt her, the thing which I have brought to her carried in my mouth.

Zanele has said she will not touch or see the children. Her husband says that if she continues in this manner he will take his children from her and place Zanele on 23rd Avenue. He says he will leave her "on 23rd" as though he will dump her in the middle of the road. The hospital for mental patients is on 23rd Avenue. It is as old as the country. Africans were sent there in Rhodesia for inciting revolutionary behavior.

Zanele's new mother calls her a lunatic who will murder her children like a crocodile which can even chew its young and swallow them. She likens Zanele to a confused hen which can be seen dripping with the yellow yolk from its own eggs as though it has been offered a feast. The mention of eggs makes Zanele resent the children even more. Zanele's nipples crack with wounds. The milk is trying to escape from her body.

A door opens. Gogo returns. She has tied a blue scarf over her head, the one I bought for her when I finished my journalism course in Harare and she had asked me what kind of work I was going to do. When I said I was going to write important things down she said, "The things which are not written down are also true." Gogo walks with me through the gate, past the lemons, the dangling pawpaws, towards the place where land meets water. We walk. We walk on the crest of a wave. We see the beauty of the sea.

Gogo is going to talk to Zanele at the clinic, she says. I must take her there quickly.

While her husband Zenzo is leaning over the two cots with the two identical faces in them, Zanele bends towards me and forgets about the plate of porridge in her arms now tipping, now spilling over the metal bed-frame, now she whispers to me that she, Gogo, she our very own Gogo, drowned her day-old infant in a bucket of water. Gogo, our very own Gogo. The memory weighs like a mountain.

"You are too young to carry a mountain on your head," Gogo says to Zanele.

NIQ MHLONGO

· South Africa ·

❖

from DOG EAT DOG

THE SWEET KWAITO music blaring from a white CITI Golf passing along De Korte Street helped to bring me back from my reminiscence. I looked at the time. It was ten minutes to six in the evening. The gliding amber of the sun was sloping down to usher in the evening.

I searched the pockets of my jeans and took out the packet of Peter Stuyvesant that I had just bought at the supermarket and unsealed it. I lit a cigarette and inhaled the stress-relieving smoke.

When I had finished I threw the butt into the road and took out my Walkman. I pressed the play button and began to listen to Bayete. The name of the song was *Mbombela*. I lifted my bottle of beer; it was almost half-empty.

When I raised my eyes from the beer bottle, the police car had already stopped in front of me. I hadn't heard them arrive because of the fat beats coming from my Walkman. I pulled the earphones off and let them dangle around my neck.

At first I thought that they wanted some smokes, but then I realised that the police officers had caught me with an open beer. In two ticks both front car doors were flung open and I shrank like a child caught masturbating by its single mother as they moved hastily to accost me.

"Evening, sir."

"Evening."

"How are you, sir?"

"I'm alright."

"Enjoying yourself, hey?"

"Yep."

"Do you realise that what you're doing is against the law?"

"Excuse me? You mean relaxing under this tree?"

"No. I'm talking about public drinking."

"I'm not drinking anything."

"The evidence is in your hand."

I looked at the bottle that I was still holding. I never expected policemen to be patrolling that quiet street. I thought that they would be attending to more serious crimes elsewhere. But there they were, spoiling the party that I was beginning to enjoy with my other self. *Why can't these people just leave a person to do his own thing?* I asked myself. I moved my eyes away from the bottle and looked at the pimple-faced Indian police officer.

"I'm just holding an open beer bottle that I was drinking when I was in the bar, sir. But I'm not drinking it now. And if that's a crime I didn't know."

"We stopped the car because we saw you drinking, my friend. Do you think we're stupid?"

Silence fell while I looked at his tall, white, moustached colleague, who was mercilessly chewing some gum. He staggered forward and I could tell from his bulging bloodshot eyes that he was already drunk. His face was also bright red, as if he had lain in the sun for too long, and the golden hair on his skull stood up like a scrubbing-brush.

"Are you denying that we saw you drinking?" asked the red-faced officer.

"It is just a misunderstanding, sir; I wasn't drinking this beer."

"Ohh! You think you're clever, né?" the red-faced officer asked contemptuously. He leaned forward and shook his large head slowly as if he was feeling sorry for me.

"What is your name?"

"Dingz."

"Are you a student?"

"Yep."

"Where?"

"Wits."

He studied my face for a while. When he started to talk again, his words were accompanied by the heavy smell of liquor and cigarettes.

"OK. Listen, Dingz. We have been asked to patrol this area because lately there have been complaints about students who abuse alcohol. They drink and throw the empty bottles into the street and that's not good for the environment. Look there!" he said pointing at some empty Coca-Cola cans on the other side of the road. "Is that not disgusting?"

"So what does that have to do with me?"

"You say you're a student?"

I nodded.

"And you're holding a beer?"

"But I'm not one of those students you are looking for. If you'll excuse me, gentlemen, I have to go."

I thought I had succeeded in talking myself out of trouble, but before I could even raise myself from the ground the red-faced officer asked me yet another question.

"What are you doing at Wits?" he asked, sprinkling my face with saliva.

"Law," I lied. "Why?"

I thought that maybe then they would leave me alone, but the white officer continued looking at me; he was sizing me up. Then the Indian officer started to lecture me in a patronising tone of voice.

"I wonder if you're aware that a student was arrested last week on a charge like this one. Fortunately he was not doing law." He paused and gave me a sympathetic look. "I understand you guys studying law are not allowed to take a legal job if you have been convicted of a criminal offence. It would be bad for you if we take you in now."

I was realising the seriousness of my situation. I started to reflect on my future; all my efforts to get a place at varsity would prove futile if I was arrested now. *Oh shit! Me and my drinking!*

The white officer was nodding along to everything his friend was saying. I remained silent, but they could see that they had managed to scare me. The white officer leaned closer to me.

"Listen! Here is a deal, pal." He lowered his tone to a confidential whisper. "Either you come with us now to spend three months in a prison cell, or face a one thousand rand fine . . ." He paused and looked at my reaction. I kept my cool. "Or we can sort this thing out right now, out of court, by reaching a gentlemen's agreement." A pause again. "Which means you can stop our mouths with only seventy rand, my friend."

The Indian officer was nodding to support what his colleague was saying as I debated with my other self about the best step to take. I had never been in jail before. I had only heard scanty rumours about the Big Fives, the Twenty-Sixes, Apollos and other prison gangs that sodomise and kill other inmates. But at that moment I was more worried about my family at home. *What will they say if they learn that I was arrested for public drinking?*

There was a moment of silence between the two corrupt officers and myself. Then the red-faced officer bent over and grabbed my beer bottle and two of my grocery bags. He was mumbling something in Afrikaans. The other officer grabbed me by the scruff of my neck and picked up my other plastic bag with the sealed beers inside.

"It seems my friend it is that time again, when you have the right to remain stupid and silent because everything that you say can be used against you in court."

"Whaa! I can't believe how some people can be stupid. We gave you a chance my friend and you blew it. Boom!" said the Indian officer.

They opened the rear door of the police car and pushed me inside with my grocery bags. The walkie-talkie inside the car started belching and cutting. The red-faced officer retrieved it and muttered something in Afrikaans as they got inside and started the engine.

By then I realised that I had messed up my chances of buying myself out. I still had about one hundred and fifty rand that I had taken out at the ATM that afternoon. I knew that the officers would try everything to incriminate me. *They are used to the system. They are also the ones who corrupt it. They know how it works and how to exploit it in their favour. Even if it means that I sleep in a cell just for one night for my disrespect, it would please them.*

The earphones that were lying on my shoulders were still blasting music. I groped inside my pocket in an attempt to find the stop button on my Walkman. I was familiar with the buttons because I had owned my Walkman for the past four years, but suddenly I changed my mind about switching the music off. I opted just to rewind the tape. I found the button I was looking for and rewound the tape.

The car hadn't moved even five metres when I began to plead with them to stop. "I'm terribly sorry, officers. I don't want to go to jail. I think I have eighty rand for you."

The red-faced officer smiled and stopped the car.

"Now you talking sense."

Pleasant smiles broke quietly on their lips as I searched my pockets for my wallet. I unzipped it and handed them four twenty-rand banknotes, money that my mother sacrificed from her pension every month to help me through my cashless varsity life.

The two officers looked at each other and took the cash. I groped inside my pocket again to reach the play and record buttons on my Walkman. Simultaneously, I pressed the two buttons down. Then very politely, in a friendly tone as if I was admitting my guilt, I asked them, "Are you sure that you'll be fine with only eighty rand? I have a feeling that this is a very serious offence?"

"You're right. You can add more if you have it. But do not make the same mistake again next time. OK, my friend?" said the white officer.

"I won't."

I looked at the nametags on the pockets of their blue police shirts.

"Sergeant Naicker and Sergeant Vilijoen, I'm terribly sorry for the inconvenience that I've caused you. Because of my behaviour I will add twenty rand just to apologise."

I offered them another twenty-rand note. Sergeant Naicker took it. He smiled at me and said, "Ja. If it wasn't for Sergeant Vilijoen we would have taken you in today."

"You're a really lucky bastard, my friend. Do you know that? This is what we call being clever. Ask Sergeant Naicker here. We normally fine people two hundred rand for a case like this. We just thought that you are a poor student and decided to fine you less, my friend."

"Hmm! Are you sure a hundred is fine because I can add another twenty."

"Just give us another ten and disappear. One hundred and ten from a student who cares about his future is fine. The next time you're in trouble you must call us or come straight to our police station along this road. You know the station, mos? Ask to speak to either Sergeant Vilijoen or Sergeant Naicker here and you'll be safe."

"Thanks a lot."

The engine was running and the right indicator light was flickering. I opened my rear door to leave.

"Sorry we can't drive you to our place. We are in a hurry for an emergency in Hillbrow. I'm sure you can manage."

I took my grocery bags out of the car and closed the door behind me. The car moved slowly to join the flow of traffic heading for the CBD. I stood on the pavement and began to wave goodbye. Then suddenly I signaled at them to stop the car, as if I had forgotten something inside. I put my grocery bags down and approached the driver's side door, while they both looked at the back seat to see if there was something I had left there. I took my Walkman out of my pocket; the record and play buttons on it were still pressed down, and the red record light was flickering. I showed it to Sergeant Vilijoen.

"What now?" he asked, perplexed.

"Are you stupid? Can't you see that our conversation is recorded on this cassette?"

"Shit! You fucking bastard! You will pay for this."

"Hey! Mind your language, Sergeant Vilijoen! This thing is still recording."

"F-fuck!" swore Sergeant Naicker from the other side.

"He's only trying to scare us. There's nothing there," said Vilijoen to console his colleague.

"Suit yourselves, I'll see you in court then."

I turned my back and pretended I was leaving, but before I could go very far they called me back. "Hey you! Come here, you."

Within the blink of an eye the two officers were out of the car. I thought they were going to negotiate a deal with me, but that was not the case. Suddenly Naicker's big hand was around my balls and I was standing on my toes with pain. Vilijoen grabbed the Walkman from my pocket. I tried to resist, but Vilijoen's fist struck me across my mouth. I tasted blood. Naicker let go of my balls and I staggered and fell down.

I lay still on the pavement pretending I had lost consciousness, but Vilijoen's boot struck me in the ribs. A few minutes later I was hand-cuffed and bundled inside the car.

"Never fuck with the police again, my boy," warned Vilijoen as the car turned past Hillbrow Hospital.

I didn't have the nerve to utter even a single word. I looked at my grocery bags on the floor of the car next to my legs. The brick of butter that I had bought had melted and was almost flat. One of us must have stepped on it. The bottle of mayonnaise had been broken and there was the smell of it inside the car.

At Esselen Street the car turned to the right in the direction of Berea. Ahead of us were about half a dozen police vans with flickering lights parked next to a tall block of flats. The handcuffs were very tight and I felt like the blood wasn't circulating properly in my hands. I looked at the time on the dashboard. It was already twenty minutes past seven in the evening. I had missed my dinner at the Y.

"These things are too tight, please loosen them," I pleaded.

"That serves you right, boy," said Naicker as the car came to a standstill next to the other police vans.

There were lots of people standing around. All eyes were on the block of flats. Policemen were all over the place with sniffer dogs. Naicker and Vilijoen got out of the car without saying a word to me, locked the doors and walked towards the entrance.

After about an hour some policemen came down through the door with some guys who were handcuffed. Deep in my heart I was hoping that Naicker and Vilijoen were amongst them, but they weren't. I sat there wondering what the guys might have done. They had probably been arrested for a much more serious offence than mine. I looked at my plastic bag again and spotted the Black Label. *No more drinking,* I told myself.

At about ten minutes to ten, I spotted Vilijoen coming towards the car. He opened the driver's door and sat inside. "Where do you stay?" he asked.

"YMCA," I answered.

Without asking my permission he opened one of my Black Label dumpies. He drank about half of it without taking a break and gave a loud disgusting belch. "Do you want some?" he asked, as if he was going to give me the one that he was holding in his hand.

I nodded, but all that I really wanted was for him to set my hands free. In a while I saw Naicker coming towards the car as well; he stopped in the middle of the road and lit a cigarette. Vilijoen put the bottle on the dashboard and searched his pockets. He took out some keys and unlocked my handcuffs. Naicker opened the front door and within seconds we were on our way back in the direction of Braamfontein. Vilijoen tossed a cold beer to me and twisted the bottle open. Naicker offered me a cigarette, but I found it too difficult to smoke with my swollen lips.

At half past ten they dropped me at the entrance of the Y with my plastic bags. My ribs were still very painful. My front teeth were loose and my left eye was nearly shut. I had lost my Walkman, my beers and my money.

NADINE GORDIMER

· *South Africa* ·

❖

A BENEFICIARY

CACHES OF OLD papers are like graves; you shouldn't open them.

Her mother had been cremated. There was no marble stone incised "Laila de Morne, born, died, actress."

She had always lied about her age; her name, too—the name she used wasn't her natal name, too ethnically limiting to suggest her uniqueness in a cast list. It wasn't her married name, either. She had baptized herself, professionally. She was long divorced, although only in her late fifties, when a taxi hit her car and (as she would have delivered her last line) brought down the curtain on her career.

Her daughter, Charlotte, had her father's surname and was as close to him as a child can be, when subject to an ex-husband's conditions of access. As Charlotte grew up, she felt more compatible with him than with her mother, fond as she was of her mother's—somehow—childishness. Perhaps acting was really a continuation of the make-believe games of childhood—fascinating, in a way. But. But what? Not a way Charlotte had wanted to follow—despite the fact that she was named after the character with which her mother had had an early success (Charlotte Corday, in Peter Weiss's "Marat/Sade"), and despite the encouragement of drama and dance classes. Not a way she could follow, because of lack of talent: her mother's unspoken interpretation, expressed in disappointment, if not reproach. Laila de Morne had not committed herself to any lover, had not gone so far as to marry again. There was no stepfather to confuse relations, loyalties; Charlie (as her father called her) could remark to him, "Why should she expect me to take after her?"

Her father was a neurologist. They laughed together at any predestinatory prerogative of her mother's, or the alternative paternal one—to be expected to become a doctor! Poking around in people's brains? They nudged each other with more laughter at the daughter's distaste.

Her father helped arrange the memorial gathering, in place of a funeral service, sensitive as always to any need of his daughter's. She certainly didn't expect or want him to come along to his ex-wife's apartment and sort the clothes, personal possessions to be kept or given away. A friend from the firm where she worked as an actuary agreed to help for a weekend. Unexpectedly, the young civil-rights lawyer with whom there had been a sensed mutual attraction, taken no further than dinner and a cinema date, also offered himself—perhaps a move toward the love affair that was coming anyway. The girls emptied the cupboards of clothes, the friend exclaiming over the elaborate range of styles women of that generation wore, how many personalities they could project—as if they had been able to choose, when now you belonged to the outfit of jeans and T-shirt. Oh, of course! Charlotte's mother was a famous actress!

Charlotte did not correct this, out of respect for her mother's ambitions. But when she went to the next room, where the lawyer was arranging chronologically the press cuttings and programs and photographs of Laila in the roles for which the wardrobe had provided, she turned over a few programs and remarked, more to be overheard by him than to him, "Never really had the leads she believed she should have had, after the glowing notices of her promise, very young. When she murdered Marat. In his bathtub, wasn't it? I've never seen the play." Confiding the truth of her mother's career, betraying Laila's idea of herself—perhaps also a move toward a love affair.

The three young people broke out of the trappings of the past for coffee and their concerns of the present. What sort of court cases does a civil-rights lawyer take on? What did he mean by "not the usual litigation"? No robberies or hijackings? Did the two young women feel that they were discriminated against? Did the plum jobs go to males? Or was it the other way around—did bad conscience over gender discrimination mean that women were now elevated to positions they weren't really up to? Women of any color, and black men—same thing? What would have been a sad and strange task for Charlotte alone became a lively evening, an animated exchange of opinions and experiences. Laila surely would not have disapproved; she had stimulated her audience.

There was a Sunday evening at a jazz club, sharing enthusiasm and a boredom with hip-hop, Kwaito. After another evening, dinner and dancing together—that first bodily contact to confirm attraction—he offered to help again with her task, and on a weekend afternoon they kissed and touched among the stacks of clothes and boxes of theatre souvenirs, his hand brimming with her breast, but did not proceed, as would have been natural, to the beautiful and inviting bed, with its signature of draped shawls and cushions. Some atavistic taboo, a notion of respect for the dead—as if her mother still lay there in possession.

The love affair found a bed elsewhere and continued uncertainly, pleasurably enough but without much expectation of commitment. A one-act piece begun among the props of a supporting-part career.

Charlotte brushed aside any offers, from him or from her office friend, to continue with the sorting of Laila's—what? The clothes were packed up. Some seemed wearable only in the context of a theatrical wardrobe and were given to an experimental-theatre group; others went to the Salvation Army, for distribution to the homeless. Her father arranged with an estate agent to advertise the apartment for sale; unless you want to move in, he suggested. But it was too big; Charlie couldn't afford to, didn't want to, live in a style not her own, even rent-free. They laughed again in their understanding, not in criticism of her mother. Laila was Laila. He agreed, but as if thinking of some other aspect of her. Yes, Laila.

The movers came to take the furniture to be sold. She half thought of inheriting the bed; it would have been luxurious to flop diagonally across its generosity, but she wouldn't have been able to get it past the bedroom door in her small flat. When the men departed with their loads, there were pale shapes on the floor where everything had stood. She opened windows to let out the dust and, turning back suddenly, saw that something had been left behind. A couple of empty boxes, the cardboard ones used for supermarket delivery. Irritated, she went to gather them. One wasn't empty; it seemed to be filled with letters. What makes you keep some letters and not others? In her own comparatively short life, she'd thrown away giggly schoolgirl stuff, sexy propositions scribbled on the backs of menus, once naïvely found flattering, a polite letter of rejection in response to an application for a job beyond her qualifications—a salutary lesson on what her set called the real world. This box apparently contained memorabilia that was different from the stuff already dealt with. The envelopes had the look of personal letters: hand-addressed, without the printed logos of businesses, banks. Had Laila had a personal life that wasn't related to her family-the-theatre? One child, the product of divorced parents, hardly counts as "family."

Charlotte—that was the identity she had in any context relating to her mother—sifted through the envelopes. If her mother had had a personal life, it was not a material possession to be disposed of like garments taken on and off; a personal life can't be "left to" a daughter, like a beneficiary in a will. Whatever letters Laila had chosen to keep were still hers; best to quietly burn them, as Laila herself had been consumed, sending them to join her. They say (she had read somewhere) that no one ever disappears, up in the atmosphere, stratosphere, whatever you call space—atoms infinitely minute, beyond conception of existence, are up there forever, from the whole world, from all time. As she shook this one box which was not empty, so that the contents would settle and not spill when it was lifted, she noticed some loose sheets of writing paper lying face down. Not held in the privacy of an envelope. She picked them out, turned them face up. Her father's handwriting, more deliberately formed than Charlie knew it. What was the date at the top of the page, under the address of the house she remembered as home when she was a small girl? A date twenty-four years back. Of course, his handwriting had changed a bit; it does with different stages in one's life. His Charlie was twenty-eight now, so she would have been four years old when he wrote that date. It must have been just before the divorce and her move to a new home with Laila.

The letter was formally addressed, on the upper left-hand side of the paper, to a firm of lawyers, Kaplan McLeod & Partners, and directed to one of them in particular: "Dear Hamish." Why on earth would Laila want to keep from a dead marriage the sort of business letter that a neurologist might have to write to a legal firm—on some question of a car accident maybe, or the nonpayment of some patient's consultation fee or surgery charges. (As if her father's medical and human ethics would ever have led him to the latter. . . .) The pages must have got mixed up with the other, truly personal material at some time. Laila and Charlotte had changed apartments frequently during Charlotte's childhood and adolescence.

The letter was marked "Copy":

"My wife, Laila de Morne, is an actress and, in the course of pursuing her career, has moved in a circle independent of one shared by a couple in marriage. I have always encouraged her to take the opportunities, through contacts she might make, to further her talent. She is a very attractive woman, and it was obvious to me that I should have to accept that there would be men, certainly among her fellow-actors, who would want to be more than admirers. But while she enjoyed the attention, and sometimes responded with a general kind of social flirtation, I had no reason to see this as a more than natural pleasure in her own looks and talents. She would make fun of these admirers, privately, with sharp remarks on their appearance, their pretensions, and, if they were actors, directors, or playwrights, on the quality of their work. I knew that I had not married a woman who would want to stay home and nurse babies, but from time to time she would bring up the subject. We ought to have a son, she said, for me. Then she would get a new part in a play and the idea was understandably postponed. After a successful start, her career was, however, not advancing to her expectations. She did not succeed in getting several roles that she had confidently anticipated. She came home elated one night and told me that she had been accepted for a small part in a play overseas, in the Edinburgh Fringe Festival. She had been selected because the leading actor himself, Rendall Harris, had told the casting director that she was the most talented of the young women in the theatre group. I was happy for her, and we gave a farewell party at our house the night before the cast left for the United Kingdom. After Edinburgh, she spent some time in London, calling to say how wonderful and necessary it was for her to experience what was happening in theatre there and, I gathered, trying her luck in auditions. Apparently unsuccessfully.

"Perhaps she intended not to come back. But she did. A few weeks later, she told me that she had just been to a gynecologist and confirmed that she was pregnant. I was moved. I took the unlikely luck of conception—I'd assumed, when we made love on the night of the party, that she'd taken the usual precautions; we weren't drunk, even if she was triumphant—as a symbol of what would be a change in our perhaps unsuitable marriage. I am a medical specialist, a neurological surgeon.

"When the child was born, it looked like any other red-faced infant, but after several months everyone remarked how the little girl was the image of Laila, her mother. It was one Saturday afternoon, when she was kicking and flinging her arms athletically—we were admiring our baby's progress, her beauty, and I joked, 'Lucky she doesn't look like me'—that my wife picked her up, away from me, and told me, 'She's not your child.' She'd met someone in Edinburgh. I interrupted with angry questions. No, she prevaricated, all right, London, the affair began in London. The leading actor who had insisted on her playing the small part had introduced her to someone there. A few days later, she admitted that it was not 'someone,' it was the leading actor. He was the father of our girl. She told this to other people, our friends, when through the press we heard the news that the actor, Rendall Harris, was making a name for himself in plays by Tom Stoppard and Tennessee Williams.

"I couldn't decide what to believe. I even consulted a colleague in the medical profession about the possible variations in the period of gestation in relation to birth. Apparently, it was possible that the conception had taken place with me, or with the other man a few days before or after the intercourse with me. Laila never expressed any intention of taking the child and making her life with the man. She was too proud to let anyone know that he most likely wouldn't want her or the supposed progeny of their affair.

"Laila has devoted herself to her acting career and, as a result, I have of necessity had a closer relation than is customary for the father with the care of the small girl, now four years old. I am devoted to her and can produce witnesses to support the conviction that she would be happiest in my custody.

"I hope this is adequate. Let me know if anything more is needed, or if there is too much detail here. I'm accustomed to writing reports in medical jargon and thought that this should be different. I don't suppose I've a hope in hell of getting Charlie; Laila will put all her dramatic skills into swearing that she isn't mine!"

That Saturday: it landed in the apartment looted by the present and filled it with blasting amazement, the presence of the past. That Saturday, coming to her just as it had come to him. Charlotte/Charlie (which was she?) received exactly as he had what Laila (yes, her mother—giving birth is proof) had told.

How do you recognize something that is not in the known vocabulary of your emotions? Shock is like a ringing in the ears; to stop it, you snatch back to the first page, read the letter again. It says what it said. This sinking collapse from within, from your flared, breathless nostrils down to your breasts, stomach, legs, and hands, hands that not only feel passively but go out to grasp what can't be. Dismay, that feeble-sounding word, has this ghastly meaning. What do you do with something you've been told? Something that now is there in the gut of your existence. Run to him? Thrust his letter at him, at her—but she's out of it now, she has escaped in smoke from the crematorium. And she is the one who really knows—knew.

Of course, he didn't get custody. He was awarded the divorce, but the mother was given the four-year-old child. It is natural, particularly in the case of a small girl, for a child to live with the mother. Despite this "deposition" of his, in which he was denied paternity, he paid maintenance for the child. The expensive boarding school, the drama and dance classes, even those holidays in the Seychelles, three times in Spain, once in France, once in Greece, with the mother. Must have paid generously. He was a neurologist, more successful in his profession than the mother was on the stage. But this couldn't have been the reason for the generosity.

Charlotte/Charlie couldn't think about that, either. She folded the two sheets, fumbled absently for the envelope they should have been in, weren't, and with them in her hand left the boxes, the letters, Laila's apartment locked, behind the door.

He could only be asked: why he had been a father, loving.

The return of this Saturday—it woke her at three, four in the morning, when she had kept it at bay through the activities of the day, work, navigating alone in her car through the city's crush, leisure time occupied in the company of friends who hadn't been told. She and her father had one of their regular early dinners at his favorite restaurant, went to a foreign movie by a director whose work she admires, and the news of that Saturday couldn't be spoken, was unreal.

In the dark, when the late-night traffic was over and the dawn traffic hadn't begun: silence.

The reason.

He believed in the chance of conception, that one night of the party. Laila's farewell. Even though his friend, the expert in biological medicine, had implied that if you didn't know the stage of the woman's fertility cycle you couldn't be sure—the conception might have been achieved a few days before or after that unique night.

I am Charlie, his.

The reason.

Another night thought, an angry mood: Who do they think they are, deciding who I am to suit themselves? To suit her vanity—she could, at least, bear the child of an actor with a career in the theatre that she hadn't attained for herself. To suit his wounded macho pride—refusing to accept another male's potency; his seed had to have been the winner.

And in the morning, before the distractions of the day took over, shame, ashamed of herself, Charlie, for thinking so spitefully, cheaply about him.

The next reason that offered itself was hardly less unjust—confusedly hurtful to her. He had paid one kind of maintenance, and he had paid another kind of maintenance, loving her in order to uphold the conventions before what he saw as the world—the respectable doctors in white coats who had wives to accompany them to medical-council dinners. If he had married again, it would have been to a woman like these. Laila was Laila. Never risk another.

The letter that belonged to no one's daughter was moved from place to place, to a drawer under sweaters, to an Indian box where she kept earrings and bracelets, behind books of plays—Euripides and Racine, Shaw and Brecht, Dario Fo, Miller, Artaud, Beckett, and, of course, an annotated "Marat/Sade." Charlotte's inheritance, never read.

When you are of many minds, the contention makes someone who has been not exactly what one wanted, who doesn't yet count, the only person to be told. In bed, yet another night, after lovemaking, when the guards were down, along with the physical tensions. Mark, the civil-rights lawyer, who acted in the mess of divorce litigation only when it infringed constitutional rights, said, in response, of the letter, "Tear it up." When she appealed (it was not just a piece of paper): "Have a DNA test." How to do that without taking the whole cache that was the past to the father? "Get a snip of his hair." All that would be needed to go along with a sample of her blood. Like whoever it was in the Bible cutting off Samson's hair. But how was she supposed to do that? Steal up on her father in his sleep somewhere?

Tear it up. Easy advice from someone who had understood nothing. She did not.

But a circumstance came about, as if somehow summoned. . . . Of course, it was fortuitous. . . . A distinguished actor-director had been invited by a local theatre to direct a season of classical and avant-garde plays, taking several lead roles himself. It was his first return to the country, to the city where he was born and which he had left to pursue his career—he said in newspaper interviews and on radio, television—how long ago? Oh, twenty-five years. Rendall Harris. Newspaper photographs: an actor's expression, assumed for many cameras, handsomely enough late-middle-aged, a defiant slight twist to the mouth to emphasize character, the eyebrows raised together amusedly, a touch of white in the short sideburns. Eyes difficult to make out in newsprint. On television, alive; something of the upper body, gestures, coming into view, the close-up of his changing expressions, the deep-set long eyes, gray darkening with some deliberate intensity, almost flashing black, meeting yours, the viewer's. What had she expected? A recognition? Hers of him? His, out of the lit-up box, of her? An actor's performance face.

She couldn't ignore the stir at the idea that the man named by her mother was in the city. Laila was Laila. Yes. If she had not gone up in smoke, would he have met her again, remembered her? Had he ever seen the baby, who was at least two when he went off for twenty-five years? What does a two-year-old remember? Had she ever seen this man as a younger self, been taken in by those strikingly interrogative eyes, received?

She was accustomed to going to the theatre with friends or with the lawyer-lover, though he preferred films, one of his limited tastes that she could at least share. Every day—every night—she thought about the theatre. Not with Mark. Not beside any of her friends. No. In a wild recurrent impulse, there was the temptation to be there with her father, who did not know that she knew, had been told, as he was that Saturday. Laila was Laila. For him and for her.

She went alone when Rendall Harris was to play one of the lead roles. There had been ecstatic notices. He was Laurence Olivier reincarnated for a new—the twenty-first—century, a deconstructed style of performance. She was far back in the box-office queue when a board went up: "House Full." She booked online for another night, an aisle seat three rows from the proscenium. At the theatre, she found herself, for some reason, hostile. Ridiculous. She wanted to disagree with the critics. That's what it was about.

Rendall Harris—how do you describe a performance that manages to create for the audience the wholeness, the life of a man, not just "in character" for the duration of the play but what he might have been before the events chosen by the playwright and how he might be, alive, continuing after? Rendall Harris was an extraordinary actor, man. Her palms were up among the hands applauding like the flight of birds rising. When he came out to take the calls, summoning the rest of the cast around him, she wasn't in his direct sight line, as she would have been if she'd asked for a seat in the middle of the row.

She went to every performance in which he was billed in the cast. A seat in the middle of the second row; the first would have been too obvious.

Though she was something other than a groupie, she was among the knot of autograph-seekers one night, who hung about the foyer hoping that he might leave the theatre that way. He did appear, making for the bar with the theatre's director, and for a moment, under the arrest of programs thrust at him, happened to encounter her eyes as she stood back from his fans—he had a smile of self-deprecating amusement, meant for anyone in his line of vision, but that one was her.

The lift of his face, his walk, his repertoire of gestures, the oddities of his lapses in expression onstage that she secretly recognized as himself appearing, became almost familiar to her. As if she somehow knew him, and these intimacies knew her. Signals. If invented, they were very like conviction. At the box office, there was the routine question, "D'you have a season ticket?" She supposed that was to have been bought when the Rendall Harris engagement was first announced.

She thought of a letter. Owed it to him for the impression that his performances had made on her. His command of the drama of living, the excitement of being there with him. After the fourth or fifth version in her mind, the next was written. Mailed to the theatre, it was most likely glanced through in his dressing room or at his hotel, among the other "tributes," and would either be forgotten or taken back to London for the collection of memorabilia it seemed actors needed. But, with him, there was that wry sideways tilt to the photographed mouth.

Of course, she neither expected nor received any acknowledgment.

After a performance one night, she bumped into some old friends of Laila's, actors who had come to the memorial, and who insisted on her joining them in the bar. When Rendall Harris's unmistakable head appeared through the late crowd, they created a swift current past backs to embrace him, to draw him with their buddy, the theatre director, to a space made at the table, where she had been left among the bottles and glasses. The friends, in the excitement of having Rendall Harris among them, forgot to introduce her as Laila's daughter, Laila who'd played Corday in that early production where he'd been Marat; perhaps they had forgotten Laila—best thing with the dead if you want to get on with your life and ignore the hazards, like that killer taxi, around you. Charlotte's letter was no more present than the other one, behind the volumes of plays. A fresh acquaintance, just the meeting of a nobody with the famous. But not entirely, even from the famous actor's side. As the talk lobbed back and forth, the man, sitting almost opposite her, thought it friendly, from his special level of presence, to toss something to the young woman whom no one was including, and easily found what came to mind: "Aren't you the one who's been sitting bang in the middle of the second row, several times lately?" And then they joined in laughter, a double confession—hers of absorbed concentration on him; his of being aware of it or at least becoming so at the sight, here, of someone out there whose attention had caught him. He asked, across the voices of the others, which plays in the repertoire she'd enjoyed most, what criticisms she had of those she didn't think much of. He named a number that she hadn't seen. Her response was another confession: she had seen only those in which he had played a part.

When the party broke up and all were meandering their way, with stops and starts in backchat and laughter, to the foyer, a shift in progress brought Rendall Harris's back right in front of her. He turned swiftly, as lithely as a young man, and—it must have been impulse in one accustomed to being natural, charming, in spite of his professional guard—spoke as if he had been thinking of it: "You've missed a lot, you know, so flattering for me, avoiding the other plays. Come some night, or there's a Sunday-afternoon performance of a Wole Soyinka you ought to see. We'll have a bite in the restaurant before I take you to your favorite seat. I'm particularly interested in audience reaction to the chances I've taken directing this play."

Rendall Harris sat beside her through the performance, now and then whispering some comment, drawing her attention to this and that. She had told him, over lasagna at lunch, that she was an actuary, a creature of calculation, that she couldn't be less qualified to judge the art of actors' interpretation or that of a director. "You know that's not true." Said with serious inattention. Tempting to believe that he sensed something in her blood, sensibility. From her mother. It was or was not the moment to tell him that she was Laila's daughter, although she carried Laila's husband's name, a name that Laila was not known by.

Now, what sort of a conundrum was that supposed to be? She was produced by—what was that long term?—parthenogenesis. She just growed, like Topsy? You know that's not true.

He arranged for her a seat as his guest for the rest of the repertoire in which he played the lead. It was taken for granted that she would come backstage afterward. Sometimes he included her in other cast gatherings, with "people your own age," obliquely acknowledging his own, old enough to be her father. Cool. He apparently had no children, adult or otherwise, didn't mention any. Was he gay? Now? Can a man change sexual preference, or literally embrace both? The way he embraced so startlingly, electric with the voltage of life, the beings created only in words by Shakespeare, Strindberg, Brecht, Beckett—oh, you name them, from the volumes holding down the letter telling of that Saturday. "You seem to understand that I—we—actors absolutely risk, kill ourselves, trying to reach the ultimate identity in what's known as a character, beating ourselves down to let the creation take over. Haven't you ever wanted to have a go yourself? Thought about acting?"

She said, "I know an actuary is the absolute antithesis of all that. I don't have the talent."

He didn't make some comforting effort. Didn't encourage magnanimously—Why not have a go? "Maybe you're right. Nothing like the failure of an actor. It isn't like other kinds of failure. It doesn't just happen inside you; it happens before an audience. Better to be yourself. You're a very interesting young woman, depths there. I don't know if you know it, but I think you do."

Like every sexually attractive young woman, she was experienced with the mostly pathetic drive that aging men have toward young women. Some of the men are themselves attractive, either because they have somehow kept the promise of vigor—mouths filled with their own teeth, tight muscular buttocks in their jeans, no jowls, fine eyes that have seen much to impart—or because they're well known, distinguished, yes, even rich. This actor, whose enduring male beauty was an attribute of his talent—he was probably more desirable now than he had been as a novice Marat in Peter Weiss's play; all the roles he had taken—he had emerged from the risk with a strongly endowed identity. Although there was no apparent reason that he should not make the usual play for this young woman, there was no sign that he was doing so. She knew the moves; they were not being made.

The attention was something else. Between them. Was this a question or a fact? They wouldn't know, would they? He simply welcomed her like a breeze that blew in with this season abroad, in his old home town, and seemed to refresh him. Famous people have protégés, a customary part of the multiply responsive public reception. He told her, sure to be indulged, that he wanted to go back to an adventure, a part of the country he'd been thrilled by as a child, wanted to climb there, where there were great spiky plants with red candelabras. She told him that it was the wrong season—those plants wouldn't be in bloom in this, his kind of season—but she'd drive him there; he took up the shy offer at once, and left the cast without him for two days, when the plays performed were not those in which he had the lead. They slipped and scrambled up the peaks he remembered, and, at the lodge in the evening, he was recognized, took this as inevitable, autographed bits of paper, and quipped privately with her that he had been mistaken in the past for a pop star he hadn't heard of but ought to have. His unconscious vitality invigorated people around him wherever he was. No wonder he was such an innovative director; the critics wrote that in his hands the classic plays, even the standbys of Greek drama, were reimagined, as if this were the way they were meant to be and never had been before. It wasn't in his shadow that she stood but in his light. As if she had been reimagined by herself. He was wittily critical at other people's expense, and so with him she was free to think—say—what she found ponderous in those she worked with: the predictability among her set of friends, which she usually tolerated without stirring them up. Not that she saw much of her friends at present. She was part of the cast of the backstage scene now, a recruit to the family of actors in the coffee shop at lunch, privy to their gossip, their bantering with the actor-director who drew so much from them, rousing their eager talent.

The regular Charlie dinners with her father, often postponed, were subdued; he caught this from her. There wasn't much for them to talk about. Unless she wanted to show off her new associations.

The old impulse came, unwelcome, to go with her father to the theatre. Suppressed. But returned. To sit with him and together see the man commanding on the stage. What for? What would this resolve? Was she Charlotte or Charlie?

Charlie said, "Let's see the play that's had such rave reviews. I'll get tickets." He didn't demur, had perhaps forgotten who Rendall Harris was, might be.

He led her to the bar afterward, talking of the play with considering interest. He had not seen Beckett in ages; the play wore well, was not outdated. She didn't want to be there. It was late, she said. No, no, she didn't want a drink, the bar was too crowded. But he persuaded gently, "We won't stay. I'm thirsty, need a beer."

The leading actor was caught in a spatter of applause as he moved among the admiring drinkers. He talked through clusters of others and then arrived.

"Rendall, my father."

"Congratulations. Wonderful performance—the critics don't exaggerate."

The actor dismissed the praise as if he'd had enough of that from people who didn't understand what such an interpretation of Vladimir or Estragon involved, the—what was that word he always used?—risk. "I didn't feel right tonight. I was missing a beat. Charlotte, you've seen me do better, hey, m'darling."

Her father picked up his glass but didn't drink. "Last time I saw you was in the play set in an asylum. Laila de Morne was Charlotte Corday." Her father told.

"Of course, you always get chalked up in the critics' hierarchy by how you play the classics, but I'm more fascinated by the new stuff— movement theatre, parts I can take from zero. I've sat in that bathtub too many times, knifed by Charlotte Cordays. . . ." The projection of that disarmingly self-deprecating laugh.

She spoke what she had not told, had not yet found the right time and situation to say to him: "Laila de Morne is my mother." No more to be discarded in the past tense than the performance of the de Sade asylum where she had been Charlotte Corday to his Marat. "That's how I was named."

"Well, you're sure not a Charlotte to carry a knife, spoil your beautiful aura with that, frighten off the men around you." Peaked eyebrows, as if he were, ruefully, one of them—a trick from the actors' repertoire contradicted by a momentary, hardly perceptible contact of those eyes with her own, diamonds, black with the intensity that it was his talent to summon, a stage prop taken up and at once released, at will.

Laila was Laila.

When they were silent in the pause at a traffic light, her father touched the open shield of his palm to the back of her head, the unobtrusive caress he had offered when driving her to boarding school. If she was, for her own reasons, now differently disturbed, that was not to be pried at. She was meant to drop him at his apartment, but when she drew up at the entrance she opened the car door at her side, as he did his, and went to him in the street. He turned—what's the matter? She moved her head—nothing. She went to him and he saw, without understanding, that he should take her in his arms. She held him. He kissed her cheek, and she pressed it against his. Nothing to do with DNA.

MARLENE VAN NIEKERK

· South Africa ·

❖

from AGAAT

IT'S A WIND-STILL evening. 'Agaat has opened the swing doors so that I can hear the yard-noise of milk cans and the returning tractors and the closing of shed doors.

Now it has gone quiet. Now I hear only the sprinklers and the pump down by the old dam, that Dawid will go to switch off at ten o'clock. Closer by is the twilight song of thrushes and Cape robins, a light rustling every now and again in the bougainvillea on the stoep, a few slight sleeping sounds of the small birds, sparrows, white-eyes, that settle there for the night in the centre of the bush.

On the mirror an abstract painting is limned, midnight-blue like the inside of an iris, with the last dusk-pale planes and dark stains from which one can surmise that the garden is deep and wide, full of concealed nooks, full of the silence of ponds, full of small stipples of reflected stars on the wet leaves, full of the deep incisions of furrows.

Green, wet fragrances of the night pour into the room, from water on lawns and on hot-baked soil and dusty greenery.

I smell it, Agaat. Everything that you have prepared before me.

She removes the spray of roses in the little crystal vase from the tray and places it next to my bed on the night-table with the candle.

Had enough? Was it good? Are you feeling better now? No way you could have gone to sleep on such a hungry stomach.

She clears away the tray, switches off the main lights.

Now how about warm milk, with sugar and a drop of vanilla? That's good, later, I gesture.

On her way out she takes her embroidery out of the basket. She looks in the little blue book lying on the chair. She reads the last page and sighs. She searches through the pile, pulls out another. She puts it down on the embroidery. I can always tell when she wants to give up the reading, when she becomes disheartened with it. But these are her two projects. She doesn't leave a thing half-done. Especially when she doesn't yet know how it is to end.

The candle casts a glow on the wall next to my bed. In it stirs the shadow of the crepuscule in the glass vase. Longer and shorter stretch and shrink the buds. Stirred by the air that freshened from the window.

It billows the gauze lining at the open doors outwards and inwards. The flame stirs, casts a silhouette of stems on the wall, crystal and water and tiny air bubbles trouble the light. Doubly magnified in the shadow on the wall where he perches in the rose twigs, front feet clasped together, I see the praying mantis.

She wouldn't bring a thing like that in here without intention. The most exemplary motionless creature she could think of. Little hands folded in prayer. The green membranous wings like coat-tails draped over the abdomen, the triangular head with the bulbous eyes.

I look at the mirror. I see the candle flame and its yellow glow, the shadows, the coruscation of the water, the vase, the rose, the spriggy limbs of the praying mantis. These then are the things reflecting in the three panels where the garden has now darkened. When the flame stirs, the shadows dance, the reflections of the shadows dance, the supplicant raises its front legs in the rose.

Does a mirror sometimes preserve everything that has been reflected in it? Is there a record of light, thin membranes compressed layer upon layer that one has to ease apart with the finger-tips so that the colours don't dissipate, so that the moments don't blot and the hours don't run together into inconsequential splotches? So that a song of preserved years lies in your palm, a miniature of your life and times, with every detail meticulous in clear, chanting angel-fine enamel, as on the old manuscripts, at which you can peer through a magnifying glass and marvel at so much effort? So many tears for nothing? For light? For bygone moments?

A floating feeling takes possession of me, to and fro I look between the shadow picture on the wall and the reflection in the mirror. A story in a mirror, second-hand. About what was and what is to be. About what I have to come to in these last days and nights. About how I must get there over the fragments I am trying to shore. I step on them, step, as on stones in a stream. Agaat and I and Jak and Jakkie. Four stepping-stones, every time four and their combinations of two, of three, their powers to infinity and their square roots. Their sequences in time, their causes and effects. How to join and to fit, how to step and to say: That is how I crossed the river, there I walked, that was the way to here. How to remember, without speech, without writing, without map, an exile within myself. Motionless. Solid. In my bed. In my body. Shrunken away from the world that I created. With images that surface and flow away, flakes of light that float away from me so that I cannot remember what I have already remembered and what I have yet to remember. Am I the stream or am I the stone and who steps on me, who wades through me, to whom do I drift down like pollen, like nectar, like a fragrance, always there are more contents to be ordered into coherence.

Through the open doors I smell the night ever more intensely. It permeates my nose like a complex snuff. Can one smell sounds? I hear the dikkops, from a northerly direction. Christmas, christmas, christmas, they cry in descending tones, christmas comes. The yard plovers cry as they fly up, a disturbance at the nest? The frogs strike up, white bibs bulging in the reeds. Under the stoep a cricket starts filing away at its leg-irons. Here next to my head something prays in the void. That I may be permitted to make the journey one more time, on stippled tracks for my eyes, pursuing place names that are dictated to me, the last circuit, a secret, a treasure that neither moth nor rust can destroy, a relation, a sentence hidden amongst words.

Suddenly I see Agaat. In the dark door-cavity with the tray in her hands. She's watching me from the shadows, I can't make out her face, just the cap, a small white tomb in the air.

Would she sometimes simply be curious, an onlooker at a fainting incident in the street, a visitor to a cage in which a snake is shedding its skin? How would I ever know? How could I hold it against her? How would I want her to look at me here where I am lying?

I close my eyes. I thought she'd already left for the kitchen. I wouldn't, after all that, have dared look around again. Not if I had known she was still there. I hear her walk down the passage, turn round, walk back slowly. She's in the spare room. She stands still.

I count to twelve before she moves again. I hear her put down the tray in the kitchen but then none of the usual, the sounds of clearing the tray on the work surface, of scraping leftovers into the bin, filling the washbasin with water, washing and drying and packing away dishes, taking her own plate out of the warming oven, the sound of the kettle being filled for her tea, pulling out and pulling up the kitchen chair and then, as always, the silence as she eats her evening meal. None of this I hear.

She walks around the house, every now and again she stops, a few paces to this side, a few paces to that, and then stops again. In the dining room, in the living room, in the sitting room, in the entrance hall I hear the floorboards creak and then again down the passage on her rubber soles she walks, tchi-tchi-tchi past my door, a glance at my bed, further along to Jakkie's room, to the spare room, a hesitation before the walk to the back room, and back again down the passage and back and stop and carry on. I can hear her thinking. I can feel her looking for empty spaces. The already-cleared house that echoes lightly. Out at the back door now. Keys. It's the big bunch. First the storage rooms in the back, then round the front.

What is she whistling for me to hear there where she is in the dark? Oh ye'll tak' the high road and I'll tak' the low road . . .

What is that rattling under my bed? The cellar door? Here right beneath me in the right wing? What would she be looking for there?

Muffled from below the floorboards, under the concrete floor layer, the whistling sounds just loud enough so that I can make out the tune.

An' I'll be in Scotland before ye' . . .

The extra mile, Leroux said, that woman walks the extra mile for you.

ZAKES MDA

· *South Africa* ·

✦

from WAYS OF DYING

I

"THERE ARE MANY ways of dying!" the Nurse shouts at us. Pain is etched in his voice, and rage has mapped his face. We listen in silence. "This our brother's way is a way that has left us without words in our mouths. This little brother was our own child, and his death is more painful because it is of our own creation. It is not the first time that we bury little children. We bury them every day. But they are killed by the enemy . . . those we are fighting against. This our little brother was killed by those who are fighting to free us!"

We mumble. It is not for the Nurse to make such statements. His duty is to tell how this child saw his death, not to give ammunition to the enemy. Is he perhaps trying to push his own political agenda? But others feel that there is no way the Nurse can explain to the funeral crowd how we killed the little brother without parading our shame to the world. That the enemy will seize hold of this, and use it against us, is certainly not the Nurse's fault. Like all good Nurses, he is going to be faithful to the facts.

Toloki belongs to the section of the crowd that believes strongly in the freedom of the Nurse to say it as he sees it. He has been to many funerals, and has developed admiration for those who are designated the Nurse at these rituals. They are the fortunate ones, those who were the last to see the deceased alive. Usually they are a fountain of fascinating information about ways of dying.

He moves forward a bit, for he wants to hear every word. The muttering about the Nurse's indiscretion has become so loud that it is beginning to swallow his words of anger. Toloki thought he would need to elbow his way through the crowd, but people willingly move away from him. Why do people give way? he wonders. Is it perhaps out of respect for his black costume and top hat, which he wears at every funeral as a hallmark of his profession? But then why do they cover their noses and mouths with their hands as they retreat in blind panic, pushing those behind them? Maybe it is the beans he ate for breakfast. They say it helps if you put some sugar in them, and he had no sugar. Or maybe it is the fact that he has not bathed for a whole week, and the December sun has not been gentle. He has been too busy attending funerals to go to the beach to use the open showers that the swimmers use to rinse salt water from their bodies.

"Merrie kressie, ou toppie," whispers a drunk, the only one who is not intimidated by whatever it is that people seem to fear from his presence. Merry Christmas, old man. Old man? He is only thirty-eight years old. He might even be younger than the drunk. "It is the perfume, ou toppie. It is too strong." He hears a woman snigger. Why would anyone hate his sacred fragrance? It is the perfume that he splashes all over his body as part of the ritual of his profession before he goes to a funeral. On this fiery Christmas day, its strong smell is exacerbated by the stench of sweat, not only from his body, but from those in the crowd as well.

Toloki is now very close to the makeshift podium where the Nurse defiantly stands, but he still cannot hear a word he is trying to say. Some of us are heckling the Nurse. Some are heckling the hecklers. So, we do not hear one another. Toloki never thought he would live to see the day when a Nurse would be heckled. This is a sacrilege that has never been heard of before. And at the funeral of an innocent little boy, on a Christmas Day too.

Then he sees her, the mother of the boy. She is a convulsion of sobs, and is surrounded by women who try to comfort her. She lifts her eyes appealingly to the feuding crowd, and Toloki thinks he has seen those eyes before. But how can it be? He must approach and speak with her. Only then can he be sure. But people close around her and stop him.

"I just want to speak with her."

"We know who you are. You are Toloki the Professional Mourner. We do not need your services here. We have enough of our own mourners."

"It is not on a professional basis that I want to see her. Please let me speak with her."

"Ha! You think you are going to convince her behind our backs to engage your services? I can tell you we have no fees to pay a Professional Mourner. We can mourn just as well."

Who are these people, anyway, who won't let him see the woman he strongly suspects is from his home village? He learns that they are members of her street committee. They are determined to protect her from all those who want to harass her with questions about the death of her son. Newspaper reporters have been particularly keen to get close to her, to ask her silly questions such as what her views are on the sorry fact that her son was killed by his own people. They are keen to trap her into saying something damaging, so that they can have blazing headlines the next day. The street committee is always vigilant.

The Nurse cannot go on to tell us the story of the death of the deceased, this our little brother. The din is too loud. The church minister says a quick prayer. Spades and shovels eat into the mound of earth next to the grave, and soon the hole that will be the resting place of this our little brother forever more amen is filled up. Those nearest the grave sing a hymn, while a man with a shovel delicately shapes the smaller mound that has risen where the hole used to be. Wreaths are laid. Someone wants to know if the messages on the wreaths will not be read for the public as is customary, and in any case where are the relatives of this bereaved mother? She has no relatives, someone else shouts back. The street committee are her relatives. Then a procession led by the van that had brought the coffin to the graveyard is formed, in preparation for the solemn march back to the home of the mother of the deceased in the squatter camp, where we will wash our hands and feast on the food that has been prepared by the street committee.

Toloki decides that he will rush to the home of the deceased, wash his hands and disappear from the scene. He will have nothing to do with people who have treated him with so much disrespect. Hungry as he is, he will not partake of their food either. If he did not have so much reverence for funeral rituals, he would go home right away, without even washing his hands. People give way as he works his way to the head of the procession, which is already outside the gates of the cemetery. By the time he gets to the street, the procession has come to a standstill, and people are impatiently complaining about the heat. Others attempt to sing hymns, but their voices have gone hoarse from the graveyard feud. Those who can still come up with a feeble note or two are overwhelmed by blaring hooters in the street.

These come from a wedding procession of many cars and buses, all embellished with colourful ribbons and balloons. They are going in the opposite direction, and will not give way to the funeral procession. The funeral procession will not give way either, since out of respect for the dead, it is customary for funeral processions to have the right of way. The wedding party is enjoying the stalemate, and they sing at the top of their voices. Their heads, and sometimes half their colourfully clad bodies, appear from the windows of the cars and buses, and they beat the sides of these vehicles with their hands, creating a tumultuous rhythm. The driver of the convertible car in front, which carries the bride and the bridegroom, argues with the driver of the van which carries the mother of the dead child.

"You must give way!"

"But we are a funeral procession."

"We are a procession of beautiful people, and many posh cars and buses, while yours is an old skorokoro of a van, and hundreds of ragged souls on foot."

"It is not my fault that these people are poor."

No one will budge. There might be a violent confrontation here, since the driver of the convertible, who is a huge fellow, is beginning to call certain parts of the van driver's mother that the slight van driver never even knew she had. Toloki walks to the convertible. He greets the bridal couple, and is about to give them a stern lecture on funeral etiquette, when the ill-humoured driver of the convertible suddenly decides that he will give way after all. He signals to the other drivers in the wedding procession to park on the side of the road so that the funeral procession can pass peacefully. Toloki smiles. He has this effect on people sometimes. Perhaps it is his fragrance. And the black costume and top hat of his profession. It cannot be that the driver of the convertible is intimidated by his size. He is quite short, in fact. But what he lacks in height he makes up for in breadth. He is quite stockily built, and his shoulders are wide enough to comfortably bear all the woes of bereavement. His yellow face is broad and almost flat, his pointed nose hovers over and dwarfs his small child-like mouth. His eyes are small, and have a permanently sorrowful look that is most effective when he musters up his famous graveside manner. Above his eyes rest thick eyebrows, like the hairy thithiboya caterpillar.

The driver of the van approaches him. "The mother of the child we have just buried wants to thank you for what you have done."

So he goes to the van, and his suspicion is confirmed. He has no doubt that this is Noria, the beautiful stuck-up bitch from his village. She has grown old now, and has become a little haggard. But she is still beautiful. And she too recognizes him.

"Toloki! You are Toloki from the village!"

"Yes, Noria, it is me. I wanted to see you at the graveyard, but they wouldn't let me get near you."

"You can't blame them, Toloki. Ever since my son died, all sorts of people have been pestering us."

Then she invites him to come and see her at the squatter camp when the sad business of the funeral is over. Toloki walks away with a happy bounce in his feet. He will wash his hands and leave quickly. He will see Noria tomorrow, or maybe the day after. My God! Noria! He has not seen her for almost twenty years! How old would she be now? She must be thirty-five. He remembers that he was three years older. A hard life has taken its toll since she left the village. But her beauty still remains.

• • •

It is not different, really, here in the city. Just like back in the village, we live our lives together as one. We know everything about everybody. We even know things that happen when we are not there; things that happen behind people's closed doors deep in the middle of the night. We are the all-seeing eye of the village gossip. When in our orature the storyteller begins the story, "They say it once happened . . . ," we are the "they." No individual owns any story. The community is the owner of the story, and it can tell it the way it deems it fit. We would not be needing to justify the communal voice that tells the story if you had not wondered how we became so omniscient in the affairs of Toloki and Noria.

Both Toloki and Noria left the village at different times, and were bent on losing themselves in the city. They had no desire to find one another, and as a result forgot about the existence of each other. But we never stopped following their disparate and meagre lives. We were happy when they were happy. And felt the pain when they were hurt. In the beginning, there were times when we tried to get them together, like homeboys and homegirls sometimes get together and talk about home, and celebrate events of common interest such as births, marriages, ancestral feasts, and deaths. But our efforts disappeared like sweat in the hair of a dog. Indeed, even in his capacity as Professional Mourner, Toloki avoided funerals that involved homeboys and homegirls. Since his bad experience with Nefolovhodwe, the furniture-maker who made it good in the city, and now pretends that he does not know the people from the village anymore, Toloki has never wanted to have anything to do with any of the people of his village who have settled in the city. He is not the type who forgives and forgets, even though his trouble with Nefolovhodwe happened many years ago, during his very early days in the city. Noria, on the other hand, has always lived in communion with her fellow-villagers, and with other people from all parts of the country who have settled in the squatter camp. So, we put the idea of getting Noria and Toloki together out of our minds until today, at the funeral of this our little brother.

· · ·

The distant bells of the cathedral toll "Silent Night," as Toloki prepares to sleep for the night. The strikes are slow and painful, not like the cheery carol that the angel-faced choirboys sang that very morning on the steps of the church. He was on his way to the funeral, and he stopped and listened. Christmas Day has no real significance for him. Nor has the church. But he enjoys carols, and always sings along whenever he hears them. He could not stop for long, since he did not know what time the funeral would be. He was not involved in this funeral in his professional capacity. In fact, until that morning he was not aware that there was going to be a funeral on this day. It is not usual to hold funerals on Christmas Day. He thought he was doomed to sit in utter boredom at his quayside resting place for the entire day, sewing his costume and putting his things in readiness for the busy coming days in the cemeteries. Then he heard two dockworkers talk of the strange things that were happening these days, of this woman whose child was killed, and who insisted that he must be buried on Christmas Day or not at all. Toloki there and then decided to seize the opportunity, and spend a fulfilling day at the graveside. He did not have an inkling that a home-girl was involved in this funeral, otherwise we know that he would not have gone. But after all, he was happy to see Noria.

At regular intervals of one hour the bell tolls "Silent Night." At the window of the tower, perhaps in the belfry, Toloki can see a Christmas tree with twinkling lights of red, green, blue, yellow, and white. The cathedral is a few streets away from his headquarters, as he calls the quayside shelter and waiting-room where he spends his nights. But since it is on a hill, he can enjoy the beauty of the lights, and tonight the bells will lull him to a blissful sleep with carols. But first he must prepare some food for himself. From the shopping trolley where he keeps all his worldly possessions, he takes out a packet containing his favourite food, a delicacy of Swiss cake relished with green onions. He pushes the trolley into one corner, where he knows it is always safe. Though his headquarters are a public place, no one ever touches his things, even when he has gone to funerals and left them unattended for the whole day. Everyone knows that the trolley belongs to Toloki who sleeps at the quayside, come rain or shine. No one ever bothers him and his property. Not the cleaners, nor the police. Not even the rowdy sailors from cargo ships and the prostitutes who come to entertain them.

He takes a bite first of the cake, and then of the green onions. His eyes roll in a dance of pleasure. He chews slowly, taking his time to savour each mouthful. Quite a tingling taste, this delicacy has. It is as though the food is singing in his mouth. Quite unlike the beans that he ate this morning. Those who have seen him eat this food have commented that it is an unusual combination. All the more reason to like it.

Although it is of his own composition, it gives him an aura of austerity that he associates with monks of eastern religions that he has heard sailors talk about.

Sometimes he transports himself through the pages of a pamphlet that he got from a pink-robed devotee who disembarked from a boat two summers ago, and walks the same ground that these holy men walk. He has a singularly searing fascination with the lives of these oriental monks. It is the thirst of a man for a concoction that he has never tasted, that he has only heard wise men describe. He sees himself in the dazzling light of the aghori sadhu, held in the same awesome veneration that the devout Hindus show the votaries. He spends his sparse existence on the cremation ground, cooks his food on the fires of a funeral pyre, and feeds on human waste and human corpses. He drinks his own urine to quench his thirst. The only detail missing is a mendicant's bowl made from a human skull, for he shuns the collection of alms. Votary or no votary, he will not collect alms. It is one tradition of the sacred order that he will break, in spite of the recognition of the shamanistic elements of almstaking. When he comes back to a life that is far from the glamour of the aghori sadhu in those distant lands, he is glad that even in his dreams he is strong enough not to take a cent he has not worked for. In his profession, people are paid for an essential service that they render in the community. His service is to mourn for the dead.

He curls up on the bench and sleeps in the foetal position that is customary of his village. Although he has been in the city for all these years, he has not changed his sleeping position, unlike people like Nefolovhodwe who have taken so much to the ways of the city that they sleep in all sorts of city positions. In all fairness, he has not seen Nefolovhodwe in his sleep, but a man like him who pretends not to know people from his village anymore now that he is one of the wealthiest men in the land is bound to sleep with his legs straight or in some such absurd position. Unlike the village people, Toloki does not sleep naked, however, because his headquarters are a public place. He sleeps fully-dressed, either in his professional costume or in the only other set of clothes that he owns, which he calls home clothes. Since his mourning costume is getting old, and the chances of his getting another one like it are very slim indeed, he often changes into his home clothes in the

public toilet as soon as he arrives back from the funerals. He would like
to save his costume, so that it lasts for many more years of mourning.
This is December, and the weather is very hot and clammy. So he does
not cover himself with a blanket. For the winters, when the icy winds
blow from the ocean, he is armed with a thick blanket that he keeps in
his shopping trolley.

Sleep does not come easily, even with the hourly lullaby of the bells.
He thinks of the events of today. Of course he is piqued. What self-
respecting Professional Mourner wouldn't be? Why did they treat him
so at this boy's funeral? He is well-known and well-liked all over the city
cemeteries. Only yesterday he surpassed himself at the funeral of a man
who died a mysterious death.

Normally when he is invited to mourn by the owners of a corpse,
he sits very conspicuously on the mound that will ultimately fill the
grave after prayers have been made and the Nurse has spoken, and weeps
softly for the dead. Well, sometimes the Nurse and other funeral orators
speak at the home of the corpse, or in church if the corpse was a Christian in its lifetime, before it is taken to the graveyard. But in any case,
he sits on the mound and shares his sorrow with the world. The appre-
ciative family of the deceased pays him any amount it can. One day he
would like to have a fixed rate of fees for different levels of mourning, as
in other professions. Doctors have different fees for different illnesses.
Lawyers charge fees which vary according to the gravity of the case. And
certainly these professionals don't accept just any amount the client feels
like giving them. But for the time being he will accept anything he is
given, because the people are not yet used to the concept of a Professional Mourner. It is a fairly new concept, and he is still the only prac-
titioner. He would be willing to train other people though, so that when
he dies the tradition will continue. Then he will live in the books of
history as the founder of a noble profession.

Yesterday saw the highlight of a career that has spanned quite a few
years. As we have told you, the man in question died a mysterious death.
The family of the deceased gave Toloki a huge retainer to grace the funeral with his presence. It was the biggest amount he had ever received
for any one funeral. Not even at mass funerals had he earned such an

amount. So, he made a point of giving of his very best. Throughout the funeral, orator after orator, he sat on the mound and made moaning sounds of agony that were so harrowing that they affected all those who were within earshot, filling their eyes with tears. When the Nurse spoke, he excelled himself by punctuating each painful segment of her speech that sent the relatives into a frenzy of wailing.

The Nurse explained that no one really knew how this brother died. What qualified her to be the Nurse was not that she was the last person to see him alive; she was the only person who went out of her way to seek the truth about his death, and to hunt his corpse down when everyone else had given up. People should therefore not expect of her what they normally expected of the Nurse: to hear the exact details of what ailed this brother, of how he had a premonition of his death, of how he died, and of what last words he uttered before his spirit left the body.

This our elder brother, we learnt from the Nurse, left home one day and said he was visiting his beloved sister, who now found herself standing before this grieving multitude in the person of the Nurse. But since the day he stepped out of the door of his house, no one had seen him alive again. For the first two days, his wife and four children did not worry unduly. "After all," said the Nurse, "men are dogs, and are known to wander from time to time."

Now, this part was not pleasant to the ears of the men. "How can a young girl who still smells her mother's milk say such disrespectful slander about us? What kind of an upbringing is this?" they grumbled among themselves. But the Nurse brazenly continued on the scandalous behaviour of the male species. Then she went on to say that after two days, the wife phoned the sister, and all the other relatives, but none of them had seen him. He had never reached his sister's house. As is the practice, they searched all the hospitals in the area, and all the police stations and prisons. None of them had any information about their brother. This was a process that took many days, since prisons and hospitals were teeming with people whose relatives didn't even know that they were there, and the bureaucrats who worked at these places were like children of one person. They were all so rude, and were not keen to be of assistance to people—especially to those who looked poor. "And you know what?" the Nurse fumed. "These are our own people. When they get these big jobs in government offices they think they are better than us. They treat us like dirt!"

The family sat down together and decided that this brother was lost, and there was nothing that could be done. But his sister said, "How can a human being be lost when he is not a needle? I say someone somewhere knows where my brother is. We have not even completed the custom of searching. We have not gone to the mortuary."

And so she went to the big government mortuary. There were many people there, also looking for relatives who were missing and might be dead. She joined the queue in the morning when the offices opened. At last her turn came at midday. The woman at the counter looked at her briefly, and then took a pen and doodled on a piece of paper. Then she shouted to a girl at the other end of the office, and boasted to her about the Christmas picnic she and her friends were going to hold. They discussed dresses, and the new patterns that were in vogue. They talked of the best dressmakers, who could sew dresses that were even more beautiful than those found in the most exclusive and expensive city boutiques specializing in Italian and Parisian fashions. The girl said she was going out to the corner café to buy fat cakes, and the woman at the counter said, "Bring me some as well." Then she went back to her doodling. A kindly old man standing behind this our sister who was looking for her beloved brother whispered, "My daughter, maybe you should remind her royal highness that we are all waiting for her assistance."

"Miss, I am looking for my brother."

"Oh, is that so? I thought you were paying us a social visit, because I see you just standing there staring at me."

She was led by a white-coated official to a corridor where there were a dozen corpses lying naked on the floor. None of these were her brother. She was led to another room, with more naked bodies on the floor. These, she was told, had just been delivered that morning. Altogether there were perhaps twenty bodies of old and young men and women, beautiful girls with stab wounds lying in grotesque positions, children who were barely in their teens, all victims of the raging war consuming our lives. "I tell you, mothers and fathers, there is death out there. Soon we shall experience the death of birth itself if we go on at this rate." People were not thrilled at the Nurse's constant editorializing. They wanted her to get to the marrow of the story: how she got the corpse of this our brother. But she felt that these things had to be said nevertheless.

The white-coated official led her to another room with corpses in trays almost like oversized filing cabinets. It was a very cold room. The official said, "Most of these are the bodies of unidentified persons. I can only open two trays at a time, and then we must run away quickly to get to the warmth of the sun outside. If we don't we'll freeze to death in here." And so he opened two trays, and she looked at the bodies. She shook her head, and they rushed out to stand in the sun. After a few minutes, they went inside again and repeated the process. It was obvious that this procedure was going to take many days. The fact that new corpses were brought in all the time, while others were taken out for burial, complicated things. But she was prepared to go through all the distress, even though her stomach was turning, and she was salivating, ready to throw up. It was late in the afternoon, and she had gone through the procedure more than ten times when a saviour came in the form of another white-coated official who looked senior both in years and in rank. "You can identify your brother by the clothes he was wearing," he said. He explained that all the clothes that the dead people were wearing were stacked in a room, with numbers on them corresponding to the numbers on the trays.

The sister did not know what clothes her brother was wearing. After phoning his wife, who described them to her, she went to the pile of clothes. She was relieved to find them there after just a few minutes of looking; relieved not because her brother was dead, but because at last the search was over. "These are the clothes my brother was wearing when he was last seen by his family," she told the official. They went back to the cold room, and the official pulled out the tray. But the body was not there. The tray was empty!

The white-coated official was concerned. On investigating the matter, he found that the body that had been in that tray had been released that morning, obviously by mistake, to a family which lived in another town. It had been given to their undertaker. It was late in the evening, and the only thing the sister could do was to go home and sleep.

The next morning, accompanied by a few male relatives, she got onto a train that took them to the town where her brother's body had been dispatched. To their horror, the body was already in the graveyard, and a funeral service was already in progress. A strange-looking man, the very man who could be seen sitting on the mound mourning with them today for their beloved brother, was sitting on a mound in that distant town, weeping softly. The body of their brother was about to be buried by strangers, when they got there and stopped the funeral service.

"What is wrong with these people? What is their trouble?"

"I tell you, people of God, it is a wrong body you are burying there. It is the body of my brother."

"Who are these people who want to steal our corpse?"

A fight nearly ensued, with the undertaker insisting that it was the right body, and that the madwoman accompanied by her mad delegation must be arrested for disrupting a solemn occasion. But the sister stood her ground. "Kill me if you will," she said. "I am not going away from here until you release the body of my brother." She was determined that if they refused, they should bury her there with him. The strange-looking man saved the day. "Please," he appealed to the indignant crowd, "let us not desecrate this place where the dead have their eternal sleep by fighting here. It is easy to solve this problem. Open the coffin to prove once and for all that this is the right body." The undertaker, supported by some members of the family that supposedly owned the corpse, refused and told the minister to continue with the funeral service. But some members of the crowd advised that the coffin be opened so as to avoid the scandal of a fight in the graveyard. The coffin was opened, and indeed this our brother was in it.

Before the delegation took the body home, the sister spoke with the strange-looking man who had helped them by suggesting that the coffin be opened.

"Who are you, father, who have been so helpful?"

"I am Toloki the Professional Mourner." Then he explained about his profession, and told them that, in fact, this was his very first job in this small town so far away from the city cemeteries where he regularly worked.

"You are a good man. We shall engage your services for the funeral of this our brother."

"It will be my pleasure to mourn for him a second time."

That was why they were seeing him there, mourning his heart out.

But this was not all that the Nurse wanted to say about this our brother. The sister had gone further in investigating who had brought her brother's body to the mortuary. It was brought in by the police, she found. She went to the police station to inquire where the police had found her brother's body. It was found, she was told, near a garage next to the hostels where migrant workers from distant villages lived. In the morning, the garage nightwatchman noticed something that was not there the previous night. He went closer and discovered a man's body. The head had been hacked open, and the brain was hanging out. There were bullet wounds on the legs. He phoned the police, who came and took the body. They said more bodies with similar wounds had been found nearby. They were all packed into the police van and dumped in the mortuary.

"Yes, it must be the migrant workers from the hostels," various people in the crowd shouted angrily. "They have killed a lot of our people, and all we do is sit here and keep on talking peace. Are we men or just scared rats?"

There was no one who did not know that the vicious migrants owed their allegiance to a tribal chief who ruled a distant village with an iron fist. They came to the city to work for their children, but the tribal chief armed them, and sent them out to harass the local residents. Sometimes they were even helped by the police, because it helped to suppress those who were fighting for freedom. Nobody seemed to know exactly why the tribal chief did these ugly things, or where his humanity had gone. But others in the crowd said that it was because he wanted to have power over all the land, instead of just his village. He wanted to rule everybody, not just his villagers, even though he did not have support from the people. Throughout the land people hated him and wished him dead. People knew who their real leaders were, the crowd said, and if the tribal chief wanted to play a rough game, then he would find himself facing his age-mates.

This politicking was interfering with Toloki's inspired mourning. He calmed the crowd down, and told them to concentrate on the business of mourning. Although the issues that the people were angry about were important, they could always discuss them when they got back to the squatter camps and townships. They had grassroots leadership in the form of street committees, which had always been effective in calling meets to discuss matters of survival and self-defence. Everybody in the crowd agreed with him. He felt very proud of the fact that people had listened to his advice. Perhaps he was gaining more importance in the eyes of the community. Before these incidents where he found himself actually acting in an advisory capacity, his role had been to mourn, and only to mourn. He must keep his priorities straight, however. The work of the Professional Mourner was to mourn, and not to intervene in any of the proceedings of the funeral. It would lower the dignity of the profession to be involved in human quarrels.

. . .

That was yesterday. Today he was treated with the utmost disrespect, and now he is annoyed. He sleeps, and in his dreams he sees the sad eyes of Noria, looking appealingly at the bickering crowd.

IVAN VLADISLAVIĆ

· South Africa ·

❖

THE WHITES ONLY BENCH

YESTERDAY OUR VISITORS' book, which Portia has covered in zebra-skin wrapping-paper and shiny plastic, recorded the name of another important person: Coretta King. When Mrs. King had finished her tour, with Strickland herself playing the guide, she was treated to tea and cakes in the cafeteria. The photographers, who had been trailing around after her trying to sniff out interesting angles and ironic juxtapositions against the exhibits, tucked in as well, I'm told, and made pigs of themselves. After the snacks Mrs. King popped into the gift shop for a few mementoes, and bought generously—soapstone hippopotami with sly expressions, coffee-table catalogues, little wire bicycles and riot-control vehicles, garish place-mats and beaded fly-whisks, among other things. Her aide had to chip in to make up the cost of a set of mugs in the popular "Leaders Past and Present" range.

The honoured guests were making their way back to the bus when Mrs. King spotted the bench in the courtyard and suggested that she pose there for a few shots. I happened to be watching from the workshop window, and I had a feeling the photographs would be exceptional. A spring shower had just fallen, out of the blue, and the courtyard was a well of clear light. Tendrils of fragrant steam coiled up evocatively from a windfall of blossoms on the flagstones. The scene had been set by chance. Perhaps the photographers had something to prove, too, having failed to notice a photo opportunity so steeped in ironic significance.

The *Star* carried one of the pictures on its front page this morning. Charmaine picked up a copy on her way to work and she couldn't wait to show it to me.

The interest of the composition derives—if I may make the obvious analysis—from a lively dispute of horizontals and verticals. The bench is a syllogism of horizontal lines, flatly contradicted by the vertical bars of the legs at either end (these legs are shaped like h's, actually, but from the front they look like l's). Three other verticals assert their position: on the left—our left, that is—the concrete stalk of the Black Sash drinking-fountain; in the middle, thrusting up behind the bench, the trunk of the controversial kaffirboom; and on the right, perched on the very end of her seat, our subject: Mrs. King.

Mrs. King has her left thigh crossed over her right, her left foot crooked around her right ankle, her left arm coiled to clutch one of our glossy brochures to her breast. The wooden slats are slickly varnished with sunlight, and she sits upon them gingerly, as if the last coat's not quite dry. Yet her right arm reposes along the backrest with the careless grace of a stem. There's an odd ambiguity in her body, and it's reflected in her face too, in an expression which superimposes the past upon the present: she looks both timorous and audacious. The WHITES ONLY sign under her dangling thumb in the very middle of the picture might be taken up the wrong way as an irreverent reference to her eyes, which she opens wide in an expression of mock alarm—or is it outrage? The rest of her features are more prudently composed, the lips quilted with bitterness, but tucked in mockingly at one corner.

The photographer was wise to choose black and white. These stark contrasts, coupled with Mrs. King's old-fashioned suit and hairdo, confound the period entirely. The photograph might have been taken thirty years ago, or yesterday.

Charmaine was tickled pink, she says her bench is finally avenged for being upstaged by that impostor from the Municipal Bus Drivers' Association. I doubt that Strickland has even noticed.

There seems to be a tacit agreement around here that *Mrs.* King is an acceptable form, although it won't do for anyone else. When I pointed this out, Charmaine said it's a special case because Mr. King, rest his soul, is no more. I fail to see what difference that makes, and I said so. Then Reddy, whose ears were flapping, said that "Mrs. King" is tolerated precisely because it preserves the memory of the absent Mr. King, like it or not. He said it's like a dead metaphor.

I can't make up my mind. Aren't we reading too much into it?

Charmaine has sliced the photograph out of the unread newspaper with a Stanley knife and pinned the cutting up on the notice-board in reception. She says her bench has been immortalized. "Immortality" is easy to bandy about, but for a while it was touch and go whether Charmaine's bench would make it to the end of the week.

We were working late one evening, as usual, when the little drama began. The Museum was due to open in six weeks' time but the whole place was still upside down. It wasn't clear yet who was in charge, if anyone, and we were all in a state.

Charmaine was putting the finishing touches to her bench, I was knocking together a couple of rostra for the Congress of the People, when Strickland came in. She had been with us for less than a week and it was the first time she had set foot in the workshop. We weren't sure at all then what to make of our new Director, and so we both greeted her politely and went on with our work.

She waved a right hand as limp as a kid glove to show that we shouldn't mind her, and then clasped it behind her back. She began to wander around on tiptoe even though I was hammering in nails, swiveling her head from side to side, peering into boxes, scanning the photographs and diagrams pinned to chipboard display stands, taking stock of the contents of tables and desks. She never touched a thing, but there was something grossly intrusive about the inspection. Strickland wears large, rimless spectacles, double glazed and tinted pink, and they sometimes make her look like a pair of television monitors.

After a soundless, interrogative circuit of the room she stopped behind Charmaine and looked over her shoulder. Charmaine had just finished the "I," and now she laid her brush across the top of the paint tin, peeled off the stencil and flourished it in the air to dry the excess paint.

I put down my hammer—the racket had become unbearable—and took up some sandpaper instead. The people here will tell you that I don't miss a thing.

Strickland looked at the half-formed word. Then she unclasped her hands and slid them smoothly into the pockets of her linen suit. The cloth was fresh cream with a dab of butter in it, richly textured, the pockets cool as arum lilies.

"What are you doing?" Strickland asked, in a tone that bristled like a new broom.

Charmaine stood back with the stencil in her hand and Strickland had to step hastily aside to preserve a decent distance between her suit and the grubby overall. Unnoticed by anyone but myself, a drop of white paint fell from the end of the brush resting across the tin onto the shapely beige toe of Strickland's shoe.

The answer to Strickland's question was so plain to see that it hardly needed voicing, but she blinked her enlarged eyes expectantly, and so Charmaine said, "It's the WHITES ONLY bench." When Strickland showed no sign of recognition, Charmaine added, "You remember the benches. For whites only?"

Silence. What on earth did she want? My sandpaper was doing nothing to smooth the ragged edges of our nerves, and so I put it down. We all looked at the bench.

It was a beautiful bench—as a useful object, I mean, rather than a symbol of injustice. The wooden slats were tomato-sauce red. The arms and legs were made of iron, but cleverly moulded to resemble branches, and painted brown to enhance a rustic illusion. The bench looked well used, which is often a sign that a thing has been loved. But when you looked closer, as Strickland was doing now, you saw that all these signs of wear and tear were no more than skin-deep. Charmaine had applied all of them in the workshop. The bruised hollows on the seat, where the surface had been abraded by decades of white thighs and buttocks, were really patches of brown and purple paint. The flashes of raw metal on the armrests, where the paint had been worn away by countless white palms and elbows, turned out to be mere discs of silver paint themselves. Charmaine had even smeared the city's grimy shadows into the grain.

Strickland pored over these special effects with an expression of amazed distaste, and then stared for a minute on end at the letters WHI on the uppermost slat of the backrest. The silence congealed around us, slowing us down, making us slur our movements, until the absence of sound was as tangible as a crinkly skin on the surface of the air. "Forgive me," she said at last, with an awakening toss of her head. "You're manufacturing a WHITES ONLY bench?"

"Ja. For Room 27."

Strickland went to the floor plan taped to one of the walls and looked for Room 27: Petty Apartheid. Then she gazed at the calendar next to the plan, but whether she was mulling over the dates, or studying the photograph—children with stones in their hands, riot policemen with rifles, between the lines a misplaced reporter with a camera—or simply lost in thought, I couldn't tell. Did she realize that the calendar was ten years old?

Charmaine and I exchanged glances behind her back.

"Surely we should have the real thing," Strickland said, turning.

"Of course—if only we could find it."

"You can't find a genuine WHITES ONLY bench?"

"No."

"That's very hard to believe."

"We've looked everywhere. It's not as easy as you'd think. This kind of thing was frowned upon, you know, in the end. Discrimination I mean. The municipalities were given instructions to paint them over. There wasn't much point in hunting for something that doesn't exist, so we decided at our last meeting—this was before your time, I'm afraid—that it would be better if I recreated one."

"Recreated one," Strickland echoed.

"Faithfully. I researched it and everything. I've got the sources here somewhere." Charmaine scratched together some photocopies splattered with paint and dusted with fingerprints and tread-marks from her running-shoes. "The bench itself is a genuine 1960s one, I'm glad to say, from the darkest decade of repression. Donated by Reddy's father-in-law, who stole it from a bus-stop for use in the garden. It was a long time ago, mind you, the family is very respectable. From a black bus-stop—for Indians. Interestingly, the Indian benches didn't have INDIANS ONLY on them—not in Natal anyway, according to Mr. Mookadam. Or even ASIATICS. Not that it matters."

"It matters to me," Strickland said curtly—Charmaine does go on sometimes—and pushed her glasses up on her nose so that her eyes were doubly magnified. "This is a museum, not some high-school operetta. It is our historical duty to be authentic."

I must say that made me feel bad, when I thought about all the effort Charmaine and I had put into everything from the Sharpeville Massacre to the Soweto Uprising, trying to get the details right, every abandoned shoe, every spent cartridge, every bloodied stitch of clothing, only to have this jenny-come-lately (as Charmaine puts it) give us a lecture about authenticity. What about our professional duty? (Charmaine again.)

"Have we advertised?" Strickland asked, and I could tell by her voice that she meant to argue the issue out. But at that moment she glanced down and saw the blob of paint on the toe of her shoe.

I had the fantastic notion to venture an excuse on Charmaine's behalf: to tell Strickland that she had dripped ice-cream on her shoe. Vanilla ice-cream! I actually saw her hand grasping the cone, her sharp tongue curling around the white cupola, the droplet plummeting. Fortunately I came to my senses before I opened my big mouth.

It was the first proper meeting of the Steering Committee with the new Director. We hadn't had a meeting for a month. When Charlie Sibeko left in a huff after the fiasco with the wooden AK-47s, we all heaved a sigh of relief. We were sick to death of meetings: the man's appetite for circular discussion was insatiable.

Strickland sat down at the head of the table, and having captured that coveted chair laid claim to another by declaring the meeting open. She seemed to assume that this was her prerogative as Director, and no one had the nerve to challenge her.

The report-backs were straightforward: we were all behind schedule and over budget. I might add that we were almost past caring. It seemed impossible that we'd be finished in time for the official opening. The builders were still knocking down walls left, right and center, and establishing piles of rubble in every room. Pincus joked that the only exhibit sure to be ready on time was the row of concrete bunks—they were part of the original compound in which the Museum is housed and we had decided to leave them exactly as we found them. He suggested that we think seriously about delaying the opening, which was Portia's cue to produce the invitations, just back from the printers. Everyone groaned (excluding Strickland and me) and breathed in the chastening scent of fresh ink.

"As far as we're concerned, this date is written in stone," Strickland said, snapping one of the copperplate cards shut. "We will be ready on time. People will have to learn to take their deadlines seriously." At that point Charmaine began to doodle on her agenda—a hand with a stiff index finger, emerging from a lacy cuff, pointing at Item 4: Bench.

Item 2: Posters, which followed the reports, was an interesting one. Pincus had had a letter from a man in Bethlehem, a former town clerk and electoral officer, who had collected copies of every election poster displayed in the town since it was founded. He was prepared to entrust the collection to us if it was kept intact. Barbara said she could probably use a couple in the Birth of Apartheid exhibit. We agreed that Pincus would write to the donor, care of the Bethlehem Old-Age Home, offering to house the entire collection and display selected items on a rotating basis.

Item 3: Poetry, was Portia's. Ernest Dladla, she informed us, had declined our invitation to read a poem at the opening ceremony, on the perfectly reasonable grounds that he was not a poet. "I have poetic impulses," he said in his charming note, "but I do not act upon them." Should she go ahead, Portia wanted to know, and approach Alfred Qabula instead, as Ernie suggested?

Then Strickland asked in an acerbic tone whether an issue this trivial needed to be tabled at an important meeting. But Portia responded magnificently, pointing out that she knew nothing about poetry, not having had the benefit of a decent education, had embarrassed herself once in the performance of her duties and did not wish to do so again. All she wanted was an answer to a simple question: Is Alfred Qabula a poet? Yes or no?

No sooner was that settled than Strickland announced Item 4: Bench, and stood up. Perhaps this was a technique she had read about in the business pages somewhere, calculated to intimidate the opposition. "It has come to my attention," she said, "that our workshop personnel are busily recreating beautiful replicas of apartheid memorabilia, when the ugly originals could be ours for the asking. I do not know what Mr. Sibeko's policy on this question was, although the saga of the wooden AK-47s is full of suggestion, but as far as I'm concerned it's an appalling waste of time and money. It's also dishonest. This is a museum, not an amusement arcade.

"My immediate concern is the WHITES ONLY bench, which is taking up so much of Charmaine's time and talent. I find it hard to believe that there is not a genuine example of a bench of this nature somewhere in the country."

"Petty apartheid went out ages ago," said Charmaine, "even in the Free State."

"The first Indian townships in the Orange Free State were established way back in October 1986," said Reddy, who had been unusually quiet so far, "in Harrismith, Virginia and Odendaalsrus. Not many people know that. I remember hearing the glad tidings from my father-in-law, Mr. Mookadam, who confessed that ever since he was a boy it had been a dream of his to visit that forbidden province."

"I'll wager that there are at least a dozen real WHITES ONLY benches in this city alone, in private collections," Strickland insisted, erasing Reddy's tangent with the back of her hand. "People are fascinated by the bizarre."

"We asked everyone we know," said Charmaine. "And we asked them to ask everyone they know, and so on. Like a chain-letter—except that we didn't say they would have a terrible accident if they broke the chain. And we couldn't find a single bench. Not one."

"Have we advertised?"

"No commercials," said Reddy, and there was a murmur of assenting voices.

"Why ever not?"

"It causes more headache."

"Oh nonsense!"

Reddy held up his right hand, with the palm out, and batted the air with it, as if he was bouncing a ball off Strickland's forehead. This gesture had a peculiarly mollifying effect on her, and she put her hand over her eyes and sat down. Reddy stood up in his ponderous way and padded out of the room.

Pincus, who has a very low tolerance for silence, said, "Wouldn't it be funny if Charmaine's bench turned out to be the whites' only bench?"

No one laughed, so he said "whites' only" again, and drew the apostrophe in the air with his forefinger.

Reddy came back, carrying a photograph, a Tupperware lunch-box and a paper-knife. He put the photograph in the middle of the table, facing Strickland. She had to lean forward in her chair to see what it was. I wondered whether she fully appreciated the havoc her outsize spectacles wreaked on her face, how they disjointed her features. She looked like a composite portrait in a magazine competition, in which some cartoon character's eyes had been mismatched with the jaw of a real-life heroine.

Everyone at the table, with the exception of our Director, had seen this routine before. Some of us had sat through it half a dozen times, with a range of donors, do-gooders, interest groups. For some reason, it never failed to involve me. I also leant forward to view the eight-by-ten. No one else moved.

I looked first at the pinprick stigmata in the four corners.

Then I looked, as I always did, at the girl's outflung hand. Her hand is a jagged speech-bubble filled with disbelief. It casts a shadow shaped like a howling mouth on her body, and that mouth takes up the cry of outrage. The palm Reddy had waved in Strickland's face was a much more distant echo.

I looked next at the right hand of the boy who is carrying Hector Peterson. His fingers press into the flesh of a thigh that is still warm, willing it to live, prompting the muscle, animating it. Hector Peterson's right hand, by contrast, lolling numbly on his belly, knows that it is dead, and it expresses that certainty in dark tones of shadow and blood.

These hands are still moving, they still speak to me.

Reddy jabbed the photograph with the point of his paper-knife. "This is a photograph of Hector Peterson, in the hour of his death," he said. Strickland nodded her head impatiently. "The day was 16 June 1976." She nodded again, urging him to skip the common knowledge and come to the point. "A Wednesday. As it happened, it was fine and mild. The sun rose that morning at 6:53 and set that evening at 5:25. The shot was taken at 10:15 on the dot. It was the third in a series of six. Hector Peterson was the first fatality of what we could come to call the Soweto Riots—the first in a series of seven hundred odd. The photographer was Sam Nzima, then in the employ of the *World*. The subject, according to the tombstone that now marks his grave, was Zolile Hector Pietersen, P-I-E-T-E-R-S-E-N, but the newspapers called him Hector Peterson and it stuck. We struck out the 'I,' we put it to rout in the alphabet of the oppressor. We bore the hero's body from the uneven field of battle and anointed it with English. According to the tombstone he was thirteen years old, but as you can see he looked no more than half that age . . . Or is it just the angle? If only we had some other pictures of the subject to compare this one with, we might feel able to speak with more authority."

This welter of detail, and the offhand tone of the delivery, produced in Strickland the usual baffled silence.

"Not many people know these things." Reddy slid the point of the knife onto the girl. "This is Hector's sister Margot, aka Tiny, now living in Soweto." The knife slid again. "And this is Mbuyisa Makhubu, whereabouts your guess is as good as mine. Not many people know them either. We have come to the conclusion, here at the Museum, that the living are seldom as famous as the dead."

The knife moved again. It creased Mbuyisa Makhubu's lips, which are bent into a bow of pain like the grimace of a tragic mask, it rasped the brick wall of the matchbox house which we see over his shoulder, skipped along the top of a wire gate, and came to rest on the small figure of a woman in the background. "And who on earth do you suppose this is?"

Strickland gazed at the little figure as if it was someone famous she should be able to recognize in an instant, some household name. In fact, the features of this woman—she is wearing a skirt and doek—are no more than a grey smudge, continuous with the shadowed wall behind her.

I looked at Hector Peterson's left arm, floating on air, and the shadow of his hand on Mbuyisa Makhubu's knee, a shadow so hard-edged and muscular it could trip the bearer up.

The child is dead. With his rumpled sock around his ankle, his grazed knee, his jersey stuck with dry grass, you would think he had taken a tumble in the playground, if it were not for the gout of blood from his mouth. The jersey is a bit too big for him: it was meant to last another year at least. Or is it just that he was small for his age? Or is it the angle? In his hair is a stalk of grass shaped like a praying mantis.

"Nobody knows."

Strickland sat back with a sigh, but Reddy went on relentlessly.

"Nevertheless, theories were advanced: some people said that this woman, this apparent bystander, was holding Hector Peterson in her arms when he died. She was a mother herself. She cradled him in her lap—you can see the bloodstains here—and when Makhubu took the body from her and carried it away, she found a bullet caught in the folds of her skirt. She is holding that fatal bullet in her right hand, here.

"Other people said that it didn't happen like that at all. Lies and fantasies. When Nzima took this photograph, Hector Peterson was still alive! What you see here, according to one reliable caption, is a critically wounded youth. The police open fire, Hector falls at Mbuyisa's feet. The boy picks him up and runs towards the nearest car, which happens to belong to Sam Nzima and Sophia Tema, a journalist on the *World,* Nzima's partner that day. Sam takes his photographs. Then Mbuyisa and Tiny pile into the back of the Volkswagen—did I mention that it was a Volkswagen?—they pile into the back with Hector; Sam and Sophia pile into the front with their driver, Thomas Khoza. They rush to the Orlando Clinic, but Hector Peterson is certified dead on arrival. And that's the real story. You can look it up for yourself.

"But the theories persisted. So we thought we would try to lay the ghost—we have a duty after all to tell the truth. This is a museum, not a paperback novel. We advertised. We called on this woman to come forward and tell her story. We said it would be nice—although it wasn't essential—if she brought the bullet with her."

"Anyone respond?"

"I'll say."

Reddy opened his lunch-box and pushed it over to Strickland with the edge of his palm, like a croupier. She looked at the contents: there were .38 Magnum slugs, 9mm and AK cartridges, shiny .22 bullets, a

.357 hollow-point that had blossomed on impact into a perfect corolla. There were even a couple of doppies and a misshapen ball from an old voorlaaier. Strickland zoomed in for a close-up. She still didn't get it.

"If you'll allow me a poetic licence," Reddy said, as if poetic licence was a certificate you could stick on a page in your Book of Life, "this is the bullet that killed Hector Peterson."

So we didn't advertise. But Strickland stuck to her guns about the WHITES ONLY bench: we would have the real thing or nothing at all. She made a few inquiries of her own, and wouldn't you know it, before the week was out she turned up the genuine article.

The chosen bench belonged to the Municipal Bus Drivers' Association, and in exchange for a small contribution to their coffers—the replacement costs plus 10 per cent—they were happy to part with it. The honour of fetching the trophy from their clubhouse in Marshall Street fell to Pincus. Unbeknown to us, the Treasurer of the MBDA had decided that there was a bit of publicity to be gained from his Association's public-spirited gesture, and when our representative arrived he found a photographer ready to record the event for posterity. Pincus was never the most politic member of our Committee. With his enthusiastic co-operation the photographer was able to produce an entire essay, which subsequently appeared, without a by-line, in the *Saturday Star.* It showed the bench in its original quarters (weighed down by a squad of bus drivers of all races, pin-up girls—whites only—looking over the drivers' shoulders, all of them, whether flesh and blood or paper, saying cheese); the bench on its way out of the door (Pincus steering, the Treasurer pushing); being loaded onto the back of our bakkie (Pincus and the Treasurer shaking hands and stretching the cheque between them like a Christmas cracker); and finally driven away (Pincus hanging out of the window to give us a thumbs-up, the Treasurer waving goodbye, the Treasurer waving back at himself from the rear-view mirror). These pictures caused exactly the kind of headache Reddy had tried so hard to avoid. Offers of benches poured in from far and wide. Pincus was made to write the polite letters of thanks but no thanks. For our purposes, one bench is quite enough, thank you.

You can see the WHITES ONLY bench now, if you like, in Room 27. Just follow the arrows. I may as well warn you that it says EUROPEAN ONLY, to be precise. There's a second prohibition too, an entirely non-racial one, strung on a chain between the armrests: PLEASE DO NOT SIT ON THIS BENCH. That little sign is Charmaine's work, and making her paint it was Strickland's way of rubbing turpentine in her wounds.

When the genuine bench came to light, Charmaine received instructions to get rid of "the fake." But she refused to part with it. I was persuaded to help her carry it into the storeroom, where it remained for a month or so. As the deadline for the opening neared, Charmaine would take refuge in there from time to time, whenever things got too much for her, and put the finishing touches to her creation. At first, she was furious about all the publicity given to the impostor. But once the offers began to roll in, and it became apparent that WHITES ONLY benches were not nearly as scarce as we'd thought, she saw an opportunity to bring her own bench out of the closet. The night before the grand opening, in the early hours, when the sky was already going grey behind the mine-dump on the far side of the parking lot, we carried her bench outside and put it in the arbour under the controversial kaffirboom.

"When Strickland asks about it," said Charmaine, "you can tell her it was a foundling, left on our doorstep, and we just had to take it in." Funny thing is, Strickland never made a peep.

I can see Charmaine's WHITES ONLY bench now, from my window. The kaffirboom, relocated here fully grown from a Nelspruit nursery, has acclimatized wonderfully well. "*Erythrina caffra,* a sensible choice," said Reddy, "deciduous, patulous, and umbrageous." And he was quite right, it casts a welcome shade. Charmaine's faithful copy reclines in the dapple below, and its ability to attract and repel our visitors never ceases to impress me.

Take Mrs. King. And talking about Mrs. King, *Mr.* King is a total misnomer, of course. I must point it out to Reddy. The Revd. King, yes, and Dr. King, yes, and possibly even the Revd. Dr. King. But Mr. King? No ways.

It seems unfair, but Charmaine's bench has the edge on that old museum piece in Room 27. Occasionally I look up from my workbench, and see a white man sitting there, a history teacher say. While the schoolchildren he has brought here on an outing hunt in the grass for lucky beans, he sits down on our bench to rest his back. And after a while he pulls up his long socks, crosses one pink leg over the other, laces his fingers behind his head and closes his eyes.

Then again, I'll look up to see a black woman shuffling resolutely past, casting a resentful eye on the bench and muttering a protest under her breath, while the flame-red blossoms of the kaffirboom detonate beneath her aching feet.

Biographical Notes

❖

At age eighteen **Chris Abani** was arrested in Nigeria as the mastermind of an alleged coup based on the "evidence" of his first novel. He was imprisoned two more times, tortured, and escaped assassination. Abani has published four volumes of poetry and four novels, including *Graceland* and *Virgin in Flames*. His numerous awards include the PEN USA Freedom to Write, PEN Hemingway, and PEN Beyond Margins awards. He currently teaches at the University of California–Riverside. More information on Abani can be found at Chrisabani.com.

Leila Aboulela was born in Cairo in 1964 and grew up in Khartoum, Sudan. After receiving a master's degree from the London School of Economics (where she studied statistics), she moved to Aberdeen, Scotland, and currently resides in Abu Dhabi. She is the author of the novels *Minaret* and *The Translator,* as well as the short story collection *Colored Lights.* Her story "The Museum" won the 2000 Caine Prize for African Writing (often referred to as the African Booker).

In 1957, at the age of twenty-seven, **Chinua Achebe** sent the only copy of his handwritten manuscript of *Things Fall Apart* to a typing service in London, where it languished for months until it was retrieved by a colleague traveling on business. Luckily the British publisher Heinemann took a chance on Achebe, and today, after dozens of books of fiction, poetry, and essays, he is the most widely read African writer in the world. Achebe has been actively involved in Nigerian politics as well as engaged in taking on Western perceptions of Africans in writing. Since the early 1990s, he has been a professor of languages and literature at Bard College.

Perhaps the fastest rising star on the African literary scene, **Chimamanda Ngozi Adichie** has been hailed as the heir to Chinua Achebe. Adichie not only grew up in the same university town (Nsukka) as Achebe but in the very house he once lived in. Her debut novel, *Purple Hibiscus,* won the 2005 Commonwealth Prize for Best First Book, and her follow-up, *Half of a Yellow Sun,* won the Orange Prize. She was named a MacArthur fellow in 2008.

José Eduardo Agualusa was born in Huambo, Angola, and works as a writer and journalist in Angola, Portugal, and Brazil. Of his numerous books, three novels—*Creole, The Book of Chameleons,* and *My Father's Wives*—have been translated into English.

Writer and musician **Mohammed Naseehu Ali** is the son of an emir in Ghana. Ali chose to be educated in the United States, studying at the Interlochen Arts Academy and Bennington College. He has published one story collection, *The Prophet of Zongo Street,* and now lives in Brooklyn, New York.

Doreen Baingana is the author of *Tropical Fish: Stories Out of Entebbe,* which won the Associated Writers and Writing Programs Award in Short Fiction and the Commonwealth Prize for Best First Book, Africa Region. She holds an MFA from the University of Maryland and a law degree from Makerere University in Kampala, Uganda. After working for several years in Washington, D.C., for the Voice of America, Baingana moved to Kampala and teaches there.

Aziz Chouaki was born in Algiers in 1951. His mother bought him a guitar at the age of ten and he learned to play the Beatles, the Rolling Stones, and Jimi Hendrix—music that was forbidden by the repressive

Algerian regime. Playing in nightclubs and studying literature soon became his focus. When Islamic terrorism appeared in Algeria in the 1990s, he began to receive death threats and moved to France. *The Star of Algiers* is the first of his three novels written in French to be translated into English. He currently lives in Paris.

Nobel laureate **J. M. Coetzee** is the idiosyncratic and reclusive author of twelve works of fiction, five nonfiction collections, and two volumes of memoirs. The novels *The Life and Times of Michael K* and *Disgrace* each won the Booker Prize (the commonwealth's most prestigious literary award), though Coetzee did not attend the award ceremonies. He did, however, attend the Nobel award ceremonies, where he gave an acceptance speech about the nature of duck calls. Coetzee received a PhD in linguistics from the University of Texas, but he was denied permanent residence in the United States because of his anti–Vietnam War protests. Although he is considered one of South Africa's greatest living writers, since 2002 he has lived in Adelaide and in 2006 became a citizen of Australia.

Mia (António Emílio Leite) Couto, Mozambique's foremost novelist, was active in his country's mid-1970s revolution against colonial Portugal, and has gone on to become a literary hero of his liberated country. Couto's most celebrated novel, *Under the Frangipani,* draws readers into the world of the dead to find spirits old and new wrestling over the soul of Mozambique. Formerly the director of the news agency AIM, Couto was also editor in chief of the newspapers *Tiempo* and *Notícias de Maputo.* In 1985 he resigned from these posts to study biology; he currently works as an environmental biologist at Limpopo Transfrontier Park.

Fatou Diome was born on the Senegalese island Niodior, where she was raised by her grandmother. She attended college in Dakar, supporting herself by working as a housekeeper. Diome moved to France in 1990 and has published two novels and a short story collection. She lives in Strasbourg, where she is completing a PhD.

Born in Dakar in 1951, **Boubacar Boris Diop** is a prolific author of novels, plays, screenplays, and political works. He founded the independent Senegalese newspaper *Sol*. After twelve works written in French, Diop wrote his latest novel in Wolof, the dominant language of Senegal.

Somali novelist **Nuruddin Farah** has said, "I have tried my best to keep my country alive by writing about it, and the reason is because nothing good comes out of a country until the artists of that country turn to writing about it in a truthful way." Farah has lived in exile since 1976, when the Somalian government pronounced his second novel, *The Naked Needle,* treasonable. The author of more than a dozen works, including the novels *Maps, Knots,* and *From a Crooked Rib,* Farah currently resides in South Africa.

Nadine Gordimer was a founding member of the banned African National Congress and has been called "the conscience of South Africa." For nearly half a century her epic novels and short stories have articulated the real-life ramifications of apartheid on the lives of ordinary men and women. She is the author of nineteen story collections, as well as numerous novels, essay collections, and memoirs, winning many awards, including the Booker Prize. Despite her international fame, the South African government still banned her novels *Burger's Daughter* and *July's People.* When Gordimer received the Nobel Prize in 1991, Nelson Mandela still did not have the right to vote.

Helon Habila credits E. M. Forster's *Aspects of the Novel* for spurring him back to school and writing. In 2001 Habila won the Caine Prize for African Writing for a selection from his first novel, *Waiting for an Angel,* as well as the Commonwealth Writers Prize. Due to a lack of publishing venues in Nigeria at the time, Habila, like many other authors, had to self-publish his novel. Since then he has achieved international success and published a second novel, *Measuring Time.* He currently teaches at George Mason University in Fairfax, Virginia.

Laila Lalami was born and raised in Morocco. She earned her BA in English from Université Mohammed V in Rabat; her MA from University College, London; and her PhD in linguistics from the University of Southern California. Her highly acclaimed debut story collection, *Hope and Other Dangerous Pursuits,* was published in 2005, and her first novel, *Secret Son,* was published in early 2009. She currently teaches at the University of California–Riverside.

Alain Mabanckou's 2003 novel *African Psycho,* a comical and macabre take on a would-be Congolese serial killer, was the first of his seven novels to be translated into English (from his native French). Winner of the Prix Renaudot, France's equal to the National Book Award, Mabanckou currently teaches Francophone literature at the University of California–Los Angeles.

Algerian **Mohamed Magani** is at the epicenter of the Maghrebian literary landscape, which is made up of North African nations and includes Morocco and Tunisia. In 1987 Magani won the prestigious Grand Prix Littéraire International de la Ville d'Alger for his novel *La Faille du Ciel.* While it is nearly impossible to get your hands on hard copies of his and other Maghreb authors, excellent translations can be accessed online, courtesy of the heroic efforts of Words Without Borders (www.wordswithoutborders.org).

Zakes Mda is the pen name of Zanemvula Kizito Gatyeni Mdais. The author of numerous plays and five novels, including *The Whale Caller* and *The Madonna of Excelsior,* Mda has a PhD from the University of Cape Town and teaches at the University of Ohio.

Niq Mhlongo was born Murhandziwa Nicholas Mhlongo in Midway-Chiawelo Soweto, South Africa, in 1973, the eighth of ten children. His parents sent him to the Limpopo Province to escape violence and get an education. Despite the chaos and school closings surrounding Nelson Mandela's release from prison, Mhlongo managed to graduate from the University of the Witwatersrand in Johannesburg. *After Tears* is his follow-up novel to the cult classic *Dog Eat Dog*. Mhlongo now works as a writer and journalist in Soweto.

Patrice Nganang was born in Yaoundé, Cameroon, in 1970, and holds a PhD from Johann Wolfgang Goethe University in Frankfurt. Poet, novelist, and scholar, he is regarded as one of the most promising young Francophone writers, and has won several French awards, including the Prix Marguerite Yourcenar and the Grand Prix Littéraire de l'Afrique Noire. His novel *Dog Days* has been translated into English. Nganang is a resident of Brooklyn, New York, and teaches at Stony Brook University.

Considered one of the leading contemporary Afrikaans writers, **Marlene van Niekerk** was born in 1954, on the farm Tygerhoek near Caledon in the Western Cape, South Africa. A poet, playwright, and fiction writer, she is best known for *Triomf,* her graphic and controversial novel about a poor Afrikaner family in post-apartheid Johannesburg. She is a professor at the Department of Afrikaans and Dutch, Stellenbosch University, in South Africa.

Ondjaki was born in Luanda, Angola, in 1977, and attended university in Lisbon. He has exhibited as a painter, has worked as an actor, and has published five novels, two story collections, and a volume of poetry. His novels *The Whistler* and *Good Morning Comrades* have recently been translated into English.

E. C. Osondu worked in advertising in Lagos before receiving his MFA in fiction from Syracuse University in 2007. He teaches at Providence College in Rhode Island and is completing a story collection and novel.

Nawal El Saadawi is an Egyptian writer and psychiatrist. The author of more than two dozen award-winning novels, plays, and memoirs, she has been at the forefront of Arabic women's rights. Her work has been banned, and she was sent into exile (for five years), arrested by the Anwar Sadat government, and included on various assassination lists of terrorist organizations. She has also served as Secretary General of the Egyptian Medical Association, and ran for president in 2004. Saadawi lives in Cairo.

Never one to cast a blind eye at government corruption, the prolific Kenyan writer **Ngũgĩ wa Thiong'o**'s 1977 play *I Will Marry When I Want* earned him a prison cell, in which he penned an entire novel, *Devil on the Cross,* on toilet paper, and also stopped writing in English, switching to the Niger-Congo language Kikuyu, or Gĩkũyũ. As much a novelist and an intellectual as a social activist, Thiong'o is also a playwright, journalist, editor, and academic. The recipient of seven honorary doctorates, Thiong'o is currently the Director of the International Center for Writing and Translation at the University of California–Irvine.

Zimbabwean **Yvonne Vera** was part of the vanguard of writers addressing the varied and complex roles of women in contemporary African society. From former Southern Rhodesia, she received a PhD from York University in Toronto before moving back to her hometown to become the director of the National Gallery of Zimbabwe in Bulawayo. The author of the short story collection *Why Don't You Carve Other Animals* and five novels, including *Butterfly Burning,* Vera sadly succumbed to AIDS in 2005 at the age of forty. "I am against silence. The books I write try to undo the silent posture African women have endured over so many decades."

The South African novelist and short story writer **Ivan Vladislavić**'s most recent book is *Portrait with Keys: The City of Johannesburg Unlocked,* a series of 138 nonfiction portraits of his hometown, a widely praised portrait that won the *Sunday Times* Alan Paton Award for Nonfiction. Vladislavić works as an editor and writer in Johannesburg.

Abdourahman A. Waberi has written nine works of fiction, two of which—*The Land Without Shadows* and *The United States of Africa*—have been translated into English. From Djibouti, which gained its independence from France in 1977, Waberi came to France when he was twenty-one, and now teaches English in the French city of Caen.

Binyavanga Wainaina is the firebrand editor of *Kwani,* a young Nairobi-based literary magazine at the heart of the burgeoning Kenyan literary scene. He won the Caine Prize for African Writing in 2002, and his memoir, *Discovering Home,* is due out from Graywolf Press in late 2009. Wainaina's stingingly smart satire "How to Write About Africa," originally published in *Granta,* has become a touchstone for young African writers.